Linda Gillard lives on the Black Isle in t
been an actress, journalist and teach
novels, including Kindle bestseller H
GAZING, short-listed in 2009 for *Romantic Novel of the year and the*
Robin Jenkins Literary Award.

Also by Linda Gillard

Emotional Geology
A Lifetime Burning
Star Gazing
House of Silence
Untying the Knot
The Glass Guardian

www.lindagillard.co.uk

CAULDSTANE

Linda Gillard

First published as a Kindle e-book in 2014
This paperback edition 2014

Copyright © 2014 Linda Gillard

ISBN 978-1496147110

Cover design by Nicola Coffield

www.lindagillard.co.uk

For my son Ralph

Ghost: The outward and visible sign of an inward fear.
The Devil's Dictionary
Ambrose Bierce (1842-1914)

PART ONE

Chapter One

Sometimes I think I can still hear – very faintly – the strains of a harpsichord. Impossible, of course. There's been no harpsichord at Cauldstane for over a year now. Meredith's has never been replaced. Never *will* be replaced.

I suspect it's not so much that I hear music, rather that I remember it. It's proved impossible to forget, though God knows, I've tried. We've all tried.

It's tempting to think I'm experiencing some sort of aftershock, hearing the ripples of a "big bang" that will echo down the years, perhaps until I die. If sound waves went on and on, becoming weaker, then I might believe I could actually hear something, hear those keys touched by long-dead fingers, years after the sound was made. But Rupert, who knows about such things, says sound doesn't go on forever. Eventually it's absorbed, both by the medium it passes through and by the things the sound waves encounter. In the physical world we know, nothing lasts forever – a thought I find strangely comforting.

Meredith's harpsichord is long gone, so if her music persists, it's only in my head.

But Meredith? Where is *she* now?...

By rights, Sholto MacNab should have been dead. Several times over. The fact that he wasn't, that he was very much alive, furnished me with a career opportunity, a modest fee and a remarkable home. He invited me to come and stay at Cauldstane Castle so I could ghostwrite his memoirs for him. Dyslexic in an age when few had even heard the word, Sholto had grown up unable to spell and had only a nodding acquaintance with punctuation – an affectation, he said, for which he had neither time nor use.

Sholto was more familiar with short wave radio than email, so when I received my contract of employment, it was accompanied by a misspelled covering note that I now treasure. It said, *So glad your*

1

on board. Evry castle should have its ghost.

Just as every old Highland family should have its curse – something Sholto failed to mention. But even if he had, I would still have taken the job. I didn't believe in curses. Or, for that matter, ghosts.

If you were of a superstitious turn of mind, you might claim Sholto's life had been devastated – twice – by the MacNab curse, but he himself had managed to cheat death at the South Pole and death in the desert. He'd been bitten by poisonous snakes and mauled by a grizzly bear. ("Not *badly*," he'd said with an airy wave of his hand, as if his insane tendency to put himself in harm's way was behaviour typical of a Highland laird.) Frostbite, starvation, dehydration and life-threatening injury had been Sholto's constant companions during a lifetime of global adventure. Another was a family snapshot – torn, creased and stained with something that might have been blood. The photograph showed his late, long-suffering wife, Liz with their two sons: Alexander and Fergus.

A radiant Liz looks down at her younger son, Fergus, who waves his teddy at the photographer. In the background, half obscured and seemingly unaware of the camera, Alexander scowls and brandishes a plastic sword at an invisible enemy.

I never met Liz. I wish I had. Even in an old photograph she looks the sort of woman you'd like to have as a best friend. Kind. Understanding. Forgiving. (With Sholto for a husband, she'd have needed those qualities.) But Liz died many years ago, not long after that battered snapshot was taken. It was very hard on the children, but it was especially traumatic for Alexander – only eight when the accident happened – because the poor boy grew up believing it had been his fault.

Sholto MacNab didn't advertise. He approached the Society of Authors and asked if they could refer him to a discreet ghost writer who'd be prepared to come and live *en famille* in a draughty Highland castle with primitive plumbing. He was frank about that at least. There were other things I had to find out for myself.

Sholto had said he didn't want a biographer as he wished to

take credit for the book and all the profits from its sale. He was equally clear he didn't want a woman. His life story was testosterone-fuelled and some of his anecdotes were distinctly off-colour. There were rumours of the castle being haunted, so Sholto had told the SoA he didn't want some neurotic woman having hysterics, or worse, ghost-hunting in her spare time as part of her research for a gothic romance.

I've always been careful to conceal my gender in the professional sphere. Readers and editors are inclined to jump to conclusions about content and style, so I write as "J. J. Ryan". Until they meet me, everyone assumes I'm a man, even though my CV includes "autobiographies" of both male and female celebrities and I've been careful to cover a wide spectrum, from fashion to the Foreign Office.

The profile the SoA had on record indicated that I was interested in writing about travel and extreme sport. I'd ghostwritten a popular memoir for a busy scientist who didn't believe in God, curses or things that went bump in the night. Sholto concluded therefore that J. J. Ryan was sceptical, adventurous and male. He was right about two out of three.

We didn't communicate by phone. To begin with, the SoA put us in touch and I was thrilled to receive a letter of inquiry from the Laird of Cauldstane Castle, Sholto MacNab, adventurer and eccentric. As he loathed computers – Sholto tended to dismiss anything at which he was not expert – we communicated by fax. Shortly before I set off for the Highlands, I received an email from Fergus, Sholto's younger son. Replying to his questions about travel arrangements, I signed off as I always did for professional purposes: "J. J. Ryan".

When I alighted from the sleeper in Inverness, I found Fergus MacNab waiting at the barrier with a sheet of paper saying RYAN in large letters. I approached, smiling, delighted by the sharp northern air, the sunshine and the swooping gulls. I was in holiday humour. Everything had gone well so far. Even the sleeper was on time.

As I approached, Fergus smiled back. I'd done my homework and knew him to be thirty-eight (my junior by a few years) and single. I knew he'd been educated at Gordonstoun and had studied at the College of Agriculture in Aberdeen. Even at a distance I could see he resembled neither of his parents, but was a throwback to his

3

grandfather, Ninian, who'd been dark, blue-eyed and handsome, but compactly built in a typically Celtic way. However something about his easy and appraising smile suggested Fergus might have inherited his father's mantle as a ladies' man.

I deposited my case at his muddy-booted feet and offered my hand. 'How do you do? I'm Jenny Ryan.'

The smile vanished. He gazed over my shoulder as other passengers approached the barrier and I watched hope fade from his eyes. He looked at me again and said, '*You're* J. J. Ryan?'

'Yes, that's right. Is something wrong?' I indicated his piece of paper. 'You appear to be expecting me.'

'We were expecting a *man*.'

'Really? Oh dear. I hope you aren't too disappointed.' Fergus was now looking at me as if I presented an enormous problem, one he hoped wouldn't be his. I began to feel embarrassed and slightly annoyed. 'Women can write too, you know. Some of us quite well.'

'Oh, aye, I don't doubt. I mean, of *course* you do! I'm sorry, Miss Ryan—'

'Please call me Jenny. You, I assume, are Fergus MacNab?'

He took my hand and shook it firmly. 'Aye, that's right. Sholto sent me to fetch you. I must apologise for my manners, Miss Ryan.'

'Jenny. Or J.J. if that's less painful for you.'

'Och, no, Jenny's fine! It's just that we – that is, Sholto was expecting a man. He was definitely *wanting* a man.'

'I see. Well, I'm afraid that crucial piece of information wasn't passed on to me and I suppose the Society of Authors didn't realise I was female. It's not a dark secret, it's just that I don't like to be pigeonholed as a writer, so for work purposes, I try to disguise my gender. I have to say, people aren't usually dismayed when they meet me. Sometimes they're pleasantly surprised.'

Fergus recovered graciously. 'I'm sure if anyone could turn my father's chaotic life into a coherent narrative, it would be you, Miss Ryan. I was just anticipating his...'

'Disappointment?'

'*Wrath* was more the word I had in mind. He's very anxious to get on with this book. We're running out of time.'

'Oh? I hope he's not unwell?'

'No, he's fine, just short of cash. He's convinced himself these memoirs will become a bestseller. He's already wondering who'll play him in the TV series.'

'I see. So no pressure then.'

He smiled. 'If you took it on, Jenny, this would be no easy writing assignment, but I can promise you it would be very entertaining.'

'But you think I'm unlikely to get a rapturous reception at Cauldstane.'

His expression was pained. 'I'll break the news to him as gently as I can.'

'I'm not sure I want to put you to the trouble. Mr MacNab has already paid my expenses so I can just turn round and go home if you think meeting him would be a waste of time. But I insist on a cooked breakfast before I do. Would you care to join me for coffee? You can watch me eat while you decide whether your father can cope with the terrible shock of meeting me.'

I reached for the handle of my case but Fergus got there first. 'I don't know what to advise. My father has pretty old-fashioned ideas about working with women. He's seventy. He can be... unpredictable. And rude. The fact is, he's always been a law unto himself. And he still is.'

'I can't wait to meet him,' I said, as we set off across the concourse, heading for the station café. 'I'm sure our encounter will be highly educational – on both sides. But first I need sustenance. ScotRail's idea of breakfast certainly isn't mine.'

Fergus held open the door to the café and the blessed aromas of coffee and bacon hit my nostrils, persuading me that the day – and possibly my trip – might yet be salvageable.

I got the impression my stock rose with Fergus as he watched me demolish the full Scottish breakfast he'd insisted on buying me. I despatched a second cup of coffee, then claimed I was ready for anything, including the wrath of Sholto MacNab.

I followed Fergus out to the station car park where he indicated a muddy Land Rover that had seen better days and many miles. I climbed in, telling myself I didn't really want this job anyway. Writing the memoirs of a cantankerous old chauvinist who couldn't spell? And for a niggardly fee too. Who in their right mind would want to spend months doing that?

5

I was clear it was just curiosity taking me to Cauldstane – that and a desire to show Fergus MacNab I wasn't intimidated by his illustrious father.

I was quite clear. Until I saw Cauldstane.

I'd seen pictures of Highland castles of course, but I'd never visited one, let alone one that was still a family home. I think of myself as well-travelled and hard to impress, but Cauldstane impressed me. Entranced me.

If I say, "Think of Disney", you'll envisage something colourful and vulgar. But remove the colour from a Disney castle, but not the quirkiness; batter it with centuries of weather, most of it wet; ravage its walls with cannon balls hurled by Cromwell's army and you might end up with a typical Scottish tower house, sixteenth-century in origin, surviving – only just – into the twenty-first as family home, money pit and national treasure.

Unfortunately Scotland is littered with them in varying states of dilapidation, so they aren't regarded as national treasures except by their devoted owners and admirers. The National Trust for Scotland maintains the best and Historic Scotland maintains some that are architecturally significant but ruinous. Anything in between depends for its survival on the dedication and funds of the family who are faced with hard choices. They can watch their home decay. They can try to sell up to someone with more cash and less sense, who might care to exploit centuries of history as a picturesque background for wedding photographs. Or the family can invest money they don't really have and go down the wedding venue/spa hotel/conference centre route themselves. At least that way they get to stay on site, albeit in an attic flat or one of the estate houses.

I knew little about all this then. When I first caught sight of Cauldstane, I didn't see a building and a way of life in its death throes. Cauldstane stood, heroic, long-suffering, defying all that the centuries had thrown at it. (Wet and dry rot have proved more damaging to many a castle than the depredations of enemy artillery.) I saw an ivy-clad tower, much taller than it was wide, with more windows than I could easily count, the whole topped by conical-roofed turrets and looking, from a distance, like a child's toy.

6

As the Land Rover bounced up the tree-lined, pot-holed drive, I noted that the lower half of the castle looked as bleak and four-square as a prison, but as the eye travelled upwards, ornamentation became apparent. Richly carved gargoyles and canon water spouts carried rain-water well away from the walls. Heraldic beasts emerged from the creamy-pink harling that clothed the granite walls. A deep belt of decorative brickwork, known as corbelling, ran all the way around the castle, supporting turrets and spacious upper storeys.

Arriving at the foot of the castle, I discovered it was much larger and more forbidding than I'd expected, but by then, I'd seen enough. I found myself regretting the decision to go through with the interview. This was no failure of nerve. I just knew if I didn't get this job, I'd be gutted.

As I craned my neck for a better view, I told myself the secret of a happy life was low expectations. I would simply regard my trip as an interesting excursion. A chance to meet a celebrity and spend a night in a Highland castle before catching the train back to London.

Fergus drove round the castle, past the main entrance and through a stone arch at the rear. As he swung into the courtyard, I saw from the corner of my eye a figure move rapidly across the cobbles, waving something in the air. As Fergus manoeuvred into a parking place, I turned my head to see a man spring across the courtyard, wielding some sort of sword, cutting the air and thrusting at an invisible opponent. He was dressed in a blue boiler suit, wore plastic safety glasses on top of his head and appeared completely oblivious of our arrival.

I was so surprised by this incongruous sight, I nearly burst out laughing. Then I realised I'd stopped breathing. Mesmerized by the swordsman's grace and the ballet of this duel with an imaginary foe, I stared through the windscreen, following every move. As Fergus switched off the ignition, the man delivered what appeared to be a *coup de grâce* at full stretch. Then he straightened up, turned and saluted us, holding his sword in front of his face, aligned with his nose. Fergus tooted the horn in response, but the man was already striding towards one of the outbuildings, slicing the air with his sword, cutting to left and right. Somehow he managed to make the action look casual. He disappeared through a wooden door and it slammed shut.

I swivelled round in my seat and faced Fergus. 'What was *that*?'

'He was trying out a new weapon. He finished it this morning. It was a commission for an American who wanted a replica of the rapier they used in *The Princess Bride*.' I blinked in astonishment. Fergus misunderstood and added, 'It's a kids' movie.'

'You make *weapons* at Cauldstane?'

'Aye.' He pointed. 'In that workshop. It used to be the stables, but we haven't had horses for years, so the building's been re-cycled. We call it the armoury now.'

'And who was he? The swordsman. He really looked as if he knew what he was doing.'

'Aye, he does. That was my brother. The heir to Cauldstane. Alexander John Balliol MacNab. We call him Alec.'

Chapter Two

Fergus led the way to the castle's back door. I registered a twinge of disappointment that I was entering Cauldstane via the tradesmen's entrance, but that was after all what I was: a jobbing writer, plying my trade. And practising to deceive. If this was the door the MacNabs themselves used, it was good enough for the likes of me.

There was a stone slab by the door, propped up against the wall. Next to it stood a rusted horse shoe. According to Fergus there hadn't been horses at Cauldstane for years, so I assumed this one had been placed at the entrance to invite good luck. I took a moment to examine the stone. The edges were uneven and damaged, as if it had been removed or fallen from a wall. It portrayed a naked, muscular arm gripping a short sword. The hand was well carved and looked quite realistic, apart from the over-long thumb, of which the first joint seemed unnaturally extended. Beneath the disembodied arm was a scroll engraved with a Latin motto, *Timor omnis abesto*.

'Fergus, what does that mean?'

'The motto?'

'Yes. I don't know much Latin. Is it something to do with fear? *Timor?*'

'Aye. *Timor omnis abesto* means, "Let fear be far from all".'

'Is that the family motto?'

'Aye.'

'It's a nice one. Not too aggressive. Some of them sound as if they're just spoiling for a fight, don't they? The stone looks ancient. Where was it originally?'

He pointed over my shoulder at the archway through which we'd driven into the courtyard. 'It used to be set into the wall above the arch over there, but it fell down. No one's got round to putting it back up again.'

'When did it come down?'

'Och, it must have been...' Fergus frowned as he calculated. 'About two hundred and fifty years ago.' I laughed and he looked a little shamefaced. 'Aye, we really should get it fixed, I suppose. But we've grown fond of it here.' He gave the stone an affectionate kick. 'It keeps fear from the door,' he said with a smile. Then less certainly, 'We like to think so anyway. But as you see, we hedge our bets with the horse shoe.' He pushed the back door open, held it for me and with a little bow of his dark head said, 'Welcome to Cauldstane, Jenny.'

It took me a moment to adjust to the low level of light in the hallway and the drop in temperature. It was actually colder inside the castle than outdoors where sunshine had warmed the courtyard air. I hoped better provision had been made for the guest rooms, but I'd taken the precaution of bringing my hot water bottle. I never travelled without it.

Sometimes I wondered whether my attachment to its cashmere cosiness was related to the absence of a regular man in my bed. It was some years now since Rupert had vacated the position and embraced instead the Anglican Church. This was no temporary fling. Rupert had decided to train for the ministry. I'd wished him well and we'd parted ways. I had no desire to live in a vicarage and to do that I would have had to marry him – a step I wasn't sure I wanted to take. Rupert and I had been through a lot together over the years and we'd both been changed by it. Events could have bound us closer together. Instead they drove us apart.

He had sought comfort in the arms of the Church. My refuge had been work, interesting and relatively undemanding work, if not well paid. I had no difficulty inhabiting the minds of my subjects, seeing their point of view. An overactive imagination had always been my besetting sin, as was my ability to empathise to, at times, a disabling degree.

I'd done my internet homework and as I walked behind Fergus along the dingy corridor, I wondered idly why he was unmarried. Instinct told me he was probably straight and he could hardly have been short of female admirers. Was he a philanderer like his father? (Sholto's messy personal life had made entertaining reading until I thought about his poor wives.) Fergus had said Sholto was hard up. Was the family as a whole strapped for cash? Did Fergus have a place of his own? Did Alec? Or did they all live at Cauldstane?

Google had been vague about what Fergus did for a living. Estate management seemed to be his main occupation, though whether that meant he managed the Cauldstane estate, I had no idea. I knew that Alec, the heir apparent, was forty and *had* married. By digging around, I'd discovered his wife had apparently committed suicide some years ago, before she'd produced an heir.

Nothing about the MacNab set-up suggested they were rolling in cash. My writer's imagination – both blessing and curse – suggested to me that the younger MacNabs could do with marrying money. Was that why Fergus was still single? Was he holding out for an heiress? As for Alec, he must surely be under a certain amount of pressure to produce an heir. Was that why his wife had committed suicide? Had she been infertile and despaired? Who would inherit Cauldstane if the MacNab brothers died without issue?...

My mind teemed with questions and as my imagination attempted to answer them, I realised I was drafting the novel of the MacNabs' lives. I chided myself for getting carried away with the romance of an old Highland family, shackled to its ancestral home. I needed to stick to facts. That was my business now. Not fiction.

Fergus and I emerged from a dark corridor into a spacious hall – or it would have been spacious had it not been over-full of furniture and bric-a-brac which seemed to cover every historical period and style. I'd seen better organised junk shops.

The hall was dominated by a stag's head on the wall. The animal looked disgruntled, as well it might. Its antlers were apparently used as a hat rack, except that the head was surely out of reach for even the tallest man. I suspected it was used for recreational purposes, as a sort of hoopla. Some of the hats, which included a straw boater and a pith helmet, looked as if they'd been there for some time. The stag was positioned above an ancient, lumpy sofa that had literally had the stuffing knocked out of it. It was adorned with a motley selection of cushions, unrelated in theme or colour, a testament to someone's passion for needlepoint. Unlike the sofa, the cushions looked exceedingly well stuffed, but just as uncomfortable.

A bookcase was topped by an outsize stuffed seabird in a glass case. An albatross, I assumed. There were several sickly houseplants, all inclining towards the only window. Here and there, wallpaper was peeling. Some might have described it as ochre, but it made me think of tobacco stains. It certainly did nothing for the balding moss green carpet on which lay a series of equally threadbare rugs.

Every surface was cluttered with knick-knacks and framed photos, mostly of children, but there were a few expedition shots of Sholto and one of him in evening dress, pictured with a striking brunette. I knew this wasn't his first wife, Liz and assumed it must be her successor. Everything was old, much of it worn, but nothing was dusty, not even the frames surrounding paintings so dark with varnish, it was difficult to discern their subject. Despite the general shabbiness, the objects in the hall looked well cared-for. Apart from the poor stag.

I followed Fergus, minding my feet as we climbed the stairs. When we reached the half-landing, I looked up and found myself face to face with an almost life-size portrait of a standing woman. It wasn't the kind of painting you could just walk past, so I stood and stared.

It was unashamedly theatrical. The woman appeared to be wearing some sort of classical fancy dress. Dazzling white Grecian drapery clung to her body and her elegantly posed feet were clad in leather sandals. Her abundant black curls were piled high on her head, but artfully arranged so they cascaded over her shoulders. Her body was turned away slightly from the viewer, but her wide, dark eyes faced front. As I shuffled across the half-landing, her eyes held mine in a most unsettling way.

The sitter had been painted in front of classical columns which framed an idealized landscape, more Suffolk than ancient Greece. Perhaps the landscape was meant to look artificial? The quantity of make-up around the woman's eyes suggested the portrait had been painted since the sixties, but the artist had chosen to present her in an anachronistic, non-naturalistic setting. I suddenly recalled a romantic portrait by Alma-Tadema of the actress Ellen Terry playing Shakespeare's Imogen...

That would explain it. I was looking at a portrait of someone *playing a part*. She was in costume and she was on stage. So was this Sholto's second wife, Meredith, the opera singer?

With some reluctance I turned my back on the portrait to find Fergus waiting on the landing above me, holding open a door.

'This is your room, Jenny. It has a good view and there's a bathroom next door. I hope you'll be comfortable.'

I hurried up the remaining stairs, eager to see more of Cauldstane.

It was a pretty room, evidently situated in a corner of the castle. There were double aspect windows set into the thick walls and one was furnished with a cushioned window seat. I headed straight over to look at the views. One window looked out over the grounds in the direction of a walled garden. The other, at the rear of the castle, looked out over the River Spey, which had carved a gorge out of the rock. The gradient was steep and the brown, peaty water flowed furiously over projecting rocks, then under an arched stone bridge further downstream. The bridge led to a path that followed the river bank for a while, then disappeared into woodland on the other side of the river.

I turned away from the windows and surveyed the contents of my room: an old brass bedstead, but when I prodded it, the double mattress felt comfortable; a chest of drawers displaying a pair of chipped Staffordshire spaniels and other figurines; no dressing table, but a large gilt mirror hung on the wall between the windows, giving an indirect view of the river. I felt like the Lady of Shalott. Later, when I checked my appearance and discovered the mirror was badly cracked, I felt even more like that unfortunate Lady.

A bookcase housed volumes selected for the entertainment of Cauldstane's guests. My eye was taken immediately by the anonymity of *Days on the Hill* by "An Old Stalker", shelved between *Scotch Deerhounds and their Masters* and *Biggles Defies the Swastika*. I'd always been a martyr to insomnia, but could see plenty of reading matter here that would amuse me and some that might induce sleep in a matter of minutes.

A writing table with shallow, brass-handled drawers was positioned in front of one of the windows. It had been thoughtfully cleared for action, apart from a jug of red and white roses. The fireplace was concealed by a chaotically cheerful découpage screen on which smiling Victorian maidens cavorted with tigers, birds, kittens, cherubs and smartly dressed rabbits delivering Easter eggs.

I was setting up my laptop on the writing desk when there was a gentle tap at the door. I called, 'Come in' and turned to see a short, plump woman of indeterminate age standing in the doorway. She carried a tray bearing coffee and a plate of cakes and biscuits.

'Good morning, Miss Ryan. I'm Wilma Guthrie, the housekeeper. Mr Fergus thought you'd like some coffee. But if you'd prefer tea, you've only to say.'

'No, coffee will be fine, thanks. It smells delicious. So does the home baking. Are *all* of those for me, or are you off to feed the five thousand elsewhere?'

She chuckled. 'Och, you've come a long way! We won't see you starve while you're here.'

Wilma Guthrie wouldn't see forty again, possibly not fifty, but it was difficult to guess her age. Her plumpness ironed out any giveaway wrinkles and her fine greying hair was cut in an unflattering pudding basin style that she might have worn since childhood. Most of her clothes were hidden under a tabard apron, but I registered thick ankles below her pleated woollen skirt and was surprised to see her feet shod in trainers.

'Now if there's anything else you want, just let me know. You'll most likely find me in the kitchen. Go down the stair and follow the sound of the radio. It's always on. We serve lunch in the dining room at one o'clock. Just a buffet, quite informal. Now, d'you have everything you need?'

'Yes, thank you. I'm sure I shall be very comfortable.'

'Then I'll pop back later to collect the tray.' She cast her eyes round the room as if checking it a final time, then she bustled out, splay-footed, but swift and silent in her running shoes.

Shortly before one, I emerged from my room just as a man came jogging up the stairs. It was Alexander MacNab. I recognised him not from his face, which I'd hardly registered in the courtyard, but from his very upright bearing. That was the thing about Alec MacNab. You wouldn't look at him twice. Not until he moved.

Boiler suit and safety glasses were now gone. He was wearing a faded T-shirt and old jeans. His hair was an unexceptional brown, rather long and untidy, swept back from his forehead and curling round his ears and temples. His features, though regular, could hardly be described as handsome. Comparing him with his younger brother, you wouldn't hesitate to say Fergus was the good-looking one. Alec, though much taller, would blend into the background, ceding the field to Fergus who, as I was to learn, wielded charm and a pair of bright blue eyes with as much panache as his brother handled a sword.

When Alec saw me, he paused, unsmiling, at the top of the stairs. There was a moment's awkwardness and I stepped forward.

'Hello. I'm Jenny Ryan. I'm here to talk to your father. We might produce a book together.'

'Ah, the ghost,' Alec said, with a faint smile.

'Yes, that's me.'

He extended his hand. 'How d'you do, Miss Ryan.'

'Oh, please call me Jenny.' I took his hand and felt rather than saw that two of his fingers wore plasters at the end. I supposed accidents must be one of the hazards of producing sharp blades. I glanced down at his hand and registered the same extraordinary long thumb joint that I'd seen on the stone carving above the MacNab motto. For reasons I couldn't fathom, I felt absurdly thrilled, as if I'd shaken hands with history.

Alec was still looking at me, his head on one side. 'Have we met before?'

'I don't think so. This is only the second time I've been to Scotland.'

'You look familiar. Are you famous?'

'No, quite the opposite! No one's supposed to know who I am.' I was beginning to feel disconcerted by his direct gaze. 'I mean, that's the point of being a ghost writer. Anonymity. You should be invisible.'

His eyebrows shot up. 'How d'you manage that?'

'Well, my name doesn't appear in the book and I'm contractually bound not to reveal who I've written for. It's a point of honour anyway that ghosts don't reveal who their subjects are. If you did, you'd never work again.'

'So someone else takes all the credit for what you write?'

'Yes. That's what we're paid for. But I take a more positive view. I see it as a sort of facilitation job. I enable people to tell their stories — stories which wouldn't find a reader unless someone ghosted them. Do you sign your swords?'

He looked surprised. '*Sign* them? Like paintings, you mean? No, I don't. But there's a mark on them that identifies me as their maker.'

'Exactly. Well, there's a sort of mark – a literary one – in all the books I write. It identifies me as their author.'

'Clever. What is it?'

I paused for a moment before saying, 'I *could* tell you… but then I'd have to kill you.'

He laughed and suddenly I saw his father, the Sholto MacNab of the early expeditions, grinning as he was hauled out of an Antarctic crevasse. *Timor omnis abesto.* "Let fear be far from all."

I know I wasn't feeling faint and I certainly didn't stumble – in fact my feet felt oddly rooted to the spot – but I experienced a vertiginous sensation, as if the floor was giving way or some invisible force was trying to sweep me off my feet. The past had somehow telescoped, as if Alec, Sholto and the anonymous stone swordsman in the courtyard had become one person. Ridiculous, of course. My imagination was running away with me as it always did – though I have to say, I'm not usually that susceptible to men laughing at my jokes.

Alec looked concerned and leaned towards me. 'Are you all right?'

'Yes, I'm fine!'

'You look a wee bit pale. Did Wilma bring you coffee?'

'Oh, yes, I got the works. Coffee and three varieties of home baking. Really, I'm fine. I had a horrible virus recently and I think I'm still not a hundred per cent.' To change the subject, I pointed down the stairs to the portrait on the half-landing. 'Who's the woman in that portrait?'

Alec didn't turn to look but said, 'Sholto's second wife.'

'Your stepmother?'

'Aye. Meredith MacNab.'

'I had no idea she was that beautiful.'

'She wasn't. A certain amount of artistic licence was employed by the artist.'

'Did Sholto commission it?'

'Och, no! My father has no interest whatever in paintings. We've attics full of them. Meredith sat for the portrait, then gave it

16

to Sholto as a Christmas present. She also gave him the bill. That was her idea of generosity.'

I looked down at the portrait and studied it in a new light, as an expensive exercise in personal vanity. 'It's very striking. There's something about the eyes. They seem to follow you, don't they?'

'Aye, they do. The picture used to hang in the dining room, but after she died Sholto said it put him off his food, the way the eyes seem to watch you.'

'I believe she died in an accident? A car crash, wasn't it?'

'On my wedding day. Meredith always had a wonderful sense of timing.' I must have looked shocked at the callous remark because Alec apologised immediately. 'I'm sorry, I shouldn't sound so bitter. But Meredith died because she chose to drive when she was dead drunk. She hit a tree on a notorious bend. It was a horrific crash and my poor father had to identify her body.'

'How dreadful... Did she kill anyone else?'

Alec stared at me for a moment, then studied the floor, as if choosing his words carefully. 'Meredith was the only one in the car, thank God. But I'm not sure my wife ever got over the tragedy. It was a hell of a way to start a marriage. With your mother-in-law's wake.' The sound of a gong reverberated up the stairs. 'That's Wilma summoning us for lunch. I need to get cleaned up. D'you know your way down to the dining room?'

'I'm sure I'll find it, thanks.'

'Turn left at the foot of the stair and cross the hall. Tell Zelda I'll not be long.'

'Zelda?'

'Have you not met her yet? My aunt Griselda. She hates it when we're late.'

'I'd better get going then.'

'You're sure you're up to it now? Wilma could bring you lunch on a tray.'

'No, I'm fine. I'm looking forward to meeting the rest of the family.'

Alec was looking beyond me now, scanning the corridor as if distracted, then he regarded me again, his grey eyes serious. 'Go carefully now.' He made it sound like an instruction, almost an order. 'The carpet's worn into holes.'

'Thank you. I will.'

17

He glanced round the passageway once more, then opened a door and was gone.

Chapter Three

The dining room was dark, oppressively red-walled and filled with polished mahogany pieces that looked as if they'd been in position for centuries. Possibly they had. It would have taken a small army of men to move them. Fergus was pouring sherry from a decanter for a woman who I assumed must be his Aunt Griselda.

Zelda — as she was known — was Sholto's younger sister and had been married in her youth to Jean-Claude Fontaine, a Formula One racing driver. She'd lived a glamorous jet-set life in southern France for many years, but maintained her independence by training as a chef, then running her own restaurant. She eventually divorced Jean-Claude but had never re-married. Zelda had sold up and moved back to her childhood home to help Sholto run the estate after his wife Liz had died. Since Sholto was often abroad on expeditions, sometimes for many months, the management of Cauldstane and the supervision of her nephews' boarding school education had fallen to Zelda. Even after Sholto re-married, Zelda stayed on while Meredith MacNab pursued her singing career. It seemed she'd turned readily to Zelda for advice and support and they'd become good friends.

Zelda's warmth and generosity were immediately apparent when Fergus introduced us. I declined his offer of sherry so he set about carving cold ham at the sideboard where a buffet lunch was laid out. Zelda shepherded me towards the table. We sat down, she at the head of the table and I to her left. Mrs Guthrie brought us soup, then hovered at the side of the room, doing her best to look invisible, but I noticed her eyes scanned the table, making sure we had all we needed. I wondered how often she sat down in a normal working day. Running shoes for travel on stone floors and polished wooden boards now seemed sensible attire. I was beginning to get the measure of Cauldstane.

Zelda put me at my ease, chatting about books and how busy she was in retirement, running a secondhand bookshop for the Highland Hospice charity. I wasn't fooled. I knew that, in the nicest possible way, I was being vetted. As I answered her numerous, sometimes probing questions, the writer in me couldn't help noting that Griselda Fontaine must once have been a beautiful woman. Her outfit was the kind worn by smart countrywomen for the last fifty years: tweed skirt, cashmere twin-set and unobtrusive pearls. Her hair, which didn't appear to be dyed, was a pale apricot colour, held back from her face by a black velvet Alice band. Her flawless skin was gilded with tiny freckles, so that even without a scrap of make-up, her face glowed, forming the perfect setting for a pair of opal-blue eyes. She was tall, slim and, despite a pair of mannish brogues, elegant. According to the MacNab family tree Zelda was sixty-seven, but she looked at least ten years younger.

I tucked into ham salad while Zelda played a version of Twenty Questions, trying to wheedle the names of my subjects out of me, working her way through the list of celebrities whose memoirs apparently formed semi-permanent stock in the Hospice bookshop.

'Now I do love a good biography but – forgive my being frank, Jenny...' I doubted Zelda was ever anything else. '*Some* of these celebrity books are good for nothing more than lining a budgie's cage. I mean no disrespect to their authors, whoever they may be. It's just that these folk haven't lived! There's a wee thing, an actress or model, I don't remember her name now, but from the look of her, she can't be long out of school. How can *she* possibly merit an autobiography?'

Zelda turned her attention to her lunch, so I assumed the question had been rhetorical. I asked what kind of books *did* sell at the Hospice shop.

'Well, you can't even give hardbacks away now, not since everyone got those reading devices. In fact I'm thinking of selling them off in sacks for firewood!'

'Or even kindling,' I said, not looking up from my plate. I thought the pun might go over her head, but she whooped with laughter. 'Och, *kindling*! Very good, Jenny! I must remember that one. *Kindling!* Fergus, did you hear that?'

She was still chuckling when the dining room door opened. Alec walked in and closed the door quietly behind him. The others had their backs to the door, so I don't know if they even registered his arrival. He ignored us and headed for the sideboard where he helped himself to soup from a tureen. Zelda and I were talking when Fergus got up and started to carve more ham. I don't remember now what question I'd just asked her – something about the books in my room, I think – when Fergus spun round to chip in, knocking over a large jar of pickles. It crashed on to the handle of the carving knife which flipped into the air and fell from the table, spinning.

Then Alec moved. He lunged easily and caught the big knife by its handle just before it hit the floor. It was only as he straightened up that I realised he was still holding his full soup plate and hadn't spilled a drop. He replaced the knife carefully on the platter and stood the jar upright again.

Oblivious to the side show, Zelda was barking instructions as Alec approached the dining table.

'Alec, come and sit down. Let me introduce you to our guest.' He set his plate down on the other side of the table, opposite me. 'Jenny, this is Alexander. He's always late for lunch because he forgets to eat... Alec, this is J. J. Ryan. *Jenny*. She's to be interviewed by Sholto this afternoon, so we must all be very kind.'

'We've already met,' Alec said softly.

'You have?' Zelda looked surprised.

'That's why Alec's late,' I explained. 'It's my fault. We were chatting upstairs. I was telling him why I'm here.'

He sat down and helped himself to bread. 'I hope someone's warned you about Sholto. He can be difficult.'

'So I gather. Fergus filled me in when he picked me up at the station. I do realise I'm completely the wrong gender.'

'Only as far as *Dad's* concerned,' said Fergus, treating me to one of his winning smiles, which Zelda quelled with a look.

'But since I've come such a long way, I thought it would be nice to meet him. In a masochistic sort of way.'

Alec tasted his soup, then ground some pepper into it. I watched and counted the plasters. There were three, all very grubby. 'Sholto can be rude, I'm afraid.'

'But not unkind,' said Fergus. 'Or unfair.'

'True. Just give as good as you get, Jenny. He likes folk to stand up to him. Is that not so, Wilma?'

'Oh aye, Mr Alec,' said Mrs Guthrie, taking my empty plate.

'And she bears the scars to prove it, don't you, Wilma?' Fergus added.

'Emotional only, Miss Ryan,' she confided with a wink.

'Och, my brother's bark is far worse than his bite,' said Zelda. 'It's just that he's addicted to *drama*. He refuses to grow old gracefully.'

'Or grow old at all,' said Alec.

Zelda ignored him and continued. 'You see, Jenny, Sholto misses the adrenalin rush of the old days, so when he meets you, he'll likely make a fuss to begin with. Take no notice. He'll come to his senses, you'll see. My brother's never been able to resist a pretty face. More's the pity,' she muttered, shaking her head.

There followed a profound silence, broken eventually by Alec, Fergus and me as we all began to speak at the same time. Embarrassment gave way to more awkward silence until Mrs Guthrie saved the day with a few quiet, deferential words, 'Will I serve coffee in the drawing room, Mrs Fontaine?' She pronounced the name without a hint of a French accent.

'Thank you, Wilma, that would be grand,' Zelda said briskly, getting to her feet. She strode towards the door and Fergus followed. Alec remained seated, stirring soup he showed little inclination to eat. When they'd gone, he looked at me, his grey eyes solemn and said, 'Don't take this job unless you really want it.'

'Well, that's the trouble. I *do* really want it.'

'Already?' That soft laugh again. 'Well, you can't say we didn't warn you.' I stood up and, in what seemed one fluid movement, Alec rose, walked to the door and held it open for me. As I passed he said, 'I'll see you later. I hope.'

As I stood in the hall, feeling slightly bewildered, I heard Zelda's voice coming from upstairs. 'Fergus, will you please go and look for Jenny. The poor girl must be lost already.'

Was I? Lost already?...

At half past two Fergus led me to the library on the second floor, knocked, then opened the door. He indicated with a nod that I should go in and I realised he wouldn't be following. I stepped forward with a nervous glance over my shoulder and saw him mouth the words, "Good luck".

If it had been Sholto's intention to intimidate me, he succeeded. The cavernous library was lit by a log fire and a series of tall, north-facing windows running along one side of the room. The MacNab book collection covered the other walls from floor to ceiling. There must have been thousands of volumes. Sholto sat at an enormous kneehole desk, silhouetted against the windows, so at first I couldn't see his face in any detail. He occupied a massive wooden chair resembling a throne. Perhaps this was going to be more of an audience than an interview, but I wasn't one to duck a challenge. It seemed there was little chance of my securing the commission, so I decided to relax and play along with whatever games Sholto MacNab had planned for me.

'Ah, Miss Ryan! Do come in and sit down.'

The first surprise was the English drawl. I'd never heard Sholto speak, I'd only read interviews and seen film footage of him smiling at the camera through a frozen beard as he dragged a sledge bigger than himself across Antarctica. I'd seen him parachuting out of planes and abseiling down national monuments. I'd even seen him bleeding and unconscious on a stretcher, but I'd never heard him speak.

When Sholto was a boy, an English public school education would have been regarded in certain circles, even in Scotland, as an essential qualification for life. I knew he'd been sent to Eton, but it hadn't occurred to me his Scots accent would have been bullied out of him. It's easy to forget that, in the class-ridden dark ages, if you wanted to get on, you ditched a regional accent in favour of RP. As old Pathé newsreels demonstrate, even a humble newsreader was expected to sound like a member of the royal family.

As I approached across threadbare Persian rugs, I savoured the musty smell of old books and lavender polish. A bowl of late, blowsy roses dropped a few exhausted petals as I passed between two wooden globes – one terrestrial, the other celestial. A longcase clock chimed the half hour and Sholto rose to his feet, which I suspect cost him an effort. That was my second surprise – how tall he was, even leaning heavily on his stick. He reached across the desk and offered me a gnarled hand. As I took it I felt an urge to check for the long thumb, but I knew it was important to look my prospective employer in the eye. What was it Alec had said? "Give as good as you get." So I returned his father's firm handshake and met his searching gaze.

Sholto MacNab was a handsome man still, though now into his

seventies. His shoulders were a little bowed, but he had the same lean, rangy frame as his elder son and something of his physical poise, an ability to be quite still, as if watching and waiting. He and Alec shared the same high forehead and curling hair, though Sholto's was much fairer and turning white. I knew he'd been blond in his youth and could see now why the blue-eyed golden boy had been a magnet for women. My research indicated Sholto was still giving his second wife the run-around in his late fifties.

He was clean-shaven and his face was very lined, which didn't surprise me. His skin had weathered a lifetime's exposure to extremes of heat and cold and Sholto, as a male Highlander, would have been a stranger to sunscreen and moisturiser. His nose and cheekbones were mottled with purple broken veins which might have been caused by hard living or exposure. Both probably.

But the photos hadn't done him justice. Parka hoods, rampant facial hair and snow goggles had concealed the man from public view. His arresting face was not merely handsome, it was heroic. Sholto had lived a full and often troubled life. The years were graven on his face, but the deep lines were offset by a liveliness in his eyes, a humorous intelligence that I warmed to immediately. It would be a challenge interpreting him for a general reader, but it was a job I knew I'd relish if only he'd allow me to take it on. I braced myself mentally and resolved to go down fighting.

Sholto released my hand and said, 'Delighted to meet you, Miss Ryan. Thank you so much for coming. Do sit down.' He indicated a wing chair, studded with brass, facing his desk. 'I hope you had a pleasant journey?'

'Yes, thank you.'

He waited until I was seated, then sank back on to his wooden throne. 'Wilma gave you lunch, I trust?'

'Yes. I've been well looked after, thanks. Mr MacNab, can I start by saying I'm very sorry the Society of Authors didn't inform you I was a woman. They wouldn't have known, you see. People just make assumptions.' He looked embarrassed and started to shuffle some papers. Undeterred, I continued. 'They didn't actually mention that you were looking for a male writer, so there was plenty of scope for misunderstanding. That's the downside of email. The anonymity. I don't want to waste your time – or mine for that matter – so if you're convinced a woman can't do the job—'

'Not at all! My *preference* was for a man, but your credentials certainly qualify you.' He glanced at his notes. 'You seem to have considerable experience in the fields of travel, sport and family history. These are subjects I hope will be of interest to my potential readers. Do *you* think they'll be interested, Miss Ryan?'

'Please call me Jenny. Yes, I do. I think they'll be very interested. That is, if I can persuade you to avoid the traditional understatement employed by intrepid explorers.'

'Understatement?' Sholto looked intrigued.

'Quiet British heroism doesn't sell. Not any more. You need to bear in mind that, in an age when television brings natural disasters and real life heroics into our sitting rooms, readers look for something more when they open a book such as the one you propose to write.'

'Really?' Sholto was watching me carefully. 'What are they looking for, Miss Ryan?'

'They're looking for *you*.'

'Me?'

'Sholto MacNab. And if you choose to employ me to write your story, that's what I would give them. The man.'

'I see.' He looked doubtful. 'Not... the deeds?'

'Of course, the deeds, but those are already documented. Your remarkable achievements are well known. What readers don't know – and what I think they'll want to know – is *why*?'

Sholto looked puzzled. 'Why what?'

'Why did you do it? Why did you put your life on the line so many times? What drove you on? What made you go back to places like Antarctica where you'd almost died? Why did you know no fear?'

'Oh, is that what you think?' he said, narrowing his eyes. 'That I'm fearless?'

'No, it's not what *I* think. I know a mountaineer who says he learned to climb as a way of conquering a crippling fear of heights. But I'm sure the average book buyer thinks you're fearless. Writing about your fear – terror, even – would be much more gripping than any Captain Scott stiff-upper-lip heroics.'

'Is that so? Do I understand you to be suggesting some sort of "warts and all" portrait then?'

'I'm suggesting you tell the whole story. Present yourself as an ordinary man with both strengths and weaknesses. That can only serve to highlight your outstanding courage and leadership, not to mention your astonishing powers of endurance. If you'll forgive my saying so, Mr MacNab, you should be dead. I'd like to help you write a book that explains exactly why you're not.'

Sholto regarded me with some suspicion, then said, 'And what about my personal life? Are you proposing a confessional approach there too?'

'I am, though of course I realise this might make uncomfortable demands on you and other members of your family.'

'They're dead.'

'I beg your pardon?'

'My wives. They're both dead. They can't suffer any more,' he added, avoiding my eyes.

I thought it best not to comment and there followed a pause in which Sholto was obviously considering something. He regarded me and said, 'Do we really have to dredge up all the old stories? The gossip about my second wife?... And my poor daughter-in-law. You know people thought it was suicide?' I nodded and Sholto passed a hand across his face, dragging the flesh across the fine bones. 'I'm really not concerned about myself. I'm thinking of Alec. He's never been – now how shall I put this? Between you and me, Jenny, Alec has never been mentally *robust*. His mother's death... Then Coral's... The lad took some hard knocks.'

'Mr MacNab, if I may speak freely—'

He spread his hands. 'Go ahead. That's what this meeting's for. Putting all our cards on the table.'

'I am in no way advising you what to do. That's not within my remit. My job would be to help you tell your story in whatever way you wish to tell it. Any moral or artistic decisions must ultimately be yours.'

'Of course. It will be my name on the dust jacket.'

'Indeed. But Fergus has already mentioned you'd like your book to sell a lot of copies.'

'Oh, yes, that's the whole point! Only reason I'm doing it, in fact. You think I want to spend weeks cooped up indoors poring over old scrapbooks, talking about the adventures I used to have? The man I used to be?' His laugh was a humourless bark. 'I do not! Delightful though I'm sure your company would be, Jenny,' he added graciously.

'Well, if you want us to produce a bestseller, I suggest you're absolutely frank with me and allow me to give the reader the inside story.'

'Because scandal sells,' he said wearily.

'It certainly does. But I think there's a way to tell your story without resorting to vulgar sensationalism.'

'You do?'

'Oh, yes. We need to present the *man*. The whole man, in all his endearing fallibility. I'm not suggesting we expose feet of clay, simply that we explain exactly why you did what you did. After all, to understand is to forgive.'

Sholto smiled. 'That's what Liz used to say. My first wife. You know, she's been dead for more than thirty years and I still miss her.' He shook his head. 'I was a bastard to her. A complete bastard.'

I said nothing but my silence must have been eloquent. He shot me a defensive look, then went on quickly. 'I was going to finish with Meredith. It was only ever meant to be a fling. Nothing serious. Liz understood that, I think. But then she went and died. And I never had the chance to explain.'

'You do now, Mr MacNab. You can explain everything and readers will lap it up.'

'You think so?'

'I do.'

'Well, you've given me a lot to think about, Jenny... Your vision of my book isn't quite what I had in mind, but I have to admit, I can see the sense in what you say. I mean, one has to compete with a lot of other memoirs these days. I'd been wondering what my angle – is that what you call it?' I nodded. 'I wondered what angle we could exploit.'

'Sholto MacNab: soldier, sportsman, husband, father, laird and lover. The complete man.'

'Warts and all.'

'If you can bear it. And if you think your family can bear it.'

'You know, there will be rather a *lot* of warts.'

'The more the merrier. Everyone loves a bad boy.'

He beamed. 'I think you've just talked yourself into the job I was convinced I wouldn't offer you. That is, if you still want it?'

'I do. Very much.'

'On the terms we agreed?'

'Yes.'

'When can you start?'

'As soon as you like. I'll have to go back to London to fetch my stuff, but I can come back in a few days' time, or whenever you think you might be ready to start.'

'Come back as soon as you can. I shall be raring to go. I thought preparing this book would be rather a chore. A necessary evil. But now I think... Well, I think it could be rather fun, don't you?' His blue eyes were bright and full of mischief.

'I certainly do. And I'm hugely excited at the prospect of working with you.'

'The feeling's mutual, I do assure you.'

I stood and Sholto hauled himself to his feet, limping round the desk to stand beside me. As he vacated his chair, I noted with a thrill that the carved oak bore the date 1663.

'Welcome to Cauldstane, Jenny. I hope you'll feel at home with us.'

'It's been a pleasure to meet you, Mr MacNab.'

'Call me Sholto. Ridiculous name, isn't it? My father was called Ninian. I suspect he named his children as an act of revenge.'

'Your brother was Torquil, wasn't he?'

'You've done your homework, I see. You can imagine what they made of Torquil and Sholto MacNab at Eton. Actually, you probably can't, a nice well-brought up girl like you.'

'Torquil inherited first, didn't he? He was your older brother?'

'Yes. Cauldstane should have been his. And so should all the problems that came with it. He was trained up for it, you see. I wasn't. I was the madcap younger son who was going to have to make his own way in the world. And I was the one everyone thought likely to die young. The Cauldstane mantle was never meant to fall on my narrow shoulders. But Torquil was what they used to call a "confirmed bachelor". He was also a chain smoker and a heavy drinker.'

'Was it cancer?'

'Lung, then liver. It was a slow business... I miss him too, you know. He was a splendid fellow. Bizarre sense of humour though. You saw the albatross in the hall?'

For a moment I was thrown by his question, then I remembered. 'Oh – the stuffed bird?'

Sholto chuckled. 'Torquil sent me that when he realised he was dying and I'd have to take on Cauldstane. Oh, we had a lot of laughs… And some of his boyfriends were quite charming. Not that I ever indulged, of course. Always been one for the ladies myself – as you'll know if you're familiar with my press cuttings.'

'It's certainly going to be a colourful story, Mr MacNab. And it has all the ingredients of a bestseller.'

'You think so? That's what Cauldstane needs, Jenny. Needs badly.' He smiled and took my hand again and this time I allowed myself to look down. And there it was. The MacNab thumb.

I decided it was a good omen.

Chapter Four

I emerged from the library cock-a-hoop. It wasn't just that I'd managed to secure the commission against the odds. I was already smitten with Cauldstane and the MacNabs – all of them, even the dead ones. I estimated this job would take me two or three months, depending on Sholto's degree of co-operation. He'd offered me bed and board at the castle and I knew he couldn't afford to pay hotel expenses, so I was perfectly happy to stay as a guest and save myself a lot of driving. If I got to know the family it couldn't fail to add depth to what promised to be a fascinating and, at times, emotional story.

I went back to my room, hurled myself on to the bed and wallowed in my sense of triumph. For all of three minutes. Then the professional writer dragged me off the bed and propelled me over to my laptop. I needed to make notes. Sholto had already been quite frank – about his love life, Torquil's and Liz, the long-suffering first wife. And what about Alec? It sounded as if more than ordinary grief lay behind the fragility Sholto had referred to.

I switched on my laptop and gazed contentedly out the window at the view. This was to be mine for weeks. My room. My view. My family, almost. I could have hugged myself.

The sun was lower now. The castle threw an immense shadow over the river so the water looked much darker. I looked up at the stone bridge and saw a figure standing in the middle, staring down into the river as it foamed over the rocks. His head was bowed and at this distance, I couldn't be sure who it was.

He had something in his hand, something red. He held it up to his face, then raised his arm and tossed it into the river, throwing it a long way upstream. He placed his hands on the bridge and watched as the object returned to him. As it tumbled over the rocks towards him, he leaned over and watched it disappear under the bridge. Long after it must have vanished from sight, he still stood staring down into the water. Eventually he turned and began to walk away from the river, slowly, head down, his shoulders slightly hunched.

I'd known as soon as he'd raised an arm to throw that it was Alec, but it wasn't until I turned away from the window and saw the jug of roses on my writing desk that I realised what he'd thrown into the river.

Puzzled by the gesture, I sat down at my laptop, my attention scattered. I opened a new document, called it *The MacNabs* and tapped out some notes, recording my thoughts randomly.

> *History of MacNab clan – legends/ghosts etc?*
> *"Let fear be far from all." Origin?*
> *Who shot the stag in the hall?*
> *Who painted the portrait of Meredith? When?*
> *Sholto's affairs – Liz knew. Did M?*
> *M's singing career? Rôles? Photos? Old programmes?*
> *Paintings in attic?*
> *How long has Mrs G been here?*
> *Eton & Gordonstoun. Was Sholto happy at school? Were Alec & Fergus? Bullying?*
> *What does Fergus do?*
> *Alec – mental health history.*
> *Why did Coral MacN kill herself?*
> *Visit Alec's armoury.*
> *Condition of Cauldstane – building & estate.*
> *How does Alec feel about inheriting?*
> *How do the others feel about Alec as the next laird?*
> *Debts. How bad? Financial plans for future of Cauldstane?*
> *Is Sholto under pressure to sell up and leave Cauldstane to its ghosts?*

There was a knock at the door and Mrs Guthrie appeared with a tray. 'You'll be wanting your tea, Miss Ryan. After your ordeal,' she added, rolling her eyes.

I swivelled round in my chair. 'Please call me Jenny. You're going to be seeing a lot more of me over the next few weeks.'

Her eyes widened as she set down the tray. 'Mr MacNab's given you the job, then?'

'Yes. He seemed quite happy about it too. Excited, in fact.'

'Well, that's grand! I'm glad it's all settled. We'll make sure you feel right at home here.'

'I do already. Everyone's been very kind.' Eyeing the plate of shortbread, I added, 'But I can see I'm going to put on pounds. How's a girl supposed to resist?'

'Och, you'll work it off walking round the estate and running up and down our stairs. Living in a castle keeps you fit. That's what Mr MacNab always says. A childhood spent at Cauldstane was the best all-round, all-weather physical training he could have had, he says, and Eton was the best preparation for Arctic conditions and short rations. Though I think he's a wee bit inclined to exaggerate, for the sake of a good story. You'll perhaps need to bear that in mind.'

'I will. I'm greatly looking forward to hearing all his traveller's tales.'

'Oh aye, there are some good ones. And most of them are true! Now, can I get you anything else?'

'No, I'm fine. I'm just making some notes about our meeting,' I said, indicating the laptop.

'Well, when you've had your tea, I'll show you the Music Room.

'Oh, that's OK, you don't need to give me the tour. I'm sure I'll find my way around.'

'The Music Room is where you're to work, Miss Jenny, if that suits you. It's never used now and Mr MacNab thought it would serve as a study for whoever took on the job of writing his book. I think you'll be comfortable in there. There's a desk and a fireplace and of course there's the harpsichord if you're able to play.'

'I'm afraid I'm not at all musical. Who's the musician in the family?'

'It was Mrs MacNab's instrument. The *second* Mrs MacNab. Mr MacNab bought it for her as a wedding present.'

'How lovely! Does anyone play it now?'

'No one, not since Mrs MacNab passed away. She was the only one who could get a tune out of it. The children were never allowed to touch it. Mr Alec learned the fiddle when he was a boy, but no one's ever played the harpsichord. Mr Fergus has often suggested it should be sold. It's an antique and worth a great deal, I understand, but Mr MacNab won't part with it. It's a beautiful instrument. Mrs MacNab played it every day when she was in residence.'

'She was very musical, obviously.'

'Aye, she was a famous singer before she married. Meredith Fitzgerald, she was then. She used to sing in opera mostly. Mrs MacNab was a very *dramatic* personality.' There was something about Mrs Guthrie's tone that suggested admiration, even envy of her mistress' temperament. 'I never saw her perform on the stage, but she used to organise concerts now and again at Cauldstane. For Christmas, or as charity fund-raisers. Folk used to travel for miles to hear her and her friends sing. Those were very merry occasions.' Mrs Guthrie's sad smile belied her words. 'The castle was full of guests. There were fires and lights everywhere, music and laughter. Cauldstane was full of life then. And Mr and Mrs MacNab were such a handsome couple.'

'It must have made a lot of extra work for you. Did you have help?'

Mrs Guthrie shrugged sturdy shoulders. 'Just a couple of lassies from the village. And Miss Coral, of course, Mr Alec's wife. *Fiancée* as she was then. She was always keen to help out. So we managed.'

'Coral MacNab is dead, isn't she? When did she pass away?'

It was obviously a question I shouldn't have asked. Tears formed in Mrs Guthrie's eyes and her lower lip started to tremble. 'Seven years ago. I can't believe it's seven already,' she chided herself. She stood with one hand braced on her aproned hip, the other clamped over mouth, staring at the floor.

I rose from my chair. 'I'm so sorry, Mrs Guthrie. I didn't mean to upset you.'

She took her hand away from her mouth and flapped it at me in a futile, helpless gesture. 'No, if you're to write their story, you'll need to know all the sadness this poor family's known. And I'd far rather you asked me than Mr Alec. It's just that – *today* of all days...'

I remembered Alec by the river and my heart rose up into my mouth. 'It isn't... the *anniversary* of Coral's death, is it?'

'Aye, it is.'

'How did she die?'

'She drowned.'

My voice was hardly more than a whisper. 'Did she drown... *here*? At Cauldstane?'

Mrs Guthrie nodded, unable to speak, then fled from the room as fast as her trainers could carry her.

I walked over to the window, but I couldn't bring myself to look down at the fast-flowing river. Instead, I stared at the jug of roses on my desk and counted them. Then I counted them again. I kept counting until I felt calm again, then I drew the heavy curtains, lay down on my bed and fell asleep.

I woke an hour later, feeling refreshed, but it took me a moment to realise where I was. When I remembered, I felt ridiculously happy. My mind was buzzing with more questions I wanted to ask about the MacNabs, so I got off the bed, opened the curtains and sat down at the writing table. I opened up my laptop and gazed out the window, suppressing a desire to wave at passing crows. My happiness was slightly diminished when I glanced up at the mirror above me and saw the river tearing past, in the wrong direction.

Poor Coral.

Poor Alec.

The thing was, not to get involved. That's where I'd gone wrong in the past. I'd got too involved with the stories I was telling. You have to maintain a distance, a certain professional objectivity, otherwise you'd go mad trying to get into someone else's mind, trying to think like them, live their life. This was just a job. It wasn't my life, or *anyone's* life. It was just a book.

I clicked on the document in which I'd made my earlier notes. When it opened, the screen was blank. Puzzled, I clicked back to check I'd opened the right one. I had. I clicked back to the empty screen. Surely I'd saved what I'd written? After all these years, I saved automatically. Perplexed by what looked like uncharacteristic inefficiency, I scrolled down, hoping to see my notes eventually.

I found only one line. Everything else had gone. It wasn't even a complete line. Just five words.

leave Cauldstane to its ghosts

Chapter Five

I left Cauldstane before breakfast the next morning. Mrs Guthrie was struggling visibly with the affront of someone embarking on a long train journey on an empty stomach, but I told her I wasn't hungry. As she said goodbye, she handed me a small package wrapped in tin foil. When I opened it on the train a few hours later, I discovered it was two pieces of sticky gingerbread. Interleaved with the foil was a paper napkin on which she'd written *Haste ye back*. As I sped south towards the border, I wolfed down both pieces with a cup of coffee.

No one else had been up when I left and the silence had been eerie. The night before, Fergus had offered to take me back to the station, but as it was Saturday I thought he might appreciate a lie-in. I said I was happy to travel back to Inverness by taxi and he'd looked relieved. So it was just Mrs Guthrie who waved me off from the castle's back door.

I'd heard about autumn in the Highlands. That morning the sky was a cloudless Mediterranean blue and the bright northern light seemed to shift everything into sharp focus. A big bird of prey hovered above the castle, apparently defying all physical laws by maintaining complete stillness in the air. Then with a casual flick of its forked tail, it would change its position, but hover still, watching and waiting. I watched too, hypnotized by the bird's apparent immobility.

It was only September, but there was a freshness to the air, almost a chill. When I looked up at the trees beyond the courtyard walls, I could see some leaves had already turned. Their warm, vivid colours stood out against the fresh green, like blemishes. The short Highland summer was over.

As I sat on the train I had leisure to examine the subject that had preoccupied my thoughts since yesterday afternoon, all through a rather stilted dinner and for some of a restless night. (*Scotch*

Deerhounds and their Masters had failed to do the trick.)

Who had wiped my notes? And why?

My bedroom door had not been locked. Fergus, Alec and Mrs Guthrie all knew which room I was in. Probably Sholto and Zelda did too. I didn't think I'd shut my laptop down completely. An inquisitive person could have lifted the lid and the laptop would have woken up. They'd have been able to see what I'd written.

And what exactly had I written? Was there anything that would upset or offend a family member, to the extent that they'd delete my notes? I simply couldn't remember. I recalled typing a lot of questions and topics to think about later. The only contentious thing I remembered writing was a question about Alec succeeding Sholto, but I'd expressed no opinion myself. There had also been a question about Coral MacNab's suicide. Perhaps someone thought I shouldn't be prying into private grief? Alec was the most likely candidate. It was after all the anniversary of his wife's death and hadn't Sholto hinted at his son's instability?

Then I realised something that made me sit up with a start and spill my coffee. *I hadn't left my room.* Whoever had tampered with my laptop had done it while I was asleep on the bed. They'd read my notes while I dozed, deleted them, then left as silently as they'd come. But who? Would I have heard Mrs Guthrie in her trainers? Perhaps not. Alec, with his cat-like poise, could probably get in and out of a room without making a sound.

But the most likely explanation was surely that I'd somehow wiped my own work in some semi-conscious state. Was it possible I'd woken briefly, gone over to the laptop, made a few more notes, accidentally wiped the whole document, then gone back to sleep again? This scenario seemed even less likely than an intruder entering and deleting a load of harmless questions. It would only have taken a few keystrokes: *Select all* and *Delete*.

Except that wasn't what he'd done. (I was shocked to realise I'd already fixed on Alec as the culprit.) He hadn't deleted everything. There was half a line remaining – the final line, if my memory served me. As we drew into Perth, I switched on my laptop, half hoping my notes might have re-appeared. They hadn't.

leave Cauldstane to its ghosts

Each time I read that phrase I fought back an irrational fear, a heartfelt wish that these words would also disappear, because the thought that someone had left them deliberately, that they weren't just a remnant of text, but a message, a warning even, made me feel sick and shivery – exactly how I'd felt on the landing when I was talking to Alec. Was this my damn virus getting a hold again? Or was it those words?

If they *were* a message for me, then I had to accept the possibility that someone – Alec, I supposed – didn't want me at Cauldstane.

When I got home, I watered my houseplants, checked my post, then sat down to ring Rupert. I chose my favourite spot – the sunny, plant-filled bay window of the Victorian semi I used to share with him. It had always been mine but Rupert had paid me rent and shared the running costs. It was one of the things that had prevented us calling ours a permanent arrangement. He liked to refer to me jokingly as his "landlady".

I'd met Rupert at a publishing party. He was a theoretical physicist who'd just published a popular science book. We found we got on well and one thing led to another. He eventually moved in to reduce the trekking about from his flat in Putney to my house in Crouch End. The break-up had been equally relaxed. There was no third party involved – unless you wanted to cite God – and I had many happy memories of our years together. I still kept a few photos of us on display and was gazing at one while I waited for Rupert to pick up the phone.

We were pictured on board ship, smiling at a fellow passenger who'd taken the photo for us. It was a Norwegian cruise ship, headed for the Arctic Circle and we were togged up in coats like duvets. Rupert, always self-conscious about his lack of height, looked almost as broad as he was tall, like Henry VIII, but he'd just seen a sea eagle at close quarters and was grinning like a schoolboy. I looked more Nordic than the Norwegians, dressed in white, with pale skin and long ash blonde hair, but I was slouching as I always did in photos, so I wouldn't look taller than Rupert. (I don't know if I ever really loved him, but I was always tender of his feelings.)

I looked different now. Older of course, but now my hair was very short and starting to go grey. So far I hadn't resorted to dye. I told myself it didn't really show. Yet.

At forty I'd done the inevitable stock-take. No man. No child. No ties. I was poorly paid, but self-employed and I had a very nice home. Things could have been worse. *Had* been worse, in fact. So I took each day as it came, which meant that sometimes I cried myself to sleep with loneliness and sometimes I woke full of joy that I was accountable to no one. If I couldn't write exactly what I wanted to write, in the way I wanted to write it, it seemed a small price to pay for all the other advantages. I wasn't one of those women who wanted to have it all. I was too aware how many people had very little. Having everything would have made me uncomfortable. I might have expected some kind of trade-off. I was free, but I suppose I was fearful.

So I missed Rupert, but only as a friend. He was now a curate in Newcastle so we rarely saw each other, but kept in touch by phone and email. If I'd been able to bring myself to believe in Him, I'm sure I would have resented God for depriving me of Rupert's company, but I accepted that his parishioners' need was greater than mine. So, presumably, was God's.

When Rupert finally answered the phone, he sounded breathless. 'Hello. Rupert Sheridan.'

'Hi, it's me. How's things?'

'Jen? I thought you were in Scotland?'

'I was. I'm back now.'

'Did you get the commission?' He sounded eager and I felt pleased I had good news for him.

'Yes, I did actually.'

'Congratulations! I suppose you're not at liberty to say more?'

'You know the rules. All I can tell you is, I'm going to be staying somewhere in the region of Inverness for the next few weeks.'

'So you'd like me to look after your houseplants.'

'Would you mind? I don't really want to give neighbours a key for weeks and I can't think of any friend I can ask who won't forget to water them or kill them with kindness.'

'You flatterer! You're travelling north by car, I presume?'

'Yes. The subject wants me to start as soon as possible, so I've just come home to collect some clothes and other bits and pieces. I thought I could drop off the plants on my way up. If that's OK?'

'Yes, fine. The more the merrier. The house badly needs re-painting but I have neither the time nor inclination, so adorning it with houseplants is a good disguise. Parishioners will be impressed by my green fingers. So is this going to be a good job then?'

'Well, the money's crap, but the people seem very nice. Which is just as well. I'll be staying with the family for a few weeks.'

'Won't that be a bit… intense?'

'Not really. I'll have my own room and a study. The family home is large. *Very* large.'

'So a stately pile then, somewhere-in-the-Highlands.'

'I couldn't possibly comment.'

'Spoilsport. But if the money's crap, why are you taking the job?'

'Rupert, I seem to remember asking you the very same question about becoming a minister. I don't take jobs for the money. I accept jobs that *interest* me. Which usually means *people* who interest me. Though in this case, I do think my subject has a fascinating story to tell and I think I could write him the sort of book that would sell. It has all the right ingredients.'

'Let me guess… Money. Class. Sex. Scandal. And a big country house?'

'A *very* big country house.'

'Splendid! Put me down for a copy. What's the catch?'

'Catch?'

'I assumed there must be one. You sounded as if you were trying to convince me it was a good job. Or convince yourself.'

'No, there's no catch. Not that I know of anyway. There's been a lot of tragedy in the family and a certain amount of… well, betrayal, I suppose. The subject is a widower. A very interesting man, but he's been through a lot. I don't think it's going to be an *easy* book to write. And I'm not totally convinced everyone wants me to write it.'

'So there *is* a catch.'

'No, not really. I mean, I just picked up on a few things, that's all. I suppose I could just sense… all the sadness.'

Rupert's sigh was audible down the phone. 'Oh, sweetheart… *please*. Walk away from this one. You don't want to go down that road again. That was the whole point of taking the ghost jobs. Easy money. No hassle. No comebacks.'

'Don't worry, I won't get involved. But I do have to be sensitive to – well, to *atmospheres*, otherwise I couldn't do the job. It's all about reading between the lines. Trying to find out what people want to say, but are perhaps not brave enough to say. Or strong enough.'

'Well, I'm sure you know what you're doing,' Rupert said, in a tone that implied completely the opposite. I remembered then how guilty yet relieved I'd felt when I realised we'd finally come to the end of the line.

'So can I come up and see you tomorrow? And offload the plants?'

'Of course not – it's Sunday! I won't have a spare moment to talk to you. Can you come Monday instead? I can put you up for the night if you want to break your journey.'

'No, that might scandalize your parishioners.'

'On the contrary, it might put the brakes on their relentless match-making.'

'Rupert, it will be lovely to see you, but it has to be just a flying visit. I want to get up to Scotland as soon as I can.'

'Fair enough. I'll make us some lunch – unless you'd rather go out?'

'It would be a late lunch. Is that OK? It will take me four or five hours to get to you.'

'I'll have something waiting.'

'Thanks. Oh – I've just thought of something else. Do you have a bird book you could lend me?'

'Several. Did you see something interesting in Scotland?'

'I don't know. A bird of prey, hovering.'

'A kestrel?'

'No, it was big. And very still. The only movement was a little flick of its tail.'

'Forked?'

'I'm sorry?'

'Was its tail forked?'

'Yes, I think it was.'

'Then you saw a red kite, you lucky thing. Not so rare in the Highlands now, but uncommon elsewhere. I'll lend you a book and my second best pair of binoculars on the condition you let me know about any interesting sightings.'

'It's a deal.'

'See you Monday then. You're *sure* you won't stay over? The spare bed's always made up for any passing waifs and strays. Or bishops.'

'Thanks, but I'll be anxious to get on. I want to get as far as Edinburgh, then I'll do the rest the next morning. I'm rather looking forward to that bit of the drive.'

'You sound excited about this job.'

'I am. It feels like something big for me.'

'Yes, that's what worries me.'

It was my turn to sigh. 'Rupert, I'm not your problem any more. Worry about your flock. I can take care of myself.'

'Yes, I'm sure you can,' he replied, doing that maddening contradictory thing with his voice again.

We said our goodbyes and I hung up feeling grateful, but slightly irritated. I knew Rupert was disappointed I wasn't staying over, but the truth was, I wanted to keep a circumspect distance between me and my former lover. I enjoyed being a free agent now, but I still felt I needed to prove to him I could cope on my own. That's what I'd done, for years now. There was nothing left to prove really, least of all to Rupert. Perhaps I was still trying to convince myself. If there *was* a small voice inside my head saying, "Walk away from the MacNabs, or you'll be sorry," I had no intention of listening to it.

Chapter Six

Ghostwriting is a job for an author with no ego and unlimited discretion.

I grew up wanting to be a writer. Actually I think I always *was* a writer. A storyteller, certainly. As an only child, I was often bored and lonely. If I was short of a playmate, I would devise make-believe games that entailed me acting out all the parts. If there was no one to talk to, I was prepared to talk to myself.

I was an avid and precocious reader, but if I didn't like the ending of a book, I would re-write it in my head – and sometimes on paper – with the conclusion I thought the characters deserved. Sometimes it wasn't just the ending I re-wrote. I would create parallel lives for characters I loved. So *my* Sydney Carton was saved at the eleventh hour from the guillotine. When my Katy Carr fell from the swing in the barn, she only broke her ankle and was laid up for four months, not four years. My Beth March recovered fully from her scarlet fever and – like Tiny Tim – she did *not* die.

You might suppose I grew up impervious to the greatness of the classics, that my quest for a happy ending guaranteed I would become a sentimental and clichéd writer, but the effort of unpicking Dickens, Coolidge and Alcott taught me a great deal about the structure of stories. As I grew older, my fascination with story overcame my aversion to unhappy outcomes. Predictably, I read English at university, acquiring a first class degree, which qualified me for absolutely nothing.

On the death of my widowed mother, I inherited a large house in north London, my parents' home for thirty years. There was some money too, so I was under no pressure to sell up. I could afford to freelance as a journalist or work as a publicist, developing a list of contacts that would come in useful years later.

But I always wrote. Writing was always there as the ballast that kept me stable and happy. The stories felt like my real world. Work was just something I did, something that got me out of a house now crammed with books – mine and my parents'. I couldn't bring myself to get rid of objects that had meant so much to the people I loved. To have sold their books or given them away would have seemed sacrilegious and unkind – not just to my dead parents, but unkind to their books. You probably won't be surprised to hear that I've never dog-eared a page in my life. Even as a child I found the lamentable state of some library books upsetting. I used to try to repair them with sellotape, but in the end I stopped using the library and took to re-reading my own books, then made an early start on reading adult fiction, guided by my bibliophile parents.

There was never any ego involved in my writing. I had no desire to be famous or win prizes, only a desire to satisfy my immense curiosity about people with lives more interesting than mine – which was most of them. Ghostwriting provided me with a crash course in someone else's life. I, who knew nothing about horses, could learn in a matter of weeks what it took to become an Olympic show jumper. I'd never bought a lottery ticket, but I could absorb the riches-to-rags story of a compulsive gambler who'd lost everything and found God.

As a ghost, I was allowed to ask impertinent questions. I could quiz my subjects about their infidelities and criminal activities. I could ask if there was any substance to the rumours that had destroyed a marriage or a career. I couldn't always use the information entrusted to me, but my knowledge and understanding of my subject was enriched.

I suppose if ghosting hadn't worked out and I'd been desperate for money, I could have pursued an alternative career as a blackmailer. Except that nothing would have made me break the seal of the confessional. The relationship I had with my subjects was based on trust and respect. The intimacy we shared might have been one-way (I knew almost everything about them and they knew almost nothing about me), but intimacy there was. It was something I cherished, even when my subject was a far from admirable human being. My immersion in the classics had furnished me with a staunchly-held belief in the possibility of redemption. I assumed that, like Sydney Carton, all miscreants were capable of doing a far, far better thing than they had ever done.

My job sanctioned curiosity and compassion and these enabled me to sublimate my own personality and take on temporarily the personality and voice of someone else, someone quite unlike me. Curiosity and compassion took me to Cauldstane and kept me there long after any sane person would have left.

When I returned, Sholto established a work routine that suited us both. We would talk in the morning, then he liked to lunch alone. In the afternoon he took a nap and then attended to estate business. At six o'clock I was invited for a drink and more talk in the library, then we dined at seven with any members of the family who were at home. So my afternoons and evenings were largely free for me to read, write, research and walk around the estate.

One day Sholto and I were sitting on a bench in the walled garden, sheltered from a cool autumnal breeze. He preferred to be outdoors whenever possible and liked to walk while talking, but he often needed to resort to one of the many strategically-placed benches in the grounds. The tools of my trade were just a small dictaphone and a notebook in which I would record questions that occurred to me while Sholto talked, so we could work anywhere. Today he'd chosen a favourite spot on a south-facing wall and as we rested, I could feel the warmth radiating from the stones behind me. I was enjoying the play of sunlight on the last of the roses and the fluttering dance of Painted Ladies on a white buddleia when Sholto said, 'Our family's cursed, of course.' He saw my look of astonishment and treated me to one of his roguish smiles. 'All good Scots families are.'

'Cursed?'

'Oh, yes. There's a MacNab curse. Hundreds of years old. As old as the castle. Older possibly.'

'Do people believe in it?'

'It's quite hard not to.'

'Why?'

'Our women keep dying.'

I felt a chill crawl down my back and looked at the little tape recorder I'd placed beside him. I wondered if I should stop it, but Sholto seemed unperturbed as he stared into the distance, his fingers clasping the handle of the carved rowan walking stick Alec had made for him from a dead tree on the estate. There was no indication from Sholto's demeanour that we'd strayed into dangerous personal territory. As I studied his handsome, craggy profile, I saw no clue as to how I should proceed, so I decided to leave the tape running and said gently, 'Do *you* believe in the MacNab curse?'

'No, I don't. I don't believe in any kind of hocus-pocus. Ghosts, spirits, witchcraft, what have you.' He turned to me and smiled again. 'That's quite unusual for a Scot my age. Did you know the last witch was burned in Scotland? And not that long ago. 1727. We've clung to our old superstitions. Some still won't let them go.'

'So the family actually believe in this curse?'

'We've never really discussed it. But I've come to my own conclusions. Wilma believes, of course.'

'Mrs Guthrie?'

'Yes. But she's the fourth generation to be in service here. The MacNab curse would have been dinned into her along with the Lord's Prayer and the nine times table. But generally the women don't believe in the curse. I'm sure Zelda doesn't. But it would never affect her, you see. She can afford to be sceptical.'

'But I thought you said it was the women who... who were affected?'

'That's correct. They die or they're infertile. Or both. Like poor Coral.' Sholto shook his head. 'She let the curse get to her, but she was... a depressive. Well, that's perhaps unfair. She seemed cheerful enough when Alec first introduced her to us. Meredith never took to her, but I liked her. She was a quiet girl. A bit deep, but so's Alec. We thought she'd be good for him. But the marriage got off to a bad start. It began with a death and ended five years later with another death.'

'So you're saying some people think Meredith's death — and Coral's — are to do with the curse?'

'You're forgetting poor Liz. In my lifetime alone there have been *three* deaths attributed to the MacNab curse — two accidents and one suicide. All women, all incomers. The curse doesn't affect the MacNabs, you see, just the unfortunate women we marry. So if you were to ask me why hasn't Alec married again or why a damned good-looking boy like Fergus has never even been engaged, I'd have to say, I've no idea. Their private lives are no concern of mine. But if you asked me, do my sons believe in the curse, my answer would be, I fear they *might*. And who can blame them? They lost a mother and a stepmother. Alec also lost a wife.'

Birds began to chatter noisily above our heads and I looked up to see blue tits racketing around in the branches of a huge fan-trained apple tree, like tiny feathered dodgems. The sight should have lifted my spirits, but it didn't. I took a deep breath and, keeping my voice level, said, 'So the curse says any woman marrying into the MacNabs of Cauldstane will be infertile or die.'

'Or both.'

'How dreadful! Even if you don't believe in it, it's an awful thing to have to live with.'

'Indeed. My father and grandfather took the precaution of marrying first cousins, thereby avoiding the curse.'

'Because their wives had MacNab blood in their veins?'

'Precisely. Earlier generations had married "out" and their wives had come to grief – though dying of TB or in childbirth was not uncommon. Infertility was less common and in previous centuries a few childless MacNab wives died suddenly in their late thirties. The bereft MacNab then married some girl half his age not long after, leading one to suspect the unfortunate MacNab wives might have met their maker prematurely because they'd failed to produce an heir. Either way, the curse was fulfilled. But it could have been used as a smokescreen for murder.'

'This is all horribly fascinating, Sholto, but are you all right discussing it? You don't find it upsetting?'

'No, because I don't believe in it! I'd find it easier to believe in Santa Claus than the Cauldstane Curse.'

Unconvinced, I regarded his face for a moment but saw nothing more than his usual affable expression. 'Well, if you're sure... Tell me then, what was the origin of the curse? Who did the cursing and when?'

He leaned back on the bench and crossed his legs. 'It's quite a tale. There's no documentary evidence, I'm afraid, just generations of hearsay and a peculiar stone.'

'What sort of stone?'

'A boulder. Round. Flattish. The result of glacial deposition, probably.'

'Where is it?'

Sholto gestured over his shoulder with his thumb. 'In the river. Near the bridge.'

'Oh *no*...' The words were out before I knew I'd spoken. Sholto

46

watched me for a moment. It was his turn to decide whether to continue.

'You've heard about Coral, then?'

'Mrs Guthrie told me. And I saw Alec on the bridge, the day I came up for my interview. I didn't speak to him there, I just saw him from my window, throwing a rose into the river. I wondered what it meant. It was the anniversary, I gather.'

'Yes. You wouldn't have seen Alec at his best that day.' Sholto swivelled round on the bench to face me and said, 'Are you *sure* you want to hear all this twaddle? You're looking a bit peaky. We could always leave it for another day. It's a gruesome tale and my forebears don't emerge with any credit.'

'No, I want to hear all about it. It will probably give me nightmares, but I can't resist a good yarn.'

'That's my girl,' Sholto said, chuckling. He paused, then said, 'An ancient MacNab married an outsider and she turned out to be a faithless hussy. In some versions of the story she slept with his brother. In a racier version she slept with his son. It was said she'd bewitched her lover with a magic herbal draught, but this claim could have been made afterwards to protect MacNab reputations. I doubt any herbal draught was required. To the best of my knowledge, no Cauldstane MacNab ever became a monk, or even a minister. Despite the curse, celibacy is not a path any of the males has chosen. Some of us — my brother Torquil and I, for example — have erred in *quite* the other direction. But I digress... When the cuckolded laird found out what his wife had been up to, he had her put to death. The usual version of the story is that she was struck down with the Cauldstane claymore.'

'Claymore?'

'It's a huge sword. Ask Alec to show it to you.'

'It still *exists*?'

'Oh, yes. It lives on the wall in the Great Hall. If you catch Alec in a good mood, he'll give you a demonstration.'

'Really?'

'Certainly. Historical swordsmanship is his passion. He's not too keen on the idea of this book, but I'm sure he'd be happy to show you the claymore. If you're interested.'

'I most certainly am.'

An image of Alec came to mind: Alec as he sprang across the

47

courtyard, attacking the air with a rapier. That image was succeeded by another: a snapshot Sholto had shown me of Liz with her two small boys, in which an eight-year old Alec appeared to defend his family against a foe the others couldn't see. I wasn't looking forward to asking Sholto about the accidents that killed both his wives. I would probably have to talk to Alec too, despite the possibility he didn't want me around. Undaunted, I returned to the cheery subject of summary execution.

'So the errant MacNab wife was despatched with the Cauldstane claymore?'

'Correct. Probably had her head lopped off. Or she might have been sliced in two. Ask Alec. He'd know exactly how you kill someone with a claymore. *Not* something he learned at Gordonstoun, I hasten to add... Anyway, that's when the real trouble started.'

'It gets worse?'

'But of course!' Sholto said gleefully. 'The wife's mother was reputedly a witch. When she heard what had happened to her daughter, she cursed all MacNabs, past, present and future. She declared that early death or barrenness would befall any bride not of the blood. So then the mother was condemned as a witch – and probable supplier of the aforementioned herbal draught – and they drowned her in the river, here at Cauldstane. She died cursing the family. Comprehensively.'

We sat in respectful silence for a moment – I felt slightly stunned – and I noticed that when Sholto wasn't talking, I could hear the sound of the river in the distance, rushing over the rocks. It wasn't a soothing sound, so I focussed on work again.

'Do you know the actual wording of the curse?'

'No. It belongs to an oral tradition. If it was ever written down, the document would have been burned or lost. But I doubt any MacNab would have dared commit the curse to parchment or paper. Asking for trouble! In any case, tradition has it the words were preserved on the Blood Stone.'

'The *Blood Stone?* Oh, now you're teasing me, aren't you?'

'Not at all! The Blood Stone is the one in the middle of the river bed. By the bridge. It's visible whenever the water level is low. The condemned witch was tied up, then hurled from the bridge, into the river. She smashed her skull on this stone. Legend says, once her blood and brains were washed away, the words of her curse were visible, etched on the stone in blood-red letters. They're conveniently illegible now of course, but there *are* strange reddish marks on the stone, even I have to admit that. Believers in the curse say the marks are all that's left after hundreds of years of the river eroding the stone.'

'You must point it out to me. Could I wade in and have a look?'

'Don't you dare! Not without being attached to a rope with someone on the other end. The river's fast-flowing. The Blood Stone's close to the surface because it sits on a rocky outcrop. That disguises the fact that the river's deep in the middle. In any case, there's nothing much to see. There are red veins in the rock that look something like a faint cursive hand. But I've no doubt a geologist could account for the marks.'

Struggling to absorb the impact of Sholto's grim story, I looked down at my notebook, scanned my list of prepared questions and adapted one. 'What was it like growing up with all these tales? Being surrounded by magic stones and ancient swords... You must have been less sceptical as a child, surely?'

'My father believed in the curse, so naturally I didn't, as a matter of principle. Two staid and fearful parents produced three non-conformist children who were determined to live life to the full. I suppose we were all explorers in our different ways. Zelda was perhaps the bravest.'

'You mean marrying a racing driver?'

'No, my dear – marrying a *foreigner*. My father would have preferred to see her enter a nunnery than marry a Frenchman. Zelda had no choice but to live abroad. And poor old Torquil was told he'd driven his father into an early grave with his homosexual exploits. It was made clear to me that I should be the one to produce a proper Cauldstane heir. As I had no intention of doing anything other than marrying for love, I couldn't afford to believe in the curse. But I do remember as a boy being tremendously excited by the legend of the Cauldstane claymore.'

'There's a *legend* as well?'

'Yes. You must get Alec to tell you about it.'

'I want to know now!'

Sholto rolled his eyes and muttered, 'Will I ever get my morning coffee?' Then he grinned, obviously enjoying himself. 'The claymore is supposed to have supernatural powers, power to protect the MacNabs from evil, but as is usually the case with these magical devices, there's a strict limit to the number of times the magic can be invoked. Our sword can be used only once more to defend the lives and honour of the MacNabs, then, inexplicably, its power expires.'

'How many times has it been used?'

'Twice. The execution of the adulterous wife was the first time.'

'And the second?'

'1975. When Torquil attacked a burglar.'

I couldn't help laughing. 'He attacked a burglar with a priceless antique?'

'It was probably the priceless antique the burglar was trying to steal. God knows, we don't own much else of any value. Not any more. And there's quite a market for old weapons now.'

'What did Torquil do?'

'He said he was too drunk at the time to realise the implications of using up the sword's magic quota. He just grabbed the nearest heavy object. He hadn't a clue how to handle the thing – a claymore would make the strongest of fellows look limp-wristed – but the intruder thought Torquil knew what he was doing and turned tail, then broke his neck falling down a turnpike stair. There's an uneven step, designed to trip the unwary – one of those built-in security measures you get in castles. The family know about it and outsiders don't. Simple but effective. The poor fellow went flying head first and that was that.'

'So the claymore apparently exerted its power again.'

'That's what believers said.'

'But now, thanks to Torquil, it can only be used once more.'

'According to the legend.'

'This is wonderful stuff, Sholto! It can go straight into the book, just as you tell it.'

'You think so? Will readers be interested in these ridiculous stories?'

'Of course they will!'

'Well, if you say so. It all seems a bit ho-hum to me because I grew up with it. I never really took any of it seriously.'

'Never?'

'No. Well, not until Meredith died.' Sholto clasped his stick tightly. 'I did wonder for a while then. I mean, losing *two* wives... It would make you think, wouldn't it? But accidents happen. Especially when people are drunk. And Meredith was very drunk. I didn't realise she'd driven off on her own. It was Alec's wedding reception and Cauldstane was heaving with guests. I didn't notice she'd gone. Not until it was too late.'

'Why did she drive off on her own? Do you know?'

Sholto didn't speak but he looked at me, as if assessing what he should say. I returned his gaze and waited. I've learned to wait.

'I've no idea why Meredith was so drunk, but she got into her car and drove off because Alec had told her to go to hell. Which I fear, poor girl, she duly did.'

As if on cue, a mournful bell began to toll and Sholto sat up, galvanised. 'Ah! That's Wilma telling us coffee's served.'

'That bell has a wonderful cracked note. Full of character. Is it very old?'

'No, Zelda rescued it from the local primary school in the days when there *was* a local primary school. It's a holiday home now.' Sholto struggled to his feet, then stood swaying a little. 'There'll be coffee in the summer house and some in the drawing room. Take your pick. I'm going indoors. The chill gets to my bones these days. You'd think a lifetime of roughing it would make you tolerant of cold and damp. Rather the reverse, I'd say. I hated it at Eton and I hate it now. Used to lie in my tent in Antarctica, trying to warm myself up, thinking about how I almost died of heatstroke in the Sahara. Didn't work. Still perished.' He stood staring at the ground, apparently reluctant to move. When he finally spoke, his voice sounded as cracked as the bell. 'Poor Meredith... Bloody awful way to die. *Christ*, she was a mess...'

With that he turned and walked away, setting a brisk pace that I'm sure must have caused him physical pain. I let him go on alone and headed instead for the summer house.

Chapter Seven

Sholto had indicated that the summer house was in a corner of the walled garden at the junction of the south- and west-facing walls. I didn't head in that direction immediately. Concerned he might fall, I watched until he was out of sight, then gathered up my things and shoved them into my bag. I turned and followed the path, wondering why I couldn't see the summer house. I caught sight of Mrs Guthrie on the other side of the garden, trotting off in the direction of the castle. I was about to call out and ask where the summer house was when I found it, almost obscured from view by an enormous shrub rose, taller than a man, which grew beside it. The roof and walls were additionally camouflaged by a canopy of what I later learned was a clematis, so that the wooden building resembled something from a fairy tale, a sort of tree house on the ground.

As I approached, I noticed a faint but continuous buzzing noise. I looked up and saw that the yellowy-green bell-shaped flowers of the clematis thronged with bees. I stood for a moment with my eyes shut, feeling the sun on the side of my face, listening to the hum of the bees. I inhaled the climber's elusive scent and knew a moment of sheer and simple happiness. That was dispelled a moment later when I opened my eyes and looked through the open door of the summer house. Alec MacNab, dressed for work in his worn leather apron and steel-capped shoes, was seated on one of the battered Lloyd Loom chairs, his long legs extended, his feet resting on another chair. My immediate thought was to turn and walk away, but I felt sure he must have heard my approach on the gravel path. As I stood, undecided, he turned his head and smiled, but didn't move.

'Good morning. Will you join me for coffee?' He indicated a large thermos coffee pot on the table. 'Wilma just delivered, but no one else seems to want to brave the elements today.'

'Sholto and I have been in the garden all morning, but he was tired. And a bit cold, I think. So he went back to the castle.' I hesitated in the doorway. 'You're sure you don't mind if I join you? I'd love some coffee.'

'Sit down and I'll pour you some.' He stood up and brought a chair forward and placed it in the doorway. 'If you sit just there, you'll have a good view of the roofline of Cauldstane. On a day like today, you might see a red kite if you're lucky.' He looked at me, checking I understood. 'Not the kind flown by wee boys.'

'I know,' I said, smiling as I stepped inside the summer house which was warm and musty and seemed rather dark after the bright sun outside. I sat down on the chair Alec had arranged for me. 'I have a friend who's a keen birdwatcher and some of it's rubbed off. He was quite jealous when I told him I'd seen a kite at Cauldstane.'

'They're magnificent creatures. The wing span is almost two metres. You don't notice that from the ground.' Alec poured me a mug of coffee and said, 'Milk and sugar?'

'Just milk, please.' He handed me the mug, then as he picked up a plate, I raised my hand in protest. 'Don't even think of offering me one of those biscuits! My willpower is non-existent when it comes to Mrs Guthrie's home baking.'

'Resistance is futile,' Alec said as he took a biscuit from the plate. 'How's it going with Sholto? He seems to be enjoying himself.'

'You think so?' I tried to ignore the tempting crunching noises and averted my eyes from the biscuits.

'He's in his element, re-living the past, dusting down the old traveller's tales. And it's doing him a power of good. We're very grateful to you.'

'Oh, it's nothing to do with me. I just sit there with the tape recorder.'

'It's everything to do with you that he's enjoying himself. He wasn't looking forward to it. And we all had mixed feelings about raking over the past.'

'There is rather a lot of past, isn't there?'

'Hundreds of years. But if you just look at Sholto's three score years and ten, there's a hell of a lot of ground to cover. Some of it pretty bumpy. That he's prepared to do it and appears to be enjoying the process is a testament to your tact and encouragement, Jenny.'

'Thank you.'

'You sound surprised.'

'I suppose I am a little.'

'Why?'

'Well, I don't think I can take all the credit.'

'And?...'

'And?'

He narrowed his eyes and said, 'There's something else you'd like to say, but you're not sure you should.'

I laughed to hide my surprise and embarrassment. 'Am I that easy to read?'

'In some ways, yes. In others, no.'

I waited for Alec to continue, but he just sat drinking his coffee, regarding me, as if waiting for me to speak. The silence was becoming awkward, so I took a biscuit from the plate and bit into it, playing for time. I chewed and swallowed, then said, 'Well, if I'm being honest—'

'Why be anything else?'

I broke off some small pieces of biscuit and tossed them outside where some chaffinches were strutting on the path. 'I suppose I wasn't really expecting your approval.'

'Why not? This project is good for Sholto. And if the book sells in sufficient quantities, it could help with some of our financial difficulties. Has he told you just how bad things are?'

'No, but he's dropped hints.'

'You'll find it hard to get him to talk about it. Well, *I* do.' Alec studied the contents of his mug. 'But things are bad. Fergus thinks we should put the castle on the market. For three million.'

'But it's your inheritance!'

'Aye, but Fergus is our business brain – the only business brain in the family – and he says Cauldstane's a money pit. And he's right. Which is why we'd never get three million for it. But my hope was not to have to sell up in Sholto's lifetime. That's where your book might help, you see. A wee cash injection could buy us a bit of time, enable us to maintain the fabric of the building so it would still be worth selling after Sholto's gone.'

'That's all so sad. I can't bear to think of Cauldstane going out of the family, so heaven knows how you must feel.'

Alec shrugged. 'It's an eventuality I've had to consider for half my life. Inheriting is the easy part. It's hanging on to a place that's hard. But why did you think I'd disapprove of you?'

I could think of no suitable reply. A certain reticence on his part on the day of my interview, the bitterness about Meredith – these could be ascribed to grief on the anniversary of his wife's death. But tampering with my laptop?... Looking at Alec now, his face calm, his eyes cool and enquiring, it was impossible to believe him capable of such an act. But if it hadn't been Alec, who could it have been?

I turned away and said, 'I just got the impression you weren't very keen on the idea of the book.' It sounded lame, but it was all I could say without asking him outright if he'd come into my room while I slept and deleted my notes.

'Did Sholto say I might be a problem?'

'No, not at all! He just warned me that – well, that you'd had some very bad experiences.'

'And he did that because, at some point, if you do your job properly, you're going to have to ask me to sit down and talk about death. My mother's, for a start. Because I was the sole witness. Also the cause.'

'You were only *eight*.'

'Aye, so they tell me. You'll also want to know about Meredith's death. And no one apart from me will discuss with you whether or not I was indirectly responsible for that too. But one thing they *will* all tell you is that my wife committed suicide. Which isn't actually true, though I can never prove it.'

'It wasn't suicide?'

'No.'

'So was it ... an accident?'

'*Another* accident? Aye, well, that's the inevitable conclusion, is it not? There were no injuries to her body. No sign of a fall. No broken bones or blow to the head. Her lungs were full of water, so that means she drowned. The bruises and scratches on her body were the kind that would have been inflicted as she was swept along. There'd been heavy rain for several days before she died and the river was in a dangerous condition. Her coat was found on the river bank. So it was assumed Coral waded into the river with the intention of taking her life. I understand why folk thought that. She'd fought a battle with depression for a couple of years and depression was winning.'

55

'Was it something to do with the Cauldstane curse?'

Alec cocked his head to one side and regarded me. He looked terribly pale. 'You know about the curse?'

'Sholto told me about it this morning. It must have been a dreadful thing to have to live with.'

'The existence of the curse certainly didn't help because the main cause of Coral's depression was our inability to conceive a child. We'd both had tests and it seemed there was no reason why she shouldn't conceive. She just didn't. So everyone assumed she took her life in a fit of despair. The more fancifully inclined concluded she was a double victim of the Cauldstane curse. She was barren and destined to die young.'

'But you don't believe that.'

'Damn right I don't.'

'Why? What else could have happened? How can you be so sure it wasn't suicide?'

I watched as his chest rose and fell with a great sigh, then he said, 'Three reasons. One – there was no note. Two – her camera was missing.'

'Her *camera*?'

'Aye. I gave Coral a camera to encourage her to get out and walk round the estate. I thought the fresh air and exercise would do her good. That camera was missing when she died. We lived in a wee house on the estate when she was alive and I turned the place upside down looking for it. I never found it and it's never turned up in the castle. That suggests to me she had it on her when she drowned.'

'And no one contemplating suicide would go out with a camera.'

Alec shot me a look of something like gratitude, then went on. 'The camera wasn't found with her body, so it's just a theory.'

I waited for him to continue but he said nothing, then suddenly set his coffee mug down on the tray. It made a jarring sound that startled me and the flock of small birds that had congregated around the biscuit crumbs I'd tossed through the door. My nerves were frayed; it already felt like it had been a long morning, but I had to know. 'Alec... You said there were three reasons you knew it wasn't suicide.'

'Aye, I did. You can dismiss the lack of note – they say some

56

folk don't leave them – and the camera's not evidence until it's found. But leaving those factors aside, there's no way my wife would have committed suicide, not on that day or on any day thereafter.'

'How can you be so sure?'

He turned and the look of cold anger in his eyes frightened me. 'Because the night before she died, Coral told me she was pregnant.'

I sat quite still, not knowing what to say, but it seemed important not to look away. I sensed he wanted to say more, but couldn't find the words. I held his eyes, even though I felt I was being beaten down by his pain. His words, when they came, surprised me.

'I'm sorry, Jenny.'

'Whatever for?'

'For burdening you. With – with my theories. My anger... But Sholto will talk about it as if it was suicide. And he's wrong. He has no understanding of mental frailty. Nor can he forgive it. He thought Coral was weak. Weak in the head.'

My tone was brisk. 'Well, if Sholto tries to persuade me it was suicide I shall point out to him that readers just won't buy it. There's not enough evidence. They'll think Coral had everything to live for. Inheriting Cauldstane. A loving husband. Many more years in which she could still have become a mother. That's how readers will see it. They'll prefer random tragedy to suicide any day... Sorry, Alec, I don't mean to sound flippant, I just wanted you to see that I – well, that I'm on your side.'

'That's OK. I understand.' He got to his feet. 'I'd better get back to work. Beating hell out of some steel will soon put the colour back in my cheeks.'

I stood up and put my empty mug on the tray. 'I'd love to see your workshop. Could I come and watch you work one day? At your convenience, obviously. Sholto said you'd show me the Cauldstane claymore.'

'It would be my pleasure.'

'He also said you'd tell me how to cut someone in two with it.'

'Had you anyone particular in mind?'

I felt absurdly pleased to see his grin. It was as if a weight had been lifted off my chest and I could breathe easily again. I followed

57

him out of the summer house and into the sunshine. The bees were still busy.

'No, my interest is purely academic. There's no one special.'

We set off along the gravel path, heading for the gate that led out of the walled garden. Alec turned to look at me. 'Is there anyone special in your life? If you don't mind my asking.'

'Of course I don't. I can't expect people to open up and trust me with their stories without giving something of myself.'

He pointed to my left hand. 'You don't appear to be married.'

'No. I lived with someone for a number of years, but we never wanted to make it permanent. Actually, that's not true. I think maybe he *did* want to marry me, but I didn't want to marry him. Especially when he decided he wanted to become a priest. I didn't see myself as a vicar's wife.'

'No, I don't see you as a vicar's wife either.'

'Thank you.'

I caught his sidelong glance and noted the grin again. When I'd dismissed Alec MacNab's looks as ordinary I'd possibly done him a disservice. His curling brown hair was actually tawny in the sunlight and there was nothing ordinary about that smile. It was just a rare occurrence.

'No regrets, then?' he asked.

'No, no regrets. But I think if I'd married I might have had them. Lots of them. I fear I might have sat brooding in the vicarage, railing against God and plotting my escape. You weren't married long enough to know that misery.'

'No. But I've known what it is to want to escape from someone.'

I didn't feel I could ask what he meant by this enigmatic remark, so silence yawned between us again. I was relieved when I saw we were almost back at the courtyard. As we passed through the archway, he said, 'Jenny, d'you mind if I ask you another personal question? You don't have to answer if you don't want to.'

'No, go ahead.'

He stopped walking and swung round to face me. 'Are you Imogen Ryan?'

Chapter Eight

I blinked at Alec and said nothing. He must have thought I didn't understand because he added, 'I mean, Imogen Ryan, the novelist.' I suppose I looked shocked, because he took a step towards me, then checked himself. 'Sorry. I shouldn't have asked. It's none of my business.'

'Yes, it is. I'm writing your father's memoirs for him. He's a notable and much loved man. You have every right to know who his literary *alter ego* is.' I looked around and said, 'Alec, is there somewhere we could go and sit down? Not in the castle. I don't think I want to see any of the others. Not right now.'

'Come into the armoury. There's an old sofa. It's filthy, but comfortable.'

Alec opened the door to his workshop and ushered me in. While he removed his leather apron and hung it on a peg, I looked round for somewhere to sit.

The workshop wouldn't have won any prizes for tidiness or cleanliness, but it was very warm. I felt as if I'd walked into a giant toolbox. Everywhere I looked, on walls, tables and workbenches, were tools and machinery, the function of which I could only guess. A pall of dust – or perhaps it was ash – had settled over everything in the room except some tools, which looked bright with use, and a sword blade that was obviously work-in progress. There was a furnace that looked like the mouth of a miniature hell, a machine with a big grinding wheel, two different anvils, a mallet I don't think I could have lifted, quantities of oily rags and used emery paper, several coffee mugs – one growing mould – and an open packet of biscuits.

The room was lit by a single window, bare hanging light bulbs and a dusty, black anglepoise lamp attached to a bench, its angular frame totally in keeping with all the tools, some of which looked like instruments of torture. There was something slightly sinister, almost Brueghelian about the darkness and chaos. The cleanest thing in the workshop was a notice board on which were pinned sketches, diagrams and news cuttings featuring Alec in fencing gear and various kinds of period costume. I noted in passing that he looked good in tights.

I headed for the sofa, regretting my decision to wear cream trousers, but Alec got there before me and spread a clean tea-towel. I thanked him and sat down, clasping my hands in my lap in an attempt to compose myself.

He wandered over to the window and appeared to be absorbed by the empty courtyard. Eventually he turned round and, leaning against the wall, his arms folded, said, 'So you *are* Imogen Ryan?' It wasn't an accusation, just a question.

'Yes.'

He frowned, then shaking his head as if in disbelief, he laughed and said, 'But *why*?'

'Why am I pretending to be someone else?'

'Why are you *ghostwriting*? You were a best-selling novelist. Famous! Did you not win an award?'

'Several. You know my work then?'

'Not directly, no. I'm not much of a reader of fiction. But Coral was a big fan. She had all your books. I kept one when she died. Don't know why exactly. It was very hard clearing everything out. I suppose I wanted to keep a few things that had meant something to her.'

'So you recognised me from a photo on the dust jacket?'

'I didn't. Wilma did.'

'*Wilma?*'

'She was turning out my room, dusting the books. She's very thorough. Takes them off the shelf to dust. I was in the room at the time and I heard her make a wee noise, as if she was startled. I thought maybe she'd seen a mouse. I asked what was wrong. She held up the book and said, "Is she not the living image of Miss Ryan? And what a coincidence! The same name." '

'So she guessed.'

'I'm not so sure. You look very different with short hair.'

'I decided that was my distinguishing characteristic – long blonde hair. Without it, most people wouldn't recognise me – people who didn't already know me, I mean. So you're saying Wilma didn't guess?'

'She looked at the photo for a while and then said, "Like two peas in a pod. It must be her sister. Writing obviously runs in the family." '

'And you think that's what she believes?'

'Maybe. Maybe not. But Wilma's worked for this family for more than forty years. She's learned there are some things it's best not to know. Best not to *see*. She'll say nothing more about it. And neither will I.'

'Alec, I didn't lie to Sholto. My CV was partial, I'll admit that, but I've been ghostwriting for years now and my books have enjoyed a lot of success. I'm very good at what I do.'

'I don't doubt it. But *why*, Jenny? You must have been earning a tidy sum writing bestsellers. Wasn't one of your books made into a film?'

'Two, actually.'

'Well, you can't be doing it for the money. I know Sholto will be paying you a pittance.'

'Yes, he was rather apologetic about that. I'm doing it for love really. I used to travel a lot researching my novels. But I never went anywhere extreme – the desert, Antarctica, the Himalayas. Sholto did all that and more. I wanted to hear his stories, be a part of them. So I accepted the job. I still don't know why he offered it to me. He said he would have preferred a man.'

'Aye, that's what he thought, but Sholto would always choose a woman as a companion. Especially a good-looking one. And I imagine he liked your work. Did you send him samples? Not Imogen Ryan's, your ghostwritten books.'

'Yes, but I didn't get the impression he'd read them. I think it all went on the interview. I fear I gushed a bit about Cauldstane. That's the way to his heart, isn't it?'

Alec turned and gazed out the window again. 'I don't know,' he said quietly. 'It's not a path I've trodden.'

I looked up at him but could only see his profile which gave nothing away. I gathered my thoughts and started to explain. 'Things started to go wrong for me, you see.'

He turned his head and said, 'Wrong? In what way?'

'My career. I decided I wanted to stop writing fiction.'

'Writer's block, you mean?'

'No, much worse than that. It wasn't that I *couldn't* write, I just didn't want to any more.'

61

'Why?'

'Oh, it was a gradual thing. There was a downward slide. But I know exactly when it began. I was cornered by a drunk at a party. He asked me what I did and when I said I was a novelist, he sneered and said. "There's no such thing as fiction". I think he might have been a writer himself. Or a failed writer. He said, "Don't kid yourself, darling – fiction is just somebody else's reality."

'I thought nothing of it at the time. Well, not consciously. But you know how people are always worried you're going to put them into your book? Use them as raw material?'

'No, I didn't know that. But then I've never known any writers.'

'Well, novelists do get some of their inspiration from real people, but we don't usually put them into books. *Bits* of people, perhaps. Their looks, or certain aspects of their personality. You absorb so much about people, even people you don't know. You see someone on the news and it gets you thinking, asking questions... Anyway, many of my characters can be traced back to a real person who provided the inspiration in some way. Usually it's just a sort of physical template that you have in mind while writing. The person might have nothing in common with your character. Nothing at all. I knew a terribly sweet lady who used to do the flowers at my ex-boyfriend's church. There was something about her that intrigued me. She was so obsessive about her arrangements. So *controlling*... I used her as the basis of a psychopath, poor thing. But she'll never recognise herself, even if she reads the book, because I changed so many physical things about her. And that's how people operate, you see. No one will ever recognise me as Imogen Ryan because she had long, blonde hair. And I don't.'

Alec gave me a confused, almost worried look. It reminded me of the look my hairdresser had given me when I told her I wanted her to cut off most of my hair.

'I'm guessing,' he said tentatively, 'this all went bad somehow.'

'Yes, it did. I was writing a novel about a famous TV personality. Fictional. Someone who was meant to be a household name. I needed someone with a lot of style and charisma, so I based him on a rather glamorous politician. In my story, the household name stunned his fans by coming out as gay and living openly with his partner. Well, after I'd written all that into my plot, the politician on whom I'd based my gay hero came out. I was very surprised but, naturally, I put it down to coincidence. Then when it transpired this guy had been diagnosed with terminal cancer, I got really rattled.'

'Why?'

'My fictional character came out because he discovered he was dying of cancer.'

Alec shrugged. 'Another coincidence. Cancer's common enough.'

'Of course. But for some reason, I was consumed with guilt. Even though I didn't know this man at all, when he died, I sent flowers and a card to his partner. But really I wanted to apologise, to tell him it was all my fault. That I'd killed his partner. I'd actually plotted his death. But I was still sane enough then to realise it was just a massive over-reaction to a distressing coincidence. Nevertheless, I deleted the novel from my hard drive.'

'That was drastic.'

'I even burned the print-out. Two years' work down the drain. My agent and publisher were livid because I was contracted to produce a book a year. That's what I'd always done. But they assumed it was just... a hiccup. Some sort of creative burnout.'

'But it wasn't.'

'No, it wasn't. I found I couldn't write a thing. I had no ideas – or only bad ones. I got into a dreadful state, frightened I'd never be able to write again. Then I realised, that wasn't the problem at all. I wasn't afraid I could no longer write, I was frightened of *writing*, of actually doing the thing that earned me a very comfortable living.

'By then I think I'd lost it, but my agent persuaded me to see a counsellor. She tried to persuade me it was all just coincidence. When I resisted that, she suggested I see a different counsellor. I found another one but he was a bit alternative. *Too* alternative. He told me I was obviously very sensitive and suggested I'd tuned in to something, some non-specific cosmic suffering. I decided he was battier than me and stopped seeing him. In fact I pretty much stopped seeing anyone.

'By now it seemed perfectly clear to me that the drunk at the party had been right. Fiction *was* just someone else's reality. But which came first – the fiction or the reality? Supposing everything I wrote happened to somebody, somewhere? Supposing I had the power to create *and* to destroy?... I'd always received fan letters, you see. Cries from the heart from grateful women I'd never met, telling me I'd written *their* story. Some sounded like they needed psychiatric help, but others seemed perfectly lucid and claimed they wouldn't have believed it possible anyone could make up fiction that so resembled *their* reality. I'd never really thought much about it before – I'd been too busy working – but now everything seemed to make sense. To me, anyway.'

'Sounds like it was some sort of creative overload. Allied to a very tender heart. What did you do?'

'Well, I might have been going mad, but I took my new responsibilities very seriously. I stopped writing gritty novels about wife-battering, aids and addiction and started writing books for children. Stories about a family of squirrels who lived in a wood.' I glanced up at Alec whose face was impassive. 'You're allowed to laugh.'

He continued to regard me intently. 'What did these squirrels do?'

'Collect food and eat it. That's *all* they did. They were unrelentingly nice to each other and to the other woodland animals. The biggest drama was when they ran out of beech nuts – a temporary crisis resolved by the quick thinking of a wise old owl.'

Alec laughed then and immediately looked shame-faced. 'I'm sorry. I know it's not funny, it's just the way you tell it. Could you really not see how... *bizarre* your thinking was?'

'No, I couldn't then, even though I had an agent and a partner telling me I needed help.'

'Were these children's stories published?'

'Yes, but they didn't sell. I wasn't surprised. They were crap. Nothing ever happened! Nothing dramatic, nothing violent, nothing bad. The books were sweet, but boring. The first two appeared as novelty items one Christmas, then sank without trace. I didn't mind. I didn't really need the money, I wanted peace of mind and a quiet conscience. Money and success hadn't brought me that. But I knew when I wrote those feeble little animal stories, I was doing no one any harm. Not even bloody squirrels.'

I looked around the room, scanning Alec's shelves and workbenches. Eventually I found what I was looking for.

'Could you possibly pour me a whisky? It must be lunchtime by now, surely. I think I'd feel a bit better if I had something to hold. Will you join me?'

Alec picked up a bottle and went over to a battered wooden cabinet. He took out two glasses and poured us both a finger of whisky, then sat down next to me on the sofa. My hand was shaking as I took the glass from him. He registered the tremor and took my other hand in his as he sat down.

'Jenny, you don't have to say any more. I shouldn't have asked.'

'But I'd rather like you to know. I don't want you thinking I've deceived Sholto. Or the family. Hear me out, then tell me what you think I should do.'

'If that's what you want.'

He didn't let go of my hand and I found I was glad. I took a good mouthful of whisky and said, 'The day I was committed to a mental institution I'd telephoned my publisher, asking, *begging* them to abandon the latest squirrel saga. I'd been checking the page proofs and had got to a bit where the West Wind blows down The Old Oak which comes crashing to the ground, to the sentimental dismay of all the squirrels. None of them was hurt of course, but as I read on it suddenly struck me… What about the *tree*? Do trees have feelings? When it was wrenched out of the ground, uprooted by the wind, did it suffer?… No one could reassure me on this point and no one could stop me sobbing with remorse. So my GP sedated me and when I woke up, I found myself in a white room. It was practically empty. I remember being shocked there weren't any books.

'I sat in that room, looking out the window, for six months. I watched a family of squirrels in an old oak tree. I didn't write a single word, I simply watched the squirrels, keeping an eye on them, making sure they came to no harm. I gradually got better but I knew I'd never write fiction again. It was too risky. But I still wanted to write. I still wanted to tell stories. So I decided I would tell other people's. Stories that had already been lived. Stories over which I had absolutely no control.'

There was a long silence in which I felt very foolish and had to fight an urge to burst into tears. I withdrew my hand from Alec's and cradled my glass, studying its contents, then said, 'Will you tell Sholto?'

'Of course not. Why would I do that?'

'I thought you might think I'd deceived him in some way.'

'You think Sholto would mind a bit of deception? He's a past master himself.'

'I haven't lied to him. And I never would. I don't mind if you do tell him about me. I will, if you like. It's just... well, it's just that I prefer to keep things simple now. Imogen Ryan was the novelist. The woman who cracked up. But Jenny is OK. Jenny loves what she does and feels strong. In control of her material. Because it's all been lived already. It's become a *story*. I just have to decide how best to tell it. And that suits me. It's the part of writing I really love. Telling the story. And Sholto has so many wonderful stories.'

Alec raised an eyebrow. 'Some of them possibly fictional.'

I managed a weak smile. 'Oh yes, I'm aware a certain amount of embroidering is going on. But I don't care. It's his book. Sholto's name will be on the cover, not mine.'

'I've heard it said, all biography is fiction and all fiction is biography.'

'That's a massive generalisation, but there's some truth in it. The fact that fiction could *become* biography was why I stopped writing it.'

Alec set down his empty glass. 'I wish you weren't so afraid, Jenny. There's no need.'

'I'm not afraid. Not any more. I let the fear go with the fiction-writing. I have absolutely no power now, for good or bad. Jenny is just a channel through which stories are told.'

'It's a shame we've lost Imogen's stories. My wife certainly used to love them.'

'Oh, they wouldn't have been any good – not once I'd decided I could make things happen. I was so afraid of abusing that power, I refused to wield it. I was crippled artistically.' I swallowed another mouthful of whisky. 'So... you don't think I should tell Sholto?'

'What would be the point? He's happy. You're happy.'

'And Mrs. Guthrie? Will she say anything? She seems very protective of him.'

'Och, no – she'll not say a word. If she did, it might suggest Sholto had been taken in. And by an attractive young woman.'

'Hardly young,' I protested, embarrassed by Alec's second reference to my appearance.

'To a woman of Wilma's years, you're just a wee lassie. But you can rely on her discretion and her devotion to her employer. She won't say anything. Neither will I.'

'Thanks. Though I don't know why I'm thanking you. I don't believe I've done anything wrong.'

'You haven't and I wasn't suggesting you had. I just couldn't understand how someone as successful as you had ended up at Cauldstane, writing someone else's life story. It didn't add up. And that was bothering me. But I'm pleased to hear it doesn't bother you.'

'When I came here, I wasn't sure I wanted the job. I certainly didn't think I'd get it. But I fancied an autumn trip to the Highlands and I thought it would be fun to meet Sholto. He was paying my travel expenses and offered me hospitality. How could I say no? Then of course, when I got here, I just fell in love. With Cauldstane, I mean. Once I'd seen the place and started to think about spending time here, writing about the family's history, well, I was desperate to get the commission. As you pointed out, the money Sholto offered was pitiful, but I really didn't care. I wanted the job so much, I wasn't prepared to haggle. We compromised on my being allowed to stay at the castle as a guest.'

'Which wasn't exactly a big concession. Sholto will find it very convenient having you around. Office hours have never suited him.'

'Yes, we have a fluid sort of arrangement. It wouldn't suit everyone, I suppose, but it suits me. It's so different from how I used to live. All I ever wanted to do was just write, but I became a literary commodity. It all got too big and when things get big you lose control. I mean, in London, before my breakdown, I was completely preoccupied with time. And timetables. Taking taxis, catching planes, living in hotels, giving interviews. I once gave eighteen in one day, starting with breakfast TV and ending with *The Late Late Show*. When I was on tour promoting a new book, the only time I spent alone was when I went to the loo – and more than one female journalist attempted to follow me there. I was parcelled up for consumption on radio, in women's magazines, on chat shows. I wasn't a person any more, I was "product". I felt as if I was running a race with time and time always seemed to win. I suppose it's not surprising I went under.'

'And are you happy here? Happy in your work?'

'Oh, yes. I seem to have much more time here. And an acute awareness of history. It must be Cauldstane, I suppose.'

He nodded slowly. 'Aye, it has that effect on some folk. The sense of history is... seductive. Though I'd have thought the eccentricities of our plumbing might have dampened your enthusiasm.'

'No, that's all part of the charm. I like sad, old, broken-down things.'

'Like Sholto you mean?'

'No, of course not!' Alec watched me and I knew he was waiting for me to catch up. Or be honest. 'Well, maybe that's partly why I feel so drawn to him. Why I wanted to tell his story.' Alec still said nothing and I was aware that his silence – or rather the way he listened – was encouraging me to talk. 'I always buy damaged things in junk shops. Things with cracks and chips, that look like they've really been used. And *loved*. I don't know why I'm fond of things like that. I suppose it's a form of salvage. I like rescuing things other people have cast aside and forgotten about.'

'It's still sounding like Sholto to me. He's certainly had a few rough edges knocked off over the years.'

'He's in pain, isn't he? A lot of the time.'

'He'll never complain, so you'll never know what he goes through. It's not just physical pain. I think he finds the mental stuff harder to bear. He was an adrenalin junkie in his youth and fit as a butcher's dog. Now he limps from room to room or just sits in a chair, staring out the window. He should be in a wheelchair or on one of those wee electric carts, but he won't even consider it. On a good day he walks with a stick. On a bad day he walks with two.'

'Is it arthritis?'

'Aye. He's broken so many bones and punished his body for so many years, he pays for it now. Can you imagine how hard it is to dress yourself with arthritic hands? And he lost one whole finger to frostbite, plus the tips of a couple of others. I've offered to help him in the mornings – that's his worst time – but he won't hear of it.' Alec scowled and I noticed the resemblance between father and son. 'If there's a prouder, more thrawn old man in the whole of Scotland – well, I wouldn't like to meet him.'

'Sholto could still travel, couldn't he?'

'Oh, aye, he's able, but he won't spend the money. When

you're feeling strong, get Fergus to talk you through the Cauldstane finances. I doubt Sholto will want all that included in the book, but if you want to understand Sholto and how things are here, you need to know the trouble we're in. But even if Sholto had a holiday – somewhere in the south where the sun would warm his aching bones – it wouldn't provide the thrills he needs, has always needed. I have a wee theory that despite his reputation as a Highland Casanova, he wasn't really that bothered about women. It was all about the *chase*. And the risk. Whether his wives would find out. Whether the husbands of the women he was bedding would find out. I think philandering was what Sholto did when he was home from expeditions and waiting for the next. It was just a substitute for what he really wanted to be doing. I suspect my mother understood that, but by turning a blind eye, she thwarted him in a way. She deprived him of some of the excitement he craved, some of the drama. But Meredith certainly made up for that,' he added grimly,

'She wasn't so tolerant?'

'No, indeed. Meredith was jealous, possessive and controlling. Then when Sholto lost interest in her and looked elsewhere, she got angry. When that didn't get her anywhere, she decided *she'd* look elsewhere. But Sholto didn't even notice. Or if he did, he didn't care. He'd moved on to the next challenge.'

'The next woman, you mean?'

'Aye. Or so Meredith said. My father never discussed his marriage with me.'

'But Meredith did?'

'She tried. She wanted to confide in someone, but I wasn't prepared to enter into that kind of relationship. I didn't want to have to take sides. But if I had, I'd have taken Sholto's. Meredith knew the score when she married him. She'd been his mistress for years, so she can't really have expected an old leopard like Sholto to change his spots.'

There was a knock at the door. Alec glanced at his watch, quickly got to his feet and called out, 'OK, Wilma. I'm coming over now.'

Mrs Guthrie's head appeared round the door. She looked startled to see me on the sofa. Her sharp eyes didn't miss the two whisky glasses either.

'Sorry to disturb you, Mr Alec, but I was wanting to clear away lunch and I wondered if you – and Miss Jenny,' she added with a deferential nod in my direction, 'were going to come across? I've made *quiche lorraine* today. Your favourite.'

'Thanks, Wilma, we'll be right over. I've been bending Jenny's ear with the family history and I lost track of the time.' He turned and offered me a hand up from the sofa. 'Come on, Jenny. You must be famished.'

Mrs Guthrie looked at Alec, then at me. Her smile wasn't exactly conspiratorial, but I have to say, she looked inordinately and unaccountably pleased.

Chapter Nine

As Alec and I approached the dining room we heard raised voices –
Fergus and Zelda engaged in what sounded like a heated argument.
I hesitated in the hallway, unwilling to move forward. Alec stood
beside me, listening, his brow contracted into a frown.

'Ferg sounds upset. That's not like him.'

'Perhaps I should go and eat in the kitchen. I'm sure Wilma will
let me make myself a sandwich. I don't want to intrude.'

'Och, no, you'll come and have your lunch,' Alec said, taking
my arm. 'Ferg is probably ranting about estate business. It gets him
down sometimes.'

Still unsure, I followed Alec's lead. As we reached the door of
the dining room he was almost knocked down by Fergus who burst
out of the dining room, his face flushed. But Alec side-stepped
neatly, avoiding a collision.

'Whoaa... What's up, Ferg?'

Fergus glanced across at me, then looked down at the carpet.
He plunged his hands into his jacket pockets, clearly trying to
compose himself. I wanted to make myself scarce in the dining
room, but the two men were in the way, so I just stood feeling
awkward.

Eventually Fergus managed to speak. 'She said no.'

Alec looked puzzled. 'Who said no?'

'Rachel.'

Alec's face lit up and he thumped his brother on the back. 'So
you finally asked her to—'

'She said *no*, Alec.'

His brother's face fell. 'But... why?'

Fergus looked at me again and I wished the ground would
open up and swallow me. 'Zelda will explain,' he said turning back
to Alec, then he swept past us, calling out over his shoulder, 'Look
at the *Courier*. Page six.' He disappeared and shortly afterwards we
heard the back door slam.

Alec bowed his head and exhaled. Not for the first time I

sensed frustration of some kind. It was impossible to ignore the coiled energy in him that I suspected he sometimes struggled to keep in check. But he looked up, shook his head with a little smile, as if to assure me Fergus would be all right, then opened the dining room door for me.

The sight that met us wasn't encouraging. Zelda sat at the table, her head in her hands, the remains of her lunch in front of her. To judge from what was left on her plate, she hadn't eaten much. She looked up and attempted to muster a smile.

'There you are! We'd given you two up for lost. Have you both had a good morning?'

Ignoring her, Alec strode to the end of the table and picked up a newspaper. He opened it and leafed through until he found what he was looking for. Zelda gave up all pretension to social niceties and announced gloomily, 'Rachel turned Fergus down. He proposed, she said she'd think about it, then the *Courier* did its worst.' Alec swore quietly. 'My thoughts exactly,' Zelda said, pushing her plate away. 'Jenny, I must apologise for all the drama, but the news has been a blow to poor Fergus. To *all* of us. Though by now we should be used to this sort of thing, I suppose.'

'I take it Fergus proposed to his girlfriend?'

'Aye, he did. After much deliberation. A proposal of marriage is not something a MacNab makes lightly. You've heard about our curse, I take it?'

'Yes. Sholto told me about it.'

'Rachel knew of course.' Zelda waved a bony and be-ringed hand. '*Everyone* knows! It's not something you can hush up. The Cauldstane curse has been around for hundreds of years, but we try to play it down. Because of course it's all nonsense!'

When he'd finished reading, Alec folded the newspaper and handed it to me without speaking.

I sat down at the table to read. The offending item appeared to be an article about Sholto and the headline read, *The Curse of Cauldstane Castle*. Sholto was referred to as "the literary laird" and the journalist had re-hashed old MacNab stories as a sort of trailer for the forthcoming memoirs. Unfortunately for Rachel, the journalist had chosen to illustrate the piece with photographs of three young women, all now deceased: Liz, Meredith and Coral MacNab. There were no quotes in the accompanying text about the

72

curse, which led me to believe Sholto had probably declined to comment, but that hadn't prevented the journalist dredging up the family's tragic past for sensational effect. As I scanned the piece, it struck me it would be a brave woman – or one singularly lacking in imagination – who could accept a MacNab proposal with a light heart. I lay the newspaper aside, at a loss for words.

'So Rachel read that and panicked?' Alec said, looking at Zelda.

'She said she loved Fergus very much, but didn't feel she could take this final step.'

'She surely doesn't *believe* in this crap?' Alec said angrily.

'She claims she doesn't. Though which of us knows what we really believe in our hearts? But Rachel said she wasn't prepared to live her life as a sort of sideshow, knowing folk were *waiting* for her to die. Or prove barren. Or both.' Zelda turned to me and explained. 'Rachel's a nursery teacher. She adores children. I imagine she'd be keen to start a family straight away.'

'So she just said no?'

'She gave him a sort of ultimatum, but she knew what he'd say. She knew Fergus would never leave Cauldstane. Not while Sholto was alive.'

Alec looked as if he was about to explode. 'What were her conditions?'

'She said she'd marry him if they could leave Cauldstane. Leave Scotland, in fact. Rachel's from New Zealand, Jenny. She wanted to go home. She wanted to start married life thousands of miles away from here.'

Alec snorted with disgust. 'And Fergus had to refuse because Sholto and I can't manage the estate without him.'

'Couldn't Sholto find a replacement?' I asked.

'One who'd work for nothing?' Alec snapped.

Zelda glared at him. 'That's not fair, Alec. Fergus has a cosy wee house on the estate, the use of a Land Rover and pocket money.'

'And he comes up here to eat with us to save himself money.'

'You know as well as I do that if Fergus were to quit, Sholto would have to sell up or just watch the place fall into ruins. Either way, it would kill him.'

'Could Fergus teach you how to run the estate, Alec?'

'Oh, aye, he could. And I could do it, though not nearly as well as Ferg. He knows every inch of the estate, every tenant's bairn *and* the names of their dogs. He's a damn good manager. But I could take on that job. The trouble is, Jenny, the Cauldstane Armoury is a major source of income. We'd be robbing Peter to pay Paul. If anything, I should be training up an assistant now to cope with all the orders I can't accept because I don't have time to fulfil them.'

Zelda shook her head. 'Rachel must have known Fergus wouldn't walk away. Not while Sholto was alive. But I suppose she hoped he might.'

'Does Sholto know?' I asked.

'About the article? Of course!' Alec snapped. 'It's obviously his doing.'

'I meant, did he know about Fergus and Rachel? That they were serious.'

'Why wouldn't he know?'

'You forget, Alec,' Zelda said patiently. '*I* know only because Rachel confided in me. Fergus didn't breathe a word.'

'I don't think Sholto can have known,' I said cautiously. 'When he spoke to me about the curse, he made a particular point of saying he had no knowledge of his sons' love lives. I don't think he had any idea.'

'Well, let's keep it that way,' said Zelda. 'We had no idea Fergus was going to propose, so I think we should take our cue from him. If I know my nephew, he'll want to keep the whole business quiet.' Zelda got to her feet and, supporting herself on the table, she said, 'There are days when I feel old and very tired. This is definitely one of them, so I think I'm going up to take a wee nap. I trust I'll wake feeling more cheerful. Enjoy your lunch, Jenny. And make sure Alec eats something, won't you?'

Zelda picked up the offending newspaper and walked over to the door, her tall figure slightly bowed now. She dropped the paper into a waste paper basket, opened the door and shut it quietly behind her.

I turned round and saw Alec was now standing at the window with his back to me. I poured myself a glass of water, then one for him.

'Will you come and join me for some lunch? Wilma's quiche looks delicious.' He didn't turn or speak, so I got up and went over to the sideboard where I helped myself to food, even though I wasn't hungry. It gave me something to do. Serving myself some salad, I said, 'Fergus can't expect you to take on the running of the estate, Alec. It wouldn't make any sense financially.'

He was silent for a moment, then said, 'The only thing that makes any sense financially is for us to sell up. Sell Cauldstane. Cut our losses and go.'

'Do you ever think about that?'

'All the time. So does Fergus. So does Sholto. But it would be quicker – and cleaner – to take the Cauldstane claymore and plunge it into my father's heart.' He turned, but didn't meet my eyes. 'If you'll excuse me, Jenny,' he said briskly, 'I find I have no appetite. If she asks, tell Zelda I ate something.'

Without waiting for an answer, he strode across the room and left me to enjoy a solitary lunch.

The conversation in the dining room and the sight of Fergus' unhappy face bothered me more than I cared to admit. I was beginning to get a sense of how much the MacNabs lived under a cloud, albeit an imaginary one. The restrictions of the men's lives and those of the women they chose to love were beginning to seem almost tragic. The weight of family history (with which I'd been entranced at first) now seemed oppressive.

I ate a sketchy lunch, then stood at the sideboard, making a doorstep cheese and pickle sandwich. I picked up the plate and headed for the armoury. It wasn't until later that I remembered the old adage Rupert used to quote at me after one of my rare culinary triumphs: *The way to a man's heart is through his stomach.*

I knocked on the door, but it sounded as if Alec was grinding a piece of metal, so I just walked in. He looked up, startled. I could have sworn that, for a second, he took up a defensive pose with his blade-in-progress, then his eyes travelled down to the plate I was carrying. He looked even more surprised.

'You don't have to eat it, but I've brought you a sandwich anyway. Cheese and pickle. Wilma's wonderful cooking is clearly wasted on you.'

He grinned and set down his blade. 'You made that with your

own fair hands?'

'Yes. Sorry about the doorstep dimensions. As you can see, I'm not nearly as handy with a knife as you are.'

He took the plate, wiped a grubby hand on the seat of his grubbier jeans and picked up the sandwich, which he proceeded to eat with relish. I stood and watched with something like maternal satisfaction.

'D'you want to make tea?' Alec mumbled, his mouth full of sandwich. He jerked his head towards the back of the workshop and swallowed. 'If you're not too fastidious, there's a wee kitchenette at the back.'

I headed to the back of the workshop where a small store room had been turned into a kitchen. The tiny fridge contained more beer than milk, but I managed to produce two mugs of tea. As I handed one to Alec – there was no sign of the sandwich now – he saved me the trouble of raising the topic I'd come to discuss with him.

'Sorry about the wee stooshie with Fergus. I wouldn't mention it to him, if I were you. If you need to talk about the curse – for the book, I mean – you'd best talk to me. Sholto will get upset and Ferg will get angry.'

'And you won't?'

'I've accepted it. Accepted that something which doesn't actually exist can still wreck your life. Fergus could have ignored it – MacNab men have to – but finding a *woman* who will...' He shook his head. 'I thought Rachel was made of sterner stuff. Her grandparents were Scots who emigrated to New Zealand. She comes from generations of farming stock. She'd have made a grand wife for Ferg. And nothing's going to stop that lassie having bairns, if she has to steal them from prams.'

'So you think it was just the article in the paper that did the damage?'

'Aye, that and everyone's reaction to it. Her friends. Colleagues at work. That'll be why she wants to go back home. To get away from our history.'

'Since Fergus wants to sell up anyway, I don't really understand why he doesn't just up sticks and head for the Antipodes. He must have lots of skills that could form the basis of a new career.'

76

'It's not that simple. Fergus doesn't *want* to sell, he thinks we have no choice *but* to sell. He wants to deliver the *coup de grâce* to Cauldstane. Sholto and I are prepared to witness its agonizingly slow death. But one of the reasons I won't consider pressurizing Sholto to sell – apart from the fact he'd knock me down if I did – is that Cauldstane is as much Ferg's inheritance as mine. He's worked for it. And if anything happens to me, he's the heir.'

'What could happen to you?' Alec looked up sharply as if I'd touched a nerve. Backtracking, I said, 'I mean, you look fit as a flea, despite your reluctance to eat.' He said nothing. 'I suppose your job is quite dangerous, isn't it? And those tournaments must be. But you haven't sustained an injury for years now, have you?'

He raised an eyebrow and I saw the suggestion of a smile at the corners of his mouth. 'You've been *researching* me?'

I'm embarrassed to admit I probably blushed. I had indeed spent more time googling Alec (and pictures of Alec) than was strictly necessary for researching a book about Sholto, but I recovered quickly and, I hope, confidently. 'Just as background. I need to see the bigger picture. And readers are going to love the idea of Sholto producing a son as fearless as himself.'

'Is that what you think I am? Fearless?'

An unaccountable shiver went down my spine, then I remembered those were the very words Sholto had said when I'd referred to his reckless courage. 'Have I got that wrong, then?'

Alec looked at me warily, but I sensed he wanted to talk. 'It has as much to do with fear as courage. But there's passion as well. A passion for history. For the art of making a beautiful blade.'

'But you don't deny what you do is dangerous?'

'Driving a car is dangerous. Look what happened to Meredith. Fergus could end up Laird of Cauldstane courtesy of black ice on the A9. Sholto was a younger son who didn't expect to inherit. But Fergus is ready, should the need arise and since I'm unlikely now to produce an heir, Cauldstane could end up in the hands of his family. If we don't sell up.'

'You wouldn't consider marrying again?'

'You heard what Rachel said. And a similar thing happened to me a year or so ago. I thought I might be heading towards another long-term relationship, but as soon as she found out about the curse and what happened to Coral... and Meredith... and my mother...' Alec's sigh was weary. 'Ferg is younger. He's thirty-eight and he's never been married, never even lived with a girlfriend. He wants to give it a go. And he should! A future Laird of Cauldstane could be a nephew of mine, yet unborn.'

'It's so sad you've given up hoping things will work out for *you*. You seriously underestimate women if you think all of them are as superstitious as Rachel.'

He looked at me then, his grey eyes dark and unfathomable. It was a long, incomprehensible look that sent another shiver down my spine. I thought he was about to say something, but then he seemed to change his mind. Eventually he shook his head and said, 'It's not that simple, Jenny. There are other factors... I hold myself responsible for what happened to Coral.' There was now a steely glint in his eye. 'And that's not going to happen to anyone else.'

'But, Alec, you don't *know* what happened to Coral. Not for certain.'

'No, I don't. But I saw what happened to her before she died. What happened to her mind. The curse doesn't have to be real for it to do real harm, Jenny. Look at Ferg and Rachel!'

I had to acknowledge the truth of this depressing statement. 'So you're saying your life now is just some kind of... damage limitation exercise?'

He nodded. 'Aye, that's exactly what it is. I see it as my job to make sure no one else comes to any harm through their association with the MacNabs. Now if you'll excuse me, Jenny – I've spent too much time today enjoying your company. I have orders to fulfil.'

'Yes, of course. I should get back to work too. Thanks for explaining things to me. I do appreciate it.'

He gave me a curt nod, lowered his safety glasses and turned back to the grinding wheel. As I lifted the catch on the door, he called out, 'Jenny?' I spun round, but Alec still faced the wheel. 'What *you* see as courage is in fact the opposite. Sholto put his life on the line time and again because he's terrified of death. Of becoming... *nothing*. That's partly what this book is about for him. A bid for immortality. And *this*...' Alec turned slowly and raised the unfinished blade. 'This is about fear, not courage.'

I didn't reply for a moment, then feeling quite stupid, I said, 'I'm sorry, Alec, I don't understand.'

His smile was slow and sad. 'Aye, I know. How could you? I'm just blethering on. Take no notice.' He turned back to the wheel. 'I really should get out more.'

'I would *like* to understand. Really, I would.'

He stood quite still with his back to me. There was nothing for me to do but stare at the way his damp hair curled at the back of his neck and his shoulder blades shifted as he raised the unfinished sword to the grinding wheel. I'd already turned away when he spoke again.

'If you ever need to understand, I promise I'll explain. But I trust there'll be no need.'

He flipped a switch and the noise of the machine made any further conversation impossible, so I left.

Chapter Ten

I was in no mood for work after my conversation with Alec, so I headed back to my room where I lay down on the bed feeling tired and confused. I was concerned about the MacNab brothers and their blighted lives, but I knew that wasn't the only reason for my confusion. Another was Alec.

I enjoyed spending time with him. I found him intriguing in his quiet, understated way. We'd come a long way since the awkwardness of our first meeting outside my room and I'd been quite wrong about him being hostile to Sholto's project. Alec was supportive of my work and clearly wanted to help in any way he could. In fact I thought he was enjoying spending time with me.

There was surely nothing more to it than that. Just good manners. Weren't Highlanders famed for their good manners and legendary hospitality? But holding my hand as I downed his whisky and talked about my breakdown?... No doubt I was making something out of nothing. That in itself gave me cause for concern. It was all too easy to get involved with your subject and their family. Up to a point you had to *become* family, but you also had to keep a professional distance. Apart from anything else, I was working to a deadline and didn't have time for a relationship. In any case, various hints had been dropped about Alec's emotional fragility. Someone with a history of instability was the last person I should think of getting involved with.

To my dismay, I realised I was sounding just like Rupert, giving myself a good talking to. It was all very sensible advice – Rupert would have been proud of me – but it failed to take into account that when Alec was around, my breathing changed slightly. I was always aware of his position in the room and what he was doing. I didn't watch him. I didn't need to. I automatically registered his presence and the distance, or lack of it, between us.

I rolled over on the bed and drew up my knees, trying to recall the photographs on the notice board in the armoury, photos in which Alec was demonstrating historical swordsmanship in period costume. I'd always thought that sort of historical re-enactment was for sad, geeky types. Maybe it was, but I doubted whether most blade enthusiasts looked as dashing or dangerous as Alec in doublet and hose.

Despite taking sensible precautions, I'd succumbed to the glamour of Cauldstane and the MacNab men – Alec in particular. Work would be the remedy. Putting pleasant thoughts of Alec aside, I resolved that I would get off my very comfortable bed, settle down with my notes and get some work done. *Soon.*

I must have been dozing off when the music began. It was distant and indistinct, but I thought it sounded like a harpsichord. I sat up on the bed, straining to hear. The piece was sad and stately and I assumed it must be coming from a radio or CD player. The music stopped abruptly. In the silence that followed, I decided I must have imagined it. After all, I spent a lot of time cooped up with a harpsichord in the music room and I often tried to imagine what it would sound like.

I concluded I was in need of tea and possibly some of Mrs Guthrie's restorative home baking. I'd eaten very little at lunchtime. As I swung my legs off the bed, the music began again – a different piece, frenetically complex this time. I'm sure it demonstrated great technical brilliance, but I found the jangling noise completely enervating. After only a moment or two, I felt a headache coming on and wished the music would stop – which it did, just as suddenly as it had started. I sat on the edge of the bed, braced for the music to start again, but there was nothing but silence – silence and a chill in the room that sent me rooting in a drawer for a jumper.

As I pulled it on over my shirt, I glanced out the window, across the river. On the opposite bank the leaves had already started to change colour. The wind tossed the tops of the trees and a few yellow leaves spiralled into the air, whirling madly before they drifted down to the surface of the rushing water. I watched them as they hurtled under the stone bridge and were gone. Despite my thick jumper, I shivered.

I was heading for the stairs, on my way to the kitchen, when Zelda opened her door. Her head shot out and when she saw it was me, she smiled broadly. 'Jenny! I'm glad I caught you. I've dug out some old photo albums. Come and have a look. Wilma's just brought me some tea, so we can have a wee blether.' Her head shot back inside again and I heard her say, 'Wilma, would you bring another cup, please?' Mrs Guthrie emerged carrying an empty tray and nodded to me before setting off downstairs at a lick.

Knowing Zelda, I doubted whether the blether would be all that wee, but I obeyed what was in effect a royal command to peruse the family albums. Sholto had shown no interest in choosing the illustrations for his biography, so Zelda and I had taken it upon ourselves to make a first selection.

As I entered the room, soft classical music was playing. It stopped abruptly as Zelda switched off a radio.

'Please don't turn it off on my account,' I protested.

'Och, it's just Classic FM. Wallpaper music. I have to have something on in the background. I can't bear the silence of this place. It gets on my nerves. Sholto says he loves it, but he'd live in Antarctica if he could. All that silence and no litter. He gets so worked up about that.'

'Litter?'

'Litter in Glasgow, litter on Mt. Everest. Sholto goes on and on about it.' Zelda plumped up a needlepoint cushion in an armchair and indicated I should sit. She poured a cup of tea, handed it to me, then drew up another chair and sat down. 'Help yourself to gingerbread. Wilma excels at gingerbread!'

I obeyed and, as I sat, took a moment to survey the room. When I entered, I'd expected to find Zelda's bedroom, but I found myself in a tiny sitting room which must once have been a dressing room. A closed door led, I presumed, to the bedroom. I had to admire the way she'd made herself a little den, heated by a primitive two-bar electric fire. Small pieces of furniture had been crammed in for the sole purpose of displaying bric-a-brac. Zelda was evidently a collector. I spotted lace bobbins and darning mushrooms arranged in different areas of the room, but I was unable to guess the purpose of what appeared to be a bowl of china apples. Pastel-coloured and surprisingly modern, these plain and patterned china balls turned out to be a set of 1930s carpet bowls. (Zelda told me later that her mother had allowed the children to play with them indoors on rainy days.) There was a shelf full of cookery books, many of them French, and a piece of needlepoint canvas stretched over a frame had been set down beside a sewing box, open on the floor beside Zelda's chair.

It was all very cosy, charming and feminine. I couldn't help thinking what a contrast it was to Alec's workshop and it suddenly struck me how separately all the MacNabs lived – all of them single, all in their separate areas. If Sholto wasn't in the walled garden, he'd be holed up in the library. Fergus was always out working on the estate and went home to his bachelor cottage. We rarely saw him except for the occasional meal. I wondered if the melancholy atmosphere I was beginning to sense at Cauldstane was just the family's palpable loneliness and isolation. Undoubtedly they'd known happier times, but those seemed long gone.

Mrs Guthrie re-appeared at the open door with more crockery. 'Thanks Wilma! I'll take that.' Zelda got up to take a cup and saucer, then shut the door and came back to the table. Pouring her own tea, she resumed her complaints about Sholto's anti-social tendencies.

'I just don't bother to take him out any more. It's not worth the lecture on the evils of modern society, particularly chewing gum and what Sholto would like to do to the folk who drop it. *He's* happy enough at Cauldstane, buried alive, but it's too quiet for me. I used to run a restaurant, you see. In France. I loved all the pandemonium! The *joie de vivre*! And Johnny was hard of hearing, so everything was always full blast with him. Conversation. Music. TV.'

'Johnny? That was your husband?'

'My ex. Jean-Claude. A life spent racing cars wrecked his ears. He couldn't converse below a shout. And all in French, of course. Not at all what I'd grown up with here. Our mother was one of those soft-spoken Highland women who never raised her voice, even when she was angry with us.' Zelda pushed the plate of cake towards me. 'Will you not have some more gingerbread? No? Och, well...' She helped herself to a piece. 'But you can get used to anything. I got used to the noise of the race track and the restaurant kitchen and Johnny bellowing at me across the breakfast table. I really missed it when it stopped. All that racket. It made you feel *alive*.' Zelda cast a jaundiced eye round her room. 'This place is like a morgue now. When Meredith was alive it was very different. There was always music in the air.'

'She played the harpsichord, didn't she?'

'Aye, she did. And she was always singing or playing her own CDs. Cauldstane used to be full of music.'

'She listened to her own recordings?'

Zelda nodded. 'Especially in the years before she died. That was a particular treat for her. She liked to sit in a darkened room – she was very fond of candlelight, said it was flattering – and she'd listen to her old recordings. There weren't that many if truth be told, so it got a wee bit repetitive. But she liked to have company when she listened, so I used to humour her. Sholto's tone deaf and the boys weren't interested of course, but Coral and I used to sit with her sometimes.' Zelda shook her head. 'She tried very hard to get on with Meredith.'

'Coral did?'

'Say what you like about that lassie, she did her best to fit in with the MacNabs. And Meredith didn't make it easy for her.'

'Oh? Why was that?'

'I couldn't say. Meredith liked to be queen bee, of course. She was very much a man's woman. The type who lights up when a good-looking man walks into the room – you know the kind I mean? But Coral was hardly the sort of woman to inspire jealousy. She couldn't hold a candle to Meredith. Not that she even tried.'

'So you think Meredith just didn't like women? Wasn't she Liz's friend?'

'She was the younger sister of Pamela, one of Liz's friends. Meredith and I got along well enough. We had a lot in common. We loved to swap stories about our time abroad, we both loved French food and wine. And French men! No, it was just *Coral* Meredith took a dislike to.'

'Dislike? As bad as that?'

'Och no, not really. Meredith was just impatient with her. Intolerant. But I think you have to make allowances for the artistic temperament.' Zelda paused and lowered her voice. 'Especially if the artist is no longer in demand. Meredith found that hard. Very hard when the phone stopped ringing. And, it has to be said, Sholto was *not* the most attentive of husbands, so naturally she got bored. And when Meredith got bored, she could be... well, a wee bit spiteful. Coral's only crime was to be young and very much in love. An old wifie like me was harmless enough. And of course Meredith was much younger than Liz. I suspect Meredith just had no time for younger women.' Zelda chortled, as if something amusing had suddenly struck her. 'She'd have hated *you*!'

'*Hated* me? Why?'

'Too much competition, my dear! You're pretty, blonde and *slim*. Poor Meredith fought a constant battle with her weight. She always had a generous figure, but as she got older and more indolent she became quite... *substantial*. She was always crash dieting, but being hungry made her miserable and being miserable made her eat. It was a vicious circle. Comfort-eating was what she did when Sholto was away on his travels. We used to sit and blether in here when she was bored or miserable. She liked to play with all my bits and pieces.' Zelda indicated a shelf unit behind her full of small pieces of china and porcelain – thimbles, pill boxes and something I couldn't identify.

'What are the things that look like pepper pots?'

'Holders for hat pins. I collect hat pins.' She stood up and took what looked like a large pincushion down from the top of the shelf unit. It was stuffed with long pins, each of which finished in a piece of coloured glass or ornate beadwork. 'Meredith called this my hedgehog,' Zelda said, holding it out for me to examine. 'She loved it. She bought me several of these pins, in fact. She liked to browse round junk shops and antique fairs and whenever she saw a nice hatpin, she'd buy it for me. She was very taken with them after I told her a bit of their history as a weapon.'

'A *weapon*?'

'Did you not know? They were sometimes used in self-defence. Some were ten inches long! They could be hidden in your hair – Edwardian women wore hair pieces to bulk out their own – and a hat pin could double as an impromptu weapon if the occasion arose.'

'Really? I had no idea!'

'Och, you can do a lot of damage with a hat pin!' said Zelda with relish. 'In fact by 1910 some places were actually passing laws banning their use. So they're an interesting thing to collect. They aren't *quite* what they seem. Meredith loved all that. The idea of a secret weapon. It appealed to her childish side.' Zelda sighed. 'Poor Meredith... She *was* a child in many ways. She'd led a very sheltered life. She didn't know much about anything other than music. I always thought it was a shame she never had a family. One of her own, I mean. A baby would have been good for her. Good for Sholto too. It might have made him act more... responsibly. But Meredith was so focused on her career.'

'Did she believe in the Cauldstane curse?'

'I'm not sure. She was very upset when Liz died and there was a lot of superstitious talk after the accident. Not within *our* family, but Meredith was probably aware of what was said. And she did mention the curse now and again, years later. In front of Coral, too, which was tactless of her, but that was Meredith for you. She always spoke her mind. She didn't seem to realise that not everyone was as emotionally robust as she was.'

'Do *you* believe in the curse, Zelda?'

She gave me one of her beady looks. 'Will this be going into the book?'

'Not if you don't want it to. The final content of the book will be up to Sholto not me. He's already said he doesn't believe in the curse.'

'That's right, he doesn't. But I think he wavers occasionally. Coral's death was such a tragedy. We were all pole-axed by grief, but it almost destroyed Alec. It was a very dark time. He got through it by throwing himself into work, but he still seems... och, I don't know − *haunted* is putting it too strongly, but I don't think he's himself, even now. But he certainly seems to have brightened up since *you* arrived, Jenny.' Zelda's smile was a little too knowing, so I looked down and studied the contents of my tea cup. She took the hint. 'I think we've *all* benefited from having a fresh face around. Someone new to talk to. And talk about! It makes a pleasant change from dwelling on this ridiculous curse.'

'So you think there's nothing to it?'

'I think there's nothing to the curse, but I think the curse *itself* has poisoned our lives.'

'Poisoned? How?'

'MacNab lives have been tainted by fear. Tragedies occur in many families, misfortune affects most, but constant *fear* of tragedy and misfortune − that's a hard cross to bear. None of the MacNab men lack courage. Even Torquil set about a burglar with the Cauldstane claymore. And he showed great fortitude at the end, poor man, dying a slow and miserable death. For all their faults,

MacNabs have always had plenty of fighting spirit,' Zelda said, looking and sounding the embodiment of fighting spirit herself. 'But if you're not careful, fear will weaken you and it can break you. That's why I left Johnny.'

'Johnny? What happened – if you don't mind my asking?'

'Well, this is definitely *not* going into the book, but between you, me and the gatepost...' Zelda set down her cup and saucer and folded her hands in her lap. 'Racing is a young man's game, everybody knows that, and once Johnny was too old for it, he started to drink. That made him aggressive.' Her hand fluttered to her throat where she smoothed her string of pearls. 'We had terrible rows. *Terrible!* On one occasion he even struck me. Just the once, because I packed my bags and left. Now I'll put up with a lot of things, Jenny – noise, silence, cold, solitude – but I'd had enough of living with fear. I'd spent years living with the fear of Johnny killing himself on the race-track. So when he hit me, that was the last straw. If years of living with the fear of losing him were to be followed by years spent fearing his foul temper and drunken outbursts – well, that was it as far as I was concerned. If you live in fear, you fear to live. And if you fear to live, you might as well be dead. I was only thirty-four. I still had a lot of living to do.'

'Well, good for you. How did Johnny cope?'

'Drank himself to death. But I suspect he'd have done that anyway, with or without me.'

'But you came home to help Sholto manage Cauldstane after Liz died?'

'It was a terrible time. They hadn't been here all that long. Barely got their feet under the table when tragedy struck again. So I decided to quit France altogether. I was needed here.'

'This poor family has endured so much.'

'Aye, we've surely had more than our fair share of trouble... Now, will you have more tea, Jenny?'

'No, thanks, I'm fine. I think I'd like to go and make some notes now.' I set down my tea cup, cast a last longing glance at the gingerbread and got to my feet. 'Could I take some of the photo albums away with me?'

'Of course.' Zelda picked up several leather-bound albums and handed them to me.

'Thanks. And thank you for the tea and the lovely chat. Your collections are delightful.'

'I'll get Wilma to deliver the rest of the albums to your room.'

The mention of my room jogged my memory. 'Oh, before I go... I've just remembered something I wanted to ask. It's nothing important, but I wondered whether you could remember what was on the radio before I came in. What had they been playing?'

She looked surprised, then gazed at the radio for inspiration. 'Before you came in?... I think it was a piano concerto. Mozart, I believe.'

'Piano? Not harpsichord?'

'Did Mozart write a concerto for harpsichord?'

'I don't know. I just wondered if they'd been playing harpsichord music on the radio.'

Zelda looked puzzled. 'When?'

'Just before I came in. Well, a few minutes before, actually.'

'No, it had been Mozart for a wee while. I remember now, there was a lovely slow movement.'

'Oh. I see.'

'But why d'you ask? Are you particularly interested in harpsichord music?'

'No, it's just that I thought I'd heard some. When I was in my room. And I knew no one in the family plays, so I assumed it must have been a CD. Or maybe the radio,' I added lamely.

'You heard harpsichord music?'

'Yes. At least, I thought I did.'

'Well, that's *very* odd.'

'Yes. I suppose I must have imagined it.'

'Aye, maybe. But if you did, that makes two of you.'

'I'm sorry? Two of what?'

'Two people who've heard a phantom harpsichord-player at Cauldstane. I'd forgotten all about it until you mentioned it just now, it was so long ago. No one's mentioned it in years.'

'Mentioned *what*?'

'Hearing the harpsichord. At odd times of the day and night. Just odd snatches. Almost like a conversation, she used to say.'

I took a deep breath and tried to keep impatience out of my voice. '*Who*, Zelda?'

'Why, Coral, of course.'

'Coral used to hear the harpsichord?'

'Aye, she did. Did I not explain? No one took much notice because Coral was... well, she was impressionable. Easily upset. Alec was always very protective, but I thought she needed to toughen up a bit.'

'Coral heard music no one else could hear?'

'Well, no one else ever *said* they heard it. That's why it had slipped my mind. Until you mentioned it just now.'

'Did Coral say anything about the music? What it was like?'

'No. Just that when she heard it, poor wee thing, it frightened her half to death.'

Chapter Eleven

There was apparently no explanation for the sudden bursts of music. Zelda seemed to think they were all part of the general oddness of Cauldstane. I would have been quite happy to dismiss them as some sort of auditory hallucination, were it not for the fact that I seemed to have shared the experience with Coral. But she was beginning to sound fragile, verging on unstable and I had no wish to align myself with any kind of mental instability, so I dismissed the strange music and resolved not to mention it again.

Apart from the occasional odd and unsettling experience, my early days at Cauldstane were very pleasant. I enjoyed the company of all the MacNabs and I loved my work. Despite the sad history with which I gradually became acquainted, I was quite happy. There was a lot of laughter and kindness and the bright autumn days were mostly cloudless.

But it was just the lull before the storm.

After tea with Zelda, I took the family photo albums to the music room where I did most of my work. It could not have been a greater contrast to the Cauldstane armoury, but despite the dust and heat, the bare light bulbs and the mouse droppings, I found I felt more at home in the armoury than the music room.

It was situated on the second floor and compared to some of the dark rooms at Cauldstane, it was airy and attractive, but dominated by the presence of a seventeenth-century Flemish harpsichord, its wood painted ox-blood red. Although no one played it any more, Mrs Guthrie took a certain pride in the instrument, which she dusted every week. She'd lifted the lid carefully to show me the Latin inscription inside:

Viva fui in sylvis sum dura occisa securi
Dum vixi tacui mortua dulce cano.

She hadn't known what it meant, so I googled it and came up with a sort of riddle:

I was alive in the woods. I was cut down by a hard axe.
While I lived I was silent. Now dead I sing sweetly.

It took me a moment to realise it was a tree speaking, the tree from which the wooden case of the harpsichord had been made. The quotation delighted me, as did the ornate interior of the instrument. The fact it was never played now saddened me a little, so occasionally I'd prop the lid open so I could see inside. As the dull red box spread its wings and became a giant wooden butterfly, it was as if I'd liberated the instrument. I would sit and contemplate its angular beauty and even though it remained silent, the harpsichord was a palpable presence in the room.

The walls were decorated with scuffed *faux*-oriental wallpaper and framed programmes celebrating Meredith's singing career in concert halls and opera houses. None of these was of the first rank, which perhaps explained why I'd never heard of her, even though Rupert was an opera buff and I'd lived for years, not altogether happily, with his extensive CD collection.

On the mantelpiece there were framed photos of Meredith in costume. Her wigs and makeup were outlandish, but I supposed such exaggeration had once been deemed necessary for performances in opera houses. I certainly learned a lot about the use and abuse of eye-liner. But the absurd pantomime effect did Meredith no favours. She looked harsh or just plain tacky. A picture of her in a riding outfit, looking natural and girlish showed her to much better advantage. Peering at the other woman in the photo, I saw it was Liz MacNab. Meredith was on horseback and Liz, also dressed for riding, was standing on the ground beside her.

If Meredith was already a friend of the family, I could see why Sholto might have married his mistress to provide his young sons with a replacement mother figure. I'd made a note to investigate – tactfully – the history of Sholto's relationship with Meredith. I also needed to know why things had gone sour between Meredith and Alec, but even though Alec and I were getting along well, I didn't yet feel I could ask him outright about the argument he'd had with his stepmother just before she died.

~

I'd got into a routine of listening to Sholto talk, then going for a walk while I thought myself into his mind, then I would go back to the music room and sit facing the wall, with my back to the log fire, laid for me every day by Mrs Guthrie. I'd noticed I had a tendency to gaze out the window, watching the comings and goings of various family members. Especially Alec. Such distractions were clearly not conducive to producing my best work, so I'd asked Mrs Guthrie to help me re-position the desk.

Once settled in the music room, I would listen to my tape once or twice, after which I'd type up the episode on my laptop, in Sholto's "voice". I would try to condense his account into something that would read well, but still sound like Sholto, or what I thought readers expected him to sound like.

At Eton I developed an obsessive interest in sport. This was a vain attempt to equip myself with skills that would protect me from the attentions of bullies who tormented me on account of my two heinous crimes: I'd been born a Scot and I was the unfortunate possessor of strawberry-blond hair. This all too distinguishing characteristic made me easy to spot, so I fell prey to boys seeking primitive entertainment. Predators of another kind found my blond curls and blue eyes alluring. I considered my options and concluded survival at Eton might depend on my sporting prowess, to which end I made sprinting and boxing my educational priorities. If I couldn't outrun my tormentors, I could at least bloody their noses.

It was a kind of impersonation, but one attempted in good faith, my object being to convey to a reader what it had been like to sit and listen to Sholto tell his stories. I was the channel through which the stories passed, but I had to be invisible and inaudible. If I did my job properly, no one would know I was there, standing between Sholto and his readers. The job fascinated me. It felt like a challenge, not a constraint, to keep myself out of the picture.

My current task was to edit my account of Coral's death. Sholto had said that although the family believed her death was probably suicide, he would like to refer to it in print as an accident. Knowing Alec's feelings on the matter, I was relieved to be able to present the tragedy in this light, especially as we would never know what had actually happened that day. But I wasn't happy with my draft and read it through again.

Coral was a keen photographer and the castle and grounds provided her with a great variety of subjects. With her eye for detail, she would record the first woodland violets or the texture of lichen on an old stone wall. One Christmas she presented me with an album of photographs taken at Cauldstane. They were a revelation to me. They made me see my home and family in a new light. They showed me how much I'd missed by spending so many months away from Cauldstane while I was on expeditions. These pictures reminded me how beautiful the Highlands are in every season.

Coral was taken from us at a cruelly young age. She was only thirty-three when she drowned in the River Spey, which flows alongside the castle. Whether she'd waded in to take a picture and got into difficulties, or whether she fell from the river bank and was swept away, we shall never know, but she is daily missed by all of us.

For as long as I can remember, I've pitted my wits against Nature, knowing she holds all the cards. A veteran of catastrophic accidents, I have more than a nodding acquaintance with death. I've lost friends and team members to avalanches, frostbite and shipwrecks, but Coral's death was particularly hard to bear. She hadn't put herself in harm's way, as I and my colleagues had. Her untimely death was just a random and inexplicable accident.

I reached the end of my account and felt depressed, not so much by what I'd written, as my memory of Alec's white face when he was talking about his dead wife. The music room seemed suddenly quite chilly, despite the logs burning in the grate, so I got up from my desk and went over to the window to stretch my legs and get my circulation going again.

As I looked out the window I saw a pleasant vista of rolling grass and woodland, trees that were possibly hundreds of years old, stones that were much older. The sight was timeless and calming. I didn't actually utter the words, but they formed in my mind: *Rest in peace.*

After a few moments I felt able to return to my desk in a more professionally detached frame of mind, ready to edit my account which, to my mind, sounded a little too formal. I might have to listen to the tape once again to see if I could lift a few more of Sholto's characteristic turns of phrase, though I was beginning to realise, when dealing with grief and loss, his narrative style tended to be laconic. His stiff-upper-lip version of personal tragedy was going to disappoint readers avid for vicarious thrills.

There was a knock at the door. I looked at my watch and realised the afternoon had almost gone.

Alec's head appeared. 'Am I disturbing you? I thought you might have knocked off for the day.'

'Oh, I haven't achieved very much today. I had tea with Zelda and she talked a lot about Meredith, then she gave me these photo albums to look through.' I indicated the pile on my desk. 'But I was just trying to edit something when you knocked...' I remembered exactly what I'd been trying to edit and quickly changed the subject. 'But I think I've had enough for today. I feel rather tired.'

'No doubt Zelda talked you into the ground.'

'She has a lot of energy, doesn't she?' I said tactfully as I closed the laptop and tidied my desk.

Alec smiled. 'I suppose you could say that.'

'You all do, all you MacNabs. You've all done so much living.'

'So have you, in your head. A writer must live many lives. Especially a ghost writer.'

'It does sometimes feel like that. I've often wondered whether multiple personality disorder would be a good qualification for being a writer.'

'Sounds like you need a break. I was wondering if now would be a good time for me to show you the claymore?'

'Oh, yes please! I'd love that.'

'Then follow me.'

Alec led the way along the corridor and into the very large room known as the Great Hall. I'd seen it before, but each time I entered I was struck by its scale. It was the largest room in the castle and was only used when entertaining on a grand scale, which effectively meant, as Sholto said, "when MacNabs were hatched, matched and despatched".

It was now something between a gallery and a drawing room, with massive dark wooden furniture and panelling and equally dark portraits on the walls. The carved stone fireplace was literally monumental and the floor space so big, there were no fewer than six large Persian rugs forming a faded patchwork on the floor.

Alec gestured towards the fireplace and said, 'The Cauldstane claymore,' almost as if we were being introduced. The sword hung between two studded shields and beneath a portrait of a MacNab ancestor, swathed in a great quantity of tartan and brandishing the claymore in a fearsome manner. The theatricality of the painting served only to emphasise the stark and simple beauty of the ancient piece of metal beneath. Already I felt in awe, as if I'd been conducted into the presence of something very special.

Alec reached up above the mantelpiece with one hand and lifted the sword off the first of the small brackets that held it in place. Then he raised his other hand, took the weight of the blade and lifted it off the other bracket. Holding it with both hands now, one on the hilt and the other on the blade, he lowered the sword to waist height and walked towards me, presenting it.

He said nothing. This didn't seem odd. I said nothing either. The silence wasn't what you'd call companionable with a steel blade over a metre long between us, a blade that had been bathed in God knows how many men's blood, but I felt we were sharing something. Something significant.

I was still staring at the blade when Alec said, 'Would you like to hold it?'

'May I?'

'Of course.'

I thought at first that Alec was reluctant to let it out of his hands, then, as I took the sword from him, I realised he was taking the weight until I'd registered just how heavy it was. If he hadn't done that, I suspect I might have dropped it.

'Good heavens! Men actually *fought* with these? Did they bludgeon each other to death?'

'Aye, it seems heavy if you're not used to it. It was used two-handed as a chopping weapon, not a piercing weapon like a rapier.'

'So you hacked at your opponent?'

'Aye. It's a double-edged blade. Steel. Made in Germany.' He pointed. 'You see the maker's mark there? That tells us it was made in Solingen.'

I peered at the engraving. 'It looks like a wolf running.'

'It is.'

I looked up from the blade. 'You said you had a maker's mark, didn't you? What's yours?'

'A red kite. With wings extended.'

'Oh, how wonderful... Gosh, I'm sounding trite, aren't I? But this is all so exciting, I don't know what to say. I feel very privileged to be allowed to hold a piece of history.'

'Try holding it as if you were going to use it. Take the hilt in both hands and raise the blade... If you hold it upright that will be the least strain on your arms.' With some difficulty, I followed Alec's instructions until the sword pointed straight up in the air.

He watched me a moment, then said, 'How d'you feel?'

I frowned at him. 'How do I *feel*?'

'Aye.' He shrugged. 'You look different. I wondered if you felt different.'

I stood, taking stock. 'Well, I feel... bigger.'

He nodded. 'That's because you're standing straighter. You have to, to hold the sword. And your arms have just been extended by more than a metre. So you would feel bigger.'

'I feel stronger too. And... *braver*. This is really weird, Alec!'

'Don't worry – swords often have that effect on folk when they handle them. It's often very marked with women. They're not used to feeling at a physical advantage. It's a new and heady sensation.' He smiled. 'Isn't it?'

'I don't think I've ever felt like this before. It's making me feel quite emotional... The beauty of the thing. And all the history... To think how many men it must have killed... How many, do you think?'

'Impossible to say. A great number, probably. Those it didn't kill outright would most likely have died of their wounds.'

'And this was the actual sword that was used to execute the faithless MacNab wife?'

'Reputedly.'

'And it can be used only once more to save the Cauldstane MacNabs?'

'So the story goes. Will I take it now? You're probably finding it a bit heavy.'

Alec relieved me of the claymore as if it weighed no more than an umbrella and I realised his earlier careful handling had simply been reverence.

'If you're interested, I'll tell you a wee bit about its construction.'

'You bet I'm interested. This is going to be a very long footnote in Sholto's book. He doesn't get to vote. It's going in.'

Alec grinned and I experienced a childish sensation of pride that I'd said the right thing. Not that I was seeking his approval. My enthusiasm for the claymore was genuine. It had inspired a strange mix of emotions in me and one of them was awe.

'The claymore was a Highland weapon and it appeared at the beginning of the sixteenth century. It's called a claymore from the Gaelic, *claidheamh-mór*, meaning "great sword" or broadsword and it was one of the few weapons that could fell a man in armour. The hilt's made of iron and would originally have been covered in leather. These drooping arms of the cross guard are called quillons and these strips of metal protruding on to the blade, they're called langets.' Alec pointed to the decorations at the end of the cross guard. 'You see these things that look like four-leafed clovers? They're called quatrefoil terminals and they're the defining characteristic of the Highland two-handed sword.'

'How much does it weigh?'

'Two and a half kilos.'

'And how long is it?'

'1.4 metres. That would be about the height of your shoulder.'

'It must be very valuable.'

'There are lots of references to Highland two-handed swords, but very few have actually survived. Perhaps about thirty in their original condition.'

'And this is one of them?'

'Aye.'

'My God, Alec – what is it *worth*?'

'Och, I've no idea! And I don't want to know. Sholto handed it over to me when I turned eighteen. It's mine now.' He took the hilt in both hands and swung the sword upwards, so he held it before him, like an inverted cross. 'If anyone wants to take it and sell it, they'll have to kill me first. Preferably with the claymore.'

~

97

Despite my words of encouragement, Alec declined to give me a demonstration of the claymore in action and hung it, respectfully, back on the wall. We went our separate ways: he down to his room to shower before dinner, I back to the music room.

As I entered, the room seemed very chilly and I saw the fire was almost out. A burning log shifted and collapsed with a grating sound, sending showers of sparks flying up the chimney, like a firework. I returned to my desk and opened the laptop. I remembered I'd been in the middle of a re-write of my account of Coral's death. With my hand on the cursor, ready to highlight defective passages, I scanned the screen. As I did so, I had the strangest of feelings, like a premonition, as if something bad was about to happen.

It was.

When I got to the end of my account – *Her untimely death was just a random and inexplicable accident* – I saw there was now a space, then a new sentence.

It wasn't an accident.

Chapter Twelve

I hadn't typed those words. Alec hadn't typed those words. He'd been with me. Was this my mysterious intruder again? Or *had* I typed those words? If I was capable of deleting my own notes while day-dreaming, I was presumably capable of writing a short sentence without knowing I'd done it. I was a very fast typist and my fingers moved almost as quickly as I could think. Is that what had happened? I believed Coral's death was no accident and I'd typed that?

But I *did* think it was an accident. I'd had no firm opinion until Alec had filled me in on the background, but once he'd told me about her pregnancy, nothing would have persuaded me Coral had taken her own life, not after she'd shared her news with her husband.

But supposing Alec was lying? What if Coral hadn't been pregnant?... I only had to think of his pained, white face to know he was telling the truth. Or he totally believed his own lies.

I'd believed Coral was pregnant, so she wouldn't have committed suicide. Why then had I written *It wasn't an accident?* What else could it have been? But if I hadn't typed that sentence, someone else had. Who other than Alec had an axe to grind about Coral's death? It made no sense, so by a process of elimination, I had to conclude I'd typed something I didn't actually believe.

Well, that wouldn't be a first for me as a ghost writer. Many's the time I'd had to dress up someone's fairy story and present it as fact. I once made a good living writing fiction. Nowadays it was faction.

But I could hear myself whistling in the dark... I was worried and a part of me wanted to give Rupert a ring, just for someone normal to talk to. (Could a theoretical physicist who felt he'd been called by God ever be considered *normal*?) I thought I might find it soothing to hear Rupert enthusing about Harvest Festival or grumbling about parish politics. For if I was being honest – and as Alec had said, why be anything else? – I was feeling slightly scared.

Scared I was losing it again, that my grip on reality had become shaky, despite the usual precautions I'd taken. I was writing things and hearing things – possibly imagining things too if I thought Alec MacNab was taking an interest in me.

I decided I wouldn't ring Rupert, but would have a very early night. So, after a family dinner at which I was less than sparkling company, I retired to bed with my hot water bottle and an unexciting book and was soon asleep.

I was woken by the sound of that damn harpsichord. As I surfaced, I felt angry for several seconds before fear kicked in. Then I remembered what Zelda had said about poor Coral. *When she heard it, poor wee thing, it frightened her half to death.*

Was it the harpsichord? The jangling noise now seemed to be right inside my head, drilling into my brain. Was it some kind of tinnitus? My father had complained about the stress of tinnitus towards the end of his life – strange irritating sounds that never let up. Was this what was happening to me?

The music stopped, suddenly and completely. The silence was suffocating. I lay in bed shaking with nerves, wondering if I was losing my mind again or whether I'd just taken a long time to surface from a nightmare. When my breathing was back to normal, I decided I would calm myself with my usual panacea: work. I turned on the bedside lamp – immediately I felt better – then got out of bed and switched on my laptop. Waiting for it to load up, I reached for my notebook, then noticed something sitting on top. Something long, thin, shiny and sharp.

A hat pin.

I stared at the pin and tried to work out how it could have travelled from Zelda's sitting room to my bedroom. Had it been attached to one of the photo albums? But they were still in the music room. It must have got caught up on my clothing somehow. But if so, how did it end up on top of my notebook? Had Zelda put it there? Was it a gift she'd left for me? With no explanatory note?...

My fingers were moving over the keyboard while I thought and I'd opened my draft of Sholto's biography before I remembered the last enigmatic line of text I couldn't account for. I scrolled down to check if the random words were still there.

They were. But that was no longer the last line. After a space there was now a new line of text.

You can do a lot of damage with a hat pin.

Zelda's exact words. But I hadn't written them down, not even in my notes, let alone on the laptop. I might be losing my mind, but I knew I hadn't typed those words. Which meant someone else had. Not Zelda, surely?

Whoever it was, I was now past caring. Fuming, I fired off a rude and deeply therapeutic response without even thinking how or when my reply would be read.

Is this some kind of threat? Who are you and why are you leaving me messages? Please stop creeping into my room and playing with my laptop. If you have a problem with my being here, sit down and talk to me about it! I'm here to do a job and I only want the best for this family.

I sat there, glaring at the screen. Then, to my absolute horror, words began to appear, one by one.

And I only want the worst.

Bat out of hell doesn't begin to describe it. I was out of my chair, across the room and into the hall before I stopped to think of any rational explanation. Slamming the door behind me, I leaned against it, my heart thumping, hoping none of the family had heard the racket I'd made. Standing there in my nightdress, shaking, I decided wild horses wouldn't drag me back into that bedroom now. A line had been crossed. Either I was going mad again or... Or *what*?

The words had appeared on the screen while I was watching. I *must* be seeing things – things that weren't really there. What alternative explanation could there possibly be?... My legs gave way beneath me and I sank to the floor, weeping. Gathering up some folds of my nightie, I pressed them to my mouth, trying to muffle my whimpering.

Across the hall there was a rattling sound as a door opened. I commanded my legs to move but they refused. It was dark in the corridor, so I hoped I wouldn't be visible, cowering on the floor, but as Alec's door opened slowly, a shaft of light fell on me. He stood silhouetted in the doorway. I saw his head drop as he spotted me on the floor. No doubt his jaw dropped too.

'Jenny! What's the matter?'

Blinking against the light, I couldn't think of anything sensible to say. How do you tell someone you think you're going mad – and for the second time? I wiped my nose discreetly on my nightie and, in as casual a voice as I could muster, said, 'Do you know anything about laptops?'

'*Laptops?*'

'Yes. Mine's started talking to me. In fact, I think it's possessed.'

Alec's reaction frightened me almost as much as the automatic writing. He was across the corridor in two strides, then he bent down, pulled me to my feet and dragged me into his bedroom, kicking the door shut behind him. He laid his hands on my shoulders and said, 'You'll be OK now. Nothing can harm you in here.'

When my eyes had adjusted to the light I saw that Alec was half-naked, clad in striped pyjama bottoms – a sight I was far too miserable to enjoy. In any case, my astonished eyes were torn between Alec's slim and muscular torso and the presence in his room of a mini armoury. A sword hung on the wall over the bed. There was another lying on the floor where sane people would have had a bedside rug. There was another sword on the floor at the end of the bed and propped up in the uncurtained window alcove stood yet another. My writer's eye noted an umbrella stand in the corner of the room which held no umbrellas or even walking sticks. It was full of scabbards. Well, of course. How else would Mrs Guthrie manage to get round with the Hoover?...

I started to giggle. I couldn't help myself. Then my giggle suddenly gave way to more weeping. 'It's happening, Alec,' I moaned. 'It's happening again! I'm seeing things. I can see *swords* all round this room! And I'm *hearing* things too! It's *me* – I'm making bad things happen!'

'It isn't you, Jenny.' He took hold of both my hands and said, 'It's nothing to do with you. You've just been caught in the crossfire. You're not seeing things. My room *is* full of swords.'

'*Why?*'

'It's a long story. First of all, tell me why you were crying.'

I sniffed and wiped my eyes. 'You're not going to believe this.'

'Try me.'

'My laptop's bullying me.'

To his credit, he didn't laugh. He didn't even look surprised. 'Come and sit down.' He led me over to the bed, then threw his dressing gown round my shoulders. 'Tell me what happened.'

'I've been getting strange messages.'

'How?'

'They're left on my laptop. I thought it was you to begin with. I thought you wanted me to leave.'

'*Me*? Why would I want you to leave? You know I'm very glad you came. Tell me about the messages.'

'There have been three – no, four now.'

'What did they say?'

'The first one said, "Leave Cauldstane to its ghosts." But that was what *I'd* written.'

Alec frowned. 'I thought you said it was a message left for you?'

'It was. But those words were part of a sentence I'd already written. I'd made notes about the family. For the book, I mean. But all the rest of my notes disappeared, apart from those few words. I thought it must be you. I thought you'd come into my room while I was asleep and deleted my notes.'

'What were the other messages?'

'The next one was when I'd been writing up Sholto's account of Coral's death.'

Alec's eyelids flickered, but he continued to stare at me. 'What did the message say?'

'It said, "It wasn't an accident".'

He flinched and looked away. After a moment, he faced me again. 'You're sure about that? She said it *wasn't* an accident?'

'*She*? Who are you talking about? You think this is Zelda?'

He ignored me and said, 'What was the next message?'

'It was just something Zelda had said to me. Something she'd said in jest really.'

'What?'

'It said, "You can do a lot of damage with a hat pin." '

'*Hat pin?*'

103

'Zelda and I had been discussing them. She showed me her collection and told me they could be used as weapons. Women used to defend themselves with them apparently.'

'That's three. What was the fourth?'

I shivered and Alec tucked the dressing gown round me more firmly but his eyes never left my face. 'It came up on the screen while I was just sitting there. So I knew it wasn't me doing it. The other messages – well, I thought maybe I'd written them without knowing what I was doing. But this one... I watched it appear, letter by letter!'

'What did it say?'

My mind went blank. The horror of that moment seemed to have wiped my memory, but then the words came back to me and I found I couldn't utter them.

'What did the fourth message say, Jenny?'

'I just can't believe – I mean, I *must* have imagined it! Or else I'm going mad. Alec, will you please come and look? I want to go back and see if those hateful words are still there.'

He seemed reluctant, but said nothing. He reached across to a chair and grabbed a T-shirt which he pulled on, then to my utter astonishment, he bent down and picked up one of the swords. I looked at it, then at his solemn face. 'I don't think we'll need the hardware, Alec. It's a talking laptop.'

'I promise I'll explain, but not now. Please keep close and stay behind me. Just in case.'

I struggled into his dressing gown and tied the belt. It swamped me but smelled pleasantly of Alec. 'In case of *what*?'

'Just... keep close.'

He opened the door and we crossed the passage. As he opened my bedroom door, I stood right behind him. He switched on the light and approached the desk. 'Show me the page you were on. Let me see the last message.'

The laptop had gone to sleep, so I leaned forward, got the page back up again and pointed to my indignant outburst. 'That's me... I was responding to the random hat pin message. Then as I watched, the laptop wrote *that*.' I pointed to the final words on the screen.

And I only want the worst.

As he read the words, I watched Alec's chest rise and fall in a great sigh – but not of sadness. Irritation perhaps? Anger, even?

'What's going on, Alec? How can anyone be writing to me on my laptop? And why would anyone write anything so awful?'

He turned to me, laid his free hand on my shoulder and fixed me with a look. I'd never noticed before but the irises of his grey eyes were ringed with a much darker colour and there were golden flecks around his pupils, like sparks. I drew strength from those dark, determined eyes, long before I realised how much I was going to need it.

'Jenny, I need to ask you to trust me, because what I'm going to say will almost certainly make you think I'm the one who's mad.'

'Oh, don't worry about that. I'd be glad of the company, frankly. I think I'm going completely round the bend.'

His free hand flew up to my face and he stroked my cheek. 'D'you believe in ghosts, Jenny?'

'*Ghosts?* No, I don't think so.' It took a moment for his words to sink in. 'Are you saying Cauldstane is haunted? *Really* haunted?' Alec nodded. 'And you think... it's a *ghost* leaving messages for me? Good God! Why *me*? I'm not even a MacNab!'

'And she wants to keep it that way,' Alec murmured as he glanced round the room, his sword still raised. 'She's trying to intimidate you because she wants you to leave Cauldstane. And it means you have to go, Jenny. For your own safety.'

'I couldn't possibly walk out on Sholto! It would break his heart. In any case, I have a job to do here. I have a contract and my professional reputation to consider. I know I was behaving like a total wimp just now, but it was shock. I really don't scare so easily. It's just messages on a laptop! Spooky, but just a form of cyber-bullying.'

Alec shook his head. 'It's more than that. I believe you could be in danger.'

'Don't be ridiculous! Even if there is some sort of poltergeist, I'm not in any *danger*. Danger of losing the plot, possibly, but if we can just work out how someone's leaving messages on my laptop, I'll be fine. Perhaps it's Wilma. She's very protective of the family. Maybe she resents my presence here.'

'Someone does, but it isn't Wilma.'

As I stared at the laptop, a new idea struck me. 'Do you think someone could have hacked into my account and be doing it remotely?'

'Aye, it's being done remotely – but not in the way you mean.' He handed me the sword. 'Hold that. Just take hold of it, like I showed you with the claymore. That's right. You'll be OK.'

'Alec, what on earth—'

He turned away and spread his hands. 'Show yourself, God damn you!'

For a stunned moment, I thought Alec was addressing me, then I realised he was talking to the spirit he believed was meddling with my laptop. Needless to say, nothing happened. My arms began to ache from holding the sword and I was shivering again. The room seemed freezing even though it was still only September.

Frightened I was going to drop it, I lowered the sword until its point rested on the floor. 'Alec, I'm really tired. Can we discuss this in the morning? I don't believe in ghosts and nothing is going to make me believe in them. I'm sure there's some sort of technical explanation—'

He laid his fingers on my lips and took the sword. Looking into my eyes, he said, 'Trust me.' Then he took his hand away from my mouth, cupped the back of my head and kissed me. Deeply. Passionately. And I responded. Because I'd been wanting to do that for days.

The harpsichord started up again, but this time it wasn't just in my head, it filled the room, getting louder and louder, until I thought my ears would burst. Alec was still looking at me, shouting something I couldn't hear when, over his shoulder, I saw first one, then the other Staffordshire china dog leave the chest of drawers and hurtle through the air, making for his head. As I yelled a warning, he turned, raised his sword and dashed both figurines to the floor, where they shattered. I stepped back, terrified, but Alec grabbed hold of me and bellowed over the music, '*Now* d'you believe me?' His eyes were alight. He seemed almost exultant.

Then the forgotten hat pin on my desk leaped into the air and came flying straight for my face, but Alec saw it and swiped it away with a flick of his sword arm. It bounced off the wall and fell to the floor, joining the shards of pottery. The music stopped as suddenly as it had started and left my ears ringing. Alec stood poised and alert, his eyes moving quickly back and forth, scanning the room for the source of the next attack. But I saw it first.

'*Look...*' I pointed to the laptop screen which was growing dark with text. Letters were appearing at an impossible rate, filling the screen with a silent tirade.

I clutched at Alec. 'In God's name, who *is* it?'

His mouth was set in a grim line as he watched the screen, the text scrolling now at a demented speed. Then, in a voice so deep, so angry, I hardly recognised it as his, Alec said, 'Jenny, allow me to introduce you to the ghost of my dear departed step-mother... Meredith MacNab.'

PART TWO

Chapter Thirteen

That's not even my real name. My public knew me – and loved me – as Meredith Fitzgerald. It always irritated me when the Highland peasantry referred to me as "Mrs MacNab".

Meredith Fitzgerald wasn't my real name either. (Even Sholto doesn't know that. But there's rather a lot Sholto doesn't know.) I was born "Moira", a name that never seemed quite in keeping with my musical aspirations, so when I left college I promoted myself to "Meredith Fitzgerald". I thought that had a musical ring to it. A certain "je ne sais quoi".

I was a high flyer, you see. A meteor in the musical world. That's what the Telegraph critic said. I developed early and I was ferociously ambitious. I don't mind admitting I was ruthless at times. But mine was an exceptional talent. The world was a brighter place when I sang. Fans wrote to me and said so. They waited at the stage door with gifts: flowers and chocolates (too many chocolates!), sometimes small pieces of jewellery. I brightened up their dull little lives and they wanted to show their appreciation. It was so sweet.

I used to command enormous fees. Oh, yes, I earned a lot of money, but I've no idea where it went. It just seemed to disappear. I had expenses, of course – hair, clothes, shoes. One had to be well groomed and it was necessary to be seen in the right places after a performance. It all added up – the money and the calories.

Of course I could have done much better for myself than Sholto MacNab. Much better. I had offers, believe me. But he was such a handsome man. So brave. A real-life hero. And he was besotted with me. That made him irresistible. I do believe he actually loved his dowdy wife, but he still couldn't keep his hands off me. He was quite reckless. I loved that. It was something we had in common: a love of risk.

I never knew if he would return from one of his dangerous expeditions. That was thrilling too. Quite an aphrodisiac. Even before we were married I sometimes used to think about what I would wear at Sholto's funeral. Something chic but severe, like

Jackie Kennedy. Definitely veiled.

It was all very exciting to begin with, then things settled down into a sort of clandestine routine. Sholto had everything he wanted: his loyal, boring wife stuck at home, breeding sons, and his glamorous young mistress providing entertainment and sophistication in London or Edinburgh, or wherever I happened to be performing. (We once enjoyed a night of passion in Perth of all places.)

Then Torquil finally died and Sholto became quite a different proposition. I must confess, I didn't realise then that "laird" wasn't a proper title, like Duke or Earl and I didn't know it was possible to own a castle and God knows how many acres and still be hard up. "Asset-rich, cash-poor" was an expression that meant little to me then. My fans gave me jewellery. When I needed money, I sold it. Or I asked Sholto.

I can't claim I knew anything about money other than how to spend it. I concentrated on my career and allowed Sholto to manage my finances – by which I mean I let him pick up the tab, which in the early years he was happy to do. He was so understanding. Until we married. Then things changed.

He never said so, but I knew he missed Liz. What there was to miss about that woman, I had no idea, but Sholto was clearly out of his depth trying to manage the boys. He wanted me to be a mother to those two tearaways and seemed to expect me to devote every waking hour to maintaining the ruin that was Cauldstane, as if I was some sort of housewife.

There was clearly only one thing to be done with Cauldstane Castle and that was sell it.

Never was a place more aptly named! They say "cold as the grave", but trust me, Cauldstane in January when the wind is in the east, is worse. I've never known cold like it. Even at the height of summer that place was never really warm. The cold and damp used to seep through the stone floors and walls until it had crept into your very bones. Some days I just didn't bother to get up, it was so cold. I stayed in bed and got Wilma to bring me all my meals on a tray.

She was a sweetheart. Nothing was too much trouble. Even though she didn't have a clue about music, she showed me the respect that was my due as an artist and mistress of Cauldstane.

There was never a speck of dust on any of my photographs or certificates and I think dear Wilma was more thrilled with my portrait than Sholto! She would have done anything for me. She used to stand in the music room occasionally and listen to me play the harpsichord. The music went right over her head of course, but she loved to watch me. I could understand that. I had beautiful hands. I used to look at them while I played and marvel at how lovely they looked, sparkling with rings.

I brought a little colour – and yes, magic! – into Wilma's humdrum life. Into so many lives. I really deserved better than the shabby treatment I got from Sholto. When I asked him to divorce Liz and marry me, he wouldn't hear of it. The selfish bastard liked having his cake and eating it. Well, I wasn't going to stand for that. I could have had my pick of any number of eligible young bachelors – not to mention the moneyed old men. So I delivered my ultimatum.

Do you know what he said? Sholto had the bloody nerve to tell me, he believed in marriage; that he found fidelity very difficult, but for him marriage was "till death us do part". I'd never heard anything so pathetic! Since he was sleeping with me at every available opportunity, the old hypocrite got what he deserved.

Liz died.

And that was that.

After Liz died, I had to be circumspect. I needed to make myself indispensable to the family, but I had to keep my distance from Sholto. That was no hardship. He was a bore as a grieving widower. You'd think no one had ever lost a wife before. He was the same about the boys – so concerned they were motherless, but since they spent half their lives at boarding school, I couldn't see what all the fuss was about. But I did my best to be nice to them. I knew that was the way to persuade Sholto to make me a permanent fixture.

It was an uphill struggle. Neither of the boys was interested in music and I didn't know much about anything else. Fergus loved animals and was a keen rider like me, but Alec was just impossible. I suppose feeling responsible for your mother's death would ensure you weren't the most cheerful of children, but I do think he milked the "reclusive loner" bit, especially in his teens. I mean, everyone said, you can't blame an eight-year old for causing someone's death and no one ever did. Nobody even mentioned it, so I think Alec *should have pulled himself together and got on with his life. I mean, it was a great shame, but it just couldn't be helped. Riding is a dangerous sport and horses are unpredictable. Liz wasn't the most expert of riders and her mare was temperamental. That's what I said to Sholto – to anyone who'd listen, in fact. "Accidents happen."*

Especially to the MacNabs.

I rubbed my eyes and looked away from the laptop. I felt numb. I couldn't believe what had happened, but I had to. It was as if my brain had taken a running jump at a brick wall and knocked itself out. Except that there was a tiny part of my mind that was relieved I wasn't going mad. It was only a ghost. *Only.*

Alec was sitting on the edge of the bed, his shoulders bowed. He was staring down at the sword resting across his pyjama-clad thighs. I don't know when I've seen anyone look so exhausted. Or defeated. He must have sensed my gaze because he looked up and I saw dark shadows under his eyes. I realised it must be very late, but there was no possibility of sleep tonight. Not for me.

He gestured towards my laptop. 'Looks like you'll be up till dawn if you read it all. Meredith obviously needed to get a lot off her chest.'

'You don't have to stay, Alec.'

'I'd like to. If you don't mind,' he added politely. The incongruity of this exchange made me want to laugh hysterically. It was 2.00 a.m. and the heir to Cauldstane was sitting on my bed in his pyjamas, keeping watch with a sword, while I read a ghost's crazed autobiography. This wasn't what Rupert had meant when he suggested I take up a less demanding career than writing fiction.

I managed to summon up a small smile for Alec. 'Meredith stopped throwing things ages ago. I'll be OK. I'm doing what she wants, aren't I? Reading all this.'

'I'd prefer to stay. I've taken precautions, but I don't know what power she has over other folk. I only know what she can do to me.'

'What do you mean – precautions?'

'There's a blade under your mattress... A Bible on the book shelf. And this...' He picked up a small carved wooden animal that had been placed on the bedside table. I'd thought it was an otter, but Wilma had told me it was a pine marten. Alec had carved it as a gift for Coral. 'It's made of rowan wood,' he explained, as if the words would mean something to me. 'But evidently Meredith can still get into the room.'

I swivelled round on my chair. 'Are you saying you put a *sword* under my mattress? In Heaven's name, *why*?'

'A steel blade is a traditional Highland talisman against evil. It's a time-honoured custom to take an oath upon cold iron or steel. A dirk, or *sgian dubh* was always handy for that purpose.' He shrugged. 'Some folk believe luck is associated with a horseshoe because it's a piece of iron that can be placed conveniently over a threshold.'

I remembered arriving at Cauldstane with Fergus. 'There's one at the castle's back door, isn't there?'

'I put it there. And I make sure it stays there.'

'And the rowan wood?'

'Another traditional talisman. A rowan tree would be planted in front of a house to keep evil spirits from the door.'

'Oh... Sholto told me his walking stick was made of rowan.'

'I made that too.'

I was beginning to grasp the scale of the problem and the pressure Alec lived under. 'Does Sholto know?'

'About Meredith? I doubt it. He's never said anything. But then he wouldn't.'

'But... you think Coral knew?' I saw him hesitate and said, 'You don't have to answer, Alec. I don't want to stir up any bad memories for you.'

'I think it best you know what happened, Jenny. If you're to understand what's happening now.' He looked at the laptop screen, then back at me. 'Would you come and sit on the bed? I think you'd be safer. I'll sit on one of the chairs.'

'No, I'd like you close at hand, if you don't mind. Get under the duvet – you must be freezing! You didn't even put any slippers on.' Alec turned back the bedclothes and, still grasping the sword, slid into bed, taking up a position as close to the edge as he could without actually falling out. I wasn't sure if this was out of consideration for me, or so he'd be ready for action. I stood up, cinched his dressing gown firmly round my waist, then climbed in on the other side. We sat there like bookends, facing the laptop, saying nothing. I felt a wave of terror begin to rise again, but I was determined not to give in to it, so I took a deep breath and said, 'Know any good bedtime stories?'

'Aye. This one's a cracker.' Alec laid the sword down in the space between us, the blade pointing to the foot of the bed, then he clasped his hands loosely in his lap and said, 'After Meredith died, Coral said she heard music. The harpsichord.'

'I've heard it too.'

His head turned sharply. 'You have?'

'A couple of times. I assumed it was a radio. But somehow I knew it wasn't. That's when I started to think that I... that I might be losing it again.'

'Aye, that's how it was with Coral... Then odd things started to happen. She had a few accidents. Nothing serious. And wee bits and bobs would disappear, then reappear. Nothing of any value, but she found it unsettling. It was bad enough living with the famous Cauldstane curse, but this was something different. At first Coral thought she was just imagining things, but eventually she thought she was ill. So did other members of the family.'

'Did you know it was Meredith?'

'Not then. It took me a long time to put two and two together. The MacNabs being accident prone wasn't exactly a new concept. And anyway, stuff like that can become a self-fulfilling prophecy if you believe in it. Things happened after Meredith died, but since Meredith was *dead*, I didn't think anything of it. Not to begin with.' He searched my face and must have seen my confusion. 'I'm sorry, I'm not explaining this very well... Jenny, you need to understand that Meredith and I... we have a history.'

'History?'

'Aye.' He paused, then, as if it cost him some effort, he said, 'At some point Meredith transferred her affections from Sholto to me. I was quite young. I didn't understand what was going on. Then when I *did* understand, I didn't know what to do.'

I was deeply shocked by Alec's words and my next remark was absurdly inconsequential. 'But... wasn't Meredith much older than you?'

'Twenty years. I thought she was just being overly affectionate.' He shrugged. 'She was flamboyant. Theatrical. I didn't see it as... well, sexual harassment, I suppose. Guys don't have too much experience of that kind of thing. And it was kind of hard to get my head round the idea of someone – a woman – with no shame. And no conscience.'

'Did you tell anyone?'

'Hell, no – who could I tell? And *what* could I tell? What Meredith did was embarrassing. Inappropriate. But nothing more. To begin with anyway. I don't think I even realised what was going on until Coral and I got serious. Then Meredith started confiding in me. Telling me how Sholto neglected her. Cheated on her. I didn't know whether or not to believe her, but I thought there was a good chance my father *was* up to his old tricks. It was none of my business, but Meredith wanted me to take sides. Then I realised she wanted more than that... I thought she just wanted some sort of sick revenge, but then I began to see she was jealous. Jealous of Coral. And then I realised that... well, that it was *personal*.'

The laptop screen had started scrolling again, as if Meredith was there in the room, ranting at us. In a way, I suppose she was.

'Alec, do you think Meredith was...' I struggled to find the right word, then he saved me the trouble.

'Sane?'

'I suppose "sane" *is* what I was going to say, yes. Whoever's writing that screed,' I said, pointing to the laptop, 'seems to be sick. I mean, the way she talks about your mother! And you and Fergus when you were children. It's just *horrible*.'

'I suppose it all depends on your definition of sanity. No doctor would ever have certified Meredith as insane. But even when she was alive, she wasn't living in the real world. In my teens, I just thought she was away with the fairies, obsessing about her career. And her image. Och, there used to be mirrors everywhere when Meredith was alive and she couldn't pass one without looking in it.' A slow and crooked smile spread across Alec's face. 'When he was a wee lad, Meredith heard Fergus say, "Mirror, mirror on the wall, who is the fairest of them all?" She made Sholto skelp his arse.'

'So she really was a beautiful wicked stepmother?'

'Aye, that's the way she seemed to us. But we were grieving for our mother. It was understandable. As I got older, I accepted that Meredith was eccentric and could be cruel. But she had another side. She could be charming when it suited her. Dazzling. She knew how to make folk love her. But it was all about control... And even though she's gone now, she still won't let go. Not until

117

she gets what she wants.'

'Which is?'

'Revenge. And...' I watched as Alec's long fingers curled round the sword hilt. 'She wants me.'

Alec was a tougher nut to crack than Sholto. In fact Alec is one of my failures – and there haven't been many of those, I can assure you. But I like a challenge. If you tell me I can't have something, it just makes me all the more determined to have it. I'm funny like that.

So Alec remains – how shall I put it? – work-in-progress.

It's such a long and tedious story. And I suffered so much. I can hardly bear to recall all the details now.

To begin with, I just felt neglected. No, I <u>was</u> neglected! Sholto was away a lot and when he was home, he was busy planning the next expedition, schmoozing sponsors for more cash, gallivanting round the UK putting his team together. It was all so bloody boring. He had no time at all for me and it wasn't long before I realised being married to Sholto wasn't going to be nearly as much fun as being his mistress. You see, I wasn't actually all that interested in Sholto's career, I'd only ever been interested in <u>Sholto</u>. And the most interesting thing about Sholto had been his interest in <u>me</u>.

I was horribly disappointed of course, but I threw myself into work and accepted jobs I really shouldn't have taken. They were unworthy of an artist of my calibre, but Sholto kept a tight hold on the purse strings after we married and I was damned if I was going to go cap-in-hand, asking for pin money. Once I'd sold off all my jewellery to settle my debts, I had no choice but to take whatever work was offered. And I thought absence would make Sholto's heart grow fonder. It didn't. Then I realised why.

I never found out who she was, but I knew something was going on behind my back. Well, two can play at that game. I had plenty of opportunity and no shortage of admirers. I found I had a particular affinity with younger men – singers and orchestral musicians who looked up to me. <u>Idolised</u> me. They loved all the glamour and my wicked sense of humour and for the foreigners, there was a certain cachet to living in an ancient Scottish castle. (I told them Cauldstane was haunted, which seems rather ironic now.)

My young men liked me and I liked their stamina. Sholto was ten years older than me and it had begun to tell. Or maybe it was just the routine of marriage. Perhaps it was all that polar exploration. God knows what that does to a human body. Whatever the reason, Sholto lost all interest in me. I don't think it was just because of the abortion. He was very upset about that, but it wouldn't have been at all convenient for me to have a child at that stage of my career. I was fairly certain the baby wasn't his anyway, so really it was all for the best.

We grew apart. Sholto was insensitive to my needs as a woman and as a creative artist. Things came to a head when he summoned me to the library – as if I were a naughty schoolgirl! – to tell me he was prepared to turn a blind eye to my infidelities if I would be more discreet and refrain from cuckolding him with men he was likely to bump into at his club.

That made my blood boil. I wasn't going to be spoken to like that, so I summoned the decorators and created a new bedroom for myself, one Sholto would never be allowed to enter. Not that he ever tried.

My marriage was over, but I still had my career, so I spent very little time at Cauldstane. I only returned when I ran out of money, but eventually I was spending more and more time at home because work was simply drying up. I'd made enemies, admittedly. Some philistine directors thought I was demanding. "Temperamental", they said. Designers got on my wrong side, expecting me to wear unflattering outfits on stage. I explained patiently that my fans didn't want to see me dressed up like a bag lady. But tempers got so frayed on a few occasions, I walked out of rehearsals. I also pulled out of one production at the last minute. (Actually, it might have been two.) I was traumatized by the barbaric treatment I received at the hands of whizz-kid directors who seemed bent on humiliating me. They clearly had no idea who they were dealing with. So I walked.

You can play that card a few times, but it appeared there was a limit to what some opera houses would tolerate. Possibly I misjudged it. Doors started to close quietly. Eventually they were slammed in my face. Oh, it was all so petty!

So my agent booked me for more song recitals and oratorios, but they weren't really my style and didn't pay nearly so well. In the *end I tired of playing to half-empty houses, singing to an audience of bronchitic geriatrics for a mere pittance. I went home to Cauldstane to wait for the operatic tide to turn. But I knew my career might be over. As was my marriage in all but name. So I had to find other ways to amuse myself.*

I didn't have to look far. Alec had some sort of breakdown in 1992. He dropped out of university and came home to Cauldstane.

I'd just turned forty. Alec was twenty. And quite delicious.

Chapter Fourteen

I was sitting up, leaning against the bed head, trying to assimilate what Alec had told me. He'd been still and silent for so long, I felt sure he must have fallen asleep, but then he moved, suddenly and decisively, and got out of bed. Taking his sword with him, he walked over to the writing desk and shut the laptop.

I don't think I imagined it. The temperature in the room really did drop a few degrees. I was staring at Alec's bare forearms, noting the muscle required to wield the heavy tools of his trade, when he shivered convulsively. I drew the bedclothes up around me and decided I'd felt a lot safer when Alec was in the bed.

He continued to watch the laptop, as if it might suddenly levitate. When he finally spoke, I thought he was addressing Meredith.

'You can't sleep in here.'

Belatedly, I realised he was referring to me. 'Oh, I don't think I'm in any danger. If Meredith's out to get anyone, it's you, isn't it?'

'I don't know.'

'What do you mean? Why would she hold a grudge against *me*? I'm not even family.'

'Two reasons. Of one I'm certain. The other's a guess.'

I began to feel afraid again. Cold, exhaustion and shock were starting to take their toll. 'How can you be certain Meredith means me harm?'

He glanced around the room, paying particular attention to the remaining china figurines on the chest of drawers. Having checked their position, he said, 'I'd rather deal with the guess first.'

'Oh, what difference does it make?' I said irritably. 'Please explain, Alec. I'm very tired and I admit, I'm scared. I just want to crawl under the duvet.'

'With me?'

I blinked several times and regarded him with dismay. He stood at the end of the bed, waiting, his face completely impassive, except for something in his eyes, something eager. Anxious, even.

He wanted to know. My answer *mattered* to him. Before I could absorb the implications, it dawned on me that if Alec knew, why wouldn't Meredith? And if *she* knew... Maybe Alec was right. I could be in for a bumpy night.

I cleared my throat noisily. 'Well, this is embarrassing. I won't insult your intelligence by pretending I don't understand you, but I'd like to know how I gave myself away. Am I really that transparent?'

'I didn't know for sure until I kissed you. Up till then, I thought it could just be wishful thinking on my part.'

It was 2.00 a.m. and I was thinking very slowly, but eventually I realised there was only one possible interpretation of Alec's words. I was too astonished to feel pleased.

'Are you saying that when you kissed me... you weren't just trying to make a point?'

'Did it *feel* like I was trying to make a point?'

'No. It felt wonderful.' He smiled. That was also wonderful. 'So that's how you knew? Because I responded?'

'You behaved as if it was the most natural thing in the world – until Meredith started hurling stuff around the room. Had my attentions been unwelcome, you'd have fended me off. But you didn't.'

'Oh... I see.' There was a long, rather smug silence, then I'm sorry to say a girlish little laugh escaped my lips. I looked up at Alec apologetically.

'Jenny, I think Meredith knows what's going on. Between us. And I think she's up to her old tricks.'

'You've seen this before?'

'Maybe. Meredith bullied Coral when she was alive. Now I'm beginning to wonder if she bullied her from beyond the grave.' I didn't reply and silence hung between us. Two women – both dead – also stood between us. 'But,' Alec resumed, 'I'm not leaving you in here on your own. I don't know yet what game she's playing, but Meredith obviously sees you as some sort of captive audience.'

'You think she wants to tell me her story?'

'Her version of her story. Aye, I think maybe she does.'

'And you think she also knows... how I feel about you?'

Alec's level gaze held mine. 'Even if she doesn't, she knows how I feel about *you*. I showed her. So that's put you at risk.'

122

'Oh, hell's bells, Alec, this is really crap timing! Not to mention unprofessional on my part. I assure you, I've never got involved with clients before.'

'I'm not your client. And we're not involved. Yet. In fact, I strongly suggest you maintain a professional distance. That's your best chance of avoiding the attentions of Meredith. In fact, Jenny... I think you have to go back to London.'

'I can't! I have to finish Sholto's book.'

'You can interview him on the phone, surely? Do your research from a distance. He can travel down to London or meet you in Edinburgh. You can discuss the draft on neutral territory.'

'But I love it here! Even leaving you out of it, I *love* being at Cauldstane.'

His stern expression softened. 'Och, Jenny, don't fall for the castle as well. It's just a heap of old stones.'

'No, it isn't,' I said, indignant now. 'And you of all people know that. Anyway, what possible reason could I give for leaving?'

'I don't suppose you'd consider lying? Invent some sort of domestic crisis?'

'I have no family. No attachments of any kind. My affairs are in good order. Even my houseplants are being looked after by a conscientious clergyman. In any case, I could no more lie to Sholto than – well, than I would lie to you.'

'So you insist on staying?' he said wearily

'I do. You don't think that bloody woman,' I said, pointing to the laptop, 'is going to drive me away, do you? Not now you've told me that... well, that my feelings are reciprocated. I don't scare so easily!' I folded my arms across my chest and sank back against the bed head. 'Well, actually I *do*, but I'm also very stubborn.'

Alec was round the bed in two strides and had taken me in his arms before I realised what had hit me. I'd enjoyed our first kiss hugely. The second was even more satisfying now I knew what it signified.

'Jenny, I want you to come and sleep in my room.'

'Oh, I'm not sure I—'

'No, you misunderstand me. I know this woman. Or at least, I *knew* her and it doesn't sound as if a sojourn in hell has mellowed her. I want you to sleep in my room and I'll sleep in here.'

'But supposing she tries to harm *you*? You said it's you she wants. Presumably she just wants to scare me off. I'm sure I'll be fine in here. *Really*, Alec.'

He shook his head. 'I want to get some sleep tonight and the only way that's going to happen is if you're in my room. There's a sofa. I'll take that and you can have the bed. No more arguments.' I opened my mouth to speak, but he kissed me again, effectively stifling further discussion. When I surfaced, Alec's face was very close to mine. 'And if you think *you're* stubborn, you should try crossing a MacNab.'

Alec had been an unprepossessing teenager. I'd barely registered either of the boys before their mother died, but I'd noticed Alec bore a pleasing resemblance to Sholto. Fergus was the more striking child – dark and sturdy, full of mischief, appealing if you liked small boys, which I didn't. It was just my luck to become stepmother to two boys. At least with girls one could have talked about hair or clothes.

Fergus, being younger, bounced back after Liz's death, but Alec – wracked with guilt, I suppose – remained a subdued child, frightened of animals, loud noises, just about anything in fact. Sholto said it was some long medical term I no longer remember – something to do with stress and trauma – and that Alec would suffer from it for years, possibly for ever. There had been nightmares and bed wetting, all sorts of horrors, which fortunately were past by the time I moved in. Both boys had been sent back to boarding school where it was assumed routine and the company of their friends would sort them out.

Sholto got rid of the horses, which was a crying shame as I loved to ride, but he claimed he couldn't afford the vet's bills. Since neither boy showed any interest in riding – Alec was now terrified of horses – Sholto said they had to go. Well, is it any wonder I put on weight when I was deprived of one of my healthy outdoor pursuits?

In their teens, Alec shot up and Fergus didn't. Alec was very quiet and appeared to be good at making things with his hands. He was always taking things apart and putting them back together again, or he'd be carving some piece of wood. I hardly ever saw him without a knife in his hands. It was quite unnerving, especially as I wasn't at all convinced he was right in the head.

Alec's favourite activity was fencing and he used to compete nationally even as a teenager, so I suppose he must have been good. He went to Edinburgh University to read law, but he couldn't settle. He changed to History but according to Sholto, he spent all his time researching historical swordsmanship and competing in tournaments. There was an accident of some sort and Alec's opponent was injured. I don't remember the details, but Alec's sword broke and the man he was duelling with got hurt. It wasn't Alec's fault, but he blamed himself and the quality of his sword. That was when he made his extraordinary decision – and Sholto encouraged him! – that he was going to become a swordsmith.

Sholto let him set up shop in the empty stables. I thought it would be a five-minute wonder, but Alec took it all very seriously, working with a local blacksmith, learning the basics and then travelling abroad to observe other swordsmiths at work.

When he came back from a stint of working in Germany he was a changed man. Literally. He'd gone away a slender, athletic boy with rather nice curly hair and worried eyes. He came back a man – no longer worried and no longer quite so slender. He'd put on a lot of muscle – wielding all those heavy hammers and swords, I suppose.

Alec came home confident and enthusiastic. He'd started smiling, which transformed his face and made him look much more attractive. As a boy he always looked as if someone had just died, or was about to, so I'd tried to ignore him.

But I couldn't ignore the man.

To begin with, it was nothing more than something to pass the time. To begin with. I was so <u>bored</u> at Cauldstane and Sholto ignored me completely. So I just used to flirt a little, as I always did with young men. Alec seemed a bit fazed by it, but I suppose that was the stepmother thing. Or maybe he was still a virgin. But I thought that unlikely. He was now quite attractive in a scruffy sort of way. He was always grubby and frequently unshaven, but there was something about the way he carried himself, the way he moved. I used to like looking at him. Eventually I took to watching him. I got the feeling he didn't really like that, so then it became a kind of game.

It was <u>such</u> fun.

Chapter Fifteen

In the morning I was woken by the sound of rain drumming on the windows, beating a frantic tattoo. When I opened my eyes, I had no idea where I was. I thought at first I must still be asleep and dreaming, then I turned my head towards the light and saw a sword propped up against the window like a crucifix and I remembered...

I closed my eyes. When I opened them again, I avoided the sword and looked round for Alec. He was still fast asleep on the sofa. I'd relinquished his dressing gown the night before and he'd wrapped himself in that and a tartan rug that had been covering the battered leather sofa. I suspected his night had been restless and uncomfortable, but he looked peaceful enough now. The worried frown was gone and his hands lay relaxed and long-fingered on the rough woollen blanket. One bare foot protruded at the other end, pale and elegant, like something on a statue.

I dragged my eyes away and studied the objects on Alec's bedside table. There was a photo of him with Coral, an informal shot taken outdoors, somewhere in the hills. They were dressed for walking, the sky was blue and they were both laughing. Alec's arm curved round Coral's shoulders and she leaned in towards him, resting her head on his chest. They looked young and happy and very much in love. I felt suddenly guilty occupying Alec's bed, then remembered Coral had been dead for seven years.

I averted my eyes from the photo and studied the spines of his bedside reading matter. There were a couple of historical tomes and one of my novels in hardback. It must have belonged to Coral. I reached out and lifted the book off the pile.

Alec had used the dust jacket as a bookmark and appeared to be about halfway through. I turned the book over and looked at the enigmatic, long-haired blonde my publisher had sold to readers as Imogen Ryan. She looked like my glamorous, younger sister. I struggled to remember details of the novel's plot – something to do with a childless woman and an abandoned baby – then, randomly, I recalled the dedication. Keeping Alec's place, I removed the flap of the dust jacket and turned to the front of the book where I read, *For R. With love and thanks.* By the time the book was published, we were no longer a couple, but Rupert was pleased and proud to have had a book dedicated to him.

I set the novel down and went back to staring at Alec. I wanted to recall what he'd said last night and our first kiss (and subsequent kisses), but I couldn't think about any of it without recalling *why* he'd kissed me.

To prove the ghost of Meredith MacNab was in the room and watching us.

Despite the warm duvet, I shivered. Much as I'd enjoyed the luxury of looking at Alec unobserved, I found myself wishing he'd wake up. His discarded watch lay on the polished oak floorboards and I sat up, anxious to know the time. As I reached down, the bed creaked. Alec was awake, upright and grabbing his sword before I could speak. When his eyes finally settled on me, I watched him blink as memory returned.

'I was just trying to get your watch,' I said sheepishly. 'I wanted to know the time.'

He bent down, picked up the watch and slid it over his wrist. 'Just gone eight.'

'Sorry I woke you.'

He shook his head and a tangle of curls fell forward on to his forehead. 'No bother. The slightest thing wakes me. Did you manage to sleep?'

'Oh, yes. I haven't been awake long. Was the sofa very uncomfortable?'

He ignored the question and said, 'Would you like me to accompany you back to your room? To check everything's... in order?'

'No, I'd rather you sat on the bed and talked to me.' His smile was hesitant but he obeyed without speaking. I sat up and threaded a finger through a corkscrew curl that hung above his brows. I tugged it gently and watched it spring back. 'You look quite different with your hair tousled.'

'So do you,' he said, running his fingers along my bare, outstretched arm.

'Last night... Did I dream all that?'

'No, you did not. Cauldstane has a resident ghost – though as

127

far as I know, I'm the only one who's aware of the fact.'

'Alec... do you really believe Meredith wants to kill you?'

'I don't know. It's all mind games with her. It always was.'

'Last night you said she wanted revenge.'

'Aye, I think she does.'

'What for?'

'In addition to rejecting her advances, I told Sholto what sort of a woman he was married to. And I told him he should throw her out.'

'Good grief! When did you tell him that?'

'The week before my wedding. I was to move out after our honeymoon. Coral and I were going to have one of the wee houses on the estate. Sholto had wanted us to live at Cauldstane. There was plenty of room and that would have been much more economical, but I wanted to move out.'

'Because of Meredith?'

He nodded. 'Sholto didn't understand and I wasn't telling him the whole story, so it probably didn't make much sense. He kept pressing me to explain and asking what was wrong. I couldn't tell him. I just couldn't do that to him. In the end he saved me the trouble. He said, "Is it Meredith?" I was stunned that he knew. Or had guessed. He asked me what had been going on and I didn't know what to say, whether I should tell him the truth... But he made it easy for me. He said, "If you don't tell me the truth – the *whole* truth, Alexander – then, by God, I'll knock you to the ground. I demand to know what sort of a woman I'm married to." So I told him.'

'Poor man. He must have been terribly upset.'

'I suppose so. But his face showed nothing. The only time he seemed to be in danger of losing his self-control was when he asked me how long it had been going on. I told him it had started when I was a student... You've never seen Sholto when he's angry, have you?' Alec shook his head. 'It's not a pretty sight.'

'But he believed you?'

'He was under no illusions about her. She'd had an affair with a friend of his and he'd felt humiliated. And very hurt. I think he gave up on the marriage after that. Up till then I think he'd probably been faithful to her, but afterwards... Well, I gather he started seeing other women. And Meredith's idea of poetic justice would

128

have been seducing Sholto's son.'

I hesitated before asking my next question, unsure if I really wanted to know the answer. 'She didn't succeed, did she?'

'No, she didn't, though I had to put up a physical fight a couple of times. I woke up one night and found her in my bed.'

'No!'

'I threw her out and put a bolt on the bedroom door the next day. God knows what Wilma thought when she was turning out the room. I suppose she put it down to poor Mr Alec's neuroses.'

'But Sholto believed you'd given Meredith no encouragement?'

'He knows I'm a lousy liar and he knew how I felt about Coral. We were a very happy couple. I was determined to keep it that way by moving out of Cauldstane. Sholto said he understood and thought it best for all concerned.'

'So he told Meredith he knew what had been going on?'

'No. I did.'

'When?'

'On my wedding day. She got drunk and started her usual antics, so I assumed Sholto had said nothing. Meredith told me she'd be paying regular visits to our new home and that she was looking forward to telling Coral how *close* she and I had become over the years.' Alec's expression was thunderous. 'I told her to get lost. Then she came out with it. Her pathetic attempt at blackmail. She said she would tell Sholto we'd had an affair, that it had been going on for years. She said she'd also tell Coral. Unless I... met her conditions.'

'Which were?'

He gave a derisive snort. 'You can guess.'

'What did you say?'

'Well, I'd had a fair amount of champagne too, so it was with great pleasure I informed Meredith that my father already knew what had been going on, that I'd told him a week ago and explained my reasons for wanting to move out. I told her she'd no power over me. She could tell Coral what the hell she liked. My wife would never believe I'd slept with such a shabby whore.'

'What did Meredith say?'

'She was speechless – understandably, I suppose – so she hurled her champagne glass at me. But I saw it coming and dodged.

So then she gave me an earful and said I would pay for what I'd done and so would Coral. Then she swept out of Cauldstane, got into her car and drove off. Dead drunk. And then... well, then she was just dead.'

As he exhaled, his body sagged, then he started to tremble. I leaned forward, throwing my arms around his neck. 'It's going to be all right, Alec! You don't have to go through this alone. Not any more.'

I felt his lips moving against my bare shoulder, then he lifted his head, so his mouth was close to my ear. 'You don't know what a relief it is... to be able to *talk* about it. After all this time... But when I think Coral might have known too. Known before me. But she never *said* anything!'

He was still shaking and I held him tight. 'How could she, Alec? Who would have believed her? I wouldn't have believed you if I hadn't seen what Meredith can do. And I would never have told you about my laptop messages. I wouldn't have told *anyone*.'

'Why not?'

'For the same reason Coral didn't tell you. You'd have thought I was mad! You already had good reason to believe I was mentally fragile. If you hadn't found me cowering outside my room last night, I don't know what I would have done. But I wouldn't have dared tell anyone.'

'Meredith would have found a way to make you leave. That's what her game is.' He extracted himself from my arms and took both my hands in his. 'And that's why you have to go, Jenny. If Meredith wants you out, she'll keep bullying you till you go.'

'Well, that's just tough, because now you've told me what sort of woman she is – I mean, *was* – I'm even more determined not to desert my post. And let her win? Over my dead body!'

He squeezed my hand. '*That's* what I'm afraid of.'

'Oh, don't be daft! How on earth can she harm me? She's just a *ghost*! I may be a bit unstable, but I'm hardly likely to die of fright. Now don't go smiling at me like that, Alec MacNab, or I shall haul you into bed. And that would *really* piss Meredith off.'

'Aye, but it would make *my* day,' Alec said, still smiling.

'Stop that right now. Today's a big work day for me. In just over an hour, I shall be interviewing your father in the library. Can I also point out, if you *do* want me to leave, going to bed with me probably isn't the best way to go about it.'

His smile vanished. 'I don't want you to leave, Jenny.'

'Good.'

'But I think you should. For your own safety.'

'No way.' He scowled, an expression only slightly less endearing than his smile. 'You know, you look just like Sholto when you do that. And I don't want *him* pulling that face at me, so I need to get a move on or I'll be late.' Clambering out of bed, I said, 'I want a bath and some breakfast. A bowl of Wilma's porridge will be just the job this morning. Who would have thought ghost-hunting would give you such an appetite?' I summoned up a cheerful smile, but Alec didn't respond. He looked miserable and I regretted my flippant remark. Picking up his dressing gown, I said, 'Can I borrow this to get back to my room? Just in case anyone's about.'

'Of course. Would you like me to go with you?'

'No, I'll be fine, thanks,' I replied, with more conviction than I felt. 'But you could tell me what to do about the breakages. I have two smashed spaniels to account for. Wilma might accept one was an accident, but two?'

'Leave me to deal with that. I'll clean up when you're with Sholto. Wilma won't mention their disappearance to you and if she says anything to me, I'll tell her I put them in the attic because you needed more space. Maybe you could spread your writing stuff around a bit more to make it look like it's true.'

'Were the dogs valuable?'

'Who knows? Cauldstane's full of junk, much of it loved, some of it detested. I dare say some of it's valuable. But those hounds will not be missed.'

'You'll need to sweep up thoroughly. If Wilma finds bits when she hoovers, she'll think I broke them.'

'Stop fretting and go and run your bath.'

'If you come across the hat pin...' I hesitated, remembering but scarcely believing the thing had flown through the air towards me, like a heat-seeking missile. 'Could you put it on my desk? I want to return it to Zelda and ask her about its history. I have a nasty feeling Meredith left that pin on my desk for a reason.'

'What will you say to Zelda?'

'I'll just tell her I found it. Which I did. A hat pin is the sort of thing that could suddenly turn up, isn't it? Easy to lose.'

131

Alec looked sceptical. 'If you say so.'

'Oh, I'll think of something to say! Remember, my natural bent is fiction. Making stuff up comes easily to me. Sticking to the facts requires far more discipline.'

'So which facts are you discussing with Sholto today?'

I thought about fudging the issue, but decided to be straight with Alec. I sat down again on the edge of the bed and said, 'I've asked him if he'll tell me about the deaths of his wives.'

'He wasn't there. For either of them.'

'I know. And I think that's something that bothers him. Which probably means it needs to go into the book.'

'He can tell you what he knows, but the information is secondhand. The police told him what happened to Meredith. When my mother died he wasn't even first on the scene.'

'Who was?'

Alec fixed me with a bleak look. 'Apart from me, you mean?'

'Yes.'

'Meredith.'

'And you told her what had happened?' He nodded. 'And she told Sholto?'

'She told everyone. They all came out into the courtyard at once. Because of all the racket. But Sholto was the last to know. He thought something terrible had happened to *me*. Meredith told him why I was crying, then he saw my mother lying on the ground... I can't tell you what happened then because Wilma took me inside. I sat on her lap in the kitchen until I stopped crying, then she put me to bed. She read to me for a wee while, then I must have fallen asleep.'

'I had no idea Wilma had been at Cauldstane for such a long time.'

'She's been here as long as I have. She was young when the accident happened. Well, she seemed old to me, but she wasn't. She'd been our nanny and then she stayed on as general factotum. She was promoted to housekeeper after Ma died.' There was a silence in which I struggled not to ask more questions, but Alec must have sensed how my mind was working. 'If you need to know, Jenny, I'll tell you what I remember, but it isn't much. I didn't recall much at the time and my mother died over thirty years ago.'

'I'd prefer to talk to Sholto first. It's his book. What *he*

132

remembers is what's important. For the book I mean.'

'He feels guilty he wasn't there. Guilty he betrayed her. Guilty he wasn't able to deal with a distraught son who had to be comforted by a servant. Go easy on him, Jenny. He's a sad, old man.'

'Oh, I will, don't you worry. I'm almost as fond of Sholto as I am of you.'

'Careful now,' Alec said, shaking his head. 'That was Meredith's problem.' A smile flickered briefly across his face. Just the ghost of a smile.

I'd declined Alec's offer to accompany me back to my room because I hadn't wanted him to see how frightened I was. If he'd picked up on my nervousness, it would only have strengthened his conviction I should leave Cauldstane. He was clearly concerned for my physical well-being, but since he was acquainted with my mental health history, he might also have feared for my emotional stability, so I'd wanted to give the impression I'd taken Meredith's ghost in my stride, that it would be business as usual. If Alec thought I was bluffing, he'd been too polite to say so.

Standing outside my room, I hesitated for a long moment, then grasped the door handle, turned it and walked in – actually, I *swept* in – but I left the door open, in case I needed to beat a swift retreat.

The room was just as Alec and I had left it. A tip. I was relieved to see the laptop was still shut. I didn't know when I'd have the courage to open it again, but I certainly didn't have time now, so I looked away from my desk and surveyed the rest of the room.

Two pillows remained propped up side by side against the bed head, still bearing the imprint of our bodies where Alec and I had sat in bed, trying to guess what Meredith would do next. As I picked my way through the pieces of broken china on the floor, a dark brown canine eye stared up at me, accusingly. I felt vaguely guilty, even though I hadn't been responsible. I bent and picked it up, together with the larger fragments and set them on the desk. The dogs were smashed beyond repair and I felt suddenly furious at Meredith's wanton destruction. Then it struck me: smashing ornaments was the least of the wretched woman's sins.

I began to ponder the extent of Meredith's powers. *Could* she hurt me? She'd hurled things at me, but could she do anything more dangerous? Were Alec's fears reasonable? My stomach lurched as another idea struck me: could Meredith read my thoughts?... I'd seen no evidence of that, though she'd shown she could respond to what I'd written on the laptop.

My imagination started to run wild. Could Meredith *see* me? Was she actually watching me now? Did she watch me while I slept?... I started to shake but took comfort from the fact that Alec wasn't far away and had placed a protective blade under my mattress. I didn't see how that could make a blind bit of difference, but if Alec was prepared to put his faith in ancient superstitions, that was good enough for me. It was no more irrational than Rupert's faith in the power of prayer and since I had no other means of defence at my disposal, beggars could hardly be choosers.

Feeling vulnerable and more than a little despondent, I gathered up my towel and toiletries and headed for the bathroom next door. Once inside, I locked the door. A temporary sense of security gave way to the realisation that locked doors were unlikely to deter vengeful ghosts. As I watched the bath fill with hot water, I decided to unlock the door again, in case Meredith should try to drown me and I needed to call for help.

I slid the bolt back again, reflecting that I'd known of Meredith's ghostly existence for only a matter of hours, but already full-blown paranoia had set in. I tried to laugh at myself and failed.

I bathed in record time, humming tunelessly to keep my spirits up and to warn the unwary that the bathroom was occupied. Back in my room, I dressed with some care and applied a little make-up. This wasn't for Alec's benefit, rather to give myself a bit of Dutch courage to face my day, a day which would encompass Sholto's double bereavement and before that, confronting Meredith's portrait, which I'd have to pass on my way down to the dining room.

I examined my face in the cracked mirror and was reasonably happy with what I saw. I was surprised to see I looked quite normal, not at all like someone who'd seen a ghost. A slight tendency to smirk could be curbed if I stopped thinking about Alec. (Easier said than done.) I re-touched my lipstick and told myself I didn't look bad for a woman who wouldn't see forty-two again.

My confidence lasted until I faced Meredith's portrait. Life-size, with lustrous dark eyes that followed the viewer, it was impossible to ignore. I didn't even try. I stood on the stairs, facing the picture and tried to fathom the woman.

Delusional, obviously.

Talented, evidently.

Sexually voracious, apparently.

But sociopathic? Not while she was alive, surely? Yet Alec was clearly afraid of what she might do now. After years of being bullied from both sides of the grave, he'd finally found someone in whom he could confide, yet he wanted me to leave. For my own safety. Was Alec as delusional as Meredith?...

I looked her in the oil-painted eye and muttered, 'Can't we just be adult about this?' There was no response, so I set off downstairs in search of breakfast.

Fortified by a bowl of Wilma's excellent porridge, some fruit and a pot of strong coffee, I made my way back up to the library for my daily meeting with Sholto. Mounting the stairs briskly, I ignored Meredith's portrait.

As I walked along the dingy corridor, I considered my feelings for this old man, who was endearing and exasperating in equal measure. The idea of Sholto coming to any harm made me feel angry, so I had to assume what I felt for him was a kind of love. Deep respect coupled with warm affection – wasn't that love? For a few years I'd told myself a similar cocktail of emotions would sustain my relationship with Rupert. I don't believe there had been a great deal more on Rupert's side. He'd always found science and religion more exciting mistresses than me, but I hadn't felt physically starved. My life had been one of the intellect and the imagination. Writing fiction provided me with hordes of imaginary friends, then ghostwriting had put me in touch with a wide range of subjects, their families, friends and, in some cases, their enemies.

Life had seemed full. I hadn't ever felt *hungry*, but I suspect I was malnourished. Since meeting Alec I'd become increasingly and uncomfortably aware of the years, post-Rupert, of sexual famine.

But would my professional ethics – or Alec's misgivings about my personal safety – allow me to indulge in a feast?...

Pleasant as it was, I pushed this thought to the back of my mind and assumed my professional persona. Imogen might be falling for the heir to Cauldstane, but Jenny had a job to do.

I knocked on the library door and entered.

Chapter Sixteen

Sholto was standing at one of the long windows, watching the rain. He didn't turn or give any indication he'd heard me enter, so I suspected he hadn't heard my knock. Sholto insisted he wasn't hard of hearing, but Zelda often teased him about it. I'd noticed that the best way to keep his attention was to sit somewhere he could see my face, which made me wonder if he depended to a degree on lip-reading. So I approached his desk slowly, not wishing to startle him. When he still didn't turn, I cleared my throat discreetly. He spun round, his faded blue eyes wide with surprise.

'Good Lord – Jenny! Is that the time?'

'Good morning, Sholto. I'm afraid it is. In fact, I'm a little late this morning. Sorry to have kept you waiting.'

'No need to apologise. I've just been standing here, watching the damn rain, trying to compose my thoughts. Without much success, I'm afraid.' Leaning heavily on his stick, he tapped the window pane with a finger. 'We buried Meredith on a day like this. Rained cats and dogs! Liz was luckier. She got sunshine,' he added, then lapsed into morose silence.

'We don't have to stick to our schedule,' I said gently. 'We can discuss something else if you'd rather. Or meet at another time?'

'No, let's get it over with. This bit of the story, I mean. The deaths. That's what we agreed to discuss today, wasn't it?' He sounded uncertain, as if struggling to remember.

'Only if you feel up to it. We have to talk about them some time, but it doesn't have to be today. You could talk to me instead about managing Cauldstane. The financial burden. The legacy you inherited and the one you hope to pass on to your sons.'

Sholto made a derisive noise. 'Some legacy! No, let's talk about my dead wives. At least I know how those two stories end.' He turned away again and stared at the leaden sky. 'Can't stand the rain. It depresses me. Makes me worry about the roof and the thousands it will cost to repair it. It's only a matter of time before that becomes necessary...' He fell silent again and I was wondering how to salvage our limping conversation when he suddenly asked, 'When is it time to let go, Jenny? How do you decide to let go of something or someone you love, because... because it's just no longer *possible*?'

I hesitated, then said, 'Are you talking about Cauldstane?'

'Mostly.' He turned round and waved his walking stick in the direction of his desk where there was a pile of opened mail. 'There have been a lot of bills lately and the bills are on the same scale as Cauldstane. Monumental! You wouldn't credit what it costs to heat this pile in winter. I wouldn't mind if that expenditure kept us warm, but just ask Zelda about her chilblains. On second thoughts, don't. It's rather a sore point after all her years in the south of France. But she'd tell you, we freeze in winter. Except for Alec, of course. When he's got his furnace going, *he's* cosy enough. But the rest of us – well, we just have to put up with it. Cauldstane is kept warm enough to preserve the fabric of the building and its contents, then we have to dress in layers. *Many* layers. As if embarking on a polar expedition.'

Sholto hobbled over to the fireplace and indicated I should join him in the chairs set either side of the fire. Such was the thickness of Cauldstane's walls, it was frequently warmer outdoors than in, so the fire was always a welcome sight in the otherwise chilly library. He waited for me to be seated, then settled with palpable relief into the other chair. 'It wasn't so bad when I could keep active. We used to tell the boys to run up and downstairs to keep warm! But nowadays...' He tapped one of his legs with his stick. 'I can't move fast enough to keep the circulation going. It's bloody miserable. Especially when Fergus reminds me – as he does with monotonous regularity – just how cosy I'd be in a centrally heated bungalow.'

'He wants to sell up, doesn't he?'

'And Alec and I *don't*. Alec and I are the dreamers. The fools. Fergus is the sensible one. And he has all our interests at heart.'

'I'm sure he does, but he isn't taking your heart into account. Or Alec's.'

'What?... Oh, I see... Well, he can't, can he? You only have to look at the accounts. *Shocking*. I tell you, Jenny, owning a property like Cauldstane is like having a high maintenance wife. And when I was married to Meredith, I had *two* of those,' Sholto grumbled. 'But making Cauldstane pay was always going to be a tall order. I inherited a lot of debts. The estate was not in good heart. Torquil was largely an absentee landlord and left his affairs to inadequate staff. Our father hadn't been much better organised. The poor fellow was dogged with ill health and had disastrous luck with his investments. So when I took charge, the farms had been poorly managed for years and the forestry areas neglected. The woods were all but impenetrable. Should have been thinned out, you see, but my father didn't know what he was doing. Thought timber would be a quick and easy cash crop. Sadly the trees had to be clear-felled before they reached maturity, wasting a lot of the original investment.' Sholto turned away and stared into the fire. 'Fergus and I have achieved a certain amount, but Cauldstane really needs investment now. And that means cash. Which we don't have.' He narrowed his eyes and said, 'How much do you think this book could make, Jenny?'

'Not enough, I'm afraid. I don't know what sort of offers we'll get for it. It could be a tidy sum, but I don't think the book alone would save Cauldstane. If the manuscript goes to auction – that means several publishers competing for the book – that would push the price up nicely. My agent would be able to play the bidders off against each other, but if the advance is generous, it's unlikely you'd earn any more.'

'I don't quite follow.'

'The amount you're paid is called an advance because it's an advance against future earnings. The book would have to earn that advance back before you were paid any royalties.'

'You mean it would have to sell a lot of copies?'

'Yes. But you never know – it might. If it became a bestseller, there would be all the spin-offs – translation rights, audio, serialisation for radio. You might even sell screen rights. It could mount up over the years. But I wouldn't want you to bank on it, Sholto. Publishing a book is always a gamble. No one knows what makes a bestseller, least of all publishers.'

'Would you talk to Fergus about all this, Jenny? Put him in the picture? It might get him off my back for a while.'

'Yes, of course. But I doubt it will change his mind. If you sell up, he'll be out of a job, won't he? So he must really think selling up is best for you. And Alec.'

'Oh, Fergus is undoubtedly taking the long view. He believes we'll *have* to sell eventually and says the time to let go is before you have to. "Sell up now and name your price," he says. That way you still feel you're in control of your destiny. But I don't think he really understands – he's a younger son, how could he? – that letting go of something like Cauldstane is admitting complete and utter failure. In every respect. It means I've failed the building, failed in my obligations to the estate and failed to protect my sons' inheritance.'

'You were a younger son, Sholto. *You* understood. I expect Fergus does too. He's just trying to limit the damage. And if he regards the sale as inevitable—'

'Oh, he does. He's made that quite clear. It's a question of *when*, not if, as far as Ferg's concerned.'

'Then he probably thinks the sale should take place while you're still around to enjoy that cosy bungalow. And while he and Alec are young enough to start over somewhere else.'

'Yes, I know, it all makes perfect sense,' Sholto conceded grudgingly. 'It just fails to take into account my *feelings*. And Alec's. And this place is Alec's now. I'm just hanging on, like some old family retainer. A useless custodian. The future of Cauldstane lies with Alec and his family. If he ever manages to acquire one...' His voice tailed away into silent despondency, then he suddenly slapped his thigh with impatience. 'Enough of all this maudlin talk! We must get to work, Jenny. This damn book won't earn us a penny until you've finished writing it.'

Fishing in my bag for my notebook and tape recorder, I said, 'I'd still like to answer your question, if I may.'

He looked surprised. 'Which question was that?'

'You asked me when it was time to let go.'

'So I did. Sorry. Burdening you with all our problems. Selfish of me. And a criminal waste of your time.'

'Not at all. It's all good background for the book and if I'm to write as you would have written, I need to *think* like you, feel as you do. And up to a point I do. I care about Cauldstane and this family. I may not be one of you, but I hope I'm considered a friend of the family now.'

He beamed at me. 'Indeed, you *are*, my dear.'

'Well, for what it's worth, my answer to your question would be this: perhaps it's time to let go when you can no longer hold on.

That might not be the most sensible advice, but I think it's what people do when they care passionately about a place. Or a person. They hold on until something *compels* them to let go. Then it's no longer a choice. It's taken out of our hands, so there can be no regrets. No blame. Maybe it's not the actual letting go that's hard. Maybe it's making the *decision* to let go, when you still have a choice.'

Sholto nodded his head slowly. 'You know, I should have made that decision with Meredith. I should have let go of the marriage. Of the idea that she could ever be more than a very alluring mistress. But my boys needed a mother. And I missed Liz *dreadfully*. I know I wasn't faithful to her, but I did love her. Can you understand that, Jenny? Meredith never forgave me for it. She was jealous of Liz when she was alive, jealous even after she was dead. That never seemed reasonable to me. How can you be jealous of a dead woman?'

I thought it best not to comment on Meredith's obsessive nature and instead asked, 'Did you love Meredith? If you don't mind my asking.'

It was a mark of the trust that Sholto now put in me that he could answer such personal questions without embarrassment and without demur, even though he was basically a private, rather taciturn man. We could talk frankly to each other and he appeared genuinely interested in my opinions. We shared little in terms of life experience and had almost nothing in common, apart from affection for Alec, but in a matter of weeks, we'd achieved the sort of intimacy one enjoys with old friends. How we'd achieved this was something of a mystery to me, but I'd observed the phenomenon many times now. It seemed to be a by-product of sharing stories.

'Did I actually *love* her?... That was a question she asked me all the time. I always said yes, of course, and I believed it to be true. But looking back... And that's what this book is about, isn't it?' Sholto looked up as if he needed reassurance to carry on.

'It's about looking back, but it's also about capturing how things were at the time. Wordsworth defined poetry as "emotion recollected in tranquillity". That's what I'm trying to get you to do. Recall how you felt *then*.'

He nodded and said, 'After Liz died, I realised — somewhat belatedly — what love was. What it *should* be. But I had a situation to deal with. What was uppermost in my mind was guilt. And the welfare of two motherless boys, both distraught, one of them blaming himself for his mother's death. And I had a mistress – *ex-*mistress by then – who seemed determined to re-establish herself as the new wife.'

I looked up from my notebook. 'Ex-mistress? I didn't realise you'd broken off with Meredith. Wasn't she here when Liz had the accident?'

'Yes, she was. In her capacity as a friend of the family. Her sister, Pamela was an old school friend of Liz's. When we had weekend parties and charity bashes, Pam and Meredith would come over. That's how I met her in the first place. She was a rather intense music student. Then years later, I met her again at a charity ball, when she was attached to a fellow I knew, a scientist who'd been on one of my expeditions. It was strange, the way I kept bumping into Meredith. Looking back, I wonder if she deliberately set her cap at me.'

'But by the time Liz died, Meredith was history?'

'Well, I'd made it pretty clear the affair was over. She'd asked me to divorce Liz and of course there was no question of that as far as I was concerned. She took that very badly, so I decided our relationship must end. It had run its course anyway, as these things do.' Sholto turned and gave me a shrewd look. 'That makes me sound a complete bastard, doesn't it? Well, maybe I was, but I don't think Meredith really loved me. She loved the *idea* of me. Famous explorer, Laird of Cauldstane, all that. So yes, it was all over as far as I was concerned.'

'How did she take the news?'

'Surprisingly well. I was braced for histrionics, but after the initial shock, she was very calm, very grown-up about it. She insisted we remain friends – she said she still wanted to see Liz and the boys – so I could hardly refuse, especially as she'd been so understanding about ending the relationship.'

'So that's why Meredith was still around when Liz died.'

'She and Pam and her husband were staying the weekend. There was some young man in tow, I forget his name now, but we assumed he was Meredith's latest paramour. The idea was, the men would go fishing with the boys while the girls went riding. We used to keep a few horses in those days because Liz liked to ride and wanted the boys to learn. But I had to sell them after she died. Neither of the boys would go near a horse – which was understandable – and we couldn't afford them anyway.'

'But after Liz died... you got back together with Meredith?'

'No, not immediately. She came to the funeral and was very sweet. We kept in touch. Pam was very upset by Liz's death and Meredith spent time with her, so I saw her socially. She just seemed to pop up all over the place. And it seemed natural, I suppose, to pick up where we'd left off. But this time she put her foot down about marriage. I thought she intended to give up her career to help run the estate and look after the boys in the holidays. In fact, I still think she *did* agree to all that, but later we rowed like hell about it and she claimed I'd misunderstood. I let her have her way, but I was very disappointed. I knew then that the marriage had been a mistake. So did Meredith when she realised she hadn't married money.'

'That was important to her?'

'Good God, yes! She'd thought because I spent money on her when she was my mistress that there was a lot of money to spend. She underestimated my stupidity, you see,' Sholto said ruefully. 'I'd never enlightened her about the family finances. Didn't think it would make much sense to a girl like Meredith. And in any case, you only had to *look* at Cauldstane to see it was a money pit. But she'd jumped to conclusions. She thought if the boys were at Gordonstoun and we lived in a castle, we must be loaded. Ha!' Sholto shook his head. 'Meredith liked to think she was a woman of the world, but she was actually quite naïve. Not stupid though. She was a clever girl in many ways. You might almost say *scheming*. But naïve. Lived in a world of her own. And she was the centre of her universe. But that universe shrank when she came to live here and it shrank again when the offers of work dried up. She put it down to living in the sticks, but I think there was more to it than that. I don't think her singing career had really got established. She had a meteoric few years when she was on the cover of all the music magazines. She was very good at publicity, I'll say that for her. Every inch the *diva*! But critics said she pushed her voice too soon, sang parts that were too demanding for her technically. The general opinion seemed to be, she'd peaked while still young, so it was a decline almost as rapid as her ascent. She was very bitter about that and blamed me, blamed the marriage. And she *hated* Cauldstane. With a passion! She said she'd die of boredom living here, so she used to disappear every so often. Sometimes to London for auditions or work. Well, that's what she said. I didn't ask questions. I could see how unhappy the poor girl was. I just begged her to be discreet. Which she *wasn't*.'

Sholto fell silent, but I said nothing. I knew he would resume his painful narrative when he was ready. We sat listening to the rain tapping at the window until he heaved a huge sigh, re-arranged his gangling limbs and said, 'What I have to say now, Jenny, is strictly off the record.' I switched off the tape recorder. 'If Meredith hadn't died, I would have had to divorce her. I was very sorry when she was killed and completely horrified by the circumstances of her death, but the fact is, the marriage had been over for some time. There were faults on both sides, undoubtedly, and I should have made our financial situation clearer, but by the time of her death, Meredith had become a pernicious influence on this family. I'm not prepared to go into any details. Suffice to say, she'd made herself generally unpopular and was running up bills like nobody's business. But certain information had come to light about her erratic sexual behaviour that had convinced me divorce, though expensive, was my only option. She died before I could discuss it with her.' Looking exhausted now, Sholto hung his head and said, 'I'm glad she was spared the ignominy of divorce. The papers would have had a field day.'

When it seemed clear he wasn't going to say any more, I prompted Sholto gently. 'You told me she drove off after a row with Alec.'

'That's correct.'

'Do you want to talk about that? Or perhaps I should say, do you want that information to go into the book?'

'No, I don't. Alec was in no way responsible for Meredith's death. She died because she'd been drinking heavily. Meredith being drunk was not an unusual occurrence – certainly not one for which Alec could be blamed. I'm prepared to talk about my marriages in the book, but all I'm prepared to say about Meredith's death is what appeared in the papers. She was killed in a terrible crash, she was driving and no other vehicles were involved. And that,' said Sholto with some finality, 'was the end of the whole sorry, sordid tale.'

I looked up from my notepad, startled by a distant sound.

Sholto gazed at me, puzzled. 'Is something wrong, Jenny? Did I say something that offended you? Perhaps I've been a little *too* frank—'

'No, no, it's not that. It's just— Can you *hear* anything?

He cocked his head to one side. 'Just the rain. But my hearing isn't what it used to be. Zelda's always telling me I should get a hearing aid.'

'You can't hear music?'

'No. Why, can you?'

'I'm not sure... I thought I heard music playing.'

'That'll be Wilma in the kitchen. She always has the radio on. You must have sharp ears if you can hear that.'

'Yes, I suppose so.' I smiled, acknowledging the compliment, even though I hadn't merited it. The noise I could hear – and heard intermittently throughout the rest of my interview with Sholto – was the sound of the harpsichord.

Meredith was letting me know that her sorry, sordid tale was far from ended.

Chapter Seventeen

The rain continued to fall and Sholto's mood remained subdued until Wilma brought us coffee. His face lit up when she entered. I sensed he not only welcomed the interruption, he found the predictable Cauldstane routines comforting. For that matter, so did I, especially after last night's revelations. Wilma was as solid and reliable as her home baking. (Today's treat was the splendidly named Ecclefechan Tarts.) As I watched her pour coffee, it struck me Wilma Guthrie and Meredith MacNab were polar opposites. Wilma's life had consisted of loyal service to just one family. Meredith's life appeared to have been entirely self-serving. Wilma was plain, pleasant but unmemorable, save perhaps for her trainers. Meredith had been charismatic, beautiful in her youth and, to judge from photos, she'd retained a blowsy glamour as she aged. There had been many men in Meredith's life. Had Wilma loved and lost a Mr Guthrie? She wore no ring. Was the title "Mrs" an honorary one, in the tradition of country housekeepers?

I made a note on my pad to ask Zelda whether Wilma was widowed or divorced. It wasn't something I felt I could ask Wilma herself. I could hardly claim she'd feature in Sholto's book. And that seemed unfair. Wilma had been the one to console Alec when his mother died. Meredith had evidently counted on Wilma's support and unstinting hard work for her musical soirées. Liz had entrusted the care of her boys to Wilma and I thought it unlikely Sholto could function without her. Wilma had been the backbone of Cauldstane, even though she wasn't a MacNab. I would have liked to honour her contribution in Sholto's book, but what we included or omitted was his decision.

So I thanked Wilma for the coffee and helped myself to a tart, knowing no other way to express my appreciation. I was rewarded with a shy smile, then she scuttled silently from the room. As the door closed, I attempted to pick up the threads of my conversation with Sholto.

'If you can bear it, I'd like to hear your account of Liz's

accident. I also need you to tell me how you want me to deal with it. I understand that you want to downplay Meredith's death and I think we can easily do that because her death, though very sudden, didn't have far-reaching consequences for the family...'

I paused and considered what I'd just said. It was completely untrue. The woman had been dead twelve years and was still wreaking havoc. Alec's life was still not his own. But there was no way I could handle Meredith's death other than from Sholto's point of view. As far as he knew, her death had been the end of her "pernicious influence" on the MacNabs, whereas Liz's death had led to all sorts of changes: the sale of the horses, Wilma's promotion to housekeeper, Zelda's return from France and a lifetime of guilt for Alec. It seemed clear Liz had been the love of Sholto's life, even if he had treated her badly, so I was convinced his book should accord her life some importance, likewise her death. Meredith on the other hand could – and should – be sidelined.

As Sholto fidgeted in his chair, I could tell his discomfort wasn't just physical. 'You'll have to help me out here, Jenny. I want Liz to feature in the book – it's no less than her due – but I don't want to give any credence to the idea that Alec was in some way responsible for the accident that killed her. We don't really know what happened. He was the only witness and by all accounts, he was completely distraught. Incoherent with grief.'

'You say, "by all accounts". Can you talk me through what you *do* know and how you know it?' When he hesitated, I added, 'This is your book, Sholto. Your version of the accident is the one I want and that should avoid pointing the finger of blame at Alec.'

'Well, I was the last on the scene. All I saw was absolute mayhem.'

'Who else was there?'

'Alec. Fergus. Meredith. Wilma. Meredith's young man. Pam and her husband... There was a crowd of them, all milling around. I didn't even see Liz lying on the ground, not for a while. I was trying to deal with Alec, who was wailing like a banshee.'

'You said you were the last to arrive.'

'I'm afraid I was.'

'Who was the first, do you know?'

'Meredith. She'd been in the stable seeing to her horse and when she heard all the commotion, she came running out to see what had happened.'

'Commotion? What had she heard?'

Sholto looked down at the carpet and struggled to order his thoughts. 'Alec on his bike... The horse rearing... Clattering hooves on the cobblestones... Liz's scream and then the fall... Meredith said she heard all of that, but didn't see any of it. It must have happened so quickly.'

'Liz was thrown because the horse reared? Did something startle it?'

Sholto gave me a stern look. 'This isn't going into the book, Jenny. I don't care if you make something up or just leave things vague, but Alec is not to be mentioned.'

'Of course. But it might be easier for me to write an incomplete account if I know what actually happened. That is, if you wouldn't mind telling me. I imagine you don't want me to ask Alec.'

'Definitely not! Very well then... Liz died on Alec's birthday.' I looked up, aghast. 'Yes, I know. The whole thing was quite appalling for him.... He'd been given a new bike and Zelda – who knew about the bike – had sent him one of those klaxon horns from France. You squeeze them and they make a terrible racket, like a high-pitched donkey. You know the sort of thing I mean?'

'Yes, I do.'

'Alec was delighted with it. But that horn caused the accident. Liz was probably mounting her horse – not the most docile of mares – when Alec cycled through the archway and into the courtyard, sounding his horn. The unfamiliar noise startled the mare and she must have reared up, throwing Liz to the ground. She can't have been secure in the saddle, that's why I think she might have been trying to mount at that particular moment. Anyway, the fall broke her neck, her arm and her collarbone.' Sholto paused and took a mouthful of what must by now have been cold coffee, then resumed. 'The frightened horse galloped off. It was a miracle Alec wasn't trampled underfoot, but he did fall off his bike. Meredith said, when she ran out to see what had happened, Alec and Liz were both lying on the ground. Alec was crying, so she knew there couldn't be too much wrong with him, so she went to see to Liz. She knew at once she was dead because of the angle of her head. So then she ran back to Alec and asked him what had happened. He told her the horse had reared when he tooted his horn and Liz had

148

been thrown. She said the poor lad was completely beside himself, sobbing and screaming. That was certainly still the case when I arrived on the scene, but by then Wilma had taken charge of him. She asked if she could take him inside and Meredith said he should be spared any more questions as it was pretty clear what had happened.'

Sholto exhaled and leaned back in his chair, looking pale. 'So you see, it was just a tragic accident. A most unfortunate sequence of events. But Alec has always blamed himself for being in the wrong place at the wrong time. I tried to tell him, time and again, that riding is a very dangerous sport. Liz could have had a fatal fall jumping a hedge! But he didn't see it like that. Still doesn't. If you want my opinion, Alec was so traumatized by what he saw that day, he's never been able to think straight about it.'

I could see Sholto was upset and decided he'd had enough. I closed my notebook and said, 'We should stop there, Sholto. This has been really helpful for me, but gruelling for you. It must be upsetting having to go over all these painful events, but I do appreciate your frankness. It makes my job so much easier.'

'I do feel rather tired, I'm afraid.'

'Perhaps we should have called a halt earlier. I'm sorry, you must say if you—'

'Oh, it's not just the interview. I've not been sleeping well lately. I've never been one for nightmares or even dreams. A total lack of imagination is an essential qualification in my line of work. You couldn't get to sleep on creaking Antarctic ice if you lay there thinking what would happen if it opened up beneath you! But I've been troubled by dreams lately... They disturb my nights and I find it hard to get back to sleep.'

'What do you dream about?'

'Well, that's just it. I dream about *Meredith*! Now why should that be? Until you arrived, I barely gave her a thought. Perhaps that's a shameful admission, but she died a long time ago. In fact I think of Liz far more often than Meredith, even though I was married to Meredith for much longer. I really loved her. Liz, I mean. Didn't deserve her...' Sholto's eyes were now filmed with tears. He swallowed and said, 'So it seems odd that I should dream about Meredith.'

I stood up and laid a hand on his shoulder. 'I think you should rest now. What about a nap before lunch? You've worked hard this morning.'

'You're sure you've got enough material? Because I don't think I'd want to re-visit—'

'Of course. If I have any further queries, I'll ask Zelda. What would you like to talk about tomorrow? One of your adventures? What about that time you found yourself adrift on an ice floe? I'm dying to hear about that.'

His face brightened. 'Oh, yes, that *was* interesting. The ice was breaking up beneath us and it was a mad scramble to get our tent and supplies off the detached floe and back on to *terra firma*. Fortunately when I was at Eton, I excelled at the long jump. But it was a close run thing. I don't mind admitting, I thought my number was up.'

Sholto was chuckling now, so I packed away my things, relieved to see him in better spirits. 'Same time tomorrow then? And we'll talk about your hair-raising adventures in the Antarctic.'

'Thank you, Jenny. I look forward to it.'

'So do I.'

I'd got as far as the door and as I opened it, I turned to check on Sholto, still concerned our session might have taken too much out of him. He sat slumped in his chair again and was gazing round the room, his eyes darting back and forth.

'What is it, Sholto? Are you all right?' He didn't answer, so I took a few steps back into the room and said, 'Would you like me to stay with you for a while? Or should I fetch Wilma?'

'No... No, thanks, Jenny. I'll be fine. It's just that... You know it's the damnedest thing, but sometimes I could *swear* Meredith is actually in the room.' He looked directly at me then and smiled faintly. 'Sometimes I think I can smell her perfume. Isn't that ridiculous?'

My first response was one of blind anger, that Meredith should haunt this old man and disturb his sleep, but thinking fast, I decided the best plan was to respond with comforting clichés. Sholto needed reassurance, so I said, 'The mind can play some funny tricks. I'm sure working on the book has stirred up a host of memories – many of them very painful for you. I expect your subconscious mind is disturbed. That's probably why you're sleeping badly and... imagining things,' I added, embarrassed by my lie.

'Oh, yes, very likely. Shackleton's fourth man.'

'I'm sorry?'

'It's an experience many people have had. Mountaineers. Polar explorers. Astronauts. Survivors of 9/11.'

'What is it?'

'The sense that someone else is present. A presence, encouraging you to make strenuous efforts to survive. Shackleton sensed it in Antarctica when he made that desperate trek across South Georgia. They all did. All three men thought there was a fourth. I've experienced that on expeditions, when I've been at death's door. But that was different. I couldn't identify the stranger, I was just aware of a benevolent presence, insisting I shouldn't give up.'

'So are you saying you feel as if there's someone else in the room *now*?'

'Yes. And somehow I know – or rather, I believe – that the third is Meredith. And I don't think she's feeling very benevolent. So very odd.' He looked around the room again. 'You don't sense anything?'

'No. Not in here.'

It wasn't a lie. It wasn't the whole truth either. But in that split second I had to make a decision, whether or not to confide in Sholto. I decided I should spare him. I had no reason to think he was in any danger and there was nothing I could do to protect him anyway. But I'd have to tell Alec.

I took my leave with a heavy heart.

I went downstairs and headed for my room, but before I got there I heard the distinctive creak of my door opening. I stepped back, still jumpy after my conversation with Sholto. I was relieved to see Alec emerge, holding a dustpan and brush. As he turned to close my door, I walked forward, calling his name softly.

He looked up and smiled as I approached. 'The deed's done. You'll not find a piece of china anywhere. Nor will Wilma when she does her rounds.'

'She's late today, isn't she?'

'I gave her the task of cleaning the Augean stables.'

'The armoury?'

He nodded. 'She'll have had her work cut out over there this morning and later she'll give me a row about the unhygienic state of that kitchenette. Poor Wilma takes dirt as a personal affront. She sees it as her mission in life to eradicate it and I don't make things easy for her.'

'Thanks for clearing up. Did you see... anything odd?'

'No. No sign of herself this morning.'

'And did you find the hatpin? I had a look round but I couldn't find it.'

'I put it beside the laptop.'

'Thanks. You didn't open—'

'No, I didn't touch the laptop.'

'Neither did I. Couldn't face it this morning. Did you hear any music earlier?'

'Music?'

'The harpsichord. I heard it when I was in the library.'

'No. I heard nothing.'

'Neither did Sholto. But he does sense her presence, Alec.' His eyes widened. 'He's started dreaming about her and says he sometimes senses her in the room.'

'Had you said anything about last night?'

'Of course not. We'd been talking about Meredith and Liz. I was just about to leave, when he came right out with it. He told me he sensed Meredith was in the room.'

'Could *you* sense her?'

'No, but I'd already heard the harpsichord and whenever I hear that, it's as if she's somehow got inside my head. Even when she's not around, I imagine that she is.'

Alec laid his hand on my arm. 'Jenny, d'you see now why you must leave? She's getting to you.'

'No, she isn't, I'm just being a wimp, that's all. I can handle it, Alec. I just don't want her getting to Sholto. I can look after myself, but he can't. He's old and infirm. And depressed about Cauldstane.'

'Did he discuss selling up?'

'Only to say he's not prepared to do it. Not yet anyway. Do you think that's what she wants? To drive you all out?'

'Probably. All Sholto wants now is to hand over Cauldstane in good heart to his sons. The icing on the cake for him would be if it looked likely there'd be a new generation of MacNabs prepared to keep the old place going. His legacy is all he cares about now. So I imagine it's all part of Meredith's game plan that Sholto should sell up and Ferg and I should live out our days like monks because no woman will touch us for fear of invoking the MacNab curse.'

'If you weren't clutching a dustpan and brush, I'd show you exactly what I think of Meredith's game plan.'

Without speaking, Alec bent gracefully and placed the pan and brush on the floor. When he straightened up, I put my hand up to his head, threaded my fingers through the untidy curls and brought his face down to the level of mine. We kissed.

When I came up for air, I stood with my arms round Alec's narrow waist, my head on his chest, listening to his heartbeat. Then a thought struck me and I looked up.

'Did you clean up my room without your sword?'

He frowned. 'A sword's no good for sweeping.'

'No, I meant did you venture in without any... protection?'

'Och, no, I had my wee dirk. I never go anywhere without it.'

I snuggled up again and as his arms pulled me tighter against his body, I murmured, 'Is that a *sgian dubh* in your pocket, or are you just pleased to see me?'

He laughed and we kissed again.

My lighthearted mood was short-lived. Back in my room, I switched on the laptop and while I waited for it to load, I picked up the hatpin Alec had placed on the table. I stared at it, as if close examination would give me some clue as to why Meredith had left it in my room.

I put the pin inside my pencil case and zipped it shut, then I opened up my Cauldstane notes. I'd resolved that if Meredith's rants were still there, I would delete them, but a part of me hoped they would already be gone. I scrolled to the end of my notes and was dismayed to see her rambling narrative. Furious, I highlighted the text, scrolling down, preparing to delete every word. Then I saw there was a new message at the end. A long one. I should have just carried on scrolling and deleted everything. But I didn't. I stopped and read it.

When, some time later, Alec knocked on my door and asked if I was going down to lunch, he found me lying on the bed. I told him I had a headache and wasn't hungry. He offered to make me a sandwich and bring it upstairs, but I told him I just wanted to be left alone. He asked if Meredith had left me any more messages and I said no. He looked relieved, then went downstairs for lunch.

I felt awful lying to him, but I didn't really have a choice. If I'd told him she had, he would have asked what it said and there was no way I could let Alec read what she'd written this time.

I suppose that's when things started to go wrong. Really wrong. When I had to lie to Alec. And it was all Meredith's doing.

You can have no idea what it's like to watch yourself die.

I'd watched my own death many times on videotape. My deaths as Tosca, Cio-Cio-San and Desdemona were immortalized on film. My greatest theatrical triumph was playing a dead woman: Eurydice, the beloved wife who's brought back from the Underworld by her desperate, grieving husband.

It's quite something to go into a theatre, sign in, put on your make-up and costume, warm up, knowing you're going to die later on in the evening; that you're going to be stabbed or smothered, or that you'll leap to your death from castle battlements. It's upsetting. Disturbing. Thank God for the curtain call when you can come back on stage and lap up all the applause. "I am the resurrection and the life." Well, not quite, but you know what I mean.

Except you don't, do you? A mere wordsmith like you? You can't know what I gave for my art. Nor do you know what it's like to watch yourself die for real, as I did, smashing into that tree, seeing the front of the car crumple, the windscreen shatter, feeling the driving wheel ram me back against the seat, cracking my ribs, crushing my lungs and splitting my heart.

They said, "She wouldn't have known what hit her." Oh, but I did. I knew exactly what was happening to me. I remember it as if it were yesterday. As I opened my mouth to scream, it filled with tiny pieces of glass. You don't forget a thing like that. Not even when you're dead.

That day the world lost a great artist and Sholto lost a wife of whom he was unworthy. The quiet family funeral deprived me of the recognition and adoration that was my due. And now Sholto thinks I'm going to be relegated to a mere episode in his wretched memoir!

Can he seriously think I'm going to play second fiddle – in death as in life – to that frump, Liz?

This castle is haunted, this family cursed. Nothing good will befall the MacNabs, I shall see to that. My powers are limited, but they're sufficient for my purpose. It's really very simple. Sholto was mine and will remain mine. Alec never was mine, so he will be nobody's. I allow no rivals, however paltry. I amused myself bullying Alec, then intimidating Coral. (Hardly a worthy adversary! Breaking her was too easy. I prefer a challenge. Like Alec.)

I suspect you might be made of stronger stuff, Jenny, but not strong enough. Take my advice and get out now. Last night's display was just a taster of what you're in for if you stay.

Leave Cauldstane.

Leave Alec to me.

Leave Sholto to rot – which is what he deserves.

You can never win because I have nothing – absolutely nothing – to lose. You, on the other hand, stand to lose everything. And what man is worth that? None in my experience – and believe me, I've known a few. So be a good girl. Pack your bags and go. You know it makes sense. Cauldstane women die in the end. Just look at us… Liz. Coral. Even me.

Do you really want to join us?

Chapter Eighteen

I didn't know what to do. Who could I tell? The one person who would have believed me was the one person I couldn't tell. There was no way I wanted Alec to know his wife had been bullied into breakdown, nor did I want him to suspect — as I now did — that Meredith might somehow have been responsible for Coral's death. Despite her claim to special powers, some of which I'd witnessed, I didn't see how a ghost could make a happily pregnant woman drown herself, but there was no doubt Meredith had tried to drive the poor woman to breaking point. Perhaps she'd succeeded.

Alec wanted to believe Coral's death had been an accident and that was the most likely explanation. I had no right, whatever my personal circumstances, to sow the seeds of doubt in an already troubled mind. It would only torment him further and for all I knew, this was precisely what Meredith wanted.

One thing seemed clear. I was not going to leave. I'd told Alec I was stubborn and it was true. But I *was* frightened — frightened by Meredith's threats, by what I'd seen her do and what I'd heard she'd done. She had every reason to want me out of the way. I was a rival for Alec's affections. I was the channel through which Sholto would tell his story, a story in which Meredith would feature only as a subsidiary character and possibly not to her credit. I was what stood between Meredith and her control of the MacNabs. If my book was a success, they might make enough money to hold on to Cauldstane for a bit longer. My friendship with Alec had provided him with someone who could share the burden of knowledge and suspicion he'd borne alone for half his life. He'd been trying to protect his family single-handed, but now he had a partner of sorts. I might not be of much practical use, but the laptop had provided Meredith with a channel for communicating. In common with some who were criminally insane, she talked too much and gave herself away in her grandiose, self-justifying rants. If we just ignored her threats, I felt sure we could stay one jump ahead. Meredith might be evil and devoid of conscience, but I had a hunch she wasn't all that bright. Between us, Alec and I could surely find a way to evict her from Cauldstane. I had to believe it was possible. If I allowed myself to think there was no way out, Meredith had already won.

I clung to the fact that she was mostly bluff. Alec had said, "It's all mind games with Meredith". Bullying. Threats. Emotional manipulation. She could certainly make her presence felt, but what else could she actually do? Hurl china. Make a hatpin fly through the air. Write on a laptop. Produce auditory hallucinations. Perhaps she was able to haunt dreams. It didn't amount to a great deal. The biggest weapon in her armoury was fear. Fear of what she *might* do.

Well, I knew all about fear. Meredith had chosen the wrong woman to bully because I'd lived with crippling, irrational fear for so long, I'd sworn I would never live like that again. I'd re-arranged my entire life, even changed my name, so I could live sanely, without fear. Fear of my own power to create and destroy. Fear of madness. Fear of fear itself.

Meredith evidently thought I was made of sterner stuff than Coral. I wasn't so sure, but nothing would make me abandon Cauldstane now. I had an emotional and professional stake in the place. I was going to finish Sholto's book. Even Alec couldn't persuade me to leave.

And that was something else Meredith got wrong. She claimed there was no man for whom it was worth risking everything. I begged to differ. I thought Alec MacNab probably was worth it.

Faced with dire situations like this, I suppose some people might turn to God. I did the next best thing. I turned to Rupert.

I sat down at the laptop and composed a long letter. When I'd finished, I went down to the Cauldstane office, printed it out, took an envelope and addressed it to Rupert. I sealed the envelope, got into my car and drove away from Cauldstane. I parked in a lay-by several miles away, then rang Rupert.

'Hi, it's me.'

'Jen! How nice to hear from you. How are you getting on in the Highlands?'

'Fine. Well... not *fine* exactly. There've been a few problems.'

'With the book?'

'No, the book's going to be OK, I think. If I get to write it.'

'Is the subject being difficult?'

'No, he's a dear. The problem is... his wife.'

'I thought you told me she was dead?'

'She is.'

There was a long silence then Rupert said, 'Jen, are you all right?'

'I'm fine. Really, I am. But some very strange things are going on here and I'd like your advice.'

'Of course. Anything I can do to help, just ask.'

'I am asking, Rupert and I warn you now, it's going to be a big ask.' I paused, uncertain if I could go on. Rupert would be the first to think I'd lost my marbles again – he'd watched it happen last time – but he was also the only person on the planet in whom I felt I could confide and who I knew would give me a fair hearing. He would also be able to answer the question I needed to ask.

I stared at the envelope on the passenger seat and said, 'Listen, I'm going to send you a letter. Not an email, a letter.'

'How quaint. Why not an email?'

'I don't trust my laptop. It's been playing up lately. I'd rather send you a letter and I want you to text me when you get it. And when you've read it, I want you to give me your advice.'

'You're breaking up, Jen... Are you on your mobile?'

'Yes. I'm sitting in my car. I didn't want to risk anyone at the castle overhearing me.'

'*Castle?*'

I groaned. 'Yes, but please forget I said that.'

'Said what?'

I laughed, despite myself. 'Thanks, I needed that... Look, I can't explain now, but it will all be in the letter. When you've read it, I want you to tell me what to do.'

'Well, I hope I'm qualified to do so.'

'Oh, don't worry, this is your area of expertise.'

'You're sure?'

'Positive. You see, Rupert, I need to know how to exorcise a ghost.'

'Jen, you're breaking up again. It sounded like you said you wanted to exorcise a ghost.'

'I did.'

There was another long silence, then Rupert said gently, 'I see... You know, Jen, that's not something for an amateur to tackle. You need to call in an expert. In the first instance, you should talk to the local priest. If he's not equipped to deal with it, he'll know a man who is. The Church avoids publicising these matters, but we do have procedures for delivering troubled households from the influence of unquiet spirits. *Evil* spirits even. But the local priest would be your first port of call.'

'I can't do that. I'm not family and only one other person apart from me knows the place is haunted. And he's not the owner of the property. He'd have no authority to summon ghostbusters.'

'*Please*, Jen.' Rupert sounded pained. 'Don't be flippant. This is a very serious matter.'

'You're telling me! I've seen what this ghost can do. We need help urgently.'

'You say you can't discuss this with the owner of the property?'

'No, he'd think I was barking mad and then I might lose the commission. Look, I just want your advice. I want you to tell me what can be done. By the Church, by mediums, *anyone*.'

'Oh, don't go summoning a medium! That could do more harm than good. And I absolutely forbid you to try any funny business with a ouija board. People think they're some sort of toy, but they can stir up serious trouble.'

'Oh, Rupert...' My eyes began to fill with tears. 'You actually *believe* me, don't you?'

'Of course I believe you. Why would you lie about something as disturbing as this?'

'But you're a *scientist*.'

'And a man of God. And as both physicist and man of God, I've experienced things I cannot explain, which I therefore respect.'

'Are *you* qualified to deal with... our problem?'

He hesitated, then said, 'I am, but it would be much better to consult the local chap. There are ways of doing these things, Jen. Protocols. I wouldn't want to step on any toes.'

'But I have no authority to ask anyone but you. You have to help me, Rupert! Promise me you'll help. Please come and – and...' I was weeping now. I couldn't help myself. 'Deliver us from *evil*.'

'Jen, calm down. Please don't get upset. You know I'll do my very best. I'll make sure you get appropriate help. Send me that letter and we'll take it from there.'

I wiped my eyes, looked at my watch and realised it was many hours since I'd eaten. No wonder I was feeling light-headed. 'Don't email me, Rupert. Text, then I'll ring you. I can't explain now, but I think that's the best way to communicate.'

'Of course. But are you sure you're going to be all right? You sounded... frightened just now.'

'No, I'm not. Not really. I'm just rattled, that's all. And angry. But I refuse to be frightened. That's exactly what she wants.'

'She?'

'The ghost.'

'Oh, *Jen*.'

'Look, I have to go. I'm going to post this letter now. When you've read it, you'll understand everything. My landline number is in the letter, but you're not to use it. I'm just giving it to you in case of... well, of direst emergency. It's professionally unethical for me to give you the number, but I'm making an exception because you're a clergyman.'

'Thank you for entrusting me with the information.'

'Thank you for being there. You have no idea what it means to know that maybe something can be *done* for this poor family.'

'Well, if it's all right with you, I'll pray for them. I'd also like to pray for you, Jen.'

'Be my guest. We're going to need all the help we can get.'

I thanked him again and hung up. As I drove off in search of a postbox, Rupert's words echoed in my mind.

Jen, you're breaking up again...

I sincerely hoped I wasn't. I was damned if I was going to go mad again.

When I got back to Cauldstane I found someone – Wilma, probably – had left cake and a thermos of coffee in my room. Both were welcome and I despatched them while examining the hatpin. It was about twenty centimetres long and made of silver. The decorative end was an amethyst sitting in a silver cup, cut so that it resembled a thistle.

Meredith had left it as some sort of clue, but to what? If she was taunting me with something, what did she want me to guess, or try to guess? Was she telling me something about Zelda? Did the enigmatic laptop message hint that Zelda had caused some harm? To whom? Or was it just a threat directed at *me*? I decided the best way to stave off paranoia was to give the hatpin back to Zelda.

Standing in the passageway, I listened for sounds coming from her room. I'd never thought of myself as someone who *skulked*, but increasingly, this is what I found myself doing at Cauldstane: lurking in corridors, listening, watching, as if there were a mad woman in the attic who might be on the prowl. Perhaps the mad woman was me.

Zelda's room was quiet, but I could hear female voices downstairs. If you were looking for someone at Cauldstane, the kitchen was always a good place to start. People gravitated there to warm up, snaffle biscuits and pick at leftovers. Wilma wasn't the sort of cook who drove intruders out of her domain. Her kitchen was more like a salon where family members would congregate for "a wee blether" or to listen to the news on the radio. So I headed downstairs, hoping I'd find Zelda in the kitchen.

I pushed the door open and found Wilma decorating a huge pie with raw pastry trimmings. Zelda and Alec were seated at the table with mugs and empty plates. I didn't miss the look of relief that passed swiftly across Alec's face when he saw me. Hoping my face betrayed less than his, I looked away and said casually, 'Hope I'm not disturbing anything?'

Zelda looked up from a pile of cookery books open in front of her, removed her glasses and waved me towards a chair. 'Not at all! Come in and sit down, Jenny. We missed you at lunch. Alec said you weren't feeling well.'

'Just a touch of migraine, that's all. I took some painkillers and it wore off. I came down because I wanted to return this to you.' Watching Zelda's face carefully for reaction, I produced the hatpin. 'I found it in my room.'

She frowned, reached for her glasses again and studied the pin. 'My goodness... I haven't seen this in *years*!'

'It is one of yours then?'

'It *was*, but I gave it to Meredith – och, it must be over thirty years ago now! I first met her when she sang in *Don Giovanni* at Nice Opera House. Liz had told her how much I love music, so she

161

sent me some tickets. Well, Meredith's first entrance was very dramatic. She came on carrying a lot of luggage, wearing a great big hat over her wig. The night I was there, it was more dramatic than planned, because her hat nearly came off. Meredith was livid after the show, so I suggested a longer hat pin might help. I gave her this one as a thank you present for the tickets.' Zelda looked up from the pin. 'Wherever did you find it?'

'It was behind a bookcase,' I said, avoiding Alec's eye. 'I had to retrieve one of my pens that had slipped down the back. And I found the pin.'

'Well, goodness knows how it ended up there! I swear things *walk* in this place. You can put something down and when you come back, it just isn't there. The number of sewing needles I've lost over the years! And I *always* secure my needle in my work. But still they disappear. It's maddening. I think there must be some sort of Cauldstane poltergeist. Either that or I'm going senile.' Zelda handed me back the hatpin.

'Don't you want to put it back in your collection?' I asked, dismayed.

'No, you keep it. As a souvenir of Cauldstane. If it turned up in your room, Fate meant you to have it.'

My answering smile must have looked wooden, but I thanked Zelda, declined tea and went back to my room where I lay down on the bed and tried to think. Meredith's message now seemed even more sinister. If that pin had ever done any harm, it had been wielded by Meredith, not Zelda. It seemed far more likely Meredith would be the one to put the thing to malicious use and I could imagine her wanting to gloat over what she'd done, in much the same way she'd boasted about her infidelities and her sexual harassment of Alec.

Alec was right. It *was* all mind games with Meredith. She wanted me to know something – or rather, she wanted me to know that I *didn't* know something. This was her way of demonstrating she still had power to manipulate people from beyond the grave. So I decided I wouldn't play the game. I would get on with my work as planned, pushing Meredith and her machinations to the back of my mind. I opened the laptop and settled down to type up my notes from my morning session with Sholto. But not before I'd dropped the hatpin into a deep and hideous vase where I wouldn't see it and

162

where I trusted it could do no damage.

I sat at my desk, struggling to compose an account of Liz's death. By leaving Alec out of the equation I had to omit the cause and some of the consequences of the accident. What remained was a vague description of a fatal riding accident that appeared to have no cause other than a jittery mare handled by an incompetent rider. This might have been fair to Alec, but hardly seemed fair to Liz.

As I re-read my partial account, written in the style I assumed for Sholto, I was distracted by thoughts of Meredith who, leaving Alec aside, had been first on the scene. She'd also been the one Alec had spoken to first. He'd told her what had happened and she'd told the others. Sholto had said Alec was "wailing like a banshee" by the time he arrived, so presumably the boy was beyond giving an account himself, so all anyone knew was what Alec remembered and what Meredith said he'd told her.

This realisation was unsettling, but I couldn't say why. Just a deep mistrust of Meredith, I suppose. It was spectacularly convenient of Liz to die after Sholto had refused to divorce her. But accidents do happen, as Meredith had pointed out in one of her vile rants. What exactly had she said?...

For a moment I chastised myself for deleting her messages, then remembered I hadn't actually done what I'd intended. When I'd spotted her latest communication – a death threat, virtually – I'd stopped what I was doing to read it. Afterwards I'd lain down on the bed, my heart pounding with anger and fear.

Without quite knowing why, I resolved to save all messages in future, however painful. (Was I collecting evidence to use against a *ghost*?) I opened up another window and scrolled until I found the section I was looking for.

Riding is a dangerous sport and horses are unpredictable. Liz wasn't the most expert of riders and her mare was temperamental. That's what I said to Sholto – to anyone who'd listen, in fact. "Accidents happen."
Especially to the MacNabs.

Nothing incriminating there. Callousness, yes, but no indication of anything sinister, other than a possible allusion to the MacNab curse. Nevertheless, I still felt something wasn't right, but could see no way to investigate the circumstances of the accident, not after all this time and not without bothering Alec.

I abandoned my attempt to write and turned instead to that great time-eater, Google. I put in a search for "post-traumatic stress disorder" and "children". Some of the psychiatric jargon was impenetrable, but the plain English sites were helpful, if depressing. There was a lot of stuff about physical and sexual abuse, less about witnessing or being involved in accidents. Generally it seemed children were pretty resilient, but witnessing a death, especially the death of a parent or carer, was likely to cause PTSD.

In children PTSD is associated with increased likelihood of worsening school performance and subsequent employment problems, increased risk of depression and anxiety disorders in adulthood, behavioural problems and substance misuse, increased chronic disease and problems forming stable relationships.

How much of that had Alec been through? I remembered he'd dropped out of university and Meredith had described him as a quiet, morose child, but as she clearly hated children, she was hardly a reliable witness.

I read on and found this on a discussion board...

If PTSD is still there after a year it's probably going to be lifelong in some form or another.

Could Alec *still* suffer from post-traumatic stress disorder? Probably hard to tell if you're being haunted by a ghost. Was he haunted by a ghost *because* of his mental instability, the way poltergeists are supposed to home in on troubled adolescents? But it seemed likely Coral was also haunted by Meredith. So for that matter was I. Was that what we all had in common? Mental instability? Or just some kind of fragility?

I remembered being bullied at school for being a cry-baby because I blubbed at stories and films. Even sad songs could make me well up. I moved on to high school, hoping for a fresh start, but bullies still singled me out – not for crying, but for being academic, for being more interested in books than boys, for wearing the wrong kind of shoes. Did I just emanate vulnerability? And did I still? Was that why I sensed Meredith?

I scanned another page and was astonished to discover that until the mid-1990s psychiatrists had been under the impression children didn't suffer from PTSD. Liz had died in 1980. What were the chances of any trauma in Alec being diagnosed or even noticed, especially by a father who made light of frostbite and failed to mention two cracked ribs to his expedition leader because he "didn't want to make a fuss". I imagined Alec would have been left to get on with it, especially while he was away at school, where he would doubtless have followed his father's stoical example.

I was scrolling through more Google results when there was a tap at the door, followed by Alec's voice saying. 'It's me. Are you busy?'

'Yes. But come in anyway.' I swivelled round in my chair as he entered.

'I haven't come for any reason.' He shut the door and, still holding the handle, just stood there, looking at me with a soft, shy smile. 'I just wanted to check you were OK. You seemed a wee bit nervous downstairs. But mainly I... well, I just wanted to look at you.'

'Oh, *Alec.*'

He raised a hand, palm outwards, as if to forestall my rising from the chair. 'No, I'll go now if you're working. That smile's set my mind at ease.'

'Please stay! Sit with me for a while.'

He obeyed, but as he set a chair beside me, I remembered what was on the laptop screen. I turned and quickly closed the window down, revealing my own work. I became flustered, trying to remember whether Meredith's last message would be visible, so I just slapped the laptop shut and turned back to Alec.

He eyed me with suspicion. 'More messages from Meredith you don't want me to know about? What are you trying to keep from me, Jenny? And why?'

Ignoring the question, I said, 'I've been researching PTSD. Post-traumatic—'

'I know what it stands for. And I can guess why you're researching it. But I don't know why you won't tell me what

Meredith wrote.'

I looked away. 'Oh, it was just the usual bombastic nonsense.'

'Threats?' I didn't answer. I didn't want to lie again, nor did I want to tell him the truth. 'Who was she threatening? Me? Or you? My guess it was you. That's why you didn't tell me. And that's her style. It would drive a wedge between us. Which is of course what she wants. You'd have to lie in order to stop me worrying about you.' I still said nothing and looked at Alec helplessly. He folded his arms and continued cheerfully, 'If I was Meredith and I wanted to wreck Alec MacNab's life again, I'd try to scare off his new woman. And she, being a plucky wee thing, wouldn't confide in him. Och no, she'd tough it out on her own because she really likes Alec and she doesn't want to be sent away.' He paused. 'Am I right?'

'In every single respect, damn you.'

He grinned. 'Don't be too hard on yourself! I've known this woman – this *ghoul* – for many a year. I know how she thinks. I watched her try to come between me and Coral. I knew as soon as I expressed an interest in you, Meredith would try to make me regret it.'

'Do you?'

'No. but I'm very sorry she's taking it out on you. Will you please show me what she said?'

'Not now. I'd like to talk to you about something else.'

He sighed and said, 'My mother's death.' It wasn't a question.

'Yes. Would you mind? It worries me that the only sources of information about what happened are a traumatised eight-year old and Meredith.'

'Aye, I know, but I seem to have given her a surprisingly lucid account of what happened.'

'Yes, that's what bothers me.'

'What d'you mean?'

'Oh, I don't know. It's just something about the way she wrote about Liz.'

'There was no love lost there, for sure, but my mother broke her neck falling off a rearing horse and I caused the horse to rear.'

'Could you bear to tell me what happened? I've heard Sholto's version and I've read Meredith's. He's adamant no detail is going into the book and I'm happy with that. But the nerdy researcher in me thinks I should also hear the only eye-witness account.'

'It was thirty-two years ago, Jenny. I'd only be telling you what I remember telling Meredith.'

'Don't you actually remember what happened?

'Aye, but it's hazy. It always *was* hazy. I've a clearer memory of what happened before and afterwards. I can tell you what book Wilma read me after it happened. *The Velveteen Rabbit.* I can still see the book now. It was one of my favourites.'

'I had that one too! I loved it so much.' I put my hand up to my mouth as I felt the tears come. 'Oh, this is stupid! Honestly, the slightest thing sets me off. Sorry.'

'Don't apologise. You love books. They've been your life. I feel the same way about swords. The craftsmanship of a blade can make me feel all mushy inside.'

'So you can remember that book clearly?'

'Aye. It had belonged to my father and it was in a very precarious condition. Like the Velveteen Rabbit himself.'

'But your memory of the accident is...vague?'

'It was like a series of impressions. I could make little sense of it at the time.'

'That's what I wanted to hear really. Your impressions. Sholto told me how it actually happened.'

Alec leaned forward, clasped his hands and rested his arms on his knees. His head was bowed, so I couldn't see his face. 'I just remember seeing my mother lying on the ground... and wondering what the hell she was *doing* there.'

'What do you remember before that?'

'Being excited about my bike. I'd cycled twice all the way round the castle and I came tearing through the archway into the courtyard. Then... well, there was a lot of noise.'

'What sort of noise?'

'Hooves clattering on the cobbles... the horse neighing... a woman screaming... my bloody klaxon... Cacophony.'

'That's what you remember most? The noise?'

'Aye. And Ma lying on the ground. With blood coming out of her ear.'

'But you must have seen her fall too. Sorry, Alec – just say if this is too much.'

After a moment's hesitation, he took a deep breath and, his voice matter-of-fact, launched into a speech. 'I cycled into the

167

courtyard, sounding my horn. The noise startled the mare, she reared up and Ma was thrown to the ground. Then the horse galloped off past me. I fell off my bike and lay there crying until Meredith came and asked me what had happened, what had frightened the horse. I told her it was me. It was my fault. I'd sounded my horn and that had startled the horse. She'd thrown Ma and galloped off.'

'You told her all that?'

'She made me tell her twice. I suppose I wasn't making much sense.'

'Sholto said you were wailing like a banshee.'

'Probably.'

'But you don't remember?'

'If I'm perfectly honest, Jenny—'

He hesitated again. I reached out, laid a hand on his and quoted his words to me. 'Why be anything else?'

He shook his head. 'My memories are... patchy.'

'I suppose they must have faded over the years.'

'I don't think so. What happened that day never seemed crystal clear to me. Not like the day Coral drowned. Or the day I had to go and identify her body. I suppose being a child makes all the difference. It was all so confusing... And the horse was so bloody *loud*. I'll never forget that. Or seeing Ma lying on the ground, with her eyes open. I could see all her teeth. It was like she was grinning up at me. As if she was pleased to see me. I remember that.'

'Oh, Alec, I'm so sorry.'

'Don't be. It happened a very long time ago. We've all moved on. Ferg and I had a wonderful mother. We just didn't have her for very long. Now if you'll excuse me, I have to get back to work. I'll see you at dinner?'

'You think I'd miss Wilma's pie?' He smiled in answer, but his face looked drawn. 'I think I'll go out for a walk now. I feel the need for some fresh air.'

He bent and kissed me gently. 'You take care now. You'll have your phone?'

'Of course. Stop worrying about me!' I stood up and turned to face him. Looking into those dark grey eyes, I saw concern. No, more than concern. I saw fear. Not fear for himself, fear for me. I lifted a hand to cup his face and he leaned into my palm, closing his eyes. I observed his long lashes and smooth forehead and wondered if I'd ever seen Alec look so peaceful. 'It's *you* she's after, Alec. Not me. And I really can't say I blame her. I'd fight for you too.'

He opened his eyes, took me in his arms and we stood still, saying nothing for a long time, then he said, 'Work' and I said, 'Walk'. We released each other and went our separate ways. But I double-checked I had my phone.

Chapter Nineteen

It was a relief to be outdoors, out of the castle, away from my room and my laptop. It was a positive pleasure to be moving smartly across the courtyard, out of the long shadows of Cauldstane and into the autumn sunshine. I buttoned up my thick cardigan against the chilly breeze and headed for the stone bridge and riverside walk which had become my favourite.

As I crossed the bridge, I averted my eyes from the Blood Stone projecting from the water. Instead, I gazed downstream at the brown water hurtling over the rocks. The movement and sounds entranced me, almost hypnotized me. I stared into the river from the bridge and for one vertiginous moment it was as if I was being drawn down towards the water; as if the current had the power to pull first my mind, then my body into the river.

My reverie was interrupted by a shout, a male voice hailing me. I looked up to see Fergus on the opposite bank, seated on a ride-on mower, pulling a trailer. The trailer contained a barking collie and two dark-haired children. He waved and switched off the ignition, then turned and said something to the children who climbed out of the trailer, laughing and shrieking, then ran off into the woods followed by their dog. Fergus jumped off the mower and jogged up onto the bridge.

'The Cauldstane taxi service, at your disposal, ma'am. Can I take you for a ride along the riverbank? Or into the woods? You looked a wee bit sad, staring down into the water. Is my father giving you a hard time?'

'Not at all. He's an absolute delight. Couldn't be more helpful. But Cauldstane's giving *him* a hard time, isn't it?'

'Aye, and so am I. Were you wanting to talk about that some time? As background for the book, I mean. Sholto and Alec will have given you the emotional and historical perspective. But there's another point of view. Financial. Practical.'

'Yes, I know. They've both been at pains to give me a balanced view of the problems you all face. But I'd also like to talk to you.'

170

'Now?'

'Do you have a few minutes?'

He leaned on the bridge parapet. 'Fire away.'

'You want to sell up, don't you? Put Cauldstane on the market.'

'I don't *want* to, but I think we should, aye.'

I wasn't quite sure how to proceed, how to avoid asking the bald question that would seem impertinent. I looked up at Cauldstane, at the mass of pale pink stone rising up incongruously above the steep river gorge. I gazed up at the window of my room and thought how lucky I was to be able to live here, if only for a few weeks. I thought of the MacNabs living here for centuries, then of the current incumbents having to leave. Finally, I blurted out the tactless words. 'Fergus, how can you bear to think of leaving?'

'I think of little else other than how we can *stay*. I have ideas. I've even drawn up business plans for some of them, but everything that could make Cauldstane commercially viable requires money in the first instance. We're blessed with a lot of assets here, but cash isn't one of them.'

'What would your priorities be if you came into some cash?'

'It would depend how much and whether the bank would lend us money on the strength of it.'

'But you do have some ideas?'

'Plenty.'

Reaching into my shoulder bag for a notebook, I said, 'Tell me about them. Imagine I was looking to invest in Cauldstane. How would you sell the idea to me?'

Fergus grinned and launched into his sales pitch. 'It would be a simple matter to renovate outbuildings and the empty houses on the estate. There are four houses and I reckon we have buildings that could be converted into three separate self-catering units. Let's say we could average £250 a week for each of those – that's a conservative estimate. You could charge a fortune for Christmas and Hogmanay, but you'd be unable to rent them out for much of the winter. So you're probably talking about an annual rental income of somewhere between eighty or ninety thousand a year. Even after deductions, there would be enough left over to enable Alec to take on an assistant, which would allow him to double his output and thus his income. And that's a major source of revenue for us. That money would allow us to smarten up the castle itself.

Possibly open it to visitors – maybe just a couple of days a week to begin with. We could see how it went. But if we provided all the extras – a café, a wee souvenir shop where Sholto's book would be on sale of course,' Fergus added with a smile, 'a plant stall, a picnic site, an adventure playground... You're talking about a grand day out for the family. Folk might pay handsomely for a chance to snoop round a castle that's still a family home.'

'Do you have more rooms you could open up to show?'

'Aye, and any amount of junk in the attics to furnish them. We'd need to get more toilets put in and who knows what else to comply with Health and Safety regulations, but plenty of other castle owners have done it. You need a few gimmicks of course. Falconry displays, open air concerts. Some added attraction.'

'Alec could presumably put on some sort of historical swordsmanship show with some of his mates.'

'Oh aye, he'd love that.'

'And I'm sure if she used to run a restaurant, Zelda would be quite capable of running a café, especially with Wilma to help. Perhaps you could do candlelit dinners in the evenings.'

Fergus nodded. 'We're thinking along the same lines, Jenny. Cauldstane could also be developed as a wildlife centre. We've got red kites as the main attraction, but there's other bird life. And red squirrels. Badgers. Pine martens. We could build hides in the woods and have a nature trail. And the estate could be developed for sport. The river's full of fish. Then there's always weddings... There's so much we could do, if we only had some cash. I just need someone to give me a million to get started. Then – just watch me! – I'd make this place earn its keep.'

'Does the family have anything to sell? Jewellery? Paintings? What about the harpsichord? How much is it worth?'

'A lot, but not a million. Aye, it could go, if you can persuade Sholto. But he's not good at getting rid of stuff. I know for a fact that somewhere in the attic there's a Hornby train set he and Torquil used to play with. *That* would fetch a good price on eBay,' Fergus said with a grin.

'Alec told me there are a lot of paintings.'

'There are, but I don't know if any of them are worth much. No one's ever really looked at them. Torquil started making an inventory of Cauldstane valuables because he knew we were massively under-insured. But then he became ill and abandoned it. Sholto's never bothered because he knows he couldn't afford the insurance premiums. But as far as I know, we're not sitting on any Rembrandts. More's the pity.'

Fergus fell silent but didn't seem in any hurry to depart, so I said, 'Would you mind if I asked you another question? I'd really like to know what you remember about your mother's death. I've talked to Sholto and Alec, but I'd really like to have a complete picture. If you don't mind.'

He frowned. 'I don't think I actually remember much. I was only five. It's hard now to distinguish my memories from what I was told had happened. I remember crying and Sholto picking me up. But I think I was crying because Alec was crying. I didn't know *why* he was crying and I certainly didn't realise Ma was dead. You don't really understand death at five. I mean, I'd had pets that died and I'd seen animals hanging in the game larder. Dad had friends who came and shot things for fun and I knew that was somehow OK, it was called sport. But I didn't understand about death and humans.'

'Who told you your mother was dead?'

'Dad, much later. He told me there'd been an accident and Ma was badly injured, then he took me away indoors. I remember that. I wanted to be with Alec, but Wilma had taken him off somewhere. There were other folk around. Meredith and her sister, Pam. There might have been others. It was a bit of a house party that weekend. We were supposed to be going fishing and they'd said I could come. I remember being very excited about that, but it didn't happen. That's how Dad broke the news to me. He came into the old nursery where Alec and I used to play. Pam and I were doing a jigsaw. Dad asked her to leave, then he sat down and pulled me on to his lap and held me. He said he was very sorry, but we wouldn't be going fishing after all. I started to cry again. I don't think I was crying about the fishing. At some level I think I already knew why we weren't going. Then Dad said Ma had fallen off her horse and been killed. I'd be lying if I told you I remember anything after that.'

'Did Sholto tell you Alec had caused the accident?'

'Och, no! He said it was the mare's fault. But Alec told me he'd frightened the horse with his horn.'

'When did he tell you that?'

'When he gave me his bike. He said he didn't want it any more

173

and that I could have it. I asked him why he didn't want it. First of all he said he just didn't want to ride it any more. I couldn't understand that. I thought there must be some sort of catch – it was a brand new bike! I kept asking Alec why he didn't want the bike. Made a real nuisance of myself. Then in the end he told me. About causing the accident. I was pretty angry with him, but at the same time he was offering me his *bike*... It was confusing for a five-year old. But self-interest won. I accepted the gift. I've often wondered whether that was Alec's way of saying sorry. Sorry he'd been responsible for the death of our mother. I don't know. We were two unhappy wee boys, with a grief-stricken father who wasn't coping. Wilma was very kind. So was Zelda. They both did their best to compensate, but things were never the same without Ma. Before she died, folk laughed and smiled. We were one big happy family. Then the sun went in and we seemed to enter a perpetual winter. But maybe I'm just talking about growing up. When you look back on your childhood, you think the sun was always shining.'

'Even in the Highlands?'

Fergus laughed. 'Oh, aye, even in the Highlands.'

'Did you get on with your stepmother?'

His face clouded over. 'As a kid, I hated her – and I think the feeling was mutual. Fortunately she took very little notice of me. She always preferred Alec.' I shot Fergus a sidelong glance, wondering how much he knew, but to judge from his far-off expression, he was still wrapped up in childhood memories. 'Alec was the clever one. He worked hard at school. He was good at sport, but he was quiet. He'd been the quiet one before Ma died and afterwards... well, Alec was just *silent*. I wasn't. I was noisy, dirty, naughty – as wee boys are – and I'm pretty sure Meredith detested me. So I was always keen to get back to school. Which I loved.'

'Did you get on any better with Meredith when you were an adult?'

Fergus heaved a sigh, then said, 'I'll be straight with you, Jenny – no, I didn't. When I was young, she couldn't measure up to my mother – nobody could – and when I was older, I saw that she didn't make Dad happy. And she was often nasty to Coral for some reason. We shouldn't speak ill of the dead, but if you want my honest opinion – and this is off the record, mind – Meredith was a selfish bitch. Talk to Zelda if you want a kinder assessment. Or Wilma. Meredith was good to her in a lady-of-the-manor sort of way. Meredith liked having servants, whereas the rest of us think of Wilma as family almost. She was brilliant when Ma died and she was only a young woman then. You forget, seeing her now. Wilma was much the same age as Meredith and when Ma died, Wilma took on running Cauldstane, supervising us, holding Dad together. He and Wilma became quite close I think. He grew to rely on her. We all did. If you're writing a book about Dad and Cauldstane, Wilma should have her own chapter.'

'I'd come to the same conclusion myself, but it's up to Sholto. He dictates the content. I'm just his mouthpiece.'

'Och, Wilma would *hate* the attention anyway. But she's a grand lady and we all owe her a great deal. She's an honorary MacNab. In fact, I often think how different things might have been if Dad had married Wilma, not Meredith.' He glanced at his watch and said, 'If you'll excuse me, Jenny, I need to get cleaned up before dinner. I'll see you later, no doubt.'

He walked back down to the riverbank, climbed on to the mower and turned on the ignition. He gave me a wave, then set off along the path. After a few moments he was out of sight. After a few more, the river drowned the distant sound of his engine. I decided to continue my walk and crossed over to the opposite bank.

I hadn't been walking for long when I heard another shout, a child's voice this time. I turned and saw a small dark-haired girl, about seven or eight, skipping along the riverbank, perilously close to the edge. I wasn't sure if she was one of the children I'd seen earlier. She was singing to herself, some tuneless rhyme, while hopping over stones and tussocks of grass. I waited to see if an accompanying adult would appear from the woods. When no one came, my stomach began to squirm with anxiety. I set off in the direction of the little girl, walking quickly to catch her up before she could come to any harm. Reaching into my bag, I grasped my phone, unsure who to ring. I took my eyes off the child for only a moment while I scrolled down and selected Fergus' number, but by the time I looked up again, she was gone.

I started to panic, then realised the bridge possibly obscured my view of her. I hurried on, my phone pressed to my ear, waiting for Fergus to pick up, but my call went straight to voicemail. As I listened impatiently to his recorded instructions, I heard the sound of crying. As it built to a wail, I left a breathless message. 'Fergus, it's Jenny. Could you ring me? It's urgent.'

I ran on, looking to left and right, trying to locate the crying child. I went back on to the bridge and looked up-river. To my horror I saw she was now standing on the Blood Stone, her shoes and socks soaked by the water that flowed past her, its course divided by the big flat stone. From my raised viewpoint it was obvious she'd picked her way across the water via a series of stepping stones – stones I didn't recollect seeing before, but which were now revealed just level with the surface of the water. The child screamed as the icy water splashed her legs. She hopped from one foot to the other, trying to keep her legs out of the water, then she slipped and landed on her bottom.

I cried out, expecting to see her swept away by the torrent, but she gamely clambered to her feet again. Even before she was standing, I'd descended to the riverbank again and was running towards her, shouting, 'It's all right! I'm coming to get you. Don't move!'

I still had my phone in my hand and as I stepped onto the stones at the river's edge, I selected Alec's number and put the phone to my ear. Keeping my eyes on my feet, I chose the flattest stones and tested them gingerly before letting them bear my weight. After a few steps I could see the water was suddenly much deeper and flowed faster. There was no doubt that if the child fell into the river, she'd be swept away.

Alec answered his phone but before he had time to say anything, I shouted, 'Come down to the river. By the bridge. *Now*. It's an emergency.' He hung up without asking a single question. I slipped my phone into the pocket of my cardigan and hoisted the strap of my shoulder bag over my head, so the bag hung across my body. Then extending both arms for balance, I attempted to step on to the next stone.

The child was strangely quiet now as she watched me, her chest still heaving. I smiled at her and called out, in what I hoped was a reassuring voice, 'Don't worry, I'm coming to get you. Just stand *very* still.' She said nothing, her dark eyes expressionless and her face sullen, but she folded her arms – an oddly adult gesture, as if she was waiting for me to join her, but I supposed she was trying to keep herself warm.

I had no idea how I was going to get the girl back on to the riverbank and I didn't like to think what would happen if I fell into the water. I wasn't even a good swimmer, but Alec was on his way from the armoury, only minutes away. I assumed between us we'd be able to rescue her, but I cursed myself for not telling him to bring some rope. I wished Fergus would ring back. Maybe he'd have some in his trailer.

Looking down, I saw that the next stone now lay beneath the water. It would require an act of faith to put my weight on it, but it had obviously born the weight of the girl, so I assumed it must be stable. She was watching me closely now and, seeing me hesitate, she started to whimper.

'It's all right, I'm coming! Just stand very still and I'll be right there.'

She looked up sharply in the direction of the bridge and her little face twisted into a scowl. I turned my head and saw Alec and Fergus standing on the bridge, leaning over the parapet. My legs almost gave way with relief.

Alec bellowed, 'Jenny, what the hell are you *doing*? For Christ's sake, don't move!' Then he started to run.

The girl began to sob and held her arms out towards me, her eyes wide with terror. 'Don't worry about me,' I shouted. 'Just go and get some rope before the child falls in!' With that, I raised one foot and prepared to step down into the rushing water, onto the sunken stone. As I did so, Fergus, still on the bridge, yelled, '*What child?*'

I knew then. I understood everything. The child. Coral's death. The trap that had been laid for her, then for me. I knew as my foot descended, feeling for the stone I'd seen beneath the water, that it would no longer be there.

I threw myself backwards, but it was too late. My body's momentum was too strong and I lost my balance. As I fell, I heard Alec cry out. The child clapped her hands and squealed with delight, as if I'd done something very clever. Screaming, I reached out towards the Blood Stone, but the river was already sweeping me away. My last sight and sound was the child pointing and laughing at me, then the water surged over my head.

As it dragged me downstream towards the bridge, the river slammed me against submerged rocks. I clutched at every obstacle I hit, but I couldn't stop or even slow my passage through the water. The sun disappeared as the current swept me under the bridge and towards the bank. I came to a jarring halt and fought my way to the surface. Flailing around, I tore the skin of my arms, but I quickly established that I was being held by the strap of my shoulder bag which had caught on a branch of a fallen tree lodged among the rocks. Relief was soon dispelled as I realised the river continued to submerge me. Only by kicking furiously was I able to keep my head above water and my legs were beginning to tire already.

I threw up an arm, trying to grab a branch above me so I could hang and pull my head up out of the water, but I missed and slipped down again, falling through the loop made by the strap of my bag. I twisted violently, grabbing the strap that would keep me attached to something solid. It slid suddenly and my neck was jerked backwards. As the leather noose tightened round my throat, I pulled frantically, trying to loosen it, but my body turned again, spun by the force of the current, and the strap increased its stranglehold. I kicked with all my might and managed to raise my head above water long enough to gulp down some air. Above me in the gloomy shadows under the bridge, I saw something hanging from a branch of the dead tree, something that looked like another strap, another small bag. But it wasn't a bag, it was a camera. Coral's camera. It had hung there, in its nylon case, for seven years.

I reached up again, caught hold of the thick shoulder strap and pulled on it. It yielded, then held. It bore some of my weight while I tried to free my neck with my other hand. Tugging with useless frozen fingers, I managed to loosen the leather's deadly hold, but I couldn't free myself. I tried to scream for help, but no sound came from my swollen throat.

Above the roar of the river, I suddenly heard a machine start up, not far away. I couldn't place the sound, then realised it was the whine of a chain saw. The noise stopped suddenly and beyond the arch of the bridge, I saw a tree slowly descend into the water, its topmost branches reaching out into the middle of the river. As it hit the water, there was a backwash and my head was submerged again.

As the water subsided, I heard a voice shouting my name. I turned and looked upstream. Alec was in the water, trying hard to swim towards me, but he was being swept towards the middle of the river. I thought he was going to sail past, but he plunged towards me, shouting, 'Kick out your legs! Towards me!' I obeyed and felt him grab my foot, then grasp my leg. As his weight pulled me down, the strap tightened round my neck again. He saw what was happening and quickly clawed his way over to the dead tree. He looked at me, horrified, then with one hand tried, as I'd tried, to loosen the strap that was biting into my neck. He gave up and reached down into the water. He appeared to be struggling with his sock but after a moment he produced a small knife, his *sgian dubh*.

He sliced through the strap of my bag and loosened its hold round my neck, shouting, 'Hold tight to the tree now.' He swept dark, wet curls out of his eyes and said, 'Here's what we do. We're going to stay together and we're going to float downstream till we hit that tree. Ferg is sitting on it and he's going to help us. So what I want you to do is this: just float down with the current. I'll be holding you and we're going to travel on our backs to protect our eyes from the tree. You keep yours closed, OK? It'll be like life-saving. I'll put my arm round your neck – like this – and your body will lie on top of mine. D'you understand, Jenny?' I found I couldn't speak, so I nodded. 'If we stick together, we'll be heavy and move more slowly. I'll be able to steer us towards the tree. The important thing is to stay still and stay together. Just act like you're dead.'

'That,' I croaked, 'won't be difficult.' My voice sounded strange and harsh, as if it belonged to someone else.

Alec's smile was brave, if not genuine. I realised then how afraid he was, afraid his plan wouldn't work, but I was too exhausted to care. I just wanted to sleep for ever. He shook me and said, 'Jenny, look at me! I'm going to take you down now, then we're going to hit that tree.'

It occurred to me then that, quite possibly, Alec and I were both about to die. But there was something he needed to know, something he shouldn't blame himself for. I opened my mouth to speak but the words wouldn't come. Clinging to the branch with one arm, I pointed above my head, to where Coral's camera dangled. He looked up, craning his neck. I saw him swallow, then his white, wet face seemed to turn grey. Unaccountably, I started to weep. 'The little girl... Could you see her? It was Meredith, wasn't it? She wanted to kill me too.'

He put a hand up to my face. 'Och, wheesht now! I have my wee blade. She cannot harm me and I won't let her harm you.' His words were defiant, but his dark eyes were blank with shock. 'Come on, Jenny, we can do this! Are you ready?'

I nodded, wincing at the pain in my neck. Alec worked his way behind me, holding on to the tree roots and I felt a sense of relief as the relative warmth of his body met the chill of mine. He put an arm round my neck, like a wrestler and said in my ear, 'Get ready to let go when I say so. But don't kick or use your arms. Just play dead. I'm your life raft, OK?' His left arm tightened round my neck as his hand gripped my shoulder. He pulled me back towards him and I felt his body floating underneath mine. 'Let go, Jenny. This is it.'

The gnarled branch that had preserved my life for the last few minutes slipped from my fingers and we moved off through the water, alarmingly fast. Underneath me Alec was kicking his legs, frantically trying to steer us against the current and towards the river bank. I lay on my back, motionless as instructed, staring up at a cloudless sky. It was a fine day to drown. Had it been a day like this when Coral had died? A large bird swooped into my field of vision and hovered above us, apparently still, apart from the delicate flick of its tail. I recognised the red kite and for who knows what reason, I started to cry again. The warmth of my tears startled, then comforted me.

Alec cried out in pain as we came to an abrupt halt, then he shouted in my ear, 'Grab a branch and hold tight.' I twisted in the water, impaling my arm on a broken twig. 'Work your way along the tree. Towards the bank. Can you see Ferg? When he can reach you, he'll pull you in.'

I stared at Alec, stupefied with cold. Blood was pouring from a wound on the side of his head. 'You're hurt,' I said.

'I'm fine. Move, Jenny! Work your way across but keep your eyes closed as much as you can. It will protect them from the branches. *Feel* your way across. I'm right behind you. You're going to be OK now.'

I clawed my way along the fallen tree and as the branches got thicker, I felt safer. Eventually I felt another pair of hands – warm hands – grab my bleeding arms and I opened my eyes to see Fergus, white-faced, sitting astride the trunk of the tree, his legs dangling in the water. He pulled and Alec pushed until I heaved myself out of the water and collapsed, clinging to the tree trunk where I think I would have lain until Doomsday, but the fallen tree lurched suddenly and Fergus yelled at me to move.

While he helped Alec out of the water, I crawled up the sloping tree trunk until I reached the riverbank, then both men scrambled after me. Just as Alec reached dry land, the tree, freed of our weight, began to shift, then, like a ship being launched, it slipped into the middle of the river and floated downstream, bumping and turning as it thrashed against the rocks.

The three of us stood on the river bank, dripping water and blood, shivering convulsively. Alec put his arms round me and Fergus put his arms round us both. Nobody spoke. I was too tired even to cry.

Chapter Twenty

Looking back, I can see exactly how things went wrong for Alec and me. One man went into the river, another came out. Alec emerged knowing Meredith had bullied his wife from beyond the grave, then lured her into the river by preying upon a childless woman's instinct to protect the vulnerable. Meredith had let Coral drown for no reason other than spite.

As he carried me back to the castle – Fergus offered, but Alec just shook his head – he must have realised Meredith had tried to kill me in the same way so that he would know Coral's death was neither an accident nor suicide. If Meredith had succeeded in her murderous plan, Alec would never have believed lightning could strike twice. But even though she'd failed to drown me, Alec still got the message. He'd seen his wife's camera dangling from a branch under the bridge. Would-be suicides don't leave home with a camera.

From that day on, Alec was inaccessible to me, as if he were behind some sort of invisible screen. He'd always seemed guarded and I understood why, but after he saved my life, he became distant. I sensed a deep reservoir of anger in him and I suspected the only way he could deal with it was to keep himself reined in, aloof, unresponsive – to me, or anyone else.

Zelda put it down to a knock on the head that required several stitches. Fergus attributed it to post-traumatic stress. Only I had any idea what was really going on in Alec's mind and even I had to guess because he wouldn't talk about it. What I didn't guess was that Alec, broken-hearted, angry and defeated, had decided Cauldstane must be sold. Not to save money. To save lives.

After I was rescued, Fergus rang for an ambulance, summoned the family and we all waited in the armoury. It was the warmest place. Alec and I sat huddled by the furnace, wrapped in blankets brought by a shocked and silent Wilma. Zelda was voluble and asked too many questions. Fergus did his best to field them, but since he had no idea why I'd been standing in the middle of the river, he could say little to satisfy Zelda's curiosity. I was incapable of speech and Alec sat with his eyes closed, bleeding steadily from a gash on his temple. Sholto was calm and business-like administering First Aid, reassuring Alec that it was "just a nasty cut", but he'd better get it seen to.

When Sholto announced that Alec and I would be kept in hospital overnight, ("Bang on the head. Could be concussion."), Wilma trotted off back to the castle. She returned with two bulging holdalls. Mine was packed with a change of clothes, a pair of shoes to replace the ones I'd lost in the river, a nightie and a comb. I assumed she'd performed a similar service for Alec. I gave her a wordless hug, but Alec didn't respond. He didn't even look inside his bag.

As we clambered into the ambulance, Sholto said, for my benefit, I'm sure, 'Don't worry now. You'll be in good hands.'

He was right, of course. As the ambulance sped off in the direction of Inverness, I was overwhelmed with a sense of relief that I was leaving Cauldstane – and therefore Meredith – behind; relief that Alec was with me; that we were both safe and would remain so for at least another twelve hours, maybe more.

It had been a narrow escape. But we *had* escaped.

The following day, Zelda collected us from hospital. On the drive back to Cauldstane she told me I'd had several telephone calls, all from the same man. Struggling to conceal her curiosity, she told me a Mr Sheridan had rung three times. He was concerned that I wasn't answering my mobile (which had joined my shoes in the river). Zelda explained there'd been an accident and that I was in hospital. Pressed for details, she told him I'd fallen into the river and almost drowned. Rupert had apparently sounded distressed and asked if he could ring back for updates. He'd then dictated a message which Zelda produced from her coat pocket and handed to me. I unfolded the piece of paper and read, "I received your letter and have given the contents a great deal of thought. I'll be in touch shortly. In the meantime, I shall be praying for you.'

I thanked Zelda for her trouble but had to ignore her sidelong look of enquiry. There was nothing I could say about Rupert or his carefully-worded message that wouldn't lead to questions, so we drove back to Cauldstane in silence.

Alec didn't speak throughout the journey. It didn't occur to me then to wonder what he might have made of that conversation.

Back at Cauldstane, I made my excuses and said I needed to go and check my email, but on the way to my room I picked up one of the house phones. Sitting on the bed, already exhausted, I rang Rupert. I got his voicemail, so I left a message to say I'd lost my mobile, but he should wait for me to call. I told him I would ring back in an hour, then on the hour until I got through.

I returned the phone to its cradle, then knocked on Alec's door, but there was no answer. I assumed he was already back at work. The thought of negotiating stairs and solicitous family members on my way to the armoury was sufficient deterrent. I went back to my room, lay on the bed and stared into space. I tried to think, but my mind just stuck in a groove, dwelling on the same irrational thought. I didn't believe in God – any god – but it was a source of inexplicable comfort to know Rupert Sheridan was praying for me.

When I was sure Sholto had gone for his nap and Zelda was ensconced with Classic FM, I took one of the house phones and a notebook to the library where I curled up in a chair by the fireside. The phone rang only once before Rupert picked it up.

'Jen? Is that you?' It sounded almost accusatory.

'Yes, it's me.'

'I've been so worried! Are you all right? Your people have been very tight-lipped about what happened.'

'That's because they don't really know what happened. On the face of it, I walked into a river and almost drowned.'

'You walked into a river?'

'Yes.'

'Why?'

'It's a long story.'

'Mrs Fontaine said "the boys" had rescued you.'

'The boys are grown men. Alec and Fergus. Oh—' I slipped back into professional mode. 'I really can't say any more. Unless...'

'Unless what?'

'Unless you're coming up to help us.'

'Jen, I can't. I did explain. It's the responsibility of your local priest.'

My heart plummeted and I fought back tears with indignation. 'Rupert, I nearly drowned!'

There was a moment's silence, then, his voice unsteady, Rupert said, 'Are you saying your accident was... connected with the ghost?'

'Yes.' I stared into the fire, trying to recall the scene – something I'd experienced, but could neither believe nor comprehend. 'I saw a little girl in trouble, standing on a rock in the middle of the river. She was crying and I thought she might fall in and drown. So I rang for help, then I went in to help her. There were stepping stones, you see, across the river. But... one of them wasn't real. Nor was the little girl. Only I could see her. No, that's not true. I think Alec might have seen her too. But his brother couldn't.'

'And you think this child was the ghost?'

'I know she was.'

'Jen, I'm having trouble keeping up. In your letter you said this spirit was your subject's dead wife.'

'They're one and the same. I think Meredith can manifest herself in other forms. And I have reason to believe another member of the family saw this child seven years ago.'

'Have you compared notes?'

'I can't. She's dead. She died the way I was meant to die. So you see, Rupert, you *have* to help us. It's really serious. I think we need an exorcism or something.'

'Oh, no, they're extremely rare. Outside Hollywood,' Rupert added pointedly.

'Well, we have to do something!' I heard the note of rising hysteria in my voice and reached automatically for my notebook. I tried to shoehorn my brain into fact-finding mode. 'OK, you're the expert. Tell me what we're up against here. How can the local priest help?'

Rupert explained the fundamentals of the Church's deliverance ministry in his patient voice, assuring me of its effectiveness.

185

Meanwhile I took notes, as if I believed every word. When he'd finished, I said, 'So we *are* in trouble then?'

'I think you might be. There definitely seems to be something going on. Which is why I can't help you, Jen. You must ask the local man first. If you draw a blank there, I'll reconsider, but these things have to be done properly. I know it sounds like bureaucratic red tape, but there's the issue of follow-up pastoral care. People often need support afterwards. We pray with them, or just lend a sympathetic ear until things settle down again.'

'But as far as I know, this family isn't religious. Well, the housekeeper is a churchgoer and I think Zelda – the woman you spoke to on the phone – she sometimes goes with her, but I don't think any of the men are.'

'Even if they aren't, the priest might have local knowledge that would be valuable. If it's a rural community, he might know the family socially. That would be a start. I would just be... an outsider.'

I gripped the phone, angry now – not with Rupert, with Meredith. 'There are lives at stake here, Rupert, and one of them is mine.'

'But *why*? You've only been there a matter of weeks. Do you know why you've been singled out?'

'Oh, yes. And I can show you proof. She sent me a death threat. Well, as good as.'

'In Heaven's name, why?'

I took a deep breath. The truth was always simplest and Rupert deserved nothing less. 'Because I've fallen in love with a man who rejected her. And she doesn't want anyone else to have him. I think she probably wants him dead too.'

There was a long silence at the other end of the phone, after which Rupert said, 'I shall pray for you all. But my advice is to contact the local priest as soon as possible. If he doesn't give satisfaction, then get back to me.'

'You'll come?'

'If for some reason he can't deal with it, yes, I'll come.'

'Thank you!'

'Keep me posted, won't you? I shall worry unless I get regular bulletins.'

'As soon as I get a replacement phone, I'll text. But I think I'd better get off the phone now. I can hear someone coming upstairs.'

186

'Before you go, Jen – may I ask?... This chap you say you've fallen for. Does he feel the same way about you?'

There was another long silence, at my end this time. 'I don't know. Something's going on between us, but I'm not sure what. The ghost has rather got in the way. Which is exactly what she intended.'

'Well, I hope you'll both stay safe. I'll remember him in my prayers. Is it Alec or Fergus?'

'Alec. He saved my life. But that isn't why—'

'No, of course. I understand. You'll stay in touch?'

'Yes, I will. Goodbye, Rupert. And thank you.'

'Goodbye, Jen. God bless.'

I decided it was time I talked to Alec. As I crossed the courtyard, heading for the armoury, my legs still weak from my ordeal in the river, I tried to order my thoughts. What I was about to suggest as a rescue strategy was unlikely to meet with his approval. It could provoke derision or even incur his wrath, but as I saw it, we had no other option.

I knocked on the door – superfluously, as Alec was hammering and would be wearing ear defenders – then I walked in. The armoury was dimly lit, as usual. A smith needs to see the changing colour of the red-hot metal so he can gauge its temperature and that was easier to assess in low light. As I entered, the shaft of daylight from the open door alerted Alec to my arrival. He looked up from his anvil, then downed tools and removed gloves, safety glasses and ear defenders, carefully avoiding the dressing on his temple. He was pale, dishevelled and looked very tired. After a moment, he smiled, as if he'd just remembered what his face should be doing.

It wasn't an encouraging start, but I launched into my speech. 'Alec, can I talk to you about what's happening at Cauldstane? What we can do about it.'

He turned away and headed towards the kitchenette where I heard him fill the kettle. 'I've done what can be done,' he called out. 'And as you can see, it isn't working.' He emerged again and leaned against the partition wall, his arms folded across his chest. 'But there's no evidence Meredith wants to harm anyone but me and the women I get involved with. So I think it's pretty obvious what we have to do. I have to be careful. And you...' His eyes swerved away from mine. 'You, Jenny, have to leave.' He retreated to the kitchenette and I heard the clattering of spoons and mugs.

'You can't make me go, Alec.'

'No, you're right, I can't. But Sholto can.'

'So you're prepared to tell him what's been going on?'

'No. I'm going to tell him we have to put Cauldstane on the market.' He emerged carrying two mugs of coffee and tried to hand one to me, but I was too stunned to take it. 'D'you not want coffee?' I took the mug and stared at it absently, watching the spiral of scum as it rotated. 'If I do that,' Alec continued, 'it will put you out of a job, I'm afraid. The main reason he was wanting to write the book was to raise cash, so we could hang on here. It was a daft wee idea, but Ferg and I humoured him. He's had a grand life and it deserves to be recorded. But if I back Ferg's plan to sell up, it's unlikely Sholto will hold out against both of us. He knows the writing's on the wall for us financially. But I'll see you're paid in full. It's not fair you should lose out over this. But you *will* have to leave, Jenny.'

I was speechless. When I finally found my voice, I said, 'So that's what you're prepared to do to appease Meredith? Sabotage your father's book. Put Fergus out of a job. And Wilma. And me. Abandon the business you've built up here to start over somewhere else. Sell up the historic MacNab seat — to some foreigner probably, who'll use it as a bijou hunting lodge! Good grief, Alec MacNab, have you no *pride*?'

'Aye, I've pride enough and to spare!' He set his mug down with a bang that chipped the base and spilled coffee on the workbench. 'But I'm not stupid, nor am I reckless. I've seen what Meredith can do. No one else is going to die on my watch.'

'So you admit you're beaten?'

He flinched, as if my words had stung him physically. 'Not beaten. But I think it's time for a tactical retreat.'

'No, it's time to fight back, Alec! There's a way we can deliver Cauldstane from Meredith's evil. I've been doing some research.' I set down my mug and braced myself before continuing. 'I've been talking to a priest.'

'A *priest*?' His laugh was sardonic. 'You'll be suggesting

188

exorcism next! We might live in a sixteenth-century castle, Jenny, but that doesn't mean we live in the dark ages.'

'It's called deliverance ministry and it isn't exorcism. Exorcism is actually very rare and it's only used in cases of demonic possession. That's not what we're dealing with here. This is an unquiet spirit who haunts the place where she lived. She died a sudden and violent death and she has... unfinished business. In cases like these – and they're surprisingly common apparently, even though no one ever talks about them – the Church's ancient rituals can be very effective. I know it sounds unlikely, but I have a friend who's a minister and he's done this kind of thing before. It's worked elsewhere. It might work here. Surely it's worth a try?'

Alec drank some coffee, considering, then said, 'What does it entail?'

'In the first instance, Sholto would have to talk to the local priest.'

'Sholto *doesn't* talk to the local priest. Ever.'

'Why?'

'No idea. They fell out years ago. And I don't think it was a theological argument. In any case, Sholto doesn't even know his home is haunted.'

'I'm not so sure. He told me he's aware of Meredith's presence at times, but he dismissed it as a delusion. He also described her to me as "a pernicious influence" on the family. I think he might be prepared to believe it's a genuine case of haunting. If I tell him who I saw in the river—'

'He'll think you're deranged.'

'But you saw her too, didn't you?' Alec was silent, then he nodded. 'What did you see? Tell me.'

Staring into space, his eyes dull with defeat, he said, 'A wee girl. With dark curly hair. She was standing in the middle of the river, on a stone. And she was watching you as you came out to help her.'

'What colour was her dress?'

'Red. And she was wearing long white socks. She looked like she was dressed up for a party.' He turned and looked at me. 'Is that what you saw?'

'Yes.'

'And you think Sholto would believe us?'

'He might. There's a lot of other evidence. Zelda told me Coral used to hear the harpsichord. So do I. You and I both saw the little girl. And I've got those messages on my laptop.'

'You could have faked those.'

'Of course, but why would I do that?' He didn't reply. 'Why would I fake my own near-fatal accident? And what about Coral? We both saw her camera. It wasn't suicide.'

'Why would Sholto believe us?'

'Why *wouldn't* he?'

'Because it sounds completely crazy!'

'Yes, it does, and I have a history of going crazy, but you don't. And you're his son. He knows you don't want to give up on Cauldstane. In fact, I doubt he'd believe you if you told him you wanted to sell up. He's pretty astute and I suspect you're a rotten liar.' Alec seemed less certain now, so I pressed home my advantage. 'I think Sholto will believe us if we're completely honest with him.'

'But it would mean telling him about us. I can't see that he'll buy it unless we explain her motives. He knew about Meredith and me, so I suppose he'll understand why Coral was hounded to death. But the real evidence – Meredith's hissy fit in your room, her attempt to drown you – we can only account for all that if we tell Sholto what's going on.'

'Well, if you tell him your first idea was to sell up the family seat to ensure my personal safety, I think he'll get the general idea, don't you? And I doubt he'll have any trouble believing I'm smitten with you.'

He looked at me directly then and his dark eyes flickered, reflecting the flames dancing in the furnace. 'Are you?'

'I suppose I must be if I'm prepared to give this religious mumbo-jumbo a whirl. But it has to be worth a shot, doesn't it?'

'I doubt he'll agree to it, but he'll give us a fair hearing.' He shrugged. 'We can but try.'

'Thank you!' I flung myself at him and, after a moment's hesitation, his powerful arms closed round me. We stood holding each other and neither of us spoke. I felt safe, protected by the warmth and strength of Alec's body. Shivering with emotion, I clung to him more tightly. He murmured something in my ear – my name, I think, my real name, Imogen, as if he was trying it out on his lips.

190

'I didn't believe in ghosts before I came here,' I said, my voice faint. 'And I don't think I've ever believed in God. But I do believe in you, Alec. And Cauldstane. And the MacNabs.' I laid my palms on his chest and looked up into his haggard face. 'We can do this! I know we can. Just believe in me. *Please.*'

He released me and took my hands in his. 'I do, Jenny. But I also have good reason to believe in the powers of darkness. And I fear they may be stronger than you, me and Cauldstane put together.'

'Zelda said if you live in fear, you fear to live.'

'Did she now? Well, that's probably true.'

'We mustn't be afraid, Alec. That's the real power Meredith has over us. The power to make us live in fear.'

'The only thing I fear is losing more loved ones. I lost my mother, my wife and my unborn child. And I nearly lost you too. I'd rather send you away than have you taken away. And that's what I'll say to my father. Leave it with me, Jenny. I'll choose my moment.'

Letting go of my hands, he turned away, picked up the rod of cooling metal he'd been hammering and thrust it back into the furnace. He raked the hot coals over the metal and stood staring silently into the fire.

It seemed there was nothing more to say, so I let myself out, closing the door behind me. The chilly autumn air came as a shock after the cosy fug of the armoury. As I made my way across the ancient cobblestones, back to the castle, it started to rain.

Chapter Twenty-one

With my head down to avoid the rain, I almost collided with Fergus on his way out. He held the back door open for me with a solicitous smile and, as I wiped my feet, I decided to seize the moment. Alec's talk of selling up had persuaded me other avenues must be explored, and urgently.

'Thanks, Fergus. Have you got a moment? Just a quick question.'

He removed his tweed cap and said, 'How can I help?'

'You know we were talking about Cauldstane valuables on the bridge, before... before my accident. You mentioned some paintings in store.'

'Aye, there are a fair few. Were you wanting to see them?'

'Oh, I don't want to trouble you. I just wondered if I could have a browse on my own? I'll be very careful. I do know a bit about paintings. I had dealings with a famous art forger.' He raised an eyebrow. 'All perfectly legal, I hasten to add.'

'Let me guess – you were writing his "autobiography"?'

'I couldn't possibly comment,' I said with a smile. 'But I did pick up quite a lot from him. That's one of the joys of my peculiar job. You're always learning something new.'

'I think our pictures are all genuine. Genuine rubbish mostly, including a few ancient family portraits done by travelling artists. You know the sort of thing I mean?'

'Oh, yes. The artist would arrive with a body already painted on the canvas, then the sitter's head would be painted in to finish it off.'

'Aye, we've one or two of those. They remind me of a book I had as a kid called *Heads, Bodies and Legs*. You'll see what I mean when you get up there. I suggested to Sholto we should hang them, just to give folk a laugh.'

'Where can I find them?'

'Go right up to the top floor. Have you ever been up there?'

'No. That would be the third floor?'

'Aye. There are a few rooms up there which we never use, apart from the Long Attic. Alec set that up as a gym and fencing studio. If you've ever heard music and wondered where it was coming from, that would be Alec or me in the gym.' I refrained from telling Fergus I had indeed heard music, but it had nothing to do with the brothers keeping fit. 'The Long Attic is at the east end of the corridor,' he continued. 'Next door is a lumber room where we store spare furniture, paintings and centuries of junk. We should create a museum. Folk might pay money to look at it. Or maybe we should just have the mother of all car boot sales.'

'If I get lost up there, I won't be barging in on anyone will I?'

'No, there's just the old nursery and some spare rooms.'

'Right. I'll go and have a snoop round, if that's OK?'

'When you get to the top of the staircase, turn left. You'll be facing the Long Attic. Have fun.'

'Thanks.'

As I set off along the corridor, Fergus called out, 'And don't be alarmed by the tiger.'

I wheeled round. *'Tiger?'*

'He's stuffed. Other kids had rocking horses. Alec and I rode a tiger,' Fergus said proudly. He turned up the collar of his jacket, pulled his cap down over his eyes and headed out into the rain. As he slammed the door behind him, I started the long climb up to the third floor.

When I got to the top, I turned left, as instructed. The door to the attic was open and I looked in. New floorboards had been laid and the room had been painted white, presumably to maximize the light coming from a series of small windows. At one end there was an impressive-looking sound system and an array of fearsome gym equipment and weights that made me think of torture chambers from earlier times. The rest of the very long room was given over to fencing. There were foils and epées in a wall-mounted rack. Masks and a couple of fencing outfits hung on a coat stand. The room smelled sweaty, male and foreign.

I turned away and looked for the lumber room. Fergus' instructions had been clear but incomplete. There were two rooms adjacent to the attic, one on each side. I had no idea which contained the paintings, but he'd assured me none of the rooms was occupied. Nevertheless I knocked before opening a door.

The room was completely dark and I had to grope on the wall for a light switch. When I flicked it, a crystal chandelier burst into dazzling light. Blinking, I realised this wasn't the lumber room. I'd stumbled upon some sort of shrine — a shrine to execrably bad taste.

As I entered, I was thrown by the sight of people emerging from the shadows and I stepped back in alarm. So did they. Laughing at myself, I realised the room was full of mirrors, some of them full length. The windows were totally obscured by burgundy velvet curtains of an Edwardian opulence. Swagged, frilled and embellished with gold tassels and braid, they reminded me of the Royal Opera House in Covent Garden. The stage curtains were the same colour and, when hoisted, fell into similarly extravagant folds.

The walls were covered in red damask, badly stained in places from a leaking roof. The effect was tacky rather than luxurious and I wondered if the mirrors had been hung to conceal more stains. The centrepiece of the room was a brass bedstead covered with a gold satin bedspread and piled with velvet cushions. A few threadbare stuffed toys perched incongruously on top. Above the bed hung a black and white photographic portrait of a woman, apparently at a masked ball, wearing a gown that resembled the curtains. The effect was just as depressing.

Most of one wall was taken up by an outsize walnut armoire. Every flat surface was decorated with bric-a-brac and photographs, some of them autographed. There were scrapbooks of yellowing press cuttings and theatre programmes blistered with damp. All of them were for operatic and concert performances given decades ago.

Fans, shawls, scarves and a variety of ladies' hats hung on pegs and wig stands. Good luck cards were tucked round the ornate mirror of a dressing table cluttered with silver-backed brushes, make-up, bottles of scent and ancient tins of French talc. A posy of dried flowers sat in a china jug. They might once have been rose buds. It was hard to tell. The flowers were now almost grey with age.

A dim corner of the room was fenced off with an oriental screen and I padded across the deep pile carpet to peep behind. I stepped back quickly, thinking I'd discovered someone in hiding, but it was a tailor's dummy wearing a Japanese kimono. Someone had propped up a parasol on its shoulder. The screen also concealed a silver drinks tray and a two-bar electric fire. On the wall above was a poster for *Madama Butterfly*, starring Maria Callas.

This was Meredith MacNab's bedroom. She'd been dead for twelve years but no one had ever cleared it. I was sure if I'd opened the magnificent wardrobe doors, I would have found her clothes hanging there, smelling of the stale *Opium* perfume that still sat on her dressing table.

The room was remarkable in itself, but even more remarkable was the fact that no surface was dusty. The room looked perfectly clean, though it smelled musty. Turning to a window that probably hadn't been opened for more than a decade, I dragged a curtain aside to let daylight in. The window panes were crusted with dirt on the outside, but inside, the deep sill was spotless and decorated with yet more photographs, plus a motley collection of twee china ornaments.

One of the photographs drew my eye and I picked it up. It showed a little girl at a birthday party – her own, presumably, as she was cutting a cake with eight candles. She was dark-haired, pretty and wearing a red dress. It was the child I'd seen by the river. I was looking at Meredith, aged eight, posing for the camera and wielding a large knife in a determined way. I dropped the picture frame as if my fingers had been burned.

I suppose the panic that seized me then was some sort of flashback. Spinning round, I saw myself reflected over and over in all the mirrors, my pale hair catching the light from the crystal chandelier. As I swayed, unsteady on my feet, the mirrored figures appeared to dance, leaning this way and that. I moved away from the window and held on to a bookcase till I felt calmer.

When my breathing was steady again, I examined the bookcase. There was a collection of leather bound books, journals of the kind I'd coveted as a teenager, with crisp cream pages and marbled endpapers. Meredith had probably bought them in Italy. I opened several, just scanning the pages. Each was filled with her flamboyant hand. She'd written in thick black ink with much underlining and copious use of exclamation marks. Alec's name caught my eye and I was tempted to read what she'd written.

Instead I closed the book.

Was it an invasion of privacy to read the diary of a dead person, someone you'd never known, who was a minor celebrity? And did you need to consider these niceties if the author of the journal had tried to kill you? I decided I owed Meredith MacNab nothing, not even respect, and I flipped open the journal again. The entries were dated 1999, the year before Alec's marriage. The year before Meredith's death.

If you'd asked me, I would have said Meredith could sink no lower in my estimation, but by the time I'd read a page of the rambling sexual fantasies of a middle-aged woman, lusting after her much younger stepson, my contempt for the woman was mixed with disgust and disbelief. I turned the pages, hoping to find something less degenerate, but Alec was the subject of most entries. Variety was occasionally provided by a spiteful rant about Sholto or Coral.

Sickened, I closed the book and as I replaced it on the shelf, I noticed the spines had dates. I selected another volume, 1982. The year of Meredith's marriage to Sholto. She would have been about thirty. Skimming the pages, I found accounts of shopping sprees, wedding lists, dinner parties and performances. (She always recorded the number of curtain calls she'd taken.) There were badly-executed sketches for a wedding-dress with fabric swatches sellotaped alongside. She'd cut out the announcement of her marriage in the *Times* and pasted it in. I looked for any mention of Sholto, anything to indicate she'd once loved him, but I searched in vain. The journal was devoid of romance, despite its preoccupation with a wedding. Another man's name began to appear as frequently as Sholto's, then more frequently. Soon I was reading a catalogue of assignations in which Meredith described her sexual exploits with her lover.

I shut the journal and put it back on the shelf. I felt a pressing need to wash my hands and it wasn't because the books were grubby — at least, not on the outside. Like everything else in the room, they'd been dusted recently. By Wilma, presumably. I hoped to God she'd never opened them. Knowing Wilma, she would never have indulged her curiosity about the mistress of whom she'd been so fond. I was relieved to think she'd been spared hideous disillusionment.

196

There was a sound on the stairs and I recognised it as the distinctive tap and shuffle of Sholto with his stick. Confused, I stood paralysed, wondering what to do for the best. I could see no reason why Sholto should enter Meredith's room. It seemed equally unlikely he was making his way to the gym. If I emerged now, it might startle him. I decided to stay put. If he found me, I would just tell the truth. I'd been looking for the store room and had got lost.

To my dismay, the footsteps approached the door, then it swung open. Sholto stood on the threshold, breathless and clutching a poker at head height.

'Jenny – it's *you*! Thought it must be burglars. Knew it wasn't Wilma – she's in the kitchen – but I could hear someone moving about up here. I'm underneath, you see. I heard creaking floorboards and thought I'd better come up and investigate.'

'I'm sorry, Sholto. Fergus gave me directions for the store room. I wanted to look at some of your paintings. But then I took a wrong turning. I hope I didn't alarm you.'

'Not really, I was just puzzled, that's all. Thought Meredith must have come back to haunt me!' I didn't know what to say and in the hiatus, Sholto gazed around the room. 'I expect you're wondering why I never cleared out all her stuff. Especially as I told you I was planning to divorce her when she died.'

'You don't have to account to me for your actions, Sholto. After all, it's not something that's likely to feature in the book.'

'But you must have wondered.'

'Well, yes. I was surprised to see the room so well preserved. And *clean*. Wilma, I suppose?'

'I don't ask her to do it. But she insists. She was devoted to her mistress. The only one of us who was. But Meredith was quite good with servants and that's how she treated Wilma, who didn't seem to mind. Wilma saw Meredith as a celebrity. Someone with a special gift. God-given. Which is how Meredith saw herself, of course.' He surveyed the ghastly room, barely able to conceal his distaste. 'No doubt Wilma found all these folderols... *glamorous*.'

'Was it just too painful to face clearing out?'

He sighed and said, 'I couldn't handle all the guilt.'

'*Gilt*? It's certainly not a style of décor I admire.'

Sholto chuckled. 'No, my dear. *Guilt*. I felt guilty. I mean, just look at it all! You'd have to get rid of *everything*. There's nothing here of any value, but it meant the world to her. It *was* her world. Meredith was always on stage, even in here. But she was miscast as a country wife. *Femme fatale* suited her better. I didn't want to sift through the seedy remnants of that life, nor could I entrust the job to anyone else.' He waved his stick in the direction of the bookcase. 'Those diaries, for example. They should be burned. Don't open them, Jenny, not unless you're very broadminded.'

'You know you could just get a firm to take everything away?'

'After I'd destroyed all the incriminating evidence, you mean? Yes, that's what I should have done. What I should still do. Lord knows, I don't want the boys to have to deal with it when I'm gone.'

'Would you like me to make a start for you? I don't think there's anything here worth selling apart from the furniture, but the clothes could be given to charity. I could sort them out for you. There's quite a vogue now for vintage clothing and jewellery. If you don't want to keep any of the journals or scrapbooks, what about the photos?'

'Burn the lot, Jenny. If you'd be so kind. I don't know who else to ask and I can't face doing it myself. Scared of what I might find. What I know already is bad enough. Perhaps if we get rid of all her stuff,' he muttered, 'we might be able to get rid of *her*.'

I turned sharply and looked at him. 'What do you mean?'

'Oh, nothing. It's just a tired old man's paranoia. I sense her still, you see. Her presence. Especially in here. And it's not a comfortable feeling, let me tell you! Meredith could be malicious. Vengeful, even. I thought her death would be the end of... well, of all the unpleasantness, but sometimes I feel as if she's still tormenting me.'

I pulled out the stool from under the dressing table and pushed it towards him. 'Why don't you sit down? You must be feeling tired after your climb upstairs.'

'Thank you, my dear. You're very kind.'

I relieved him of the poker which I stood in an empty waste paper bin. Once he was seated, I swallowed and, trying to sound casual, said, 'Actually, there's something I'd like to discuss with you and it relates to what you've just said. About Meredith's "presence".'

He looked up. 'You don't mean to say you can sense it too?'

'Yes, I do. So does Alec. And although I don't think she's

198

consciously aware of it, I believe Zelda has also been affected by Meredith's ghost.'

'Ghost? It's surely not as bad as that!' He searched my face, but I said nothing. '*Is* it?'

'Do you believe in ghosts, Sholto?'

He didn't answer immediately, but gave me a shrewd look, then choosing his words carefully, he said, 'Let's say I have an open mind. I know plenty of people – quite sane – who say they've seen or heard a ghost. I myself have seen some strange things in my time. On expeditions you put it down to the silence and the isolation. Or starvation. You think you must be seeing things. But I will say this. Much as I loved her, I've never sensed my first wife. And I never, ever thought Cauldstane might be haunted before Meredith died. *Cursed*, yes. There's the ancient MacNab curse and it's blighted many a relationship, one way and another, like poor Coral and Alec. But it was only after Meredith died that odd things started to happen... Have you seen something then?'

'I believe so. And I've heard things. And I can't account for what I've seen and heard. So I've been talking to a man who knows about these things. I didn't mention where I'm staying. In any case, you can rely on him to be totally discreet. He's a Church of England minister. I said I wanted to know if there was anything one could do in a situation like this. To bring peace to a troubled household.'

'What did he say?'

'He said it's something the Church can deal with. It's called deliverance ministry. It's not like exorcism. It's a question of blessing a place with prayer and holy water. There's nothing sensational about it,' I said, glancing round at the heavily-curtained room. 'He said the main thing is to let in the light.'

'Is that so?'

'It might be worth trying. If you were open to the idea.'

'I see.' Sholto was thoughtful for a moment, then said, 'What was it the Bard said? *There are more things in Heaven and Earth, Horatio, than are dreamt of in your philosophy.* Probably very true. I've never been a particularly imaginative man, but I hope I've always been open-minded... Was your fellow offering to come and sort us out?' Sholto hesitated. 'Is he – er – expensive?'

'Oh, I'm sure there's no charge, but my friend said the matter is very serious and must be dealt with by your local priest.'

Sholto looked blank for a moment, then started to laugh. 'Oh, dear me, no! That's quite out of the question!'

'You could trust him to be discreet. Apparently the Church is quite used to dealing with matters of this kind and they have people who are trained especially for it. But in the first instance, you have to approach your local priest. He will set the appropriate wheels in motion.'

'Haven't spoken to him in twenty years,' Sholto said, grim-faced now.

'I don't think that really matters. You don't even have to be a believer. They say deliverance ministry will work anyway.'

'I dare say, but James Kennedy will not be crossing the Cauldstane threshold in *my* lifetime.' Sholto's angry face softened. 'How Meredith would have enjoyed all this!' He looked up and addressed the portrait over the bed, the woman in a ball gown, smirking behind her harlequin mask. 'You might be dead, my dear, but you're certainly not forgotten.'

He struggled to his feet and tottered towards the door. Grasping the handle for support, he turned to face me. 'Jamie Kennedy was my minister and a friend. A bachelor. Perhaps not overburdened with intelligence, but a handsome devil. Loved music. He also loved Meredith.' Sholto waved his stick in the direction of the bookcase that housed the journals. 'November 1990, if you want the sordid details.'

He turned and left. A few moments later I heard the soft tap on the stairs as he made his painful descent.

Chapter Twenty-two

I rang Rupert to let him know that under no circumstances would the local minister be setting foot over Cauldstane's threshold. I didn't tell him why. He was dismayed and anxious on my behalf. This was a circumstance he hadn't foreseen and I could say nothing to account for Sholto's refusal, other than that it was a personal, not a religious matter.

I managed to convince Rupert I was in no immediate danger, but that wasn't really what I felt. I knew I *was* in danger and I believed Alec was too. This time Meredith's murderous plan had failed. Who knew what she might try next, and when? I understood why Alec wanted me to leave. I could even see why he wanted to sell up. Over the next few days I witnessed his steely determination to implement a simple but drastic plan. First he was going to cut me out of his life, then he was going to cut out Cauldstane.

I didn't flatter myself that the stillbirth of our relationship was a major loss for him, but observing his efforts to persuade Sholto to sell was like watching a man cut out his own heart.

So I mounted a counter-campaign. I didn't share my plans with Alec, who I felt sure was avoiding me. When we did cross paths, he was civil, but no more. I didn't tell him about my conversation with Sholto in Meredith's room. Alec had predicted his father would have nothing to do with the minister, so his lack of co-operation came as no surprise. I decided to spare Alec the reason for the estrangement. He hardly needed more evidence of Meredith's depravity, or the ways in which she'd hurt and humiliated the MacNabs.

Instead I talked to Fergus, Zelda and even Wilma about ways in which Cauldstane could be rescued financially, if not spiritually. If I could come up with an alternative scheme, perhaps Sholto would listen to me as well as Alec. If nothing else, my business plans might buy some time, time in which I could try to convince Alec that

Meredith could be beaten. Or if she couldn't, that he didn't have to concede defeat.

Not yet.

Taking a notebook, tape measure and my camera, I went back up to the third floor and found the lumber room. As I sorted through the fascinating and occasionally hideous junk, I could have done with a flashlight to augment the dismal light provided by a single bare light bulb. Generations of MacNabs appeared to have consigned their white elephants to the third floor and I was searching for anything that could be turned into money.

Zelda had told me Meredith found old paintings "depressing" and had banished many family portraits. These I found stacked against the wall, but far more interesting was a collection of assorted paintings wrapped carelessly in dust sheets. I lingered, amused, over a pair of his 'n' hers portraits done by the travelling painter Fergus had mentioned. I hoped the artist's fee had been as modest as his talent. The nineteenth-century MacNab and his lady had either both been blessed with massive shoulders and arms, or the artist had painted their elegant heads far too small. The effect was comic, yet somehow endearing. Mrs MacNab wore a slightly anxious expression that suggested she had less than complete confidence in the man painting her.

Next, I opened up a trunk that contained nothing but old clothes and an overpowering scent of mothballs, but another contained paintings, and of a superior quality. There was a set of small landscapes, very good and probably very old, by an artist whose name I couldn't read, but it looked Spanish. I transcribed the name as best I could and took photos of each canvas. I thought these might be worth something as a collection – not a life-changing amount admittedly, but if I could find a few assets that could be turned into cash, it might put new heart into the MacNab men. Fergus had said he could get started with a few cash injections and that's what I was hoping to find: valuables they'd overlooked, forgotten or didn't even know they had.

I got excited about an unsigned and probably unfinished portrait of a barely recognizable – and nude – Torquil MacNab. It looked like a Lucian Freud. Might he have known Torquil? Perhaps

Torquil had become ill before the portrait could be finished. He didn't look a well man in the picture, but that could be because it was painted by Freud. I carried the canvas out into the hall where it was lighter, took several photos and made a note to ask Sholto what he knew of the painting's provenance.

I continued to rummage until another painting stopped me dead. It was a portrait of a solemn young man, dressed in late eighteenth-century style, sitting in a chair, surrounded by a still life of books and papers. His hand rested on a brightly patterned Turkey rug. The painting looked slightly familiar, but I concluded that might be because it was in the style of Henry Raeburn, Scotland's greatest portrait painter. I looked for a signature. When I couldn't find one, my heart beat a little faster. Raeburn didn't sign his canvases, or at least only one is known to be signed. But surely even Meredith wouldn't have relegated a Raeburn to an attic? I looked for the characteristic single dab of white highlight on the tip of the nose that appears in all Raeburn's portraits. It was there.

Of course it could be a fake, or just a painting by an artist unknown to me. But I did know Raeburn's work and this canvas looked familiar, so I assumed it must be a copy. A pity, because an original would be worth a lot of money. Again, not enough to put Cauldstane in the black, but a significant amount nonetheless.

I photographed the canvas and made a note of its dimensions. Armed with my photos, notes and a consuming curiosity, I was ready to do some research and make some enquiries.

I headed downstairs intending to make myself a coffee, but as I approached the kitchen, I heard the snuffling sound of suppressed tears. It could only be Wilma and that put me in a quandary. She wouldn't want me to know she'd been crying. On the other hand, I didn't like to just walk away. I had a suspicion I knew why she was crying and the chances were, she knew more about the latest Cauldstane developments than I did. It would take a lot to make Wilma cry at work. Whatever news she'd been given must have been bad. Convinced no one should have to cry alone and hopeful that I could help, I knocked on the door.

'Wilma, can I come in?' I realised it was the first time I hadn't called her "Mrs Guthrie". I didn't wait for an answer and walked in.

She struggled to her feet and quickly pushed a hankie into the pocket of her apron. Avoiding my eye, she said, 'Can I get you some coffee, Miss Jenny?'

'Thank you, but how about you sit down and I'll make us both a cup? You look like you could use one. Or even something stronger.'

Her eyes filled with tears again and she sank back onto a kitchen chair. 'You're very kind, Miss Je—'

'It's just Jenny. Well, actually, it's Imogen, but Jenny will do. And if you don't mind, I'd like to call you Wilma, because I think of you as a friend now and I call my friends by their first names.'

A sad little smile twitched at the corners of her mouth. I thought I might be making some progress. As I waited for the kettle to boil, I said, 'How long have you been here, Wilma? Working for the MacNabs, I mean.'

'I've lived here all my life and I've been working for the MacNabs since 1968,' she said with a touch of pride. 'My mother, Annie Guthrie was Mr Torquil's cook and I used to help her and the housekeeper.'

'Your mother's name was Guthrie too?'

Wilma blushed. 'I never married. My mother was Mrs Guthrie and there was some confusion when Mr Sholto took over Cauldstane. He thought I was Mrs Guthrie, the cook. It was understandable because my mother took ill and died during poor Mr Torquil's last illness and I stepped in. I did explain to Mr Sholto eventually and we had a wee laugh about it, but somehow the name stuck.' She shrugged. 'I didn't mind. That's the thing with a family like this. And a place like this. The continuity. That's what we all try to preserve. That's what matters. In the long run.'

It was the longest speech I'd ever heard Wilma make and I was pleased to see it had a calming effect on her. I set a cup of coffee in front of her, then sat down beside her with mine. She stared dolefully at her mug, as if the effort of lifting it might prove too much. I nudged the sugar bowl towards her, saying, 'Did Sholto give you some bad news?'

'It was Mr Alec. Mr Sholto would never have got through the speech. I do believe Mr Alec had a tear in his eye when he left. Och, we both did!'

'What did he say?'

'He didn't give me my notice. He said they'll need me until the last box is moved out of Cauldstane.' That pride again. 'But he said the castle is going on the market. And soon. Of course, the new owners might wish to keep me on – Mr Alec said he was going to advise that they should – but he thought it only fair to give me as much notice as possible that I would lose my job. And... my home. I stay in the wee lodge at the gate,' she explained. 'I used to share it with my mother and father. Now there's just me.'

'Wilma, if you don't mind my asking, how old are you? I think you must be a lot older than you look.'

'Och, away with you!' she exclaimed, but I could tell she was pleased. 'I'm *sixty*,' she said, lowering her voice.

'Not a good age to be seeking a new position.'

'No, but Mr Alec says I can start looking immediately if I want to. And if I don't find one, he says I'll be provided for. Of course, I wouldn't accept charity, but it's very kind of him to think of me, especially when he has so much on his mind and his own heart must be broken in two.'

It was my turn to well up now and I blurted out my thoughts without considering their wisdom. 'I don't think they'll find a buyer, Wilma. And if they do, chances are, they'll want to keep you on. Sholto will give you a brilliant reference.'

'I don't wish to sound ungrateful, Miss Je— *Jenny*. But I don't know if I could bear to see another family under this roof. Or some *foreign* gentleman. Cauldstane isn't mine, but I've never lived anywhere else. I'm not sure I could bear to see it occupied by anyone other than MacNabs.'

There was something about the way Wilma said "occupied" that made me think of barbarian invaders. 'I know what you mean. Maybe a clean break would be less painful for you. But Cauldstane might never be sold. In fact, I'm going to talk to Sholto about various ideas I've been discussing with Fergus.'

Her eyes brightened. 'You mean business plans?'

'Yes. I think there are ways in which the MacNabs could make Cauldstane economically viable. But they'd need to raise some cash first. Then they'd have to invest that in making Cauldstane pay its way.'

'You mean, opening it up to the public?'

'Well, that would be one way of making money.'

'Och, you should talk to Mrs Fontaine! She and I have been planning a cookery school for *years*. She says we should have a café that serves snacks during the day and a restaurant to serve dinners in the evening. There's nowhere to get a decent meal round here if you want anything more than a fish supper.'

I blinked. 'Zelda wants to open a restaurant?'

'Aye, it's her dream. She's even got a name for it. *The Auld Alliance*.'

'Referring to the historic connection between France and Scotland? How clever!' I laughed, delighted. 'And she'd serve a fusion of French and Scottish food, I suppose?'

'Aye, that's right. She said folk would pay handsomely to eat in a castle. Her idea was to convert the library into a dining room.'

'But what would you do with all the books?'

'Mrs Fontaine said she'd leave them there. It would be cheaper than re-decorating and everyone loves to see old books, even if they don't read them.'

'It's a brilliant idea, Wilma!'

'Aye, and Mrs Fontaine would be bound to make a success of it. She ran her own restaurant in France.'

'What did Sholto say?'

'He said he thought it *might* work, but...'

'But there's no money.'

'Mrs Fontaine can put up some of the capital, but she says she doesn't have anything like enough to go it alone.'

'And in any case, converting Cauldstane to include a café and restaurant should be part of a bigger scheme, to make the castle a multi-purpose business venture.'

'Aye. We need a Master Plan. And a millionaire,' she added with a sigh.

'Well, don't start packing your bags yet, Wilma. I do have a few plans and I'm going to badger Sholto and Alec until they give in or throw me out. Fergus has a vision of this place working. So does Zelda, apparently. And I can see so much potential! We just have to persuade Alec and Sholto. They mustn't be allowed to give up.'

'Don't be too hard on Mr Alec. He's been through so much. When you nearly drowned, it fair set him back. I haven't seen him so low in years.'

'I suppose it reminded him of losing his wife.'

'There's been so much tragedy. And it began when he was so young.' Wilma shook her head. 'What can you say to comfort a motherless child?'

'I bet you thought of something.'

'Oh aye, I said my piece. I think it helped a little. Not at the time. But later.'

'What did you say? Can you remember?'

Wilma paused, then leaned back in her chair and folded her hands in her lap. 'I said someone isn't dead – not *truly* dead – until the last person has had the last kind thought about them. That's what I told the boys when their mother died. I said she would be preserved in their memories. That's why it's so important not to speak ill of the dead. If we do, they die again. In our hearts. If we remember the good, the *best*, then our loved ones will live on and on, in our hearts and in our minds. Until finally we join them. That way, they never really leave us... That's what I told the boys. Because that's what I believe.'

'I'm sure it must have helped them.'

'Maybe.' Wilma stood up and took our empty coffee cups over to the sink. 'But I think we all understand why Mr Alec wants to give up Cauldstane now.'

No, you don't, I thought. None of you has any idea why Alec is prepared to make this sacrifice.

Or why I'm not going to let him do it.

I was typing up the notes that would form Operation Cauldstane when there was a knock on my door. It was Alec. He stood in the doorway, as if unwilling to commit himself to actually crossing the threshold. I knew it wasn't fear of Meredith keeping him out. It was me.

'Hi,' I said, treating him to a bright, artificial smile. I was pleased to see him – there were times when I *ached* to see him – but already I felt nervous about the ensuing conversation.

His eyes shifted to the laptop. 'I'm not interrupting anything important?'

'Well, *you* wouldn't think so. I'm working on a business plan I want to present to Sholto. Just a few ideas, plus the results of some research I've been doing.' Alec was silent and his face betrayed nothing. Ignoring this unpromising start, I continued. 'Did you know Zelda wants to open a restaurant here? She says she can put up half the money herself, so it's a question of finding a sleeping partner, someone who wants to go halves on a top-notch French-Scottish restaurant called *The Auld Alliance*. And I think I might know just the person.'

'Jenny.' Alec stopped me in my tracks with the single word. 'Sholto says he'd like to see you. In the library.'

'Now?'

'If it's convenient.'

'You've been talking to him.'

'For days,' he said wearily.

'Alec, please don't put any more pressure on him to sell. Give me a chance to talk about the alternatives first. Fergus and Zelda are on board. So's Wilma. I just have to convince Sholto now.'

'And me.'

'Well, I can't convince you, can I? You're selling up to save the family from Meredith. I don't suppose you've shared that piece of information, have you?'

His face was stony. 'How can I?'

'But I thought honesty was your policy? "Why be anything else?" Wasn't that your line? None of the others understand why you've suddenly bailed out. Since you're doing this for them, you could at least ask them if they want rescuing. They might prefer to stand up to Meredith. If they saw the whole picture, maybe they'd be prepared to try the deliverance ministry.'

'I told you, Sholto won't have James Kennedy in the house.'

'Yes, and I now know why.'

Alec's composure slipped and his eyes widened. 'You asked him?'

'I told Sholto about the deliverance ministry and then he told me why he fell out with Kennedy. He's one of Meredith's many conquests, apparently. Quite a notch on her bedpost, that one. A minister of the Church of Scotland *and* a personal friend of Sholto's. A double whammy. I suppose that must have compensated for not being able to pull her stepson.' Alec's face was dark with anger. He looked as if he might be about to throttle me, but I assumed his murderous thoughts were directed towards Meredith. 'Alec, you surely aren't going to let that woman win? Won't you at least *try* to drive her out? I know a minister in England – a good man – who'll come and do the business. He's agreed in principle. We just have to get Sholto to say the word.'

Alec stood quite still, frowning slightly, as if he had a headache or was thinking very hard. When finally he spoke, his voice sounded oddly detached. 'My father's waiting to see you. In the library.' As he turned to go, I knew I was either about to burst into tears or be very, very angry. I chose anger.

'How can you bear to live like this? This... this *half-life*! A man like you! This isn't living, Alec. Tell me, when was the last time you felt no fear? No fear at all?'

I saw him grip the doorframe and bite back a reply, then he bowed his head and stared at the floor. 'My eighth birthday. When I came cycling into the courtyard. I felt like king of the world. Then all hell broke out. The horse *screaming*... Then my mother... The sound of the horse's hooves, galloping past me... Sparks flying up from the cobblestones... I've never been so terrified, before or since.' He lifted his head and gazed at me. 'But seeing you in the river, being swept away.... That came pretty close.'

My anger gone now, I said gently, 'Has it ever occurred to you that moving out might not be the end of it? How do you know Meredith won't follow you? Or Sholto?'

'I don't. But if we all go our separate ways, if I live alone, how much harm can she do? In any case, I know that woman. Once she knows she's won, she'll rest. It was always about conquest with Meredith.' He shrugged. 'Maybe if I'd slept with her, she'd have just moved on, left me in peace. I don't know why she became obsessed with me. Because I said no?... Maybe no one had ever said no before.'

'Sholto did. He refused to divorce Liz. And we know Meredith wasn't happy about that.'

'Aye, but she got her way in the end. I was always unfinished business. I still am.'

'And that's why you think you have to put an end to it. By giving in. But Alec, you could have the whole family on your side. And me! *Please* don't give up.'

He was silent for a long time and, though his face was impassive, I thought I saw a man struggling with emotions that threatened to overwhelm him. Eventually, his voice barely audible,

he said, 'You'd better not keep him waiting any longer,' then he
turned away and closed the door.

Chapter Twenty-three

The signs weren't good. Sholto was seated at his desk, suggesting the formality of our first interview, weeks ago. He was writing and barely looked up as I entered.

'Ah, Jenny. Thank you for coming.'

He waved me towards a chair and I sat, preparing myself for the worst. What *was* the worst, I wondered? Cauldstane being sold and Sholto having to live out the rest of his days in a cosy bungalow? (Many would relish the prospect, but the Laird of Cauldstane had slung his hammock in jungles and pitched his tent at the foot of Everest. I doubted he dreamed of deep pile carpets.) Why then did I dread whatever Sholto was about to announce? How could I begrudge the MacNabs being released from Meredith's ghostly grip? Even if I was prepared to take my chances, how could I expect Alec to take responsibility for endangering lives when he'd already lost loved ones?

When it came, I realised what the worst thing was. *Me* having to leave Cauldstane.

My employer replaced the cap on his fountain pen, set it down and said, cautiously, 'I think it's time we had a talk about the future, Jenny. You must have heard some of what's afoot, I'm sure.' He didn't pause for me to answer, nor did he meet my eye. I recalled what Wilma had said about Alec having to break the bad news to her. Sholto was evidently struggling. He folded his hands in front of him, then proceeded to address them, not me. 'It is with much regret that I've decided to abandon my memoirs. This is in no way a reflection on you or the work we've done together. My decision is a response to the changed circumstances in which I find myself.' He raised his eyes from the desk, but only to regard the ceiling. 'To cut a long story short, Jenny, after consultation with both my sons, I've decided to put Cauldstane on the market, to see if we can find a buyer.' He risked a quick look at me. Clearly he didn't like what he saw, for he looked away again immediately. 'As you're aware, my main reason for writing the book was to raise money, money that might enable us to stay on at Cauldstane. I now think that was an unrealistic goal. A pipe dream. The income from that book would have been a mere drop in the ocean of debt on which my sons and I now find ourselves adrift. As a money-spinner, my story was always rather a long shot and, I fear, something of a vanity project.'

'I beg to differ. There's definitely a market for the book. If I hadn't thought so, I wouldn't have accepted the commission. But in my view, your biography is worth writing as a record of your life, regardless of whether it made enough money to save Cauldstane. It's a good story, Sholto. It should be told.'

Finally his eyes met mine. 'You really think so?' He looked tired and confused. I wondered how many sleepless nights he'd endured before succumbing to pressure from Alec to sell his birthright.

'I do. And until you actually find a buyer, we might as well continue with the book. I hope you'll forgive me pointing out that, under the terms of our contract, you're still obliged to pay half my fee if you sack me now. Why not finish what we started?'

'Oh, you'll receive your *full* fee, Jenny, no question of that. I don't want you penalized by my sudden decision. I'd also like you to choose a little souvenir from Cauldstane, to take away as a memento of your stay with us.'

'I'll do nothing of the sort. Nor will I accept my full fee. Not unless you allow me to finish writing the book.'

Sholto narrowed his eyes and fixed me with a stern look, but he was unable to hide his amusement. 'You know, it's come to my attention in the last few days that some perfectly decent people are capable of blackmail.' The corners of his mouth twitched. 'Really, I had no idea.'

I leaned forward in my chair. 'Sholto, I know this is all Alec's doing and I think *you* know it's only half the story. Fergus is ready to sell up if you fail to raise the cash to renovate Cauldstane, but he has lots of ideas — good ones — about how this place could make money. As for Alec — well, I simply don't believe he wants to sell. Not really.'

Sholto spread his hands. 'He says enough is enough. Cauldstane is draining us of money. Energy. Life's blood, I fear. Alec and Fergus say we should sell and, let's face it, the future belongs to them. They don't need a sentimental old man getting in their way. It's all perfectly understandable. Inevitable, in fact.'

Despite the certainty of his words, I sensed he was weakening, so I decided to try another tack. 'What if you don't find a buyer?'

His face brightened a little. 'You think no one will stump up the cash?'

'It's possible. An awful lot needs doing. I've heard the phrase "money pit" used more than once. I suppose if you put it on the market at a silly price, you might find a buyer, but is that really what you want to do? Give Cauldstane away?'

'Beggars can't be choosers. The agent has warned us we shouldn't be too optimistic with regard to the sum it will fetch. Alec says we must reconcile ourselves to the sale being a damage limitation exercise.'

I cursed Alec inwardly, knowing just what kind of damage he was attempting to limit. 'Well, even if you do decide to drop the book,' I said in desperation, 'would you please allow me to stay on for a while to help with preparations for the sale? I wanted to talk to you about Cauldstane's paintings. I've been having a rummage upstairs – I hope you don't mind. Fergus said it would be all right – and I've been doing some research. I think you might have some interesting stuff up there among all the junk.'

'Really? I can't say I've ever paid much attention to our pictures. I don't have much of an eye for that sort of thing. More Torquil's area of expertise.'

'Do you know if he ever sat for Lucian Freud?'

'No idea. But they knew each other, certainly. Torquil knew everybody. Very gregarious fellow. I believe there *was* some talk of a portrait. A nude, I believe. But I assumed that was just my brother's idea of a joke.'

'Apparently not. I think that might be what you've got upstairs. And there are other paintings that I think could be worth something. You've got a lovely set of landscapes that look seventeenth-century to me. I'd be happy to get things valued for you. And if you're selling Cauldstane, you'll have to sell most of the contents, won't you?'

'Yes, I suppose we will.'

'And what about all Meredith's stuff? You wanted me to help with that, didn't you? I think I'm the only person you can ask to dispose of those journals.'

'That's very kind of you, Jenny. I do appreciate that you're trying to help us, but... well, Alec seems very keen that you should leave. As soon as possible.'

'Why?'

'I'm not sure, but I suspect he thinks you'll try to persuade me to hang on. Or that you'll try to dissuade *him*. He knows you're not in favour of his plan to sell up. And to be fair to Alec, you *are* trying to persuade me to hang on.'

I regarded Sholto, wondering just how much Alec had told him. 'Has he given any other reason for selling? Other than financial necessity, I mean?'

Sholto looked blank. 'Why, no. What other reason could there be? Our dire financial position is reason enough. It's probably something I should have done a long time ago. But one hopes...' He smiled, a little embarrassed. 'And one dreams.'

'Well, I don't think you need let go of your dreams just yet. There are various possibilities. Has Fergus talked to you about converting the empty estate cottages?'

'Converting for what purpose?'

'Self-catering accommodation for holidaymakers. Has Zelda ever mentioned that she'd like to run a restaurant again? Here.'

'*Zelda?* At her time of life?'

'I think she'd mainly manage the thing, with Wilma. You know, Zelda could oversee the whole Cauldstane project. She obviously has the vision. And the energy.'

'But all this would require a great deal of capital!'

'Of course. But if Zelda could find someone to invest in her restaurant; if your paintings *are* worth something, if you sold the harpsichord — my preliminary research suggests it could be worth up to £100,000; if Alec took on an assistant and doubled his output; if self-catering properties provided a regular income; if you hosted weddings and conferences... Well, it could be worth asking the bank how much they'd lend you. In the long term, I think Cauldstane might be able to pay its way. So does Fergus.' I opened up a folder I'd brought with me and handed Sholto a few sheets of paper. 'That's a sort of business plan I drew up. Very sketchy, but you'll get the general idea.'

Sholto reached for his reading glasses and spread the sheets out in front of him. 'Jenny, I'm touched. You've obviously given this a great deal of thought.'

'So have Fergus and Zelda. Even Wilma.' Sholto looked up, conscience-stricken. 'She's not ready to retire yet, Sholto. She's game to cook till she drops.'

'Bless that woman. You know, Jenny, I can no more think of life without Wilma than life without Cauldstane. But Alec's arguments are persuasive. He's a quiet chap, slow to anger, but when he's set his mind on something... Well, my advice is, don't ever get into an argument with Alec. He can't be budged.'

'But Cauldstane is still *yours*, Sholto. And you could live for another twenty years – and probably will! What happens to Cauldstane is ultimately *your* decision. I just wanted you to know what all the options were, if you got the whole family behind you.'

'Yes, I do see.'

'Shall I leave you to think about it? And perhaps discuss it with them? Alec will tell you it can't work, but don't take no for an answer. Ask him to explain *why* it won't work. And... can I ask you to do something else?'

'What, my dear?'

'Give me another week's grace. *Please*. Another week to interview you, so I can get all the information I need to complete the book, just in case you do decide to go ahead with it. Which I very much hope you will. If Alec wants me out, I'll go quietly, but I can still work on the book at home. Once I've completed all the interviews, I can work from transcriptions in London. Then I'll produce a draft. If you like it, we can move forward with trying to find a publisher. There would be no obligation, but if you insist on paying me my full fee, the least I can do is supply you with a draft autobiography.'

'And is that what you want to do, Jenny?'

'It's what I really, *really* want to do. So do we have a deal?'

'We do. To hell with Alec! I shall miss your company when you've gone and I'm damned if I know why I shouldn't make the most of it now. Especially when there are still so many stories to tell! Some corkers, too.' He frowned as he tried to recall. 'Did I tell you about the time Wilma found one of my toes in the bath?'

I shrieked with horror and delight. 'No, you did not! Your *toe*?'

'Just one of my little toes. Nothing vital,' Sholto explained. 'It was quite dead from frostbite. Came off in a hot bath once I was back home. I didn't notice. Then Wilma found it when she was cleaning. It had been washed into the plughole. She screamed the place down when she realised what it was.'

'Sholto, if we don't write this book, it will be a crime.'

'If you say so,' he replied with a grin. 'But I warn you, there'll be hell to pay with Alec. He wants you to leave. So very disappointing...' Sholto shook his head. 'I thought you two were getting on famously.' He shot me a sidelong glance. 'Perhaps I was just imagining things. I do want my boys to be happy. They've had rather a rough deal. Losing their mother. Absentee father. And Meredith was bloody useless of course. Simply not interested in them when they were *boys*.'

He heard the emphasis he'd laid on the word "boys" and looked nonplussed, unsure for a moment how much I knew about Meredith's distinctly un-maternal feelings towards Alec. My face was a bland mask as I said, 'Leave Alec to me. I might be able to talk him round. And if I can't, the final say is yours, surely? But can we resume our routine? Provisionally, at least? Ten o' clock tomorrow, in here? Business as usual. Until Alec boots me out.'

'Business as usual, my dear. And I'm really looking forward to it!'

I'd entered the library to find a sad, old man. I left the Laird of Cauldstane in fine form, a twinkle in those roguish blue eyes. If his future was uncertain, his past was not. For the immediate future, Sholto was content to share highlights of that past, re-living times when life had seemed happier and – mislaid toes notwithstanding – simpler.

As I walked back to my room, I was thinking about Sholto's traveller's tales and how often the most preposterous of his stories were the ones least embellished. Years of being a ghost writer, listening to the version of their life that subjects wished to present to a waiting world, meant I had a highly developed crap detector. You learned to recognise the rehearsed grief, the paranoid fantasies. You also learned to interpret silences and odd gaps in the CV.

Instinct always told me when I was listening to truth and when I wasn't. It was something that had hampered my relationships with men, apart from Rupert who, as a scientist and a priest, was preoccupied with truth. He'd said, with something like pride, that I saw right through people, but that I did it without judging. He said that was what had made me a good novelist and would also make me a good ghost writer.

Events had proved him right, but a highly developed crap detector didn't make for a comfortable life. Once the crap had been detected, it was rarely clear what should be done with it. Professionally, I was required to ignore it, unless I thought honesty would make the book better or more commercial, but in my private life I'd discovered I was able to tolerate very little toxic waste.

Now something was bothering me about Alec – in particular, his account of his mother's death.

I understood why he deemed the current coolness between us necessary. We were at loggerheads over the future of Cauldstane. That was hardly conducive to a blossoming sexual relationship, despite what you might read in lightweight romantic fiction. He might also be having second thoughts about me. I'd practically called him a coward – not my finest hour. Possibly he thought there was no future in the relationship – I lived in London and travelled a lot for work, Alec was rooted in the Highlands – but what he *said* was, he thought I might have no future at all if I didn't leave Cauldstane.

Alec struck me as a truth-teller. I didn't always agree with him, but I had always believed him. Except when he'd talked about how his mother died. The more I thought about his two accounts of the accident, the more uneasy I felt. Long experience with liars of all creeds and colours told me Alec wasn't lying. But neither was he telling the truth.

Who actually knew what happened that day, apart from Alec, aged eight? Liz MacNab and possibly Meredith, both dead. Any other evidence was hearsay. The cause of the accident was Alec's horn startling the horse, which reared and bolted, but in his most recent account, the one he'd given me when I'd goaded him into a response, Alec hadn't even mentioned the klaxon. He'd been emotional, incoherent, clearly distressed by his memories. Yet when I'd first asked him about them – under happier circumstances, admittedly – he'd given a coherent and dispassionate account, almost like a prepared speech. At the time I'd put that down to the fact he must have had to explain what happened many times. His composure hadn't seemed surprising. What *was* odd was the latest version, an account in which he didn't even mention sounding the horn, the source of thirty-two years' guilt.

Thinking back to his first account, I remembered that even then, I hadn't felt happy. My crap detector again? Hardly. I'd known Alec wasn't lying, so what had bugged me? I tried to recall exactly what he'd said. The words had made an impression on me – partly because Alec had made an impression on me, but also because I habitually listened hard. Failures with tape recorders over the years had encouraged the development of a good memory and the taking of copious notes.

Back in my room, I opened up my notebook and turned to the page where I'd recorded details of the accident.

What had Alec actually said? To begin with he'd been vague. *There was a lot of noise...*

Noise seemed to be a big factor in both accounts. Noise and fear. What had he said next? Something about the hooves? *Hooves clattering on the cobbles... the horse neighing...*

Why hadn't he mentioned sounding the horn?.. Ah, but he *did*. I remembered the phrase *my bloody klaxon* – the words of the man, not the boy. And *that* was the order in which he'd mentioned things. *Hooves clattering on the cobbles... the horse neighing... a woman screaming... my bloody klaxon... Cacophony.* Again, the adult word to describe the experience of an eight-year old.

I felt sure that's what Alec had said. Now I thought about it, I realised that even at the time, this hadn't made sense. The order was wrong. The horse was rearing *before* Alec used his horn. In fact, did it not make more sense that he would have sounded his horn because he thought he heard a horse and rider coming his way? What would a bright boy do if he thought he was about to be trampled by a horse? He might sound his horn and try to swerve out of the way. That could cause him to fall off his bike – which was how Meredith had found him.

If Alec's running order was correct, it meant he hadn't been responsible for the horse rearing, it had been startled by something else. What? And why did Alec tell everyone *he'd* frightened the horse?

There was no one to ask other than Alec, who admitted all he could remember now was what he'd told Meredith when she found him lying on the ground, crying. She was the only one who might have had an accurate idea of what happened. And she was dead.

It's hard to believe how long it took me to realise what I had to do. I'm a writer, a biographer, a researcher. I'm used to dealing with family archives on a regular basis. Well, they say love makes you blind. It must also render you stupid. That's the only explanation I can give for the time it took me to realise, if I wanted to know exactly what happened that day, all I needed to do was read Meredith's journal.

Sholto had said he wanted me to get rid of the diaries. He'd actually told me to "burn the lot", so I had no qualms about taking a couple of cardboard boxes from the recycling pile in the utility room and carrying them up to Meredith's room. No qualms, but I decided to do it early in the morning when I was unlikely to be seen or interrupted. As well as the boxes, I took a bag with my usual writing paraphernalia.

Mounting the stairs to the third floor, I realised I wasn't the only one busy before breakfast. Rock music was coming from the Long Attic – vintage Springsteen, unless I was mistaken – and once I was on the landing, I could hear rhythmic grunts. Alec or Fergus engaged in some punishing routine on the gym equipment, I supposed.

No one in the Long Attic would have heard me open Meredith's door. Nevertheless, I opened and closed it quietly. I switched on the light and experienced once again a sense of revulsion – worse this time now I knew what the journals contained and how Sholto felt about them. I hurried over to the window, eager to let daylight in, but as I tried to drag one of the thick velvet curtains aside, my fingers penetrated the cloth with an ugly tearing sound. Horrified, I surveyed the damage. The worn red fibres had parted and there was a ragged tear, but I noticed there were other threadbare patches where you would grasp the curtains to draw them. Probably I'd just made an existing tear worse. I was still mortified, but knew Sholto would very likely get rid of the curtains along with everything else. They were good for nothing, not even a jumble sale. I re-arranged the damaged curtain so it fell into its usual folds and resigned myself to working by artificial light.

I'd checked the date of Liz's death on the MacNab family tree I'd drawn up. Kneeling on the floor by the bookcase, I pulled out the journal for 1980. There was just the one. Meredith must have had an uneventful year. I felt unaccountably nervous about opening the diary and I was still worried that someone – well, Alec – might come into the room and challenge me.

Partly to calm myself, partly to make it clear I was making myself useful and not just snooping, I piled some of the diaries into a box. When it was almost full, I sat down again, picked up the journal for 1980 and turned the pages until I found May 1st, the day Liz MacNab had died. Alec's eighth birthday.

Even before I read the entry, I was struck by the change in Meredith's handwriting. Always black, bold and slanting, the entry for that day was remarkable for the number of exclamation marks and underlined words. Given the trauma everyone experienced that day, I wasn't surprised to see her writing was more erratic than usual. It sloped downwards on the unlined page, so that the overall effect, even before reading the content, was of turbulent thoughts committed to paper in a rushed, chaotic fashion.

Then I began to read what she'd written.

These were not the words of a woman in shock, grieving for someone she knew as a family friend, albeit a rival for her ex-lover's affections. As I read on, it became clear that Meredith had recorded the events of that tragic day in a state of exultation...

It's happened! My prayers have been answered. Sholto is _free_ at last. I'm so happy I could burst!

Chapter Twenty-four

Liz is dead. I thought she might only break arms or legs. But she's quite dead.

She put up a fight, I'll say that for her. She clung on for dear life, but the mare was determined to unseat her. She was panic-stricken. (Not Liz, Bella, her mare.) Horses go mad when they're startled. All they think about is getting shot of their rider and bolting, so Bella bucked like a corkscrew until Liz was thrown, screaming, through the air. She hit the cobbles from quite a height. It was terrifying, even though I'd moved back, well out of the way.

As soon as horse and rider parted company, Bella was off, galloping through the courtyard and out into the countryside. She's been gone for hours now.

I could tell Liz was dead from the way she was lying on the ground, with her limbs pointing in funny directions. She had blood coming out of her ears – from the head injury, I suppose. Those hard hats are <u>useless</u>. I don't know why people make such a fuss about wearing them – and they ruin your hair. Riding is simply a very dangerous sport. But that's why it's so thrilling! You're trying to control an animal, one quite capable of killing you, so <u>you</u> have to be the one in control. That's why I'm such a good rider. I love to be in control! And today I was. <u>Totally</u>. Everything went exactly as I'd hoped. Even the bit I hadn't planned was an absolute godsend. I feel it was all meant to be!

Poor Alec had his birthday ruined, but he'll have plenty more. It was just bad luck – his, not mine – that he should have cycled into the courtyard at that precise moment. I say bad luck, but was it Fate? Fate providing me with the final piece of the jigsaw. When I saw him come speeding through the archway into the courtyard, I thought he'd had it. (That would have been quite a coup – the laird's lady <u>and</u> his heir.) But he tooted that ridiculous horn and Bella swerved. He still fell off his bike, but I think he was howling with fright more than anything. He hadn't actually seen Liz's body at that point, so I seized my chance. I ran over and hauled him to his feet, then I grabbed hold of his shoulders and shook him. I pretended to be angry and told him he'd killed his mother. I said he'd frightened the horse and Liz had been thrown and broken her neck. 'Your mummy's dead,' I said, 'and it's all your fault, Alec!' Then I dragged him over to Liz and made him look. Oh, then he really started! Screamed blue murder. I ignored him and repeated the sequence, told him how he'd scared Bella, how she'd bucked, how he'd <u>seen</u> his mother thrown to the ground, seen her die.

I was worried stiff someone might appear at any second, but it only took a few moments to tell Alec what he'd "done". By the time I'd repeated it a couple of times, I almost believed I'd seen it myself! Then when I heard people coming out of the castle, I held him tight, so he couldn't run away. It must have looked as if I was comforting him, but all the time I was repeating the story in his ear, like a mantra. "Your mummy's dead and it's all your fault."

By the time Wilma and Sholto arrived on the scene, Alec was completely beside himself. My riding jacket was quite ruined – smeared with snot and tears. I do believe the wretched boy wet himself too. There was an ominous smell.

Everyone gathered round, of course, but I made sure it was me who told them what had happened. Fortunately Alec was in too much of a state to speak, so everyone believed me. I told them I hadn't actually seen what happened because I'd been in the stable with my own horse, but I'd heard the horn, then the clatter of hooves on the cobbles and Liz screaming. I'd rushed out (I said) to find Liz dead, the horse gone and Alec lying on the ground having fallen off his bike. I said I'd asked him what had happened and he'd given me a distraught (but surprisingly coherent!) account of the accident. I suggested we shouldn't badger him with any more questions as he appeared to be traumatised by what he'd seen. That was a bit of quick thinking on my part.

But my whole scheme was brilliant! Brilliant and daring. Even if Alec hadn't swallowed my story, what could he have said? He <u>didn't</u> see what happened, Liz was dead <u>before</u> he cycled into the courtyard, so the most he could have said was I'd shouted at him, accused him of startling the mare. But he's only eight. Who'd set any store by something said by a hysterical child? But everyone accepted my version of events. It made complete sense, thanks to Alec and his blessed bike.

I just can't believe how well everything worked out! I'd hoped Liz would be injured, crippled for life maybe. I didn't dare hope she'd die. Of course, it took some nerve. I might have been badly injured myself, but I'm used to taking risks and, as they say, "Fortune favours the bold".

Well, Fortune certainly favoured me today. When Liz was mounting Bella, I thought the mare seemed a bit nervous. Did she sense what I was about to do, I wonder? Horses are terribly clever, so maybe she did. I "helped" Liz by holding her other stirrup as she mounted. Nothing could have seemed more natural, though of course she didn't really need any help. When she was not quite in the saddle, I withdrew the hatpin concealed in my hair and stabbed the mare. I was careful not to let go of the pin and withdrew it immediately, leaping backwards as the horse bucked violently. As she clung to the reins, Liz was shouting, "Bella, stop! Stop!" which only made things worse. Bella was determined to throw her and eventually she did.

And that was that.

Unfortunately there was nowhere I could conceal the hatpin, other than putting it back into my hair. I couldn't risk anyone finding it in the courtyard, so even though it was sticky with Bella's blood, I shoved it back into my bun. I had the presence of mind to touch Liz's head, so my hands were bloody. No one would have registered the mare's blood on my hands. (After all this, if I ever get to sing Lady Macbeth, I'll be fabulous in the rôle!)

The blood came off in a nice hot bath. It was wonderful to relax after the strain of the day, though the Cauldstane plumbing leaves a lot to be desired. (I will have to get that seen to once I'm installed.) I washed the hat pin carefully, then dropped it behind a bookcase in the guest room the MacNabs allocated to me. I doubt it will ever be found. Even if it is, no one will ever know what that pin accomplished today. My happiness!

People don't realise, you see. That's what Zelda said when she gave it to me. "You can do a lot of damage with a hatpin." Indeed!

Later...
Someone just brought Bella back. She was in a terrible state, poor thing. I offered to settle her in the stable as everyone else was exhausted. She was scratched and cut, as if she'd plunged through a

hedge or a fence. All very convenient! No one will notice her stab wound, even if they look. Really, things couldn't have worked out better for me.

I shut the journal and set it down beside me, on the floor. I leaned against the bookcase and sat very still, with my eyes closed, wondering if I was going to be sick.

My initial impulse was to scream. I wanted to scream and scream at the top of my voice, so everyone would know how wicked the world was, how unjust, how cruel. But someone was on the other side of the wall – Alec, probably – and so I had to remain silent.

But I couldn't remain still. I got to my feet and, scarcely thinking what I was doing, went over to the window and swept a curtain aside. I found what I was looking for. I picked up the photo of Meredith at her eighth birthday party – the same age Alec had been – and removed it from the frame. I dropped the frame on the floor and held the photo up in front of me with both hands and then I spat on it. I ripped it in half, then in half again. I kept tearing until the pieces were tiny, then I hurled them at the portrait of Meredith hanging over the bed. They fluttered down onto the hideous gold bedspread, like confetti.

I returned to my boxes and started hurling the rest of the journals in. When there were none left on the shelf, I made a conscious effort to calm down, gathered up the pieces of photograph and dropped them into a box. My heart was still thumping with fury, but now I had to decide what to do. And it was imperative I should make the right decision.

My first coherent thought was that I must show the journal to Alec, show him he was completely innocent of his mother's death. My second thought – possibly rather more coherent – was that the truth would probably be even harder for him to bear than the lie he'd been made to believe. Since there was no possibility of Meredith being put on trial, since justice could never be done, wasn't it best to just leave things as they were, allow the family to continue to believe Liz had died in an accident?...

I found myself wondering what Rupert would advise, Rupert to whom I'd sometimes taken my moral dilemmas, even after we'd parted. But there had never been anything on this scale and given that I wasn't even family, surely it wasn't up to *me* to make a decision? I felt like Pandora after she'd opened the box. Only worse.

I had to assume Sholto had no inkling of what this particular journal contained. He evidently suspected details of his wife's extra-marital affairs, but I was certain he knew nothing of Meredith's confession. If he'd known, he would never have allowed me, or anyone else, to believe Alec was responsible.

I was just as confident Alec knew nothing. He'd twice given me an account of his version of what happened and now I knew how he'd been convinced of his own guilt. Meredith had bullied a traumatised child into believing he'd done something that would put her in the clear.

In all probability, I was the only person alive who knew what had happened that day. I was the only one who knew what this journal contained and it was up to me to decide what should be done with that knowledge. Arguably, Sholto, Alec and Fergus had a right to know what had really happened. But the incriminating evidence had existed for over thirty years. After Meredith's death, twelve years ago, anyone could have done what I'd done. But they'd all chosen not to. What right did I have to barge in with information the family hadn't sought to know?

But they had no reason to suspect foul play, no reason to doubt Alec's word – Alec, supposedly the only eyewitness. Sholto had chosen to ignore Meredith's journals because he didn't want to confront the evidence of his wife's adulterous liaisons. And Alec? Would he know of the journals' existence? Even if he did, why would he doubt his version of events when he'd grown up believing he was the only one who actually saw what happened?

So it was up to me and me alone. I could decide to show Alec. Or Sholto. (Might the shock actually kill Sholto? Did people die of shock?) Or I could do nothing. But doing nothing wasn't as harmless as it sounded. Doing nothing would be concealing, or conspiring to conceal a serious crime. Doing nothing was surely as wrong morally as revealing a hideous truth to people who might be too vulnerable to handle it.

Instinct said I should do nothing. But instinct didn't say that was the right thing to do. Instinct told me doing nothing would cause Alec the least pain and that, instinctively, was what I wanted to do: protect him, whether or not it was the right thing to do.

I didn't notice that the rock music had stopped, nor did I realise how long I'd been sitting on the floor in what was, I suppose, a state of shock. I was still feeling dazed when the door handle rattled and the door was flung open. Alec stood in the doorway, his hair dark with sweat, a towel draped round his neck. His skin was damp and his colour high – though whether this was as a result of exercise or anger, it was hard to say. As he looked down at me, sitting cross-legged on the floor, his expression seemed to change from surprise to fury.

'What the hell are you doing in here?'

I felt as if I'd been caught red-handed in some nefarious act, but my feelings of guilt were related to what I *knew*, not what I'd done. I ignored Alec's question and countered with one of my own. 'How did you know I was in here?'

'I saw the light under the door. What are you doing?'

I took a deep breath and tried to sound casual. 'Sholto asked me to help clear out this room. If you're selling up, it all has to go. So I offered to make a start on sorting things out. Obviously he can't face doing it, or he'd have tackled it before now.'

'That's a job for Wilma, not you.'

'He said he didn't want anyone else – family, I mean – looking at Meredith's journals.'

'Meredith kept a diary? Jesus, I bet that makes colourful reading.'

It was a moment before I was able to speak, then I said, 'Sholto wants them all destroyed.'

'I'm not surprised. I hope to God he's never felt tempted to read them.'

'I don't think he has. Nothing he said to me indicated that he knows... what they contain,' I said, avoiding Alec's eye. 'I think it would be a good idea to get rid of all this rubbish. Meredith's presence should be *eradicated* from Cauldstane.'

'Aye, but you'll never get rid of her smell.'

'Smell?'

'Can you not smell her sickly perfume? It's suffocating. Like something's rotting.'

'No, I can't smell anything. But the air is very stale in here. Who knows, maybe if you get rid of all her stuff—'

'You've been talking to Sholto.'

226

'Yes. He summoned me. You know he did. And he gave me the sack. I imagine that was your idea. Give up on Cauldstane and give up on Sholto's book.'

'You know why I want to get you away from here.'

'Yes, I do, but I have a contract with my employer over which you have no control and he agreed to give me a week's grace in which we will finish our interviews, after which, if he still wants me to leave, I'll go back to London and complete the book. It's up to Sholto whether he wants to seek publication. I shall encourage him to do so because I think it's going to be a damn good book, though I say so myself. I think there's every chance it could make him some money.' Alec said nothing and I got to my feet. 'One week, Alec. You surely can't begrudge me that?'

'It's not a question of begrudging, Jenny, it's about your personal safety. Meredith won't baulk at murder.'

'Believe me, Alec, I *know*.'

I could have told him then. Perhaps I should have, but looking into his dark and, yes, haunted eyes, I couldn't bring myself to do it. I couldn't bring myself to hurt that poor man any more. Instead, I said, 'Why don't you explain? Tell Sholto exactly why you want me out. I think you'll find he's got an open mind about these things. Why give up on Cauldstane before you've even tried to evict Meredith? Before you've exhausted all the commercial possibilities for the place?'

His mouth twisted into a smile. 'Aye, Ferg told me about your wee money-making schemes.'

'Some of them aren't schemes. I've suggested the sale of some valuable assets. I didn't even tell Sholto about one of the things I've found because I didn't want to get his hopes up. I could be very wrong. But I have a contact at Sotheby's who's desperate to come and find out.'

Alec couldn't disguise his interest. He folded his arms and leaned against the door frame. 'What d'you think you've found?'

'Well, there's an unsigned portrait in your lumber room that's either a long lost Raeburn or a copy of it.'

'Raeburn? You mean Henry Raeburn?'

'The same.'

'But if it's not signed—'

'Raeburn didn't sign. I sent a photo of the portrait to my friend

227

at Sotheby's and he said it conforms in size and appearance to a portrait that was lost in the 1930s. It's always been assumed the portrait was destroyed. But there are photographs of it, so we know what it looked like. And I think it's in your lumber room.'

Alec shrugged. 'It's probably a copy.'

'Unlikely. It's an early work and not his greatest.'

'Maybe someone copied it, hoping to pass it off as the lost portrait?'

'Since the 1930s?'

'I wouldn't put anything past Uncle Torquil and his impecunious bohemian pals.'

'Well, it should be simple enough to establish whether or not the painting is twentieth-century or eighteenth. But you'd need to send it to Sotheby's in Edinburgh or get them to come up here.'

'You say you didn't tell Sholto about this?'

'No. But I did tell him about some other pictures. The MacNabs might not have two ha'pennies to rub together, but in other respects, you could be sitting on a smallish gold mine. I also told him the business potential here is enormous.'

'As is the potential for injury or even loss of life. I want my family – and you, Jenny – *out*. And I'm going to make it happen. We need to start over and put all this,' he said, gazing round the room at Meredith's possessions with obvious distaste, 'behind us. We have to move on.'

'I agree, but I don't think you have to move out. I think we could stand up to her.'

'We?'

'You. The MacNabs. As a family. I think if you clear out all her stuff, including that damn harpsichord – one like that reached £100,000 at auction recently, by the way – if you get a priest in to bless the castle and do whatever it is they do to banish evil spirits, you could all have a fresh start *here*.'

He shook his head. 'Will you never give up?'

'No, probably not.'

'Stop trying to save us, Jenny.'

'Why should I? Isn't that exactly what *you're* trying to do? Save the MacNabs – and me – from Meredith? But why must you bear all this *alone*? I could help you! Or if I can't, I can at least help you share the burden.'

'Why? Why would you want to do such a thing? Put your own life in danger for a family that isn't even yours?'

'Because you've suffered enough! And... and it isn't fair. It's wrong! And *you're* wrong.'

'What d'you mean, wrong?'

'It's wrong that you... that you should have suffered your whole life. That you should have to give up everything, just to be free.'

'Och, I'll never be free! Don't delude yourself, Jenny. Even if Meredith decides to let me go, I'll never be free of the anger. Or the hatred. But I'll make sure she harms no one else. And she'll take nothing more from me.'

'*Please* let me help!'

'For Christ's sake, Jenny, why should I let you put yourself in harm's way?'

'Isn't it bloody obvious? Because I'd rather suffer *with* you than walk away. Because... because I think I might be in love with you. And I can tell you now because, thanks to you, I've been told I have to go.'

'Thanks to *Meredith*,' he said softly, looking down at the floor, so I couldn't see the expression on his face.

By now I was in so deep, I didn't care what I said. I didn't care about anything, I just wanted Alec to understand and it gave me some small satisfaction to make my declaration beneath a portrait of the woman who'd ruined lives and taken them, in the name of love for MacNab men. Oh, I said far too much to retain a shred of dignity or self-respect, but what I said was from the heart. A broken heart.

'Look, Alec, I don't want to leave. I was horrified when Sholto said he was shelving the book, but the main reason I was so upset – and I didn't realise until he said it – was that I didn't want to leave *you*. I'd thought maybe you felt the same way. Some of the things you said that night when Meredith was hurling things round my room... and the way you kissed me, not just that night, but later... Well, if I misunderstood, I don't think I'm entirely to blame. You led me to believe the main reason I was in danger was Meredith's sexual jealousy. You actually said what put me in danger was how you felt about me. Are you now saying I got that wrong?' He was silent for a long time. 'Please answer, Alec.'

'Yes. You got that wrong.'

'But you risked your life for me in the river!'

'Anyone would have done the same. Ferg would have done it if I hadn't.'

'But until Meredith made it clear she was prepared to kill me, you showed every sign of wanting a relationship with me. But it didn't happen. You *changed*. I wondered if you were trying to fool Meredith into thinking you no longer cared for me. You certainly convinced me!' He said nothing and I suddenly felt foolish. 'I'm sorry if I misunderstood.'

'Don't be. You've nothing to be sorry for. I have the highest regard for you and all you've done for my father. But if that's how you feel about me... I think it best you leave, Jenny. As soon as you can.'

'Yes, of course. I'll shut up about saving Cauldstane, but if you don't mind, I'll give Sholto all the information I've gathered. About the paintings and so on. It would be on my conscience if I didn't explain to him... give him every opportunity to—'

My voice dwindled into tearful silence. I sensed a movement from Alec at the door, a movement he curbed. I looked up, but couldn't quite bring myself to meet his eyes. 'I think Sholto's grown quite fond of me. He said he'll miss me. Wasn't that sweet? I'll certainly miss him.' I sniffed heartily. 'I'll miss all of you. Another reason I should go soon, I suppose. It's not going to get any easier to make the break. And in any case...' I managed a humourless little laugh. 'How can I stay now, after – well, after my stupid declaration?' I bowed my head and put my hand over my eyes. 'God, I've behaved like a lovesick schoolgirl. I'm so sorry.'

'No,' Alec said, so softly I almost didn't catch the word. 'There's nothing...'

If he completed the sentence I didn't hear. I was bending down to pick up my notebook and pen when I realised the incriminating journal was still lying at my feet. I had a choice and really only a split second in which to make it. The journal could sit there like an unexploded bomb, until someone detonated it by reading the contents. Or I could take it with me, back to my room, which would at least give me more time to work out what was the best thing to do with it.

Stop trying to rescue them, Jenny. I heard myself say that, quite clearly, in my head. Then I glanced up at Alec. He wasn't looking at me, but standing in the doorway, to one side, to let me pass. He looked as if he'd just been given very bad news. Actually, he looked broken. But perhaps it was acute embarrassment.

I ignored my sound advice to myself, picked up Meredith's journal and hid it under my notebook. I hugged both of them to my chest and, head down, walked over to the door. Alec didn't move aside, didn't move at all and, as I squeezed past him, my arm brushed his. My legs almost gave way, but I kept walking – across the landing, down the stairs, back to my room, where I flung my notebook and Meredith's journal on to my desk, then I lay down on the bed and allowed the tears to come.

A few moments later, I heard Alec come thundering down the stairs. When he got to my landing, his footsteps faltered. I stopped crying, stopped breathing. (I'm not proud of the pathetic hope I cherished in those few agonizing seconds.) I heard his door, opposite mine, open, then slam shut. After that there was silence.

I lay on my bed, calmer now. Or perhaps I was just numb. I strained my ears to catch any sound coming from Alec's room, but all I could hear was the distant sound of the River Spey, the river that would have claimed my life, were it not for the heroic actions of the man across the corridor, who apparently felt nothing for me.

Later – much later – I rang Rupert and told him God would not be needed at Cauldstane and neither would he. When pressed for details, I reminded him about my confidentiality clause and simply said my work was almost done. I would be driving back to London in a few days. I asked if I could break my journey in Newcastle and pick up my houseplants, then I got off the phone quickly, to avoid any more questions.

I don't remember a great deal about my last few days at Cauldstane. I did my best not to mope. If I wasn't very good company, I was at least professionally detached. Everyone talked about me coming back some time soon. Everyone except Alec, of course.

The MacNabs were so kind. Fergus gave me a book about red kites and Zelda had made me a needlepoint case for my phone. Sholto invited me to choose a souvenir from one of his expeditions and I selected a favourite photograph of him taken in Antarctica. ("Ah, *that* one was taken just before I fell into a crevasse", he announced cheerfully.) He signed it, scrawling my name and his across the desolate snowy waste.

Wilma sent me away with a fruit cake redolent of whisky which I resolved to offload at Rupert's. I'd put on several pounds at Cauldstane. When Wilma described me as looking "bonny" (a Highland euphemism for "chubby", I suspect), I decided the time had come to cut down. After my last disastrous conversation with Alec, I found I didn't have much appetite anyway, even for Wilma's baking, so I assumed the pounds would come off as easily as they'd gone on.

I wasn't expecting anything from Alec and we didn't say a private goodbye. There were hugs and a few tears on my final day, but from Alec there was only a firm handshake. I could tell Wilma was shocked.

What she didn't know — I presume nobody knew, and I didn't find out until I unpacked my case in London — was that Alec had placed a small replica of the Cauldstane claymore, wrapped in soft cloth, in one of the outside zip-up pockets of my suitcase. I examined the blade for the mark of the red kite and I found it. He'd made it himself and probably intended me to use it as a paper knife. There was a small scrap of paper wrapped up with the cloth. Written on it were the words, *Take care. Alec.*

I smoothed out the creases and put the paper, together with Sholto's photo, inside the bird book. I placed the little sword on my mantelpiece. Most days, I would pick it up at some point and stroke the blade, remembering the time I'd held the real thing; how heavy it had been; how brave it had made me feel. I remembered Alec and his smiling grey eyes, how tall and strong he'd seemed standing beside me, handling the claymore so easily. Then, when I could stand the pain no longer, I would put the little sword back on the mantelpiece and try to settle down to work.

I thought of sending a letter, or perhaps just a card, thanking Alec for his gift, but after a week spent trying to compose a short but appropriate message, I gave up and decided the moment had passed.

In every sense, our moment had passed.

PART THREE

Chapter Twenty-five

I broke my long journey south at Rupert's. I was pleased to see him again in his untidy, book-filled home. His desk was piled with paperwork, a draft sermon and copies of the parish magazine. Carrier bags full of jumble slouched in the hall beside a rusting bicycle. It was all so blessedly normal.

Over tea and Wilma's fruit cake, I filled Rupert in on the circumstances under which I'd left Cauldstane. Well, I tried. He listened attentively, comfortable in his worn cords and baggy sweater, his hair over-long and schoolboyish, but an attempt to describe my abortive relationship with Alec, to whom I'd said goodbye only hours earlier, left me feeling tearful. Rupert filled our cups and tactfully changed the subject to bird-watching. He asked if I'd seen any more red kites and told me he'd always wanted to go bird-watching in Scotland. I could think of nothing to say in reply. He helped himself to another piece of cake and said he'd heard May was a good time to spot puffins. After that, the conversation languished.

I knew he was waiting for me to take the lead, so I said, 'Rupert, can I ask you something? Have you ever felt you were in the presence of... evil?'

He was unfazed by the question and answered without hesitation. 'Yes, I have. Only once. But once was enough.'

'What did you do about it?'

'What I do about anything problematic. I prayed.'

'And did that help?'

'Oh, yes. It always does, I find.'

'No, I mean, did prayer make... the evil go away?'

'Eventually. There were other factors brought into play. Light. That's *so* important. Holy water. Salt.'

'*Salt?*'

'Yes, salt can sometimes be a very useful element. Of course, as a scientist I have to point out that I have no way of knowing if the trouble would have gone away anyway. But people prayed and observed certain rituals, then peace descended. It was quite palpable. The evil – for want of a better word – departed. Naturally, *I* don't believe that was a coincidence, but some might claim, quite reasonably, that it was. The question we should ask ourselves, I suppose, is how often can something be regarded as a coincidence before we begin to see it as cause and effect?' Rupert was clearly into his stride now and I knew I was in for an entertaining and educational digression. I let his soothing words flow over me. 'You see, for scientists to take something seriously, a result has to be reproduced under lab conditions, many times. We're not impressed by anecdotal evidence, however impressive the quantity, or impeccable the source.' Re-filling our teacups, he barely paused for breath. 'But there's so much scientists don't know! Even common or garden stuff. Take birds for instance. Why do they sing? No one knows. We understand their alarm and mating calls, but why does a blackbird perch on a chimneypot on a sunny evening and sing its heart out, apparently for no reason? And why does it *vary the tune*?' Rupert grinned, clearly enjoying his inquisition. 'It's hard to avoid coming to the conclusion that birds sing for their own entertainment or each other's. But it's a hypothesis you could never test under lab conditions.'

I leaned back in my armchair. 'Oh, Rupert, it's doing me a power of good to listen to you. I feel as if sanity is returning. Do go on.'

'Glad to be of service,' he said, cheerfully. 'My garden keeps me sane. If I'm feeling murderous towards an awkward parishioner – God forgive me, but it happens – I sit and watch the activity on my bird table for a few minutes, then I feel the milk of human kindness begin to course through my veins again. Will you have some more of this wonderful cake?'

Rupert's jokey use of the word *murderous* had put me in mind of my moral dilemma. Meredith's journal sat upstairs in my suitcase, wrapped in several plastic bags, as if it might contaminate the rest of my luggage. I had to decide what to do with it. Return it to Sholto? Hand it over to the police? Show it to Alec? I'd been told to destroy all the journals, but this one seemed quite outside my remit. If, therefore, I had to return it, I needed to decide how and to whom. This was a problem I felt I needed to lay before Rupert. If there was a right thing to do, I was sure he'd know what it was.

'I need to ask your advice, Rupert. As a clergyman. And I need you to treat this information as confidential.'

'Of course. The seal of the confessional, my dear.'

'The evil spirit I've told you about... this *ghost*... she committed a wicked crime when she was alive. She arranged a fatal accident, then made sure someone else got the blame. A child.'

'How on earth do you know all this?'

'I've read her confession. It's in a journal written on the day of the accident.'

'And you think this account is authentic?'

'Oh, yes. Authentic and quite insane. She positively gloats about what she's done. In any case, apart from a couple of details, her account coincides with what the family know happened that day. What they don't know is the *cause* of the accident.'

'You're saying they're unaware of the existence of this journal?'

'Of its contents, yes.'

'So who else knows about it?'

'Well, that's just it. I'm convinced no one knows about it but me. I think I'm the only person who's ever read this confession, even though the accident happened thirty-two years ago.'

'And you want to know who you should tell? *If* you should tell,' Rupert added.

'Exactly.'

He sipped his tea thoughtfully, then after a pause said, 'It seems very wrong that a child should have been blamed for a fatal accident. That's the sort of thing that would haunt you for the rest of your life. He or she has a right to know the truth, I'd say.'

'Yes, of course. But it's much more complicated than that.'

'I was afraid you were going to say that. Tell me the worst.'

'The person who was killed was the child's mother.'

'Good grief!' Rupert's cup rattled in the saucer as he set it down.

'So if I tell him he didn't cause the accident in which his mother died, I'm more or less obliged to tell him how she *did* die. Because I know. Know that it was effectively murder.'

'I see. And it's one thing losing a parent in an accident, quite another knowing her death was connived at.'

'Especially when there's no possibility of the criminal being brought to justice because she's dead.'

'Indeed. The son's suffering might be even greater for knowing what actually happened. In fact, I think we can be certain of that. To discover that your mother had been *murdered*... My goodness me. It's hard to imagine the impact that could have.'

'It gets worse, Rupert,' I said in a very small voice.

'Really?' He looked at me in disbelief.

'The child – now a man – is the man I've been talking to you about. Alec. We were... involved until he decided he should send me away. For my own safety. But I have reason to believe... I mean, I now have to assume he doesn't want anything more to do with me.'

'This is beginning to sound like the plot of one of your books, Imogen.'

'There's more.'

Rupert raised both his hands in a gesture of surrender. 'Do your worst.'

'The woman who killed Alec's mother married his father. If I tell Alec the truth, I'll have to explain that his stepmother killed his mother. And he already knows this same woman was responsible – in her ghost form – for drowning his wife. *And* she tried to drown me using the same method, but Alec and his brother rescued me.' Rupert stared at me, white-faced and speechless. 'The thing is, I don't know how much more Alec can take. I don't know how *anyone* processes information like this. Obviously what I'd rather do is let sleeping dogs lie – I can't bear to think of making anything *worse* for him – but does he have a right to know? Does his brother have a right to know? And what about their father? He married his wife's killer! Should I tell him?'

'No. I think there are limits to your responsibilities. The only obligation you *might* have now is towards Alec. But at this stage, I wouldn't like to commit myself, not without a great deal more thought. And prayer. Whether Alec tells his brother, his father, anybody else, is *his* decision. You might of course decide to tell someone other than Alec what you've discovered. But I'm not sure that relieves you of your moral responsibility with regard to him. Certainly, as he's been blamed for decades, it's hard to avoid the conclusion that, if anyone should know the truth about this sorry business, it's Alec.'

'Yes. That's as far as I've got – should I tell him or not?'

'Let's approach it from another angle. If you don't tell him, what will you do with the journal?'

'Well, that's just it. I don't know. I was given instructions to destroy it.'

'Well, that seems clear enough.'

'But the person who gave me the instruction had no idea what the journal contained.'

'Could you return it?'

'Well, I don't expect to go back to Cauldstane, so it would mean posting it. If I post it to Alec, he might read it. If I post it to his father – he's the one who told me to destroy it – I'd have to explain why I'm returning it. So returning the journal is tantamount to sharing the information. But I think I'd rather destroy the damn thing and have that on my conscience than dump this information on them. In the post! But that would be wrong, wouldn't it? To destroy evidence that would free Alec from a lifetime's guilt?'

Rupert was silent for a while, then said, 'Jen, could you leave this one with me? I need to give this some serious thought. Shall we discuss it again tomorrow? Over breakfast?'

'Oh, there's no hurry. I'm not rushing in to anything. I've got to get this right. If I don't, then that witch will have won.'

'I'm sure the way will become clear. It usually does. Now why don't you go and unpack your things and make yourself at home upstairs? You'll find some soothing literature by your bedside, but feel free to take a nap while I potter about in the kitchen. Will dinner at seven suit you? It's only macaroni cheese, I'm afraid, but I've made it with an excellent cheddar.'

'That will be lovely. Comfort food. Just what I need. You're an angel, Rupert.'

'Hardly. But a female parishioner did comment the other day that I was looking positively cherubic. I thought she was having a dig about the weight I've put on,' he added with a sigh.

I got to my feet and stretched, aware of how tense I'd been for the last hour, but as Rupert loaded the tea tray and carried it through to the kitchen, a thought struck me, one so momentous, I had to sit down again.

When he returned, Rupert looked at me and said, 'What's the matter? Are you feeling ill?'

'No. I've just thought of something... You know the family has refused to consider the deliverance ministry?'

'Yes.'

'Well, it just occurred to me... If I tell them what Meredith did... If I tell them *everything*, I wonder if they might change their mind? I really don't know Alec very well, but I know how angry he is. I think he might consider anything that would destroy that woman's power. But... supposing the knowledge destroyed *him*?'

Rupert folded his hands neatly in front of his generous belly and immediately looked ecclesiastical. 'Rarely have I come across a moral dilemma this complex,' he announced solemnly. 'Holmes would have called this "a three pipe problem". We must tread very carefully, Imogen. And I feel I should warn you... the temptation to do good can sometimes prove irresistible. So beware.'

I slept well, better than I'd slept in days and Rupert served kippers for breakfast. I was indeed blessed. He'd obviously been turning over my problem in his mind and, as I would be setting off after breakfast, he delivered his advice between mouthfuls in the calm and doggedly rational way that had been, at times, so comforting, at others, so annoying.

'I've tried to be clear about the moral imperatives. Not easy, but I think we must begin with the instruction you were given: to destroy the journal. You must either do that, or you must return the journal to the person who gave that instruction. Would you agree?'

'Yes. I see that.'

'Then it gets complicated. How should you return it? And should you give any reason why you've returned it?' He helped himself to a slice of brown bread and buttered it thickly. 'The easier option is to destroy the journal, as instructed.'

'I don't think I can do that. Not unless Alec, or someone other than me, knows what it contains.'

'Yes, I thought that's what you'd say. I'd feel the same. So I think your way is becoming clearer... You're obliged to return this journal and you have to decide to whom you'll give it and when, and what explanation you'll give for not destroying it.'

'I don't know if I can give my reason. It sounds so ridiculous! And it's not as if I'm even family.'

'Try me,' Rupert said, setting down his cutlery.

'Well... I think this journal could be used to free the family. I think if they understood the full extent of the evil that surrounds them, they'd fight back. And I think if we all fight back *together* – it's just a hunch, maybe just wishful thinking – but I think if the family unite and face up to Meredith – that's the ghost – and if we've got God on our side and holy water and *you*, Rupert, I feel sure something can be done. I mean, there must have been a reason why I found that appalling journal, surely?'

'Providence, you mean? I wonder... What made you look for it? The journal, I mean.'

'I thought Alec might be wrong about his mother's death. Something just didn't add up. I suspected he wasn't to blame and I thought maybe I could prove it.'

'Which you did. But you haven't yet proved it to *him*.'

'No.'

Rupert was watching me closely. 'But you think you should.'

I hesitated for a long moment before saying, 'Yes.'

'To sum up then... You think Alec should know he's innocent, so it simply remains for you to decide whether you tell him or his father and whether you inform either man in person or via some other form of communication. You say you have no reason to return to Scotland?'

'Not really. When I finish a draft of the biography, I *could* deliver it in person. That was my plan before I was sent packing. But now I think my client would expect me to post a print-out of the draft. After that it's up to him whether he wants to pursue publication or not. I'm hoping my draft will convince him that he should.'

Rupert was silent, deep in thought, then he said, 'Much as I'd like to help, Jen, I don't think I can be of further assistance. The decisions are all yours and you need to give them careful consideration. Go back to London and finish the book, then see if it's any clearer what you should do. You never know, something might happen in the interim. One of the family might get in touch, provide you with an excuse to return. Or at least open up a channel for communication. Undoubtedly, Alec thinks he's done the right thing sending you away out of the danger zone, but he might have a hard time living with the consequences.'

I shook my head. 'I think Alec is very used to having a hard time living.'

'And that's why you want to tell him about the journal. Why you want to get rid of his stepmother's earthbound spirit.'

'She's like a *disease*, Rupert! I don't know about holy water, she makes me want to go round sprinkling disinfectant!'

He smiled. 'You know, there's a lot in what you say. The popular conception of evil is a dark, majestic god, or a beautiful fallen angel. Milton has a lot to answer for, I'm afraid. But I prefer to think of unquiet spirits, poltergeists, demons and so forth as spiritual *bacilli*. They attack the soul and the personality. They cause sickness. But, I assure you, the sickness can be cured.'

'You think so?'

'I *know* so. Now, if you'll excuse me, I have to be at a meeting in an hour and I must clear up, or the kitchen will reek of kippers for the rest of the week.'

While Rupert cleared away, I got my things together and loaded up the car with my houseplants, conscious that a weight had been lifted from my shoulders. It wasn't gone completely, but sharing the burden had made a huge difference. I no longer felt I was completely in the dark, groping my way towards a decision. I knew what I had to do, I just didn't know how to do it.

When I said goodbye to Rupert, I hugged him and we stood for a moment with our arms round each other in a completely platonic embrace. There was no longer any desire on my part, but there was still, I was relieved to note, a great deal of love. I missed Rupert and suspected I always would. He claimed there was a God-shaped hole in everybody's life and people found different ways to fill it. He said mine was writing.

There's a Rupert-shaped hole in my life and so far I've found nothing to fill it. Which is why, when I bade farewell, I kissed him on the cheek and said, 'Goodbye, Rupert. You're one in a million. And when I count my blessings, you're near the top of the list.'

'It's a privilege to be able to serve,' he said, smiling broadly. 'If you need me for anything, Imogen – anything at all – just get in touch. I'll be standing by. With the spiritual disinfectant.'

Chapter Twenty-six

In the days after I returned home from Cauldstane, I felt empty, drained by grief and longing.

The thing about pain — any kind of pain, physical or emotional — is that you can't ignore it. You can *pretend* to ignore it. You can continue to function as if the pain doesn't exist and possibly no one will guess at the adaptations you make to live with that pain. But that's my point. You have to *adapt*. Things aren't the same, even if you manage to create an impression that they are. All that happens when you adapt to pain is that other people are able to ignore, even forget about it.

That was my mother's experience of widowhood. Putting on a brave show after my father's sudden death, she refused to fall apart on the outside, even though she appeared quite hollowed out by grief. The woman who eked out a life for another three years was brittle, fragile like a blown egg, but like an egg, there was no indication on the outside of the emptiness within. She just drifted, oddly weightless, without direction, through what remained of her life, as if waiting for something. I never knew what. I hoped it wasn't death.

Like her, I waited.

I wasn't prepared for how much I would miss the MacNabs. I thought as I put first miles, then days between us, the pain of separation would lessen, memories would become less vivid. I couldn't have been more wrong. In idle moments I found myself dwelling on happier times at Cauldstane. I remembered the funny things people had said, the tender things Alec had done. Trying to remember Alec became, if not an obsession, then a preoccupation. I'd taken no photos of him and could have kicked myself for that oversight, but I'd borrowed some photos from the family albums, intending to make a selection for Sholto's biography. He'd said he had no idea what would interest readers, so I'd made my own choice, mixing the adventurous with the domestic. That included a few photos of the MacNab brothers as boys and young men, but nothing recent.

Thank heavens for Google. I found a few photos of Alec online, pictured competing as a historical swordsman. There was also a photo of him in the armoury on his website, dressed in his leather apron. That was all I had in the way of mementos – those few photos and the miniature claymore.

Most of the time I was relieved we'd never got as far as sleeping together. I told myself, very sensibly, how much harder it would have been to forget him if we'd ever made love. But sometimes – usually when lying awake in the middle of the night – I chided myself for my reserve, for not seizing the moment. But which moment? When? By the time it was apparent Alec and I were headed towards bed, Meredith had decided to drown me, the one being a natural consequence of the other.

We'd missed our opportunity, but maybe it was just as well. As my feelings weren't reciprocated, our failure to graduate to a sexual relationship was probably a blessing. I told myself I wouldn't have wanted to feel used. Then I'd look at Alec's photo and think, "Yes, I would. I wouldn't have minded. Perhaps I wouldn't have *felt* used. Maybe it would have been a glorious, casual but mutually fulfilling one-night stand. And where's the harm in that?"

Since the mere possibility of sexual activity had been enough to send Meredith into full "vengeance is mine" mode, my question was perhaps naïve. I knew I'd been in danger, I just didn't care. Was that love? Stubbornness? Stupidity?

It was certainly foolish to speculate that Alec might have sent me away despite his feelings for me. That was even harder to live with, even more frustrating than believing I'd been toyed with, then cast aside. If I could convince myself Alec had exploited my emotional vulnerability, I'd at least enjoy the luxury of disapproval. But I couldn't. That old crap detector again. I would have bet a large amount of money that Alec MacNab didn't have a dishonourable bone in that rangy, elegant body. Which led me to conclude either he'd never felt more than a passing lust, or alternatively, whatever he felt when he'd kissed me, goading Meredith to reveal herself, he *still* felt, but refused to acknowledge.

Whichever way I looked at it, whatever emotional knots I tied myself in, I ended up in the same miserable place. London. Alone. Trying not to check my phone too often. Trying to ration the number of times I looked at Alec's photo.

I was just waiting. For some kind of sign.

I worked long hours on Sholto's book and struggled with the short but necessary section concerning Meredith. Taking a break, I googled "psychopath" and, wearing my researcher's hat, attempted to come to terms with what I'd seen and what I knew. But the labels didn't help. Psychopaths, it seemed, were a law unto themselves when alive, so I didn't rate anyone's chances of negotiating with a psychopathic ghost. Perhaps Alec was right to concede defeat.

Some days I could push the fear so far to the back of my mind, I began to wonder if I'd imagined how bad things were. Then I'd remember the little girl standing in the middle of the river, crying her crocodile tears and I'd start to shiver at the memory of how cold and terrified I'd been. Then I'd get angry. Angry that Meredith, who felt compassion for no one, should use other people's compassion as a deadly weapon against them. Coral had died because she wanted to help a child in distress. If I'd drowned, it would have been for the same reason. Evil was a word that hadn't really featured in my vocabulary pre-Cauldstane, but I could think of no other way to describe Meredith's actions, both when she was alive and after she was dead.

In the middle of one sleepless night, I thought of trying to write Meredith out of the story. Years ago, before I cracked up, I'd been convinced that if I put something into a novel, it would actually happen. Now, insomniac and irrational, I considered writing "Cauldstane: the novel", in which Meredith lived long enough to see the error of her ways and dandle grandchildren on her knee, but died peacefully and prematurely after a short and painless illness. Then I remembered she was only a member of the MacNab clan by virtue of having arranged Liz MacNab's death. I ended up, predictably, wishing Meredith had never been born. And that was a re-write quite beyond me.

~

The sign came. At least, that's what I told myself. I was sitting on a tube and the man opposite me was reading the *Telegraph* with the property page facing out. When I glanced up from my Kindle to see what station we were in, I came face-to-face with an article about Cauldstane, a piece designed to publicise an expensive property for sale. I couldn't see the price tag, but I recognised the distinctive outline of Cauldstane and the lanky, stooped figure with a walking stick standing in front of it.

It was a substantial article with one of those inane, punning headlines: *Laird of all he surveys*. There were interior and exterior shots of Cauldstane concentrating on its best features – the Great Hall, the library and the riverside location. A veil had sensibly been drawn over the sanitary arrangements and the Dickensian kitchen. I knew just what the agent's brochure would say. *A historic family home, full of character and charm, now in need of substantial refurbishment.* When the passenger opposite me alighted, he discarded his paper. I pounced, then leafed through the crumpled pages until I found the article.

Cauldstane was on the books of Galbraith's in Inverness and they were soliciting offers over £3,000,000. The price was ridiculous and must have been aimed at gullible foreigners with more money than sense who might buy on the internet without viewing first. No one who'd seen Cauldstane, let alone had it surveyed, would have paid three million. But perhaps there was an alternative interpretation of that unrealistic price. Sholto wasn't stupid. Had he priced it *not* to sell? If he'd finally yielded to pressure from Alec, he might have agreed to the castle going on the market, at the same time hedging his bets with the asking price. Cauldstane's ludicrous price tag could be Sholto's way of buying time.

I was hardly reassured. There might be someone mad enough and rich enough to pay three million to live their Highland dream. Cauldstane was up for sale and the Scottish legal system made buying property faster and more straightforward than in England. If I wanted to prevent the sale and foil Meredith's plan, I had to act soon. I'd already deferred what seemed like an impossible decision for two weeks while I'd worked hard at finishing the draft of Sholto's book. It was almost done and I knew if I pushed myself, I could complete it in a matter of days, after which I appeared to have little choice other than to return to Cauldstane with the draft manuscript and Meredith's journal. While I was there I had to hope I'd find an opportunity to talk to Alec and break the dreadful news about his mother.

The prospect made me feel quite ill, but I'd hashed it over with Rupert on the phone. I had to tell Alec what I knew. I had to ask him one last time if he'd let Rupert try to deliver the MacNabs from Meredith's pernicious influence. And if Alec said no, I would go over his head to Sholto. I'd tell *him* about the journal and ask him to sanction the deliverance ministry.

I'd lost a night's sleep trying to decide if I had the right to tell Sholto his wife and daughter-in-law had effectively been murdered. The only way I could square it with my beleaguered conscience was by focusing on the fact that I knew Sholto didn't want to sell up; that he wanted Alec to become the next Laird of Cauldstane. I didn't know Alec well enough to predict how he'd react to the shocking information I had to impart, but I knew Sholto. I'd spent weeks closeted with the man. I'd researched his life so thoroughly, I was probably more familiar with its details than members of his family.

I knew Sholto and I loved him. I thought he would probably rather die than give Cauldstane up to strangers. Admittedly, he'd just been holding on for Alec, who appeared to have suddenly lost interest in his inheritance, but I believed if I could show Sholto *why* Alec was no longer interested, he'd stop the sale and summon all his energies to defend Cauldstane and Alec's birthright.

That was my belief and I was prepared to put it to the test. It was a huge gamble and the stakes could scarcely have been higher. By no means confident of success, I nevertheless thought I stood a chance. But in the middle of one sleepless night, it occurred to me I might increase my chances of success if I turned up at Cauldstane with Rupert, primed and ready to perform the deliverance ministry. I could arrive without actually explaining his purpose. Even if offered hospitality at Cauldstane, I didn't think I could accept it, so it would be quite in order to arrive with a travelling companion. We'd be offered lunch or tea and I would discuss Sholto's book and return his photographs while Rupert explored the estate. I thought I could rely on Fergus to show another wildlife enthusiast around. Perhaps the red kites would put in an appearance, so Rupert's journey wouldn't be completely wasted if Sholto said no. It only remained for me to find some time alone with Alec to discuss the journal. After that, I'd just have to play it by ear.

At 3.00am it looked something like a plan. All I needed to do was book Rupert for a short trip to the Highlands, then inform the MacNabs I would be making a return visit to see Sholto and deliver his completed manuscript.

What could possibly go wrong?

When I'd finished the draft, I rang Rupert.

'Hope I haven't caught you at a bad time?' There were indeterminate grunting sounds as if he had a mouth full of food, but I pressed on. 'I wanted to let you know, I've finished the draft.'

'Congratulations,' he said, swallowing. 'Are you going to deliver it in person?'

'Yes. There are still a few things to discuss and I have to return some photos.'

'And have you decided what to do about... the other matter?'

'That's really why I was ringing. I need you to come to Scotland with me.'

'Ah... Well, it so happens I've got a few days booked off at the end of next week. I was planning to spend them in the Yorkshire Dales. Walking, perhaps some bird watching. But if your family have had a change of heart, I could cancel my break and use that time.'

There was a silence in which I struggled with my conscience. I don't know when I've felt a greater temptation to lie, but Rupert would have been the first to point out that lying in a good cause is just as wrong as lying in a bad cause. I was still choosing my words when he said, with a slight edge to his voice, 'I take it the family *have* come round?' When I still didn't reply, he said, 'Jen? Are you there?'

'Yes. I'm here.'

'Have the family changed their mind about the deliverance ministry?'

'No. At least – I don't know. They might have. I haven't asked them.'

'Why ever not? Or perhaps I should say, why are you booking my services when you don't even know if they're required?'

'Because if I ask them, I think they'll say no. But if I just turn up

248

with you—'

'No, I couldn't possibly agree to that. The Church doesn't intervene in these matters unless specifically invited to do so.'

'Oh, absolutely. But they need know nothing about your occupation. You'd simply be there as my travelling companion. But if I *should* manage to persuade them that deliverance ministry would be a better solution than selling up, then there you are, on the spot.'

'On the spot indeed,' Rupert sighed. 'No, Jen, I don't think this is a very sound idea. In any case, I really don't have time to go off on what would probably be a wild goose chase.'

'Rubbish. You just said you'd booked some time off.'

'That was for a recreational break!'

'And that's what you'll get in Scotland. The walking's terrific. And there's every chance you'll see red kites. I wasn't planning to stay at the castle, I was going to book us into a hotel. When was the last time you stayed in a decent hotel? Or ate a really good dinner? My treat, Rupert. And if the family refuse to let you do your stuff, you just get a nice little holiday in the Highlands.'

'But how will you account for my presence? I presume you won't be introducing me as a clergyman? That would be a bit of a giveaway.'

'I'll just say you're an old friend and, if anyone asks, a retired physicist – all of which is perfectly true.'

'But it's not the whole truth.'

'I promise you, I won't be asking you to *lie*, Rupert. They might not even want to talk to *me*, let alone you. The castle is up for sale now and they all know how I feel about that. Our visit could be a very short one.'

'But you're still hoping to persuade them to permit the deliverance ministry?'

'Yes.'

'Whereupon you will produce me, like a rabbit out of a hat. It will look calculating and manipulative, Jen.'

'Yes, I realise that. And if the castle weren't already on the market, I'd consider doing things properly – discussing it with them again, then inviting you to help. But any day an offer could be made that the family will accept. If they do, then we've lost and Meredith has won.'

'Is an offer likely?'

'I've no idea. They're asking three million. When I rang the agents, pretending to be a potential buyer, they said there'd been a lot of interest, but they would say that. As soon as I get talking to members of the family, I'll have more idea how things stand. I fear Alec won't want anything to do with me, but I expect the others will be eager to fill me in on developments. I just need to get up there. But I'd like to go prepared. Ready to act. Should the opportunity arise.'

'Yes, I understand, but you'll be putting me in a very difficult position. I'm not prepared to lie. If I'm asked a straight question I will have to give a straight answer.'

'I know. I don't want you doing anything you're not comfortable with, Rupert.'

'Can I have some time to think about this? You seem to have presented me with another tricky moral dilemma. Could I let you know tomorrow?'

'Of course. You must sleep on it. Whatever you decide, I'll be going, so there's really no pressure,' I said, sounding not the least bit convincing.

There was a short silence, then Rupert said huffily, 'This is all most irregular, you know. I realise you have to return the journal and you need to discuss the book, but I do wonder whether we should simply mind our own business and let the family sort out their problems in their own way – which they seem keen to do. Putting the castle on the market – that's a big step.'

'Not necessarily. The price is quite unrealistic.'

'How do you know that? Properties like that must be very difficult to value.'

'I've done some research. They seem to sit on agents' books for months, even years, then they come down in price until they're sold for a humiliating amount. This is why the family haven't tried to sell up before. But things are different now. Alec wants everyone out for safety reasons. For all I know, he could persuade his father to accept some stupid offer, just to expedite matters. So that's why I think we shouldn't hang about.'

'Well, I'll let you know tomorrow.'

'Thanks. I do realise I'm being a total pain. I'm really sorry. I'll leave you in peace now and we'll speak tomorrow.'

'Very well, but do keep thinking about the wisdom of what you're doing, Jen. The less charitable would call it meddling.'

'And what would *you* call it?'

'Oh, compassion in action, I suppose,' he said airily. 'You've always been a do-gooder. But your life would be so much calmer if you could restrict your crusades to saving your local library. Saving castles is a very tall order.'

'But I think we're up to it. Don't you?'

'I'll let you know tomorrow,' Rupert said warily. 'I have some serious praying to do first.'

Rupert said yes. Is it possible to love two men simultaneously? In that moment I did, acknowledging that my old love for Rupert was of a completely different kind from my new love for Alec. One was a warm and comfortable glow. No thrills, but no surprises either. The other was an acute stabbing pain. Inconvenient and disabling, it ambushed me while I was going about my daily business.

Rupert's leave was already booked for the end of November and he wanted to be back for Advent Sunday. I said I'd check the dates with Sholto. If they suited him, I would get the train to Newcastle, hire a car and collect Rupert. I'd return him to his door three days later.

So we had a deal.

When I spoke to Sholto on the phone he sounded delighted to hear from me. He was thrilled I'd finished the book and had even come up with a couple of possible titles, both of which I liked.

'What do you think of *A Curious Life*? It's a pun. I've *lived* a rather curious life and I've always been very curious about, well, pretty much everything. Do you think it's a good title?'

'I think if we preface it with your name, *Sholto MacNab: A Curious Life*, it would be an excellent title.'

'Good. I'm glad you like it. My other suggestion was going to be *Footsteps in the Snow*. That one's more evocative, don't you think?'

'Yes, I do. It all depends what image the publisher wants to put on the cover. I think they'll use a picture of you doing something hair-raising, or possibly a portrait, so *A Curious Life* might work best. But we can put forward any suggestions for consideration.'

'Good! So when can I read it?'

'Well, I'd like to deliver the manuscript in person on November 28th if that would suit you. It would be useful to have some time to talk to you on the 28th or 29th if you're free.'

'Yes, that would be splendid. You'll stay with us for a few days, of course? Everyone will be pleased to see you again. I must say, it's been very dull since you left. Alec's been like a bear with a sore head, but I think all this business with the sale – ah, you know about that, I suppose?'

'Yes, I saw the piece in the *Telegraph*.'

'Yes, well, Alec and I have been at loggerheads over the asking price, but as I said to him, it's not as if we're in a hurry to sell.'

'No, I suppose not,' I said cautiously, knowing perfectly well Alec thought the need to evacuate Cauldstane was pressing. 'But the thing is, Sholto, I won't be travelling alone. I'm coming up with a friend and we're going to stay in a hotel.'

'You can both stay here! We've plenty of room. She won't object to our antique plumbing, I presume? The estate agent was quite dismissive about that when he came to do the valuation. Positively scathing, in fact.'

'My friend's a *he* actually. I think he might feel a bit of a spare part as he doesn't know anyone.'

'Nonsense! We're a friendly bunch, as you know. Well, apart from Alec. But he'll make the effort for *you*, I'm sure.'

Floundering in the face of Sholto's hospitality, I made yet another effort to extricate myself from the possibility of further intimacy with Alec. 'My friend was hoping to get some walking done—'

'There are splendid walks on the estate. Fergus will show him some of our beauty spots. You must both stay here. We have a double room if that's what you'd prefer.'

'Oh, no, that won't be necessary. If we stayed,' I said, my resolve weakening, 'we'd need a room each. But I really can't put you to all that trouble.'

'No trouble at all! Can you imagine what Wilma would say if I told her you were visiting, but staying elsewhere? She'd be deeply offended and I'd never hear the last of it. So it's settled, then. You and your gentleman friend will stay with us for a couple of days. Zelda will be pleased as punch! You're *sure* you can't stay longer?'

'My friend can only spare a few days.'

'I understand. Work commitments.'

I saw the trap before walking into it and recovered quickly. 'No he's retired. But...' Rupert's aged mother saved the day. 'He has to get back to see to an elderly relative. He's arranged respite care so he can get away.' This wasn't a total lie. Rupert *had* arranged for his mother to be cared for in a Gateshead nursing home and he visited her twice a week. 'If you're sure it will be OK?'

'You would both be very welcome. Though...' Sholto hesitated. 'I should perhaps point out Cauldstane isn't exactly *cosy* in November. We light all the fires, of course, but it might be as well to tell your friend to dress warmly. November's an odd month. It can be glorious. Crisp, sunny mornings, with wonderful sunsets. Or it can be freezing. Heavy snow is not out of the question, I'm afraid, so come prepared.'

'I will.' I thought of Rupert's selection of seriously warm Scandinavian pullovers, acquired as part of his economy drive to reduce his heating bills. 'Rupert's the hardy type. He'll be fine.'

'It will do us all good to see you, Jenny. And your friend,' Sholto added. 'We don't see many new faces these days. To tell you the truth, we've not been good company for each other since you left. Don't know what's got into everyone. A lot of arguments about selling up and so forth,' he said vaguely. 'Cauldstane hasn't been a happy place lately. But I know you'll brighten up the old place.'

'Well, I'll do my best, but it *will* have to be a short visit,' I said firmly.

'I understand. You have your own life to lead. I imagine you'll be moving on to the next project soon. Who's it to be?'

'I haven't got anything lined up yet. But if I had, you know I couldn't tell you anything about it.'

'No, of course! You're bound by the seal of the confessional,' Sholto chuckled. I recalled Rupert uttering the same words when I'd confided in him about the MacNab woes and the very real confession of what I assumed the law would call manslaughter.

I knew I needed to get off the phone before I said too much and betrayed my main reason for going back to Cauldstane: to speak to Alec. So I wound up the conversation with Sholto, then emailed Rupert to tell him our trip was on.

As I closed the lid of the laptop, I felt as if I'd burned my bridges. Much to my surprise, I discovered it's possible to feel both relieved and terrified at the same time.

Chapter Twenty-seven

It was a cold grey day when Rupert and I arrived at Cauldstane. The sky was leaden with the threat of snow and I was relieved we'd managed to get there before the weather closed in. Wilma must have been keeping an eye open for us at the kitchen window, for moments after we pulled into the courtyard, she appeared, waving at the back door with Zelda. Sholto wasn't far behind, saluting us with his stick.

He looked older and thinner. So for that matter did Zelda, but perhaps it was just that she looked tired. They were all clearly delighted to see me and made Rupert very welcome. There were of course no questions as to his purpose. He'd arrived in birding gear – green waterproofs and cap, plus binoculars round his neck – so the MacNabs were in little doubt as to the purpose of his visit to the Highlands.

There was no sign of Alec or Fergus. I assumed Fergus was out working on the estate, but I wondered if Alec was keeping a tactful distance. With his ear defenders on, he wouldn't have heard us arrive, but I couldn't hear any hammering or noise of machinery coming from the armoury. I assumed the worst and tried not to let disappointment mar my pleasure at being back at Cauldstane.

Wilma shooed us all indoors out of the cold, then disappeared to put the finishing touches to what I knew would be a tea worthy of the prodigal's return. Zelda led us up to our rooms and Rupert carried our bags, his head swivelling, his eyes wide, like an owl, as we made our way upstairs.

'I thought you'd like your old room, Jenny,' Zelda said, throwing open the door to the bedroom opposite Alec's. I was indeed pleased, but concerned how much scope there would be for bumping into Alec. Zelda then took Rupert off to the third floor. 'Did you bring your oxygen mask?' she quipped as they mounted the stairs. Rupert followed gamely, declaring he needed the exercise.

I unpacked my few things and set the large padded envelope

containing Sholto's manuscript on the table. There was little daylight left now, so I drew the curtains, glancing down at the river. The water looked black and seemed to be flowing even faster than I remembered. No doubt heavy autumn rain had added to the volume of water. I shivered at the memory of being submerged in the river and felt suddenly sick with fright. What on earth was I doing, returning to the place where someone – some*thing* – had tried to kill me? Was I mad? Alec would have said so.

There was a knock at my door and I couldn't help hoping it was Alec come to greet me belatedly, but it was only Rupert. The door swung open and he entered, looking pleased with himself.

'Well, this is all quite splendid, I must say. I'm up in the eagle's nest on the third floor. A dear little room with a turret. Zelda says I'll be able to see for miles in the morning if there's no fog. And I have a wondrous selection of reading matter. Everything from seventeenth-century witch trials to the breeding of hunting dogs. If I had a spare three million, I'd snap this place up... Jen, are you all right? You've gone very quiet. Is all this going to be difficult for you?'

'I think it might be. A little. The sound of the river... Just now I was remembering the day Alec fished me out.' I put my hand up to my face and covered my eyes, but I could still see the little girl dancing with delight as I fell into the water.

I felt Rupert's arm go round my shoulders. 'You know, we *can* just do what you came to do. Deliver the book. Return the photos.' He took my hand and squeezed it. 'You really don't have to get involved.'

When I opened my eyes to reply, something – a slight movement – made me glance over Rupert's shoulder into the corridor. Alec stood in the hallway looking into the bedroom. Cat-like as ever, he'd ascended the stairs without making a sound.

I craned my head, saying, 'Hello, Alec,' and Rupert released me, turning round.

Before I could say any more, Alec stepped forward, offering his hand to Rupert. 'Alec MacNab.'

'How do you do?' Rupert replied, shaking hands firmly. 'Rupert Sheridan. Very pleased to meet you.'

'I hope you find your room comfortable?'

'Oh, yes, thanks. It's delightful. I'm sure I shall sleep very well.'

Alec didn't reply but shot me a look that would have curdled milk. I realised he thought Rupert and I were sharing my room, but there was no way I could disabuse him of the idea without suggesting it was an issue for him. Since it *wasn't*, there was no earthly reason why I should enlighten him, apart from the fact that I didn't want him to think I'd declared my feelings, then gone back to the arms of a former lover. I couldn't even recall what he knew about Rupert. Had I ever mentioned his name? If I had, would Alec have remembered it? I'd told him I knew someone who could perform the deliverance ministry, but I knew I hadn't mentioned Rupert by name.

It was ridiculous for me to be concerned. Alec wouldn't care, even if I did, but the misunderstanding and my inability to set it straight rankled, as did Alec's manner. Unsmiling, he said, 'Welcome back, Jenny. Tea's being served in the drawing room. Wilma's pushed the boat out, so I hope you're both hungry.'

'Splendid!' Rupert said, rubbing his hands together. 'I've heard a great deal about Mrs Guthrie's baking—' but Alec had already turned away, headed in the direction of the drawing room.

Wilma's spread was predictably magnificent, but Alec drank only half a cup of tea, ate nothing and left the gathering as soon as was decent. Zelda cast an anxious look at his retreating back and sighed. Rupert on the other hand despatched three of Wilma's scones and declared her strawberry jam the best he'd ever tasted. She smiled shyly and offered the opinion that hunger was the best sauce.

After tea, Zelda took Rupert on a tour of the castle. Their laughter echoed down the corridors and I could tell she was enjoying her hostess duties. Sholto and I retired to the library where I presented him with the finished manuscript and his family photographs, annotated with my suggestions for book illustrations. I left him skimming pages and poring over my post-its.

I was always apprehensive when a client read "their book" for the first time. People were normally very happy with my efforts, but this time I wasn't sure if my knowledge of Meredith's criminal and insane behaviour might have coloured the biography. It had certainly tainted it for me, but I hoped my account was still Sholto's and that there was no hint in the book that Meredith's sins went beyond occasional adultery.

Whether to enlighten Sholto was a decision I still had to make, or leave Alec to make. Normally, if my researches turn up something significant, I share the information with a client, even if I find something embarrassing or incriminating. Forewarned is forearmed. If I can discover an unsuspected skeleton in a client's cupboard, so can nosy journalists.

Did Sholto have the right to know what Meredith had done? If he knew, would it affect his autobiography? He'd asked me to downplay his second marriage in favour of the first. If he knew his second wife had despatched his first, would he even want to publish this version of his life?

Tired after the long drive and full of Wilma's cake, I lay down on my bed – a bed I'd once shared, briefly and chastely with Alec – and tried to think things through for one final time. That Alec must be freed from guilt, I was in no doubt. He might decide Sholto also needed to know the truth, though I thought it more probable he'd want his father to die in ignorance. However, over the years Sholto had shown himself to be well nigh indestructible. He might live to see his nineties. Unless Alec destroyed the journal, there was always a chance Sholto could find out. Meredith's ghost might even try to arrange it.

Rupert's continuing reservations about his rôle and Alec's distant behaviour only added to my confusion. Alec would probably never see me again after this visit, so I didn't understand why he was treating me as *persona non grata*, unless he suspected who Rupert was and why he'd come to Cauldstane.

I sat up, suddenly quite certain what I should do. I would inform first Alec, then Sholto of the circumstances of Liz's death, then Rupert and I must leave. I had no right to go against Alec's wishes and it was clear he'd not had a change of heart. I would place the journal in Sholto's hands and he must decide what should be done with it. Then I would wash my hands of the whole MacNab clan and get on with the next book.

Dinner was a cheerful affair with Sholto in fine story-telling form. The wine flowed, food disappeared and there was a great deal of laughter. Fergus and Rupert hit it off and made plans for an early morning walk the following day. I was seated between MacNab, father and son, so it wasn't too difficult to ignore the fact that Alec barely spoke two words to me. Sholto was attentive and Rupert, seated opposite, managed to engage Alec in a conversation about the geometry of sword design and the mathematical beauty of death-dealing instruments. I suspected Alec was enjoying the conversation despite himself. Rarely could he – or anyone – have had a more attentive or intelligent listener than Rupert. I found myself wishing the two men could be friends.

After dinner Sholto and I took coffee in the library and discussed what he'd read so far. He seemed pleasantly surprised. ('I had no idea I was such an eloquent fellow,' he said with a wink.) So I left him to read the rest while I tackled Alec. He hadn't gone to the drawing room with the others and I'd heard the back door bang, so I assumed he was in the armoury, working or just avoiding company. A glance out of my bedroom window confirmed there was a light on. It would be as good a place as any to break the news to him. He felt safe there and, late at night, we wouldn't be interrupted by visits from family members.

I picked up my writing bag and packed Meredith's journal. It was still swathed in plastic bags, like a gift. I wished I could believe what I was giving Alec *was* a gift, the gift of freedom, but the journal was more like a poisoned chalice. I rued the day I'd ever read it, but I reminded myself the only reason I'd checked the facts was because Alec's story didn't add up. It was my job to ensure what I wrote made sense and, if it wasn't the gospel truth, it was at least the version of the truth my subject wished to tell.

I put on my coat, hoisted the bag on to my shoulder and stepped out into the hall. Feeling nervous, I trudged downstairs and along the ill-lit corridor until I came to the back door. Grasping the handle, I suddenly wanted to turn back, but more than that, I just wanted it over with.

As I opened the door and looked across the courtyard at the light in the armoury window, I noticed it had started to snow. I picked my way carefully across the treacherously wet cobblestones, the very stones on which Alec's mother had died thirty-two years ago.

~

I knocked on the door and walked straight in. The light was low, as always, but I could see Alec, seated on a low stool beside the furnace, leaning forward, his hands clasped between his knees. There was an empty whisky glass on the floor by his feet and the bottle was to hand. He looked up as I entered and the glow from the dying furnace cast a warm light on the side of his face, throwing his even features into relief. At that moment I couldn't imagine why I'd ever thought he wasn't handsome.

As he stood, habitually polite, I noticed a silver crucifix glinting in the hollow of his throat. I'd never seen it before and wondered if he'd recently taken to wearing one. As I approached, I saw it wasn't a cross, but a miniature sword, a tiny replica of the Cauldstane claymore.

He didn't speak or smile, nor did he invite me to sit. I'd rehearsed various opening lines for this difficult conversation, but now none of them seemed appropriate. Before I could think of a new one, Alec said wearily, 'If you've come to dissuade me from selling, you're wasting your time. My mind's made up. So was Sholto's before you decided to return.'

'I had to come back, Alec.'

'You surely could have posted the manuscript?'

'Yes, I could.' I removed the bag from my shoulder and set it down on the sofa. 'Do you mind if I sit down? There's something I want to explain.'

'There's no need. You're not accountable to me. You owe me nothing.'

'On the contrary, I owe you my *life*.'

'What you've done for this family – and what you tried to do – is ample compensation. If it weren't for me and the way I feel – *felt* about you, your life would never have been in danger.' He reached down for bottle and glass and poured himself another slug of whisky. 'But I'm relieved to find you're not the sort of woman who nurses a broken heart – gratifying though that might have been to my ego.'

'What do you know or care about the state of my heart? You completely misled me, Alec—'

'No, *you* misled *me!*' He faced me, gesticulating with his glass, spilling whisky. I wondered how much he'd already drunk. 'D'you have any idea how hard it was to send you packing? How much it *grieved* me to have to lie? But I believed it was the right thing to do. I still do. Though apparently I could have spared myself the guilt of thinking I'd hurt you. You didn't waste any time, did you? And I suppose arriving with your new man in tow was a neat form of revenge.'

I stared at him, open-mouthed, overwhelmed by sudden, joyous comprehension. 'Oh my god... You think Rupert— For heaven's sake, Alec, Rupert isn't my new man, he's my very *old* man! We broke up years ago. He's just a friend now.'

'So why did Zelda put you in the same room?'

'She didn't.'

'But I saw you. You were both standing in the room. He had his arm around...' I watched his expression change from belligerence to embarrassment as realisation slowly dawned. 'I got that wrong?'

'You couldn't be more wrong. I was feeling a bit upset and Rupert – well, he's almost like a brother to me now. There hasn't been anything sexual between us for years. Zelda put him up on the third floor. He'd just dropped in when you saw us. You really have got hold of the wrong end of the stick.'

'I see... It seems I've been a prize eejit.' He swallowed some more whisky. 'Not that your love life is any of my business anyway.'

'No, wait a minute, the fact that you jumped to conclusions and say you had to *lie* to me... Well, that rather changes things, doesn't it?' He looked at me, but said nothing. 'I'd really appreciate your being straight with me, Alec, even if I'm only here for a couple of days. You can kick me out of the armoury, throw me out of Cauldstane, but I think you owe it to me to tell me what you really feel. If we can have no future, couldn't we at least have an honest ending?'

'That wouldn't be fair to you.'

'I'll be the judge of that. The truth, please. I told you I loved you before I left. My feelings haven't changed. And I'm mortified you thought I was the kind of woman who'd offer to take on a psychotic ghost, then seek consolation elsewhere when spurned.'

'Aye, I should have known... *Steel-true and blade-straight.*'

'I beg your pardon?'

'It's from a poem by Robert Louis Stevenson. About his wife.'

'Oh... What was it again? *Steel-true*?'

'*And blade-straight.*'

'Well, yes,' I said, considering. 'I think that's probably fair comment. Honesty and loyalty *are* important to me. Very important. Honesty was what made me break up with Rupert. And loyalty is why we're still good friends.' I cast an eye towards the sofa where my bag sat like an elephant in the room. 'And it's honesty that's brought me back to Cauldstane, Alec. There's something important you need to know.'

He shook his head and set down his glass. 'Och, let's have no more words, Jenny. I know that's your stock in trade, but it's not mine.' He gave me a long look and said, 'Will you not let me take you in my arms and let my body do the talking?'

I gazed at him, trying to process the meaning of what I'd just heard and the journal was forgotten. 'I'd like that very much. In fact, you have no idea how much time I've spent thinking about that very thing.'

He moved towards me and slid an arm around my waist, then he pulled me to him and kissed me, cradling my head in one of his hands. When I came up for air, I started to struggle out of my coat. Alec dragged it off me and slung it on to the sofa. When he turned back, I took his face in both hands and pulled his head down towards me, so I could kiss him again. Then he broke away and strode over to the door, where he slid the bolt and turned out the dim overhead light.

My eyes followed every movement of his body as it wove in and out of the shadows of the room, lit now by a little moonlight that entered through a grubby window pane. Alec moved back to the furnace and raked some coals so the fire revived, radiating more light and heat into the room. Having made a circuit of the room, he stood in front of me again, his eyes wide and dark, his face expectant. He looked at me, pleading, and I knew what he was asking. I laid a hand on his chest and nodded.

His expression changed suddenly. Frowning, he clasped my hand where it lay on his chest. 'I'm afraid I don't have anything. And I don't intend to produce a MacNab heir on the wrong side of the blanket. You wouldn't have...?'

The question hung between us until I said, 'Yes. I'm rather embarrassed to admit I do. That,' I said pointing to my discarded bag, 'contains my writing kit, but also my Surviving Life kit. Cheque book. Elastoplast. Safety pins. Vitamin C.'

'And condoms?'

'I've been single for most of my adult life,' I protested. 'And I've always had a bit of a girl scout mentality.'

Alec laughed softly and stroked my cheek. 'So you came prepared.'

'No, they've been in my bag for months! *Years*. Do condoms have a use-by date?' I asked uncertainly. 'They were in my bag before I set sight on Cauldstane. Their presence is nothing to do with you. Believe me, this is the last thing I expected. And it certainly isn't why I came back.'

'I do believe you. But it's what I want, Jenny. It's what I've wanted for a long while.'

He kissed me again, then began to haul the big sofa cushions on to the floor to provide us with a makeshift bed. He unhooked his leather apron from a peg, rolled it up to make a pillow and laid it at one end of the bed, then he took down a sword that was hanging on the wall and propped it against the door. As the door was already bolted, I knew he must have placed it there to protect us from Meredith.

I'd already started to undress, but when I glanced anxiously at the small, uncurtained window, Alec understood. He grabbed a dirty cloth and smeared soot across the window panes in a gesture so economically elegant, I laughed. He grinned as he wiped his hand on his jeans and said, 'I'll have trouble explaining that to Wilma.'

He undressed quickly, dropping his clothes on to the floor, while I removed the last of mine, then he stood before me, naked but for the tiny sword round his neck. He reached up and removed the necklace, then to my surprise, he started to drop it over my head.

'But… what about you?' I said, protesting.

'Och, I'll be fine.'

'But, Alec, supposing she—'

'When once we're united, Jenny, I believe that wee sword will protect us both. Which is as good a reason as you'll ever get for allowing a man to make free with your body.'

I have no idea why I started to weep then, unless it was with happiness. Alec swept me up in his arms and carried me over to the

263

cushions. As I clung to him, pressing my face against the warm skin of his chest, I could hear the thud of his heart. He knelt and set me down gently on the cushions. Gazing at me, he touched the claymore crucifix that lay between my breasts.

'I'm so very glad you came back, Jenny. I thought I had to let you go. But I was wrong.'

'You did exactly what Meredith wanted you to do.'

'Aye, I did. But I'll make up for it now. Meredith definitely doesn't want me to do *this*...'

There was a rattle at the door when Alec entered me, but it might have been the wind. The frantic tapping at the window could have been hailstones, but there was no reason why the furnace should have flared and spat. My body was covered by Alec's. If any sparks reached him, they didn't deter him from his purpose.

By the time I got back to my room, escorted by Alec, everyone else had turned in for the night. We agreed we should sleep separately to avoid scandalizing Wilma when she brought early morning tea to the guests, though Alec agreed Wilma would probably be delighted at the latest developments.

As I removed my clothes for the second time that night, the little sword swung round my neck. When I'd tried to return it, Alec had forbidden me to take it off.

'But supposing one of the others notices it?'

'I don't care. Do you?'

'No. Just as long as no one asks me how I came by it. I couldn't guarantee to maintain my composure if they do.'

'I like it when you fail to maintain your composure,' he said, stroking my cheek. 'Good night, Imogen, my love. Sleep soundly.'

I was lying in bed, fingering the little silver sword, remembering how it had felt to bear the weight of Alec's long body, wondering how soon I could repeat the experience, when I suddenly remembered.

The journal.

Alec still didn't know.

And I still had to tell him.

Chapter Twenty-eight

I slept late and when I got up I found Rupert had gone out with Fergus for a tour of the estate. Wilma said they'd be back for lunch. After a solitary breakfast, I went looking for Alec, but he wasn't to be found in the armoury. On my way back up to my room, I heard raised voices coming from the floor above. Pausing on the landing, I heard Alec and Sholto arguing in the library – about Cauldstane, I presumed.

Alec might have changed his mind about me, but there was no reason to think he'd relented about the sale. He knew I'd be gone in thirty-six hours and if he saw any future for us – even in the short term – he didn't see it taking place at Cauldstane. Alec wouldn't fight back – not for me, not even for Cauldstane, but I wondered if he might fight for his mother. Revenge was a base motive for action, but a powerful one.

Sholto's voice rose to a thunderous crescendo. I heard the library door open, then slam. Feet went bounding up a flight of stairs and another door slammed. I assumed Alec had retreated to the Long Attic. A fusillade of coughing issued from the library and I was tempted to run up and see if Sholto was all right, but I thought he'd be embarrassed to know I'd overheard the row, so I turned away and saw Zelda standing at the open door of her little sitting room.

She rolled her eyes and said, 'Sorry you had to hear all that, Jenny. Cauldstane's not a happy household these days.'

'So I gather.'

'Those two are at loggerheads. It fair breaks my heart to see it. Sholto's *done* what Alec asked. He's put Cauldstane up for sale, but of course no one wants to view it, let alone buy it. It's November, for goodness sake! But Alec wants Sholto to reduce the price for a quick sale and Sholto – well, he'd rather be hanged than *give* the old place away.' She shook her head and leaned against the door frame. 'I see both points of view, but I cannot help either man. It's so sad. And so unlike us… It's as if there's a rot at the heart of the

265

place. I don't mean dry rot – though no doubt we have that too. No, I think there's something just plain *wrong*. There haven't been rows at Cauldstane for years – not since Meredith died. I don't think it's Sholto's fault, but nor do I really blame Alec. They're just not *themselves*. Why, even Fergus is grouchy these days! He's got something on his mind, but he's saying nothing.'

'Still getting over his disappointment with Rachel, perhaps?'

'Aye, maybe. There's something afoot there, but I'm not sure what.'

'I wish I could do something to help.'

'Och, it's been a treat for everyone to see your lovely smiling face again. And Sholto's delighted with his book. You've done what you can, Jenny and we're all very grateful. We just have to sort ourselves out now. But it's times like these I miss Liz the most. She'd have known what to do. What to say.'

'What do you think she might have said?'

Zelda lowered her voice. 'I think Liz would have taken Alec aside and told him – very quietly – that the Laird of Cauldstane was yet living and not beholden to his son. She might have said that. And she'd have got away with it too! But *I* can't say that and Alec doesn't hear when Sholto says it. Poor Liz. She's been gone so many years now...'

'Thirty-two.'

'Is it as much as that? Aye, it must be. Alec's turned forty. But she's still sorely missed. Those poor wee boys needed a mother and instead they got Meredith. Not the same thing *at all*,' Zelda said with a touch of asperity. 'But you must take no notice of me, Jenny. I'm just a grumpy old woman these days, wondering why I ever left the sunny south of France.'

'Family ties, wasn't it? They needed you and you came to the rescue.'

'Well, you can't just stand by, wringing your hands. I'd rather roll my sleeves up and get on with the job. Which reminds me,' she said, consulting her watch, 'It's high time I went down and gave Wilma a hand with lunch. Now she *doesn't* change. Wilma is always good for my spirits – but very bad for my waistline!'

I watched as Zelda descended the stairs, then listened, almost enviously, to the reassuring sound of female chatter as it drifted up from the kitchen. I went into my room and sat by the window, under the cracked mirror, staring down at the river.

Alec was at war with the wrong person. Meredith was the enemy, not Sholto. Her journal was the only weapon I could use against her. I just needed to summon the courage to wield it.

I didn't do Wilma's lunch justice. Nor did Alec. Sholto took his lunch on a tray in the library, as usual. Fortunately Rupert and Fergus came home mud-spattered, red-cheeked, happy and hungry. Each man ate for two.

After lunch I went to the library for my final work meeting with Sholto. We sat either side of his desk, quite comfortable together now, sorting through photos. He'd finished reading the manuscript and claimed he was delighted with it. When he confirmed he'd like to seek a publisher, I told him he could leave everything to me and my capable agent.

'We feel fairly optimistic about our chances of selling the book.'

'I wish the same could be said about our chances of selling Cauldstane,' Sholto grumbled, his smile fading. 'You know we had an offer?'

I sat back in my wing chair, astonished. 'No, I didn't.'

'Alec didn't mention it?'

'No. But the sale is a subject I try to avoid with him.'

'Very wise. I only wish I could do the same. He probably didn't tell you because the offer was quite ludicrously low. An insult!'

'So you rejected it?'

'Rejected it and poured scorn upon it,' Sholto said loftily. 'The estate agent was *not* happy. He tried to imply we should feel grateful for *any* offer. So I reminded him he was in my employ and not *vice versa*. You know, I think I've managed to fall out with everyone over the last few weeks. Everyone except you and Wilma. But then only a fool would argue with Wilma. She's always right. I sometimes think I should go to Wilma and ask her what to do about this business – and it's a bad business, make no mistake. But I doubt she'd tell me what to do, even if I pleaded with her. She'd just say, "I'm sure you know best, Mr Sholto".'

'Well, I'm inclined to agree.'

'Now why do all you women think the same? Why does no one

think Alec knows best?'

'Because you're acting out of love. Love for your sons and for Cauldstane. Alec is motivated by fear.'

The damning words were out before I'd considered them. There was a short silence in which I realised there was no chance of turning back, so I prepared myself for Sholto's inevitable question. It came.

'Motivated by *fear*? Why do you say that?' He leaned across the desk. 'Fear of what exactly?'

'Did Alec ever talk about what happened to me in the river? Why it happened?'

'No. He didn't volunteer any information and I didn't like to press him. It was all so similar to what happened to—' Sholto hesitated and a look of anguish passed over his weary face.

'What happened to Coral?' He nodded. 'Then I imagine Alec hasn't told you why he wanted me to leave. Or why he changed his mind about selling Cauldstane.'

'Are you referring to the curse?'

'No. Alec doesn't believe in the curse. Nobody does, do they? But as Zelda explained to me, you don't have to believe in the MacNab curse for it to do you harm.'

Sholto looked confused. 'I'm not sure I follow, Jenny.'

'Before I came here, I didn't believe in ghosts. I'm still not sure I do, but I know *something* is trying to destroy this family, bit by bit. And top of her To Do list is drive the MacNabs out of Cauldstane.'

Sholto appeared to consider, then said, 'Are you talking about... *Meredith*?'

'Meredith's ghost.'

'And you think that is what she wants?'

'I know it is. And so does Alec.'

He put a gnarled hand up to his brow and rubbed his forehead. 'Let me get this straight... You're saying Meredith's *ghost* had something to do with your accident?'

'And Coral's suicide. Except that it wasn't suicide. Coral died the way I was meant to die. She was lured into the river by a child in distress.'

'A child?'

'A little girl. But there was no child. It was Meredith.'

'But—' He gave a short laugh of disbelief. 'How can you *know* all this, Jenny?'

'When I was in the river I saw Coral's camera. It was hanging under the bridge, caught on a branch. Alec saw it too. It's been missing since she drowned. He never believed it was suicide because he couldn't find her camera. He thought she just went out for a walk that day. With her camera. She didn't go out intending to die.'

Before Sholto could reply, there was a knock at the door. Fergus' dark head appeared. 'Sorry to disturb you folks. I couldn't find Zelda. Wilma says, would you like tea served in here or will you be joining us in the drawing room?'

'Oh... In here, I suppose,' Sholto replied, distracted.

'Fergus, before you go—' I called to his retreating head. He reappeared and stepped into the room. 'Could I ask you something? You remember the day I nearly drowned?'

He pulled a face. 'I'll never forget it. It haunts me still. I had a ringside seat for a double drowning that would have made me heir to Cauldstane – an honour, I do *not* covet.'

'When you were standing on the bridge, looking at me, what did you see?'

Fergus looked puzzled, but answered gamely. 'You were standing on the stepping stones. Near the Blood Stone.'

'Did you see anything else?'

'No.'

'You're sure you didn't see anyone else?'

'Well, Alec was on the bridge beside me. Until he started running.'

'But you didn't see anyone in the river with me?'

'No.'

Fergus looked uneasy, as if he anticipated my next question. 'But I referred to someone else, didn't I? And you didn't understand. Can you remember what I said?'

'Aye. You said, "Don't worry about me, just go and get some rope. Before the child falls in." Something like that.'

I nodded. 'And do you remember what *you* said in reply?'

'I think I said, "What child?" '

'Yes, you did. Thanks, Fergus. I'm sorry for the interrogation, but I'm trying to demonstrate something to Sholto. Do you happen to know if Alec's about?'

'He's in the kitchen. Or he was a few moments ago.'

I glanced at Sholto, then said, 'Would you ask him to come up to the library, please?' Fergus now looked as confused as Sholto, but he said nothing and left.

As soon as the door closed, Sholto said, 'What the hell happened that day, Jenny? Please tell me the truth, however incredible the truth may be.'

I spoke quickly, wanting to explain before Alec arrived. 'I saw the child Fergus couldn't see. She was standing on the stepping stones. She was crying and I thought she might fall in at any moment, so I rang Fergus, then Alec. I told them to come to the river, then I went in to try to rescue her.'

'Did Alec see this child?'

Before I could reply, there was another knock at the door. I fixed Sholto with a look. 'Ask him. He knows what I saw that day and I know what he saw. We compared notes.'

Sholto called, 'Come in.'

Alec smiled when he saw me. I felt mean, knowing what I was about to do, but I returned his smile, registering an impulse – a strong one – to move towards him and take his hand, but I remained seated.

Sholto had evidently clocked his son's smile and looked from Alec to me, then back again, even more perplexed. He rose and walked round his desk, so that he stood beside my chair. If Alec faced Sholto, he could hardly fail to register my reactions.

'Alec,' Sholto said, leaning on his stick. 'I've been talking to Jenny about the time you pulled her out of the river.' The remnants of Alec's smile disappeared and he looked at me for guidance. I met his helpless gaze as Sholto continued. 'She says there was a child in difficulties. That's why she went in. To rescue her. Is this true?'

The next few seconds were agonizing. I watched Alec calculate whether there was any way he could lie his way out of telling Sholto the truth and whether he'd be able to live with himself if he did. He shoved his hands in the pockets of his jeans and, his eyes cast down, said, 'Aye, that's right. She must have been one of the kids on the estate.'

'You recognised her?'

He hesitated for only a second. 'No, I didn't.'

'What happened to her?'

Alec made a show of folding his arms and gazing through the library window. I couldn't bear to watch any more and looked away.

'When Jenny fell in, the wee girl ran back across the stones. Then she disappeared into the woods. At least, I assume that's where she went. I wasn't paying any attention. I was kicking off my shoes so I could go in after Jenny. I wasn't worried about the girl,' he added, with a bitterness I felt sure would not escape Sholto.

There was a long silence. When I looked up, Alec appeared to be studying the contents of a neighbouring bookcase. Sholto gripped his stick, then cleared his throat noisily before saying, 'Alexander, I regret to say I know you are lying to me – possibly for the first time in your life. Most regrettable. You see, I've already spoken to Fergus about this and he said – *emphatically* – that there was no child. Your story makes perfect sense. Ferg's does not. Which leads me to conclude – paradoxically – that Fergus is the one who's telling me the truth.'

Alec stood very tall and looked his father in the eye. 'There *was* a child. Fergus just didn't see her.'

'Why? I'm not aware there's anything wrong with his eyesight.'

'He couldn't see her because—' Alec looked down at me in desperation. I nodded quickly. 'Because she was a ghost. I didn't see her run away. That *was* a lie and for that I apologise. The last thing I remember before I went in was the girl laughing and pointing at Jenny as she went under.'

'And *that*, I presume is why you wanted Jenny to leave,' Sholto said, gravely. 'And why you want me to sell up. Because you believe this ghost – Meredith's ghost – can kill.'

'I know she can't. If she could, I'd be dead by now. Meredith has no power to kill, but she can put folk in harm's way. I believe she was responsible for Coral's death. She tried the same trick on Jenny, who also fell for it.'

'Even supposing I can bring myself to believe there are such things as ghosts – *malevolent* ghosts! – why would Meredith wish Coral any harm? Or Jenny for that matter? She never even knew Jenny.'

'I believe Meredith wishes to hurt Jenny for the same reason she wanted to hurt Coral. She'll not tolerate any rival. I believe after she died, she haunted Coral, bullied her to the point of breakdown, then engineered her death. Even before Meredith tried the same

271

thing with Jenny, I'd suspected she might be... at risk.'

'But *why*?' Sholto asked.

'Because of the way Meredith felt about me. And... because of the way I feel about Jenny.'

'Ah! I see.' Sholto took a moment to digest Alec's words. 'Well, I'll say this for you, Alexander, you have excellent taste in women. And I presume from the way you're talking, Jenny feels the same way about you?'

Alec's mouth twisted in a wry smile. He looked at me and said, 'She's given me good reason to believe so, aye.'

'Splendid!'

'But I also have reason to believe Jenny will never be safe at Cauldstane. Possibly she'll never be safe around *me*.' I started to protest, but Alec raised a hand. 'Hear me out, Jenny.' He turned back to Sholto. 'I want to give my family a chance to escape Meredith's influence. I think she wants to break us. And I'm sick and tired of fighting her. Of *fearing* her. That's why I want out. I don't think Meredith was right in the head when she was alive and she doesn't seem any more kindly disposed towards the MacNabs in her ghostly incarnation.'

I could be silent no longer and rose from my chair. 'But, Alec, what if you knew Meredith had done far worse? That she was even more wicked than you imagined? Wouldn't you want to fight back? Wouldn't you try *anything* to rid Cauldstane of her influence?'

'You're referring, I take it,' Sholto said, 'to – what was it called? – deliverance ministry?'

'Yes, I am. Because I think this household needs to be delivered from evil. Evil you don't even know about.'

Alec stared at me. 'Are you saying you know something I don't? Something about Meredith?'

'Yes. And it's something you *should* know, Alec. Something that will set you free. But at the same time, I dread you knowing.' I looked at Sholto. 'I dread both of you knowing. But I think you should. And it's my dearest hope, that when you *do* know, you'll fight back, whatever the consequences. I hope you'll think you owe it to Liz.'

'Liz?' Sholto said sharply. 'What's Liz got to do with this?'

I got up and walked over to the door. I turned the key, then went back to my chair where I'd left my bag. I extracted the journal and as I removed its plastic wrapping, Sholto recognised it for what it was. 'That's one of Meredith's diaries... I hope you don't expect me to read that tosh.'

'Sholto, I believe I'm doing the right thing, but it's taken me a long time to come to this decision. I even consulted a priest about it. I wanted to be certain, you see. You asked me to destroy Meredith's journals, but I think you and Alec should read an entry in this one before it's destroyed. I'd like you to read the pages I've marked. And in handing over this diary, I abdicate responsibility for destroying it. It's up to *you* now what you do about this journal. What you do about Meredith.'

Sholto's lower lip quivered. 'Is this going to be something about Liz? Something *bad*?'

I nodded. 'You must prepare yourself for a shock. A dreadful shock.' I handed him the journal and he went back to sit at his desk. Alec was still standing, mystified. I moved over to him and took his hand in both of mine. We watched as Sholto opened the book at the place I'd marked and started to read. At first he frowned, as if he couldn't follow, then his mouth fell open slightly. As he read on, the tears came. At one point he had to stop. He leaned back in his carved wooden throne of a chair and closed his eyes. I was about to leave Alec's side to take the book away when Sholto mastered his emotions and continued reading to the end. Then, his chest heaving, he pushed the book away and wailed, 'God damn you to Hell, Meredith!' He started to wheeze, then gasp for air. Alec moved swiftly round the desk and attempted to put an arm round his father, but Sholto shoved him away. 'Read it! Read it, Alec. Dear God in Heaven! All these *years*... And you blamed yourself!'

Alec picked up the journal and stepped away from the desk, his face very pale. Sholto's breathing was still laboured, so I ran to the door, fumbled with the key and rushed out into the passage, shouting, 'Wilma! Zelda! Somebody – come quickly!'

I ran back into the room to find Sholto hunched over his desk, weeping into a large handkerchief. 'It can't be true... It *can't*. Alec, tell me it isn't true!' I bent over and put my arm around him, saying, 'I'm so sorry, Sholto. Please forgive me. I'm so sorry!' and I too started to cry.

Wilma ran into the room, followed by Zelda, who had a phone in her hand. She took one look at Sholto and started to tap numbers, saying, 'Wilma, help me get him to bed. I'm calling the doctor.'

'I think he might be suffering from shock,' I said. 'He's had some very bad news.'

Sholto tried to speak, then started to choke, so I filled a glass with water from a drinks tray. I handed it to Wilma who managed to calm him enough to take a few sips. Then coaxing and cajoling him out of his chair, she took his arm and draped it round her shoulders, then she put an arm round his waist to hold him steady. Still speaking on the phone, Zelda ran round to Sholto's other side. He hung between the two women, broken and bent, like an ancient crucified Christ, and they dragged him across the floor towards the door.

Looking back over her shoulder, Zelda barked, 'Find Alec. I don't know where he went, but he should be with his father. Find him, will you, Jenny?'

Astonished, I looked around the room for Alec, but he was gone. So was the journal.

I hurried out of the library and hurtled down the stairs, calling his name.

The armoury. That's where Alec would have gone. Ignoring the falling snow, I ran across the courtyard and found the door open and the light on. I went in and looked around but saw no one. Suspicious, I checked the little kitchenette at the back. There was no sign of him, but he must have turned on the light. To read the journal?... And then he'd left. To go where? His car was still in the courtyard, so he couldn't have gone far. Perhaps he'd taken the journal to the bridge, intending to dispose of it in the river. I left the armoury and closed the door behind me.

Snow was falling steadily now, but I headed for the archway and the path to the river, my feet crunching on the cobblestones. I wondered if I should return to the castle to pick up a coat from the assortment hanging by the back door, but I decided not to waste the time. I was wearing a long, chunky jumper – standard draught-excluding uniform at Cauldstane – and jogging to the bridge would keep me warm.

Moving away from the castle's lights and into the shadows, I saw a movement against the wall, near the archway. As my eyes adjusted to the darkness, a pale shape at around waist-height emerged from the dense blackness. I was frightened, but I kept walking. As I approached, I could hear a light, high voice repeating something over and over, like a nursery rhyme. Was I about to come face to face with Meredith? My nerve failed me and I came to a halt a few paces from a figure crouched against the old stone wall. In as fierce a voice as I could muster, I called, 'Who's there?'

There was no answer, nor any movement. The recitation continued. I took one step closer, then another, until I could make out the words.

'*Your mummy's dead and it's all your fault... Your mummy's dead and it's all your fault...*'

Alec was sitting on the ground, hugging his knees, rocking backwards and forwards, repeating Meredith's words. His voice was child-like, but rhythmic and toneless. He stared into space, unblinking and his face was very wet – with tears or melted snow, I couldn't tell. His eyes were wide, but unseeing.

I kneeled down and said, 'Alec, it's me. Jenny. Will you come indoors? It's very cold out here and you're soaking wet.'

He didn't respond or even pause in his heart-rending chant. '*Your mummy's dead and it's all your fault... Your mummy's dead and—*'

'It's *not* your fault, Alec. It never was. You know that now. The journal said so, didn't it?' There was a moment's hesitation, his eyes flickered and he blinked several times, very quickly, as if something had got through, but then he resumed chanting and rocking. I raised my voice slightly. 'It was *Meredith's* fault, not yours. But she blamed you. Do you remember what she said? What she told you to say?'

He broke off, threw his head back and yelped, as if in pain. Then, his voice much lower, he snapped, '*Don't try to get away. Stand still! Stop crying and listen. This is what happened...*' He started to weep, but it sounded like a child crying. I edged closer and said, 'It's all right, Alec. She's gone. It's only me. Jenny.' He screwed up his eyes and spoke quickly, the words tumbling out. 'I couldn't breathe. She was holding me tight and squashing me. And I felt sick. There was a smell. A horrible sickly smell. Meredith's smell. I couldn't *breathe*! There was just her smell and her hands holding me. Hurting me.' He covered his ears. 'And she was shouting!' He reverted to an adult voice again. *'You came through the arch and you sounded your horn. That frightened the horse and your mummy fell off. You saw it. You saw it happen. Your mummy's dead and it's all your fault. Do you hear me, Alec? Your mummy's dead and it's all your fault.'*

'No, it isn't – and it never was! Meredith *lied*. And we know it was a lie because it says so in her book. Where is that book? What did you do with it when you'd read it?' He turned and looked at me, his eyes still blank. 'Alec, will you let me hold your hand?' He offered no resistance, so I took his frozen fingers in mine and began to chafe them. 'Do you remember what you read in the diary? It explains what really happened that day. It wasn't your fault *at all*. Please believe me. I wouldn't lie to you.'

He looked confused, but then he turned, brushed away some snow with his hand and picked up the journal. 'Is this it?' he asked, still in his child's voice. 'Does it say in there what happened?'

'Yes.' I took the book and opened it at random. It was too dark to see anything, but I pretended to read. *'Alec wasn't to blame. It was all my fault. I frightened Liz's horse, she fell off and she died. It was nothing to do with Alec. He wasn't even there.* Did you hear, Alec? You weren't even there!'

'Is that book true?'

'Completely true.'

'It *wasn't* my fault?'

'No, it was Meredith's fault. And your father knows it wasn't your fault.'

'Does Ferg know?'

'Not yet, but we're going to tell him.'

'Does Wilma know it wasn't me?'

'No, but we're going to tell her too. We're going to tell everyone, just as soon as we get back indoors.'

'Does... Did Mummy think it was my fault?'

My voice failed me then, but I recovered quickly. 'No, she didn't, Alec. She knew it couldn't possibly be your fault, because you weren't even there.'

'But she *saw* me. She was lying on the ground and her eyes were looking up at me!'

'They weren't, Alec, my love. She was already dead, but her

eyes were still open. She died before you fell off your bike. Before the horse galloped past you.' I squeezed his trembling hand. 'You must have been so frightened.'

'I thought I was going to die. And then... then I wished I *had* died.' I threw my arms around him, doubting that the meagre warmth of my body would make any difference to the chill of his, but I held him anyway. His body felt rigid, then he suddenly sagged against me and started to sob. To my utter relief, I realised this was the man crying. He clung to me and I made soothing noises, stroked his wet face, told him I loved him and I don't know what else. Then a shaft of bright light fell across the courtyard. The back door was open and someone was coming out. A long, thin shadow was cast across the courtyard and Sholto stepped into the light, making an entrance like an actor onto the stage, except that he was wearing pyjamas, dressing gown and slippers.

Raising his stick and holding it aloft, he announced, in a clear voice that echoed off the ancient stones, 'I, Sholto Alexander James MacNab hereby declare war on all the powers of darkness. I will *not* be moved from this, my ancestral home – not until I leave it in a coffin! I solemnly swear that I will renounce all fear and fight in a manner worthy of the name MacNab to protect my family, my home and all those who shelter beneath my roof. *Timor omnis abesto!* Let fear be far from all!'

Alec had sat up at once, alert at the sound of his father's voice. He now got to his feet and I followed, my limbs stiff and numb with cold.

'Dad, what the hell are you doing out here? Get back inside before you fall and break something! Where's Wilma? She'll give you a row if she finds you out here in your jammies.'

Sholto peered into the darkness. 'Alexander? Just the man I wanted to see. I regret to inform you that I've changed my mind. I have decided to take Cauldstane off the market. I refuse to be driven out by that *whore*, so I shall be sitting tight until the bailiffs remove the last chair from beneath my skinny backside. Sorry if this decision fails to meet with your approval, but my mind is made up.' He brandished his stick again and shouted, 'Let that harpy do her worst! I shall be ready for her.'

'Mr Sholto!'

Sholto turned to see Wilma standing at the door, clutching a raincoat and an umbrella. She trotted across the courtyard, scolding, then opened the brolly. She wasn't quite tall enough to hold it above Sholto's head, so Alec took it and put an arm round his father to steady him. Wilma scampered back and took refuge once more in the doorway.

Sholto stared at his son. 'My dear boy, you're *soaked*. Don't tell me you fell in the river too? Which reminds me – where *is* that girl?'

'What girl?'

'The one you ought to marry. Good looking. Talks a lot of sense.'

'You mean Jenny?'

'*That's* the one!'

I stepped forward into the light, shivering convulsively. 'I'm here, Sholto.'

His face wreathed in smiles now, he beckoned me to come under the umbrella. 'Splendid! Thought you'd run away. No need, my dear. Nothing to fear now. We'll sort this business out, you'll see.'

'Mr Sholto!' Wilma pleaded from the doorstep. 'Will you come away inside? You need to see a doctor!'

'No, Wilma, I need to see a *priest*.' Sholto laid a hand on my shoulder. 'Find me one, Jenny. Find me a priest and bring him to Cauldstane.'

'I already did.'

'I beg your pardon?'

'I hope you'll forgive me, Sholto, but Rupert Sheridan is actually a minister. I brought him to Cauldstane because I think he can help us. If you'll give your permission.'

'Sheridan? You mean the bird watcher?'

'Yes.'

'But he said he was a scientist.'

'He's a minister now, but he used to be a scientist. A very clever one, actually.'

'Good! He'll need his wits about him if he's going to tackle Meredith. She's cunning, you see. Always was. Ran rings round me. But not any more, eh? *Timor omnis abesto!* Let that be our watchword.' And with that Sholto marched back into the castle, leaving us with the umbrella.

Alec looked down at me, his white face pinched with cold. 'Looks like I'm beaten.'

'No, you're not beaten, but you have no choice now but to fight.'

He shivered convulsively, then said, 'You and me, Jenny... We have a chance. Don't we?'

'Yes, we do! Whatever happens. But I know we can do this, Alec. Trust me. Trust Rupert. Love *has* to be stronger than hate.'

The wind got up then and a vicious gust sent the snowflakes spiralling. The pages of Meredith's abandoned journal turned as it lay in the snow, making a wet, slapping sound. Alec thrust the handle of the umbrella into my hand, ducked out and retrieved the sodden book. He returned and held it up to show me. In the light from the open door we could see the pages were now almost illegible. The thick black ink had run and, as we watched, words dissolved, to be replaced by grey, spreading blots.

'I wonder,' he said, his voice quite calm now. 'Did that woman ever shed a tear for anyone other than herself?'

'I very much doubt it... Can we go in now, Alec? I'm cold. And so tired.'

He shut the journal and tossed it away, into the snow. It landed in a drift by the wall and sank at once. 'OK,' he said putting an arm round me. 'Let's get this over with.'

He pulled me to him and we walked together, towards the light and warmth of Cauldstane.

Chapter Twenty-nine

Alec and I were soaked and thoroughly chilled. We took refuge in the kitchen where we clung alternately to the Aga and each other. Wilma fussed and tried to shoo us upstairs in the direction of hot water. She said whatever time we presented ourselves, we'd find a venison casserole in the Aga and celery soup on top. She'd also made my favourite blackberry and apple pie which now sat on the kitchen table, its purple juices oozing at the edge of a spectacular golden crust.

It was to have been a special family dinner and my last at Cauldstane. As it was, no one had the heart or energy to sit down to a formal meal. Over the next hour or so, people helped themselves to whatever took their fancy, which in some cases was just pieces of the bread and cheese Wilma had set out for those with no real appetite.

Sholto had been taken in hand by Zelda. He'd insisted she ring NHS 24 to cancel the request for an emergency visit. She protested but complied, then produced fresh pyjamas and insisted on putting him back to bed with supper on a tray. It returned to the kitchen untouched. I know because I was still in the kitchen putting my ruined shoes to dry by the Aga when Wilma brought the tray back. With an exasperated sigh, she set it down, reached for a bottle of whisky and poured a generous dram. I'd never seen Wilma touch alcohol, so I assumed events at Cauldstane must finally be getting to her, then she placed the glass on a smaller tray with a jug of water and set off upstairs again. Sholto had evidently asserted himself.

Alec and I dragged ourselves away from the Aga eventually – he to the shower, while I ran a bath. By the time I was out and dressed, the dead silence in his room was starting to unnerve me, so I knocked on his door. There was no answer. Concerned, I went in and found him asleep on the bed, still wrapped in a bath towel. It looked as if at some point he'd tried to pull the duvet over his chilled, damp body, but he'd managed to cover very little. Gently, trying not to disturb him, I dragged the duvet up. He didn't stir. In fact he lay there so pale and lifeless, I stood and watched his chest for a few seconds to reassure myself he was alive.

Reluctant to leave, I gazed round the room for something to do. I picked up Alec's discarded wet clothes, folded them roughly and put them on a radiator. Looking up at the sword placed in the window and others elsewhere in the room, I thought he ought to be safe, but still I didn't want to leave. In the end I switched on a bedside lamp, turned off the top light and took up a position on the sofa where Alec had once slept while I occupied his bed. It felt like a lifetime ago, but it was only a matter of weeks.

I kept watch and was very nearly completely happy. Alec was alive. He was safe – for now. We were together. If my faith in God was debatable, my faith in Rupert was considerable. I was pretty confident he'd pull us all through this.

But if he couldn't?... To distract myself from this unanswerable question, I gazed at Alec's sleeping face: the long dark lashes that flickered occasionally as he slept; the slightly parted lips I wanted to kiss; the reddish-brown stubble that was beginning to shade his face. I studied the undulating curves of his shoulders as they rose above the duvet and had to restrain myself from touching him. He needed to sleep. Alec was enjoying the first guilt-free sleep he'd known since he was eight. Every precious minute would heal. And for every precious minute, I would watch and wait, happy to do what I could to protect that sleep. As Sholto had said, 'Let that harpy do her worst.' I would be ready. And when he woke, so would Alec.

While I watched Alec sleep, Sholto was not idle. Rupert was summoned to his bedside and there ensued (so Rupert told me later) a long and painful discussion in which Sholto related the sordid and miserable details of his marriages and the violent deaths of both his wives. At some point, he must have asked Wilma to bring him Meredith's incriminating journal. When she knocked on Alec's door, I jumped up and went out into the hall. I explained he was asleep and asked if I could help. In hushed tones Wilma said, 'Mr MacNab wishes to show Mrs MacNab's journal to Mr Sheridan.' When I hesitated, she explained, 'Mr Alec was the last person to see the journal, I believe.'

I struggled to recall what Alec had done with the book, then realised it had now been sitting in a snow drift for a couple of hours.

'He left it outside, Wilma. In the snow. It will almost certainly be illegible by now.' Despite a lifetime exercising professional tact, Wilma looked shocked. 'Would you like me to explain to Sholto? Or I can go out and look for it with a torch. But it could be buried under the snow.'

She declined both my offers and scurried back upstairs, while I resumed my watch over Alec. It was gone midnight and I was shattered. I longed to climb into bed with him and sleep for a very long time, but after a few minutes there was another knock on the door. It was Wilma again with a request that Alec and I should join Sholto in the library.

'Does he have to come right away? He really needs to sleep.'

'I did tell Mr MacNab, but he just said, "Wake him." He seems to think the matter's urgent. He was quite agitated when he spoke. And he seemed very upset about the journal.'

'Well, could you tell Sholto we'll be along in a few minutes? It might take me a while to rouse Alec.'

Wilma wrestled visibly with her conscience for a moment, then set discretion aside. 'Something's wrong, isn't it, Jenny? Badly wrong. I've never seen Mr MacNab in such a state. Not since the first Mrs MacNab died.'

'Yes, something *is* wrong and it's been wrong for a very long time. But I think all wrongs are about to be set right. Mr Sheridan is a minister and a very old friend of mine, so Sholto's in good hands. You don't need to worry about the MacNabs, Wilma – any of them. But I'm not at liberty to say more, I'm afraid.'

She still looked anxious, but said, 'If there's anything I can do to help – anything at all – you'll be sure to let me know?'

'Of course. Just stand by for now. I suspect we could be in for a long night.'

I sat on the edge of the bed and shook Alec gently, then harder when he didn't stir. When he finally opened his eyes and saw me, he looked startled, then smiled. A fleeting happiness relaxed his features before memory closed in and bodily tension returned. He sat up, suddenly alert, and looked round the room.

'How long have I been asleep?'

'A while. You obviously needed it.'

He got out of bed and started to dress. I told him we'd been summoned to the library by Sholto and that Wilma knew something was up. Alec said nothing, but just before we left the room, he grabbed hold of both my hands and said, 'Thank you, Jenny.'

My laugh was nervous. 'Whatever for?'

'Everything. For being brave. And stubborn. And for caring so much about my family. And me.' Too choked to speak, I lifted my head and repaid his thanks with a kiss. 'It means a great deal to me to have you by my side.'

'That's just as well,' I said, brushing tousled hair back from his eyes. 'Because I'm not leaving now, whatever happens. We're in this together – is that understood?'

'Understood. Come on – we mustn't keep Sholto waiting.' At the door, he suddenly turned to me. There was a strange light in his eyes, something combative, even dangerous. 'It's begun, Jenny… And I'm going to finish it.' He pressed my hand to his lips and together we ran upstairs to the library.

When we got there we found Fergus and Zelda waiting with Sholto. Neither greeted us as we entered. Fergus looked shattered and to judge from the crumpled handkerchief in her balled fist, Zelda had been crying. I assumed Sholto must have informed them of the manner of Liz's death, but I wondered how much they knew about Meredith's continuing presence at Cauldstane. Rupert wasn't there. He'd retired to pray and had asked that we all reconvene at 2.00 a.m.

Sholto was brief. His hand shook a little as he refilled his whisky glass, but his speech was clear and his thinking incisive. I wasn't really surprised. He was used to being responsible for big projects and many men's lives. Though he'd never have chosen to shoulder the burden now his, there was no doubt in my mind that, grief-stricken, aged and infirm as he was, we were in a safe pair of hands. In that moment I loved Sholto almost as much as I loved his son.

'My apologies for the uncivilized hour, but I want this business

283

settled as quickly as possible, especially as there's a faint possibility that if I sleep on it, I'll wake up in a more rational frame of mind and manage to persuade myself Cauldstane is neither cursed nor haunted. It *is*. I've suspected as much for some time, but thought I was going senile. Jenny has helped me see what's really going on here – and what went on many years ago. For this painful knowledge, I'm profoundly grateful. I wish to acknowledge before you all Jenny's courage and persistence, which she's demonstrated despite great personal risk.

'Wilma knows nothing, of course. Well, I've *told* her nothing, but I'm not sure how long we'll be able to maintain her ignorance. She'll be as upset as the rest of us by these revelations. My silence is simply an attempt to spare her. Unfortunately Zelda and Fergus could not be spared. As MacNabs, they needed to know the truth. *Believing* it is, of course, another matter.' Sholto glanced at Zelda who'd started to sniff ominously, but she mastered her emotions by staring fixedly into the fire. 'I've instructed Wilma to prepare the Great Hall for our meeting. It seems only right that on an occasion as momentous as this, the MacNabs should assemble as we've always done, in our ceremonial hall, beneath the Cauldstane claymore. But I suggest you all get some rest now. Eat something, if you can face it. Wilma says there's plenty of food in the kitchen.' He glanced at his watch. 'We'll meet again at two with Rupert Sheridan. Any questions?' No one responded and Sholto looked relieved. 'Good. Stand firm, everyone. Remember the MacNab motto. *Let fear be far from all.*'

As we began to file out of the library in silence, Sholto called my name. I turned and he beckoned me over to his desk. He waited until the others had left, then said, 'Jenny, would you mind bringing your laptop to the meeting? Rupert told me you've been receiving intimidating messages from Meredith. Cyber-bullying. Isn't that what they call it?'

'When it's done by living people, yes. I'm not sure there's a name for what Meredith's been doing.'

'Ah – quite. If you don't mind, I'd like to have the laptop standing by as... well, as evidence. And – just in case...'

'In case she wants to communicate with us?'

Sholto winced slightly, but when he spoke, his voice was firm. 'There is that, of course. I don't know whether we should give her the opportunity, but frankly, I don't expect her to go down without a fight.' He shook his head and murmured, 'She was always one for having the last word.'

'I'll bring the laptop. It's no problem. I thought we should have it with us. Meredith seems keen to communicate directly with me for some reason.'

'I don't think it's a good reason – not good for you, I mean.'

'No, but I'm not afraid of her. Not any more. I'm far too angry to be afraid.'

Sholto's smile was wan but I was glad to see it. 'That's the spirit. Best get some rest, my dear, if you can.'

As I left the library, I heard Sholto mutter, almost to himself, 'I wonder if *she* ever sleeps?...'

Just before two I presented myself, with laptop, in the Great Hall. Eight dark and massive Jacobean oak chairs had been placed round an equally dark and massive table set before the fireplace, over which the Cauldstane claymore presided. A large and ancient book sat in the centre of the table – the family Bible, I presumed.

A log fire was burning in the grate and had evidently been alight for some time, dispelling the Hall's usual chill. The room was lit by an eccentric chandelier constructed of antlers and bearing fake candles, but the real thing was also in evidence. On either side of the fireplace and in the corners of the room stood huge church candles on floor-standing holders, almost as tall as me. More burning candles stood on the mantelpiece beneath the claymore and the air was scented pleasantly with wood smoke and beeswax.

I was hesitating, wondering where I should sit, when all four MacNabs entered, led by Sholto. The sight brought a lump to my throat. The men were all dressed formally, in kilts and black jackets. The MacNab tartan is bright, basically red and green, and as the family entered, the room looked almost festive. Zelda brought up the rear, also dressed for a formal occasion in a long silk MacNab tartan skirt with a sash of the same fabric tied across her body. I felt seriously under-dressed in my jeans and baggy sweater.

Sholto took his place at the centre of the table, with his back to the fire. His sons took the chairs on either side and Zelda sat at one of the short ends. I had a feeling Rupert would want to sit opposite the MacNab men, so I put my laptop down at the other end of the table, facing Zelda. That was also as close as I could get to Alec and I knew, whatever we were in for, I wanted to go through it at his side.

None of us had spoken. Sholto was pouring glasses of water from a carafe and Fergus appeared to be reading a text on his phone, then replying to it. I wondered who would text him at 2.00am, then couldn't resist a smile as he put the phone away in his sporran. I'd often wondered what men kept in their sporrans, much as one speculates about the contents of the Queen's handbag.

Zelda was calm now. She'd applied a bright lipstick and the determined set of her painted mouth suggested she was ready for anything. Alec sat silent and composed, but hyper-alert. His eyes shifting to the door told me of Rupert's approach, long before he entered.

Rupert was, in his own way, no less impressive than the MacNabs. He'd donned a dog collar, but wore no vestments or other indication of his office, yet his upright and dignified bearing inspired confidence.

He was carrying a Bible, one that I recognised. He'd bought it in a secondhand bookshop in York many years ago, long before he was ordained. I'd asked him why on earth he'd bought a Bible. He'd said something had told him to buy it. Then, looking slightly embarrassed, he'd qualified his answer and added, 'It was a voice. A persistent voice.'

That voice and the purchase of that Bible were where Rupert's life had changed direction. The Bible's presence in the room was another source of inexplicable, agnostic comfort to me. I had no particular faith in the words the book contained, but as Rupert took his place on the empty side of the table, opposite the men, I knew the book itself would be a source of strength and courage for him.

He set down his Bible, a prayer book, a notebook and pencil. Still standing, he asked Sholto for permission to open the proceedings with a prayer. Sholto nodded and stood. We all followed suit and Rupert said, 'Almighty and Eternal God, you are present in every part of your creation. Protect this home and let no evil here oppose your rule. We ask you to free all those who live in this place from the influence of wicked spirits and from all their terrors and deceptions. Guard your people and keep them safe, so they may serve you, free from fear, through Jesus Christ our Lord. Amen.'

Rupert asked us to sit again. He waited for the chairs to finish scraping the ancient wooden boards, then began his introductory remarks.

'Einstein once said, "Even if I saw a ghost, I wouldn't believe it". I assume he meant he found it easier to believe in the vulnerability of the over-taxed mind than the existence of paranormal phenomena. But Einstein lived in a pre-quantum age. I speak to you tonight as a physicist as well as a minister and I have to tell you that matters in physics have reached the point where it's difficult for a layperson to distinguish between the bogus claims of cranks and the legitimately strange claims of scientists.

'Niels Bohr, who won a Nobel Prize for physics in 1922 said, "Anyone who isn't shocked by quantum theory has not understood it." For most of us, our understanding is limited by our perception. Humans can only detect four dimensions – space and time – but many of the world's greatest minds believe there are more than four dimensions. They claim there could be eleven. Could ghosts exist in one of these other dimensions? Charlatans will try to give you answers. Scientists will admit they don't know. But some of my colleagues believe there's a connection between quantum physics and paranormal activity.

'I've never seen a ghost, but unlike Einstein, I do believe in them – or rather, I believe in what they can *do*.' Rupert paused to take a sip of water. The silence and tension in the room were palpable and I was relieved when he started to speak again in his soothing, measured tones. 'I've spoken with all of you in the last few hours. None of you said you believe in the MacNab curse, but each of you spoke to me about the detrimental effects this non-existent curse has had on various members of the family, past and present. The curse doesn't exist, but you've all seen what it can do.

'So I'd like to reassure you, that whether you believe in the existence of ghosts or in the existence of the unquiet spirit of Meredith MacNab and the malevolence of that spirit, doesn't really matter. You don't need to believe in any of these things for deliverance ministry to work. You don't even need to believe in God. I'm confident it will be possible to bring peace to this troubled household and that's what I'm here to do. I've been asked by Sholto to bless Cauldstane Castle throughout, which I shall do, saying prayers and sprinkling holy water. I hope you'll all accompany me on that journey, but it isn't necessary. In any case,' Rupert allowed himself a smile. 'I won't be alone. *Yea, though I walk through the valley of the shadow of death, I will fear no evil, for thou art with me—'*

At that point the lights went out. Zelda gasped and Sholto swore softly, but we weren't plunged into darkness. There were plenty of candles burning and my laptop, running off its battery, cast a pool of light around me. Fergus got to his feet and said, 'I'll check the fuses.'

To my astonishment, Rupert produced a small bicycle lamp from his jacket pocket. He switched it on, set it down beside his Bible and said, 'I think you'll find it's a power cut. And it's probably local. *Very* local.'

Fergus stood, confused, until Sholto said, 'Sit down, Ferg. We've light enough. Let's not get distracted by... *game-playing*.'

As Fergus took his place again at the table, Rupert said casually, 'This often happens. No one knows what ghosts are, but a popular theory is they're a form of energy. Another is that they need to batten on to some form of energy. What we do know is that electrical disturbance is quite common. And,' he added, smiling kindly at Zelda, 'nothing to worry about. So if I may,' – a look to Sholto – 'I will proceed...

'There are two people present who have seen – or believe they've seen – a manifestation of the late Meredith MacNab.' Rupert turned to me, 'Jen, would you describe for us what happened on the day you fell into the river?'

As I began my account for the benefit of Zelda and Fergus, I started to shiver, despite my thick jumper and the now considerable heat generated by the log fire. I assumed it must be the effect of re-living my freezing experience in the water, but then I recalled that a sudden drop in temperature had often indicated Meredith's presence. Sholto must have registered the change too because he got up and stood in front of the fire, leaning on his stick, gazing into the flames. I began to feel nervous, but I pressed on with my tale, occasionally seeking Rupert's eyes for reassurance.

I heard the noise long before I identified the cause. It was just a funny little scraping noise, barely audible above my voice. The others were listening to me intently and gave no sign they'd noticed it. When the candles on the mantelpiece flickered, they caught my attention. I looked up above Sholto's head and realised this was where the noise was coming from, but I could see nothing. I'd decided it must be rats scratching when something – just the slightest movement – made me look higher, at the claymore. I saw a rotating screw glint in the candlelight. Several rotating screws. As I watched, all the screws that fastened the claymore's brackets to the wall were coming loose. The tiny scratching noise was caused by their slow rotation in the plaster.

Horrified, I stopped mid-sentence. When I tried to speak again, to warn Sholto about the danger he was in, I found I couldn't speak. I just sat there, gaping, frozen with fear. Alec must have noticed something was wrong and said sharply, 'Jenny?' The single word galvanized me. I pointed to the sword and said, 'The screws!' as, one by one, they dropped out of the wall, showering Sholto below as he bent to throw another log on to the fire.

The claymore and its brackets were falling even before Alec was out of his chair, but he launched himself across the hearth, reached up and snatched the sword by the hilt as it descended, twisting the blade upwards so it missed Sholto as he straightened up, alarmed by Alec's sudden movement.

Alec stood before the fire, clasping the claymore's hilt with both hands now, pointing the blade upwards. His chest rose and fell, but not, I was sure, with exertion. He was angry, angrier than I'd ever seen him, but when he spoke, his voice was quite calm. Nevertheless, I shivered again.

'Jenny, you once asked me how you'd kill someone with a claymore. I don't believe I ever told you.' He raised the sword to shoulder height, as if about to strike an imaginary foe. 'It was made for slicing, so you'd bring the blade down diagonally where the neck meets the shoulder. Even if your enemy was wearing armour, there'd be a place beneath the helmet, near the neck, where he was vulnerable.' Alec lowered the blade, but rotated it in his hands, as if he still intended to use it. I was terrified and wondered if the strain of the last twenty-four hours had proved too much for his beleaguered mind, but he continued, sounding perfectly sane. 'The faithless MacNab wife, the one whose death was the origin of our curse, might have been formally executed. Hanged perhaps. But one version of the legend says she was struck down with a single blow from the Cauldstane claymore, by the son she was supposed to have seduced. Maybe,' Alec said, his eyes glinting in the candlelight, 'he wanted to silence her.'

Still gripping the sword, he stepped over the fallen brackets, walked past Sholto, Fergus and Zelda and left the room without a word. In the silence we heard his footsteps descend the stairs.

A tremulous voice broke the silence. It was mine. 'I think I know what he's going to do.' I stared helplessly at Fergus. 'Her portrait...'

Fergus leaped to his feet and ran to the door. I wasn't far behind. We stumbled down the stairs until we got to the first floor. Looking down, we saw Alec on the half-landing, facing the life-size portrait of Meredith. As he raised the claymore, Fergus yelled, 'Alec – no!', but the blade came down accurately and diagonally, slashing the canvas from head to foot, severing Meredith's head and shoulder from the rest of her body. Alec lowered the sword and stood contemplating his handiwork.

'For Christ's sake, Alec!' Fergus hissed. 'What have you *done*?'

I turned and was astonished to see his angry, white face. 'But, Fergus – it wasn't a very *good* painting. I doubt it would have fetched much at auction.'

'You misunderstand, Jenny,' Alec said, turning round, his face impassive. 'Fergus doesn't give a damn about the portrait. He's appalled because I've used the Cauldstane claymore for the third and last time. If it ever had any power to protect us, it's gone now. Sorry, Ferg.' He gave his brother a wry smile. 'But I knew exactly what I was doing. And the claymore is mine to use. Or abuse.'

I pointed to the wrecked portrait. 'You think doing that might have got rid of her?' Alec was about to answer when I heard a distant but familiar noise, coming from upstairs. 'Listen! Can you hear that? Dear God, please tell me I'm imagining it!'

As if reeling from a blow, Alec sank down onto the stairs. He bowed his head and placed the claymore across his thighs, laying his palms reverently on the blade. 'No, you're not imagining it,' he murmured. It's the harpsichord.'

As the music got louder, Fergus exclaimed, 'What the hell is that?'

'It's Meredith's ghost,' Sholto bellowed. 'She's honouring us with a recital.' We looked up to see him standing on the landing above. 'The tune is *Scotland the Brave*, Jenny. Meredith's idea of a joke, I suppose. Also her way of letting us know the claymore didn't work. Never mind, Alec. It was worth a try. I never could abide that ridiculous portrait anyway.'

Alec got to his feet and, still holding the claymore, he mounted the stairs, taking them two at a time.

'No, Alec!' I called out as he passed. 'Can't you see? That's exactly what she wants you to do. The portrait was worthless, but the harpsichord could fetch a small fortune. Don't destroy it. Sell it – just to spite her!'

He paused on the stairs, then a voice above us called out, 'Jen?...' I looked up from the half-landing and saw Rupert's round face leaning over the banister on the second floor. 'I think you'd better come back up. It's your laptop... Meredith has started writing to you again.'

Chapter Thirty

'Well, I must say, this is all vastly entertaining. It reminds me of when I used to host soirées at Cauldstane. It's gratifying to find myself the centre of attention once again – and calling the tune. I do hope you all enjoyed the musical interlude, especially Alec with his ridiculous sword. What a pointless and pathetic gesture, destroying my portrait. I'm glad I—'

I stopped reading aloud and looked up at Rupert and the MacNabs who had reassembled round the table in the Great Hall. 'I'd rather not read this out. It's too horrible.'

Alec reached across the table for the laptop. 'If you won't, I will.'

I laid my hand on his. 'No – I'll do it. If that's what everyone wants.' I looked round the table from one grim face to another and each nodded. I resumed my reading in a leaden monotone that did little to reduce the sickening impact of Meredith's words.

'I'm glad I killed Alec's boring little wife. Remorse is not a character weakness I was prone to anyway, but seeing what he's done, I now rejoice that Coral suffered as she did. It wasn't quick. She was carried along by the river for some time before she drowned. I suppose it must have been terrifying. Well, of course, you would know, wouldn't you, Jenny?'

I looked up from the screen at Alec's profile. It might have been carved from stone. I don't know which was more frightening – the torrent of vile words appearing on the screen or Alec's absolute immobility. Reluctantly, I resumed my reading.

'I see you've now brought a priest in to dispatch me. How amusing! I'm actually rather fond of priests, as Sholto will confirm. I look forward to witnessing his efforts on your behalf, but they're doomed to failure, I'm afraid, because someone is keeping me here.'

I stared at the screen, waiting for Meredith to continue, then said, 'She's stopped writing.'

'She's playing a game,' Sholto growled. 'Ask her who it is. And how.'

I typed "Who is keeping you here?"

She answered immediately. *'Someone who loves me. Someone who has never let me go.'*

Without waiting for permission or corroboration, I typed, "Nobody here loves you."

'Someone does.'

Reading aloud as I typed, I wrote, "The MacNabs detest you." Then, for good measure, I added, "So do I."

'The feeling's mutual, sweetheart. But do all the MacNabs hate me? Why don't you ask them?'

"This is just a bluff."

'It's not. You can't get rid of me. Not till I'm released. Do you think I want to hang around this ghastly dump, watching the men I adored flirt with other women? Do you realise just how bloody boring it is waiting in some sort of spiritual ante-chamber? Hell would be livelier, I'm sure, and teeming with fascinating people. I'd be bound to bump into old friends. And lovers! But my punishment for a colourful life appears to be a sentence of perpetual boredom. As if I hadn't already suffered enough in that department! But I'm tethered to this hideous half-life until Sholto lets me go.'

As I looked up, Alec's head turned towards his father. Sholto snorted, then narrowed his eyes and nodded at the laptop. 'Read on, Jenny.'

'She's stopped.'

'Pausing for effect, I suppose.' He shook his head. 'Ask what the deluded creature means.'

I typed, "You think Sholto still loves you?"

'Of course. Who else could it be?'

When I read out this exchange, Sholto exclaimed, 'It's simply not true!'

Zelda fixed him with a look. 'Are you sure? You were infatuated with her for years.'

'Absolutely certain. It's true I've sensed her presence here from time to time and I've wondered... But it's certainly not *me* keeping her here, I assure you. I'm rather ashamed to admit I didn't even love Meredith when I married her. I only proposed to her after— well, after another woman turned me down. Someone who would have made a much better stepmother for the boys. Meredith was a last resort, frankly.'

The candles flickered and a downdraught of wind in the chimney blew a puff of smoke into the room. At the same time, words began to appear on the screen at tremendous speed. I looked at them, then averted my eyes. 'I'm not going to read this out. It's just foul-mouthed abuse of Sholto.'

Sholto's laughter was mirthless. 'Oh, yes, Meredith she could swear like a trooper! But you don't have to protect me, Jenny. My capacity to wound her ego is greater than her power to hurt mine. I ignored her and that she couldn't forgive. Or forget. She'd rather be hated than ignored, you see. Meredith was an inveterate show-off — just an overgrown child in many ways. She wanted to be loved and admired by *everyone*, even people she despised. There was a sort of desperation about her. She'd do anything to get attention, or steal someone else's limelight. Like getting blind drunk on Alec's wedding day. Dear God, that was a dreadful business... The random horror of it... I had to identify her by her jewellery. There was no face left to speak of. I remember thinking then that whatever bad things she'd done — and there had been a few — the poor woman had paid for them. Of course, I didn't know then that she was responsible for Liz's accident.' Sholto's voice faltered and he passed a hand across his eyes. 'Which puts a rather different complexion on things, doesn't it? But after Meredith's death, all I felt was vague feelings of guilt. And pity. Because you wouldn't want your worst enemy to die like that.'

Sholto fell silent and fidgeted in his chair, clearly uncomfortable discussing his private life in front of family members and a minister, but he struggled on gamely. 'Perhaps I did love her once, before we were married... But what do *I* know about love? How did I manage to go off to the ends of the earth, leaving behind a wife — whom I *did* love — and two young sons, knowing there was a good chance I might not return? You know, there was never a word of recrimination from Liz. She said she knew what she was taking on when she married me. But I did wonder if I was just plain selfish. More in love with exploration and danger than with my family.'

'Liz said, if you gave up travelling, you'd shrivel up and die,' Zelda said, matter-of-fact. 'And she was right. You were an apology for a human being between expeditions — you know you were — until you started planning the next trip. Then you came alive again.

294

Adventure's in your blood. Liz knew it. So did the boys.'

'When you got to the South Pole,' Alec said, without looking at his father, 'I was so proud of you, I thought I'd burst.'

Sholto turned and stared at him, speechless, then Fergus spoke up. 'You know those stupid "My dad's bigger than your dad" arguments kids have? I used to say, "Aye, well, *my* Dad's climbed Everest. *And* K2." ' He grinned and folded his arms. 'That used to shut them up.'

'MacNabs like to be busy!' Zelda said. 'We have to be *doing*. I'm sure if we all set our minds to it, we could turn this old place round in no time. We're none of us afraid of hard work. Time was, we weren't afraid of *anything*. That's why Meredith didn't fit in.'

'Because despite all her amoral bravado,' Alec said softly, 'she was a coward.'

'Aye, she was.'

'What was she afraid of, Zelda?' I asked. 'Is there something we can use against her?'

Zelda threw her head back and laughed. 'Och, what was Meredith *not* afraid of?... Ageing. Losing her voice. Losing her looks. Poverty. Sleeping alone. Having no friends. Having powerful enemies. She feared other singers' youth and talent. She even suffered from stage fright! That lassie lived in fear – fear of being ignored and fear of being forgotten. Relegated to a musical footnote. A *short* one,' Zelda added. 'I told her, if you live in fear, you fear to live. And I know about that. I left a husband I loved rather than live with fear – may his alcoholic soul rest in peace,' she added, with a sidelong look at Rupert, who said nothing but continued to listen intently, turning his head from one speaker to the next, like a spectator at Wimbledon.

'Meredith didn't live', Sholto said. 'She kept busy. She had a lot of lovers, but I don't think she ever fell in love. She travelled the world, but what did she see? The inside of dressing rooms, beauty salons and hotel bars. I once offered to take her to the Arctic, just for the experience. Do you know what she said? "But what would I *do* there?" I said, "*Be!*" She said she didn't know what that meant. And she didn't. Meredith didn't know how to be. She was always playing a part. The diva. The *femme fatale*. The laird's lady... Who was she underneath all that rôle-playing? I never knew. She was a good actress, you see, on stage and off. But was there a real face behind the mask?' Sholto paused for a moment, then sounding mystified, said, 'I was married to the woman for eighteen years, but I'm damned if I can remember now what her face actually looked like.'

Words began to appear on the screen again. As soon as I saw Alec's name, I looked away, filled with dread. 'She's started up again. But, I'm sorry, I don't think I can—'

'What is it?' Alec said sharply. 'Something about me?' He got up and came and stood behind my chair, reading over my shoulder. Then he crouched down beside me and said, 'You don't believe her, do you?

'I don't want to, but... she said *someone* is keeping her here.'

Sholto tapped the table impatiently. 'Alec, kindly tell us what Meredith has written.'

'She says, "So it's Alec. Well, what a surprise! I'd always assumed it was dear old Sholto." Jenny, you surely cannot believe I feel anything for that ghoul other than hatred.'

Meredith started to write again and Alec and I read together.

I suppose he told you he turned me down. It's true he put up a token show of resistance, but that was all part of the game. He lied to you, Jenny. And Sholto. Alec was indeed my lover. On many pleasurable occasions.

'It isn't true!' Alec grabbed my hand. 'You have to believe me!'

'Alexander, will you please read what it says on the screen? That's an order,' Sholto barked.

'Shall I?' Rupert asked gently, reaching across to take the laptop. As he read out Meredith's vile accusation, I felt close to tears, tears of exhaustion and despair. I gazed round the room and saw the MacNabs in disarray: Sholto and Alec, standing now, were shouting at each other. Zelda was also on her feet, leaning across the table in an attempt to remonstrate with them. Fergus sat in miserable silence, his head in his hands.

Rupert slid the laptop back over to me and, in the din, I didn't catch what he said, but I looked at the screen and read, *This is the most fun I've had in years. See how I can make the MacNabs dance to my tune?*

I slapped the laptop shut, leaped to my feet and yelled, 'Stop it! Stop it, all of you! This is what Meredith wants. *She's* doing this, can't you see? She's sowing doubts. Setting us against each other.'

The lights flickered, then came back on again. Four blank MacNab faces stared at me, blinking. Fergus was the first to recover. 'She's right. Sit down, folks,' he said, producing his phone. 'I'm going to read you a text message.'

'*What?* In heaven's name, Ferg—' Sholto thundered.

'Bear with me, Dad.' As the others sat, Fergus got to his feet, clutching his phone. 'I've some news I want to share with you. I didn't think today was the right time and I really wanted Rachel to be with me when I told you.'

'Rachel?' Sholto looked vague.

'My girlfriend, Dad. I proposed recently, but she turned me down. Because of the curse.'

Sholto was clearly about to embark on an apoplectic rant, but Fergus raised his hand. 'Keep your hair on, Dad. Circumstances have changed and I think now *is* the right time to tell you. And Rachel,' he said, raising his phone, 'has given me permission.' He looked down at the screen and read, '*Yes. You can tell them. Only hope they're pleased. It's due 24th May.*' He looked up, cleared his throat and said, 'She's referring to our baby.' Zelda squealed and Fergus shot her an anxious look, followed by an enormous grin. 'Aye, Rachel's pregnant. But we're not going to marry. We're just going to live together. We don't need marriage, but we do want a family. So that's how we're going to beat the MacNab curse. Rachel will never be a MacNab. As for bloody Meredith – she'll not take any more away from me. She took my mother and my sister-in-law. That's enough! No damn ghost – or curse – is going to stop Rachel and me being happy. Och, what's the worst that fiend can do? Make us live in fear? Well, just let her try!'

Zelda got up and took Fergus in her arms, weeping and laughing. 'I'm so thrilled for you both! I can't tell you how cross I was when Rachel said no. But you're going to beat it, Ferg. Beat that wretched, *stupid* curse!'

'He's already beaten it,' Alec said, moving to his brother's side to shake his hand. 'Rachel's pregnant. Congratulations, Ferg.' He clapped his brother on the back, then both men hugged each other.

Alec made way for Sholto who pumped his son's hand, but seemed too overcome to speak. Lastly, Rupert and I offered our congratulations. As I returned to my chair, I looked round for Alec and saw him standing gazing into the fire, his face solemn once more. As I watched, he lifted his head, then regarded me for some time without smiling, then said, 'Jenny...'

'Yes? What is it?'

His expression softened. 'My wee brother has shown me the way.' He looked across at Fergus who was now busy texting Rachel. 'I've no desire to steal your thunder, Ferg, but this was something I'd planned to do today. Your news and Meredith's false accusations have convinced me the time is right for me to speak. But I confess, never in my life have I felt more fearful.' He turned back to me and continued. 'Jenny, I hope you'll forgive the public nature of my declaration, but it seems important to say this in the presence of my loving family and in the Great Hall of Cauldstane.' He picked up the claymore and walked slowly round the table towards me, his eyes never leaving mine. When he reached my chair, he stood the sword on the floor, point downwards, then grasping the hilt, he kneeled at my feet. His face was now level with mine and close enough for me to see the amber sparks that lit up his grey eyes. They burned with an intensity that made me want to look away, but I held his gaze and watched rather than heard him say, 'We haven't known each other for very long, but there's no doubt in my mind about the rightness of what I'm about to say. Jenny, would you do me the very great honour of becoming my wife?'

There was a collective intake of breath, but no one spoke. My mouth fell open and my mind went blank. As I gazed at Alec, stunned, I saw his resolution falter. Fear began to stalk him again. I was about to speak when there was a scream, followed by a loud crash on the stairs, then the sound of a woman crying.

Wilma.

Alec got to his feet and, still clutching the claymore, he headed for the door, with Fergus right behind him.

We found Wilma sitting on the stairs in front of Meredith's portrait, sobbing and wiping her eyes with her apron. She was surrounded by the wreckage of the refreshments she'd been about to deliver. The vacuum coffee pot hadn't spilled its contents, but the milk jug and sugar bowl had. Plates of sandwiches and cake were now scattered over the shabby stair carpet, together with crockery and cutlery.

Wilma looked up when she heard our footsteps on the stairs and struggled to her feet, sniffing. 'I'm very sorry, Mr Alec, but it's poor Mrs. MacNab's portrait. It's been *vandalized!*' She clapped a hand to her mouth, closed her eyes and started to cry again. Alec descended the stairs and, side-stepping the spillages, he put an arm round Wilma. Fergus picked up the big wooden tray and together we started to clear up the mess.

'Sit down now, Wilma,' Alec said in soothing tones. 'You've had a shock, but it's not as bad as it looks.'

Wilma was not mollified. 'But the portrait's *ruined*, Mr Alec! Someone's done this deliberately.' She pointed to the bisected figure of Meredith. 'That's no accident.'

'You're right, Wilma, it *was* done deliberately.'

'Just mindless destruction! And it was such a beautiful portrait. The living image of Mrs MacNab. D'you think it could be restored?'

'I'm sure it could, but first you need to hear why I destroyed it.'

'*You?* Och, Mr Alec – never say it was you!' Wilma began to weep again.

'Aye, it was me. And I used the claymore.'

The words turned Wilma's tears off like a tap. She stared at Alec, wide-eyed. In a sepulchral whisper, she said, 'You used the *claymore?* For the third time?... Mr Alec, are you unwell?'

'No, Wilma, I'm fine. In better spirits than I've been in years. But there's a lot I need to explain. When you feel steady on your feet, I'd like you to come up to the library. Sholto and I need to talk to you.'

'But why did you use the *claymore?* What will save the MacNabs now in their hour of need?'

'Don't you worry now,' Alec said with a smile. 'I believe the claymore's already done its work and the MacNabs will soon be out of danger.'

'*Danger?*'

'Aye. We've been living through some rough times, Wilma, but I think the tide's about to turn.'

'That's what Miss Jenny said.' She summoned up a little smile and directed it at me. 'She told me something was going on.'

'We're all indebted to Jenny – as you'll hear in a wee while. Now, don't worry about the supper things, Ferg and Jenny will clear up. Jenny, could you make some fresh sandwiches and take them up to the Great Hall?' Alec lifted his head and saw Sholto, Zelda and Rupert looking down from above. 'Dad, would you and Zelda go to the library? You too, Ferg. I'd like to explain to Wilma what's afoot. I think maybe she can help us.'

As Alec took Wilma's arm, he turned to me and said in an undertone, 'I meant what I said, Jenny. Please consider my proposal.'

Unable to think of any suitable response, I called up the stairs, 'Rupert, could you come and give me a hand in the kitchen?'

'Certainly.' He trotted downstairs, relieved Fergus of the heavy tray and continued on down to the kitchen.

I watched as Alec helped Wilma up the stairs. When Sholto met her on the landing, she began to apologise again, but he cut her off with a question. 'Tell me, Wilma – were you very fond of Meredith? Is that why you've kept her room just as she left it?'

I lingered on the stairs, listening to Wilma's anxious reply. 'I hope you didn't mind, Mr Sholto, but you never asked me to clear out her room. And it didn't seem right to let it get dusty. Mrs MacNab couldn't bear dust! She said it was very bad for her voice.'

'That's fine, Wilma. I'm just sorry you made extra work for yourself.'

'Och, it was no bother. It was a pleasure to look after her lovely things. Mrs MacNab was so good to me. So generous. She gave me wee presents – things she had no use for – and one Christmas she presented me with a signed photograph – in a frame!'

'Indeed?'

'She once said I was like a sister to her. An *older* sister.'

'You and Meredith were born in the same year, Wilma.'

'Is that so? Well, of course, Mrs MacNab looked so much *younger*. I'll never forget her, Mr Sholto, nor the terrible way she died. When I saw the portrait just now, ripped in two, it made me think of what happened... I just don't understand how Mr Alec—'

'Don't worry about that now,' Sholto said as he opened the library door. 'Come in and sit down. We need to talk to you about Meredith. Things are not quite as they seem. And I'm afraid, Wilma, it's my duty to inform you that you must prepare yourself for a shock. For several shocks...' There was a whimper from Wilma, then the door closed.

As I went downstairs to the kitchen, I considered the latest developments. We'd found the person whose devotion kept Meredith tethered to Cauldstane, but the thought uppermost in my mind was the proposal I'd received from Cauldstane's heir. Was I prepared to tether myself to his ancestral home? And could I accept – or decline – without telling him the truth about Imogen Ryan?

Chapter Thirty-one

Rupert and I made sandwiches in silence. It was the middle of the night, we were very tired and we both needed space in which to think. We'd made an impressive stack of sandwiches before Rupert finally broke the silence with the question I'd been expecting.

'You haven't told Alec, have you? About Imogen Ryan.'

'Yes, I have. Well, actually, he recognised me. His wife used to read my novels. In hardback. So he'd seen my photo. But he doesn't realise... the implications. Well, I assume he doesn't. I don't think he'd have proposed if he'd known.'

'So will you enlighten him?'

'Only if I accept.'

'You think you have to tell him?'

'Well, if I don't, I think he'll withdraw when he finds out.'

'Are you sure about that?'

'No, I'm not sure. But Alec's a proud man. I'm sure he wouldn't have proposed if he'd known.'

We fell silent again while I poured milk into a jug and put sugar in a bowl. Rupert cut up the sandwiches with mathematical precision, then arranged them on plates, alternating white and brown bread. He stepped back to admire his arrangement, then washed his hands at the sink. 'My goodness, this water's freezing!'

'It's winter in the Highlands. You can die of old age waiting for the hot water to come through. Use the water in the kettle.'

'No, this is very bracing. It'll keep me awake for a few more hours.' He took a towel from the Aga rail to dry his hands and said, 'Do you love Alec enough to marry him?'

'This is turning into an inquisition, Rupert.'

'Sorry. I was just curious. He's clearly potty about you.'

'How on earth can you tell?'

'I've married a lot of couples. You can tell who's in love and who wants a big white wedding.'

'Well, yes, since you asked. I think I do love him enough to marry him.'

'But do you love him enough to take on this place?'

I looked round the dingy barn of a kitchen, with its huge arched fireplace, cracked floor tiles, chipped paint and mushroom-coloured walls. 'Yes, I do. I love Cauldstane almost as much as I love Alec.'

Rupert shrugged. 'Well, it all seems perfectly clear to me. You should accept.'

'But I do have to tell him.'

'Oh, yes, at some point. But I think you should accept his proposal first. In any case, I doubt a gentleman would withdraw a proposal of marriage just because of... unforeseen circumstances.'

'And you think Alec is a gentleman?'

'Most definitely. And I *think*,' Rupert said carefully, 'he's also a realist. Don't you?'

'Apart from believing in ghosts. And the magical power of an ancient sword. Yes, I think he is.'

'Good. That's settled then.' Rupert beamed and rubbed his chilled hands together. 'I look forward to dancing at your wedding. Now, shall we take these sandwiches upstairs? I imagine everyone will be in need of fortification by now. Especially poor Wilma.'

He loaded the tray and we started the climb upstairs to the Great Hall.

We found the MacNab men seated in silence at the table. All three looked as if someone had just died. Alec sat with his head resting on the back of his throne-like chair, staring at the ceiling. As we entered the Hall, he looked up and I smiled. The relief that flooded his face might have been occasioned by the sight of coffee and sandwiches, but I thought it was probably a response to me. To normality. To a possible future without Meredith.

Rupert poured coffee and I delivered it to the MacNabs, who murmured their thanks. As I deposited a cup in front of Alec, I laid a hand on his shoulder and his hand came up quickly to touch mine. Hearing the sound of footsteps in the corridor, he got to his feet and, as I took my place at the table, he walked round behind me and pulled out the next chair for Wilma, so she would be seated between me and Rupert.

Wilma entered leaning on Zelda's arm. She had removed her

303

apron, but her hair was awry and her face ravaged by tears. Zelda sat her down and Rupert poured another cup of coffee. He placed it in front of Wilma, together with the milk jug and sugar bowl, but she just stared at them, dazed, as if she'd been presented with the Japanese tea ceremony. I knew how Wilma liked her coffee, so I added milk and sugar, stirred and nudged the cup towards her. She seemed to come to then and whispered, 'Thank you, Miss Jenny.' When she picked up her cup, her hand trembled and coffee slopped into the saucer.

Wilma now looked every one of her sixty years. Her usually bright eyes were dull and pink-rimmed with crying. I wanted to give her a hug, but I knew any overt show of affection might shatter her fragile composure. What Wilma wanted most right now was to hang on to her dignity.

My laptop sat in front of me, closed. I knew as soon as I lifted the lid I'd see Meredith's last message, or perhaps a new one. I experienced a strong urge to take the laptop to the window and hurl it into the river, but just then, the overhead lights flickered and one of the candles guttered and went out. Meredith was rattled and I smiled inwardly.

Sholto leaned forward and broke a long silence. There was an unexpected tenderness in his voice as he addressed the woman who'd served his family all her working life. 'Wilma, is there anything you'd like to say to the assembled company? I'm sure I speak for Jenny and Rev. Sheridan when I say we're all heartily sorry to have to involve you in these proceedings, but I know you very well. I know you'd want to do all you can to free Cauldstane and the MacNabs from what I'm afraid I must call the forces of evil.' Wilma said nothing, but raised her eyes to regard Sholto with something like adoration. 'I know things seem pretty grim at the moment, but this is – literally – the darkness before the dawn. I'm confident that between us, we shall overcome all obstacles, but it might be a painful process.' He paused, then said, 'Feel free to speak, Wilma, if you so wish. But I must inform you that we believe Meredith's spirit is present in the room and able to hear what we say and observe what we do.' Wilma sat up in her chair and gazed round the room in alarm. 'Don't be frightened. She has no power to harm us. She's really no more than a particularly malicious poltergeist, but she's able to communicate with us via Jenny's laptop, so whatever you say could elicit some sort of response. Another power cut. Or she might type something nasty on the laptop.'

Wilma's lower lip began to quiver. Alec got up, retrieved the claymore from the hearth where he'd set it, and walked round to Wilma's chair. He crouched down beside her and said, 'Hold the claymore, Wilma. It will make you feel strong. And while you're holding it, Meredith cannot harm you. With the sword in your right hand and a minister on your left, you're unassailable.' He laid the sword on the table so Wilma could touch the hilt.

'Thank you Mr Alec. You're very kind. I'd like to say something – if I may.' She cast an anxious look at Sholto, who nodded.

'Go ahead, Wilma. Say what needs to be said.'

As Alec returned to his seat, Wilma placed her right palm on the hilt of the claymore. She paused to gather herself, then said, 'I wish to apologise to you all for any part I have played in prolonging the suffering of the MacNabs. As most of you know, I've dedicated my life to serving this family and...' Wilma lowered her eyes. 'I have loved Mr Alec and Mr Fergus as if they were my own bairns. I loved and served both Mr MacNab's wives. All I've ever wanted was to make his life run smoothly and happily.'

Wilma seemed to struggle, then she surveyed the company and continued with a tearful smile. 'There has been so much love in this family! But I see now there has also been hate. Deceit. And betrayal. I've kept the memory of Meredith MacNab in my heart, just as I have cherished the memory of Elizabeth MacNab, my first mistress. But I hereby renounce my misplaced loyalty and affection. I curse the memory of Meredith MacNab and I pray that God will deliver us from this evil enchantment and send her spirit to... wherever it belongs.'

The wind howled in the chimney and another cloud of smoke enveloped the MacNab men where they sat with their backs to the fire. Sholto began to cough and Zelda got up and opened a window. Leaning back in her chair, Wilma folded her hands in her lap and turned to me. With a nod in the direction of the laptop, she said, 'What does she have to say to that?'

'Are you sure you want to know, Wilma? She's abused Sholto and said many dreadful things.'

'I think this is between Mrs MacNab and me now, so I'd like to know what I'm up against. What can she do to me? If she took my life, it's only something I'd give gladly in the service of the MacNabs. But Mr Alec says she can't harm me and I believe him. My conscience is clear. I've done nothing wrong. But *she* has betrayed my loyalty – in life and in death.'

I opened the laptop and looked at the screen. There was no message from Meredith. Had we beaten her?... I was about to share the good news when the cursor stopped winking and letters started to appear.

Well, that was a nice little speech. I didn't realise you had it in you, Wilma. But you've been a teeny bit economical with the truth. Your devoted service to the MacNabs isn't quite what it seems, is it? Sholto is and always has been the love of your pathetic little life. Did you think I didn't know?

I looked up from the screen and said, 'Wilma, I think you'd better read this first. Meredith's written something that, even if it's true, you might not wish to make public.'

'Read it, Jenny. I have nothing – *nothing at all* – to hide. If she's written something that shames me, it's not true.'

I read out Meredith's latest attack. No one moved or spoke until Sholto, visibly shaken, said, 'Wilma – my dear – is this true?'

'Aye, it is. I've never loved another man. But the fact that you didn't know, Mr Sholto, is proof I've never done or said anything to be ashamed of. I never wanted you to know, but since the cat's out of the bag, I'll not deny the truth of Mrs MacNab's words.' Wilma cast her eyes sideways to the laptop and said with disdain, 'I wouldn't give her the satisfaction!'

'But Wilma, if you have indeed always loved me...' Sholto paused and his blue eyes were bright with tears. 'Why on earth did you turn down my proposal? You could have been – *should* have been – the second Mrs MacNab.'

Zelda made a gulping noise and pulled out her handkerchief. Fergus stared at his father open-mouthed, but Alec watched Wilma, unblinking.

'It's a decision I've never regretted, Mr Sholto. Not until today. After the first Mrs MacNab died, you were in a terrible way. You couldn't cope. You relied on me to look after the boys and keep things running smoothly. And I think I made a fair job of that.'

'You were magnificent, Wilma. I don't know how we'd have managed without you.'

'We worked together closely, Mr Sholto, as you know. We became friends, almost. When the worst of your grief was past, it was natural you should want a mother for the boys and someone to help you run Cauldstane. And that's why you proposed to me. Because I was a suitable candidate for the job. But you didn't love me, did you?'

'No, Wilma. I didn't... Not then.'

It was a moment or two before Wilma could speak. When she did, her voice was low and hoarse with suppressed emotion. 'I believed there was a higher goal in life than personal happiness. That was the happiness of those I loved. It was clear to me I could still serve you and the boys without being married to you and if I turned you down, it would leave you free to find a woman you truly loved. I believed Meredith Fitzgerald to be that woman. When you announced your engagement, I was pleased because I hoped and believed she'd make you and the boys happy. In that I was deceived, but I meant all for the best. I could never have married a man who didn't love me, Mr Sholto. I have my pride. And I'd seen how much you loved your first wife, how you grieved for her. I'd had little enough experience of love, but I knew the real thing when I saw it.'

'I was a damned fool!' Sholto exclaimed. 'But heaven knows, I've paid for my folly. Unfortunately, others have paid for it too. It's true I didn't love you when I proposed. Your analysis of my motives was quite correct. It appears you knew me better than I knew myself. I was a fool again when I realised, years ago, after Meredith died, that I *did* in fact love you. I should have proposed then, but I feared if I did, you might turn me down again and give notice. You see, I thought you'd only stayed on to look after the boys. I didn't realise...' Sholto exhaled and shook his head. 'What a hideous mess...' Then slowly his expression changed. When he looked up, I saw hope in his eyes. 'But I'm going to put things right! It's never too late, is it, to do the right thing? Look here, Wilma, I'd like you to reconsider my offer – ah, but do bear in mind I might not be making you mistress of Cauldstane. If Jenny's business plans come to naught, our home could be a humble bungalow. But wherever I end my days, I'd be mad to think I could manage without you, even for a week. You've bailed me out before and I'm going to have the damn cheek to ask you if you'll do it again. What do you say?'

In a very small voice, Wilma said, 'Before I answer, may I ask one question, Mr Sholto?'

'Oh, please! *Sholto.*'

'Do you love me, Sholto?'

'Yes, Wilma, I do. With all my heart.'

'Then...' She glanced nervously at Alec and Fergus who were both smiling their encouragement. 'This time, Sholto, my answer is yes.'

The MacNabs whooped and broke into applause, apart from Sholto who limped round the table until he got to Wilma's chair. As she lifted her face to look up at him, he bent and kissed her, then took her hand and helped her to her feet. Fergus stood and pulled out his chair, vacating it for Wilma who, arm in arm with Sholto, walked round the table to take her place at his side, her face shining with happiness. One by one the MacNabs kissed her and voiced their congratulations. Then it was my turn to hug her and Sholto and wish them every happiness. Finally Rupert shook their hands and offered his congratulations.

As he turned away, Rupert announced to the room at large, 'As Wilma so rightly said, there has been much love in this family. Such loyalty. And courage. My friends, this love is surely strong enough to defeat hatred, envy and fear. *Timor omnis abesto*, as the MacNabs say,' and he resumed his seat chuckling.

'So, Jenny,' Sholto said pointing to the laptop. 'Any word from Meredith?'

I was back in front of the laptop, but I'd avoided looking at the screen until now. What I read made my heart plummet.

But you haven't given Alec your *answer, Jenny. What's stopping you? There's something you don't want him to know, isn't there? And now you're wondering if he loves you enough and you're frightened that he doesn't. Just how much love* is *there in this wretched family? Enough to send me packing? Do you dare put Alec to the test, Jenny? I wonder... Do you have the guts?*

'I do.'

I'd said the words aloud, firmly, without reading Meredith's latest message aloud. When I looked up, Alec was watching me. 'Was that for my benefit?' he asked. 'Was it – I hope – my answer?'

My heart began to pound as I struggled to order my thoughts. 'I was answering Meredith. She's... she's needling *me* now. About your proposal.' A hush descended on the room and I knew it was now or never. I looked round the table at all the expectant faces and said, 'Before I can give Alec his answer, I have some explaining to do. Rupert and Alec know, but I believe the rest of you don't, that I have an *alter ego*, Imogen Ryan. Actually, that's my real name. J.J. Ryan is the *alter ego*. Imogen was a very successful novelist who cracked up some years ago. She overcame her fear of writing fiction by coming back as Jenny the ghost writer. Alec, do you remember you once asked me what I put into my ghosted books to identify Imogen Ryan as the real author? I said I always left my mark, just as you mark your swords with a red kite. Well, I include a little quotation from Shakespeare's *Cymbeline*. The heroine of that play's called Imogen. There's a scene where people think she's dead and they sing a funeral song over her lifeless body. But she's not dead, she's just taken a sleeping potion that makes her appear to be dead.'

'What's the quotation?' Alec asked.

'It's from that funeral song. *Fear no more.*'

'You're kidding me.'

'No, I'm not. I always manage to get that phrase in somewhere, even if there's a full stop between *fear* and *no*. It's surprisingly versatile. I'm telling you all this because fear has been... well, it's been my issue for many years now. And that's why I always put that phrase in my J.J. Ryan books. It was a little nod to Imogen, my other self, my *real* self, who's fearful. And that's what I want to say to you about your proposal. Jenny very much wants to accept... but Imogen is afraid.'

'You've nothing to fear, Jenny. The MacNab curse is nothing but superstition and I'm confident Meredith cannot touch us now.'

'Actually, I'm not afraid of her. Not any more. I'm afraid that you don't know what you'll be taking on.'

'I agree we haven't known each other long, but—'

'No, that's not what I mean. Alec, I don't want to sound as if I'm testing you, but if I accept your proposal, it has to be on one condition.'

'Which is?'

'That no future disclosure will make you withdraw your proposal in the light of... well, of information received.'

Alec considered. 'I take it you're not already married?'

'No man's ever proposed to me, let alone married me. It would be perfectly legal for us to marry. But there's something that *you* personally might regard as an obstacle.'

'Would Sholto regard it as an impediment?'

'No. Definitely not.'

'Would Zelda?'

'No.'

'Rupert?'

'No. And he knows what it is. In fact he's tried to persuade me I should accept your proposal.'

'Thank you, Rupert,' Alec said with a smile. 'OK, then, I'll repeat my offer.' He stood and reached across the table for the claymore, raised it before him and said, 'Imogen Ryan, for better or worse and under any conditions you care to name, I swear on this ancient and beloved blade that no future disclosure will make me withdraw or even regret my proposal.' He lowered the blade and grinned. '*Now* will you marry me?'

'With the very greatest of pleasure.'

Applause broke out again as Alec put down the sword, strode round the table and took me in his arms. He kissed me thoroughly and, still holding me tight against his pounding chest, declared, 'Go ahead and do your worst, Meredith. If you bring the stones down around our ears, you'll not touch us. The MacNab men have chosen their women and their women are "steel-true and blade-straight". They don't fear death and they certainly don't fear you. Nor do I. There's only one thing I fear and that's fear itself. I will make only one concession to fear: I will fear to lose my loved ones – all of whom are in this room – but I won't let that fear prevent me from loving them, from living with them and for them.

'So you see, Meredith, you've lost. You'll not be able to kill us because we all know – as my poor wife and mother did not – what we're up against. We are united against you. We shall be looking out for each other. Whatever you put us through, none of us will have to go through it alone. So go ahead. Hurl your hatpins. Chuck your china ornaments. Plague us with your wee tunes. I shall eradicate all physical trace of you from my home and it will be as if you never lived. And if it takes me the rest of my life, Meredith, I promise you, as God is my witness, *I will forget you.*' He reached for my hand and raised it to his lips. 'And so will my wife.'

Sholto wiped a tear from his eye and said, 'I wonder if I might just say a few words?... They're for Meredith's benefit, but I'd like you all to hear them.' He got to his feet and leaned on the table. 'Alec, could you hand me the dear old claymore for a moment? I'd like to hold it on this momentous and very happy occasion.'

Alec returned to his father's side and handed him the claymore. Raising the sword, two-handed, like a crucifix, Sholto said, 'This is your last chance, Meredith. The last time anyone will find it in their heart to forgive you. God's mercy and forgiveness might be infinite. The rest of us are mere mortals. You died a terrible death. A worse death than Liz, though you at least were responsible for your own death. It could have stopped there. It *should* have. You might say you paid for what you'd done. Though some would argue, anyone who blighted a child's life the way you blighted Alec's deserves to die many times. I'm not saying that. I'm saying you have *already* died many times. Each time you chose evil instead of good. There are people in this room who had reason to remember you fondly and there's one among us,' Sholto said, looking at me, 'who never knew you, but wanted to tell your story. You could have lived on, Meredith, in the kindly memories of your family and your loyal friend and servant, Wilma. Instead, you chose spite and revenge. You chose to bully. To destroy. You had a talent for making people adore you, but instead you have tried to make us fear you.'

Visibly tired now, Sholto laid the sword down on the table. 'But you haven't succeeded. No one is afraid of you. Or the curse. Not any more. To flout the curse, Fergus and Rachel are prepared to reject marriage. There's already a MacNab heir on the way. And as she's about to become part of our family, I hope Jenny will forgive my saying, she's not so old that there might not be *another* MacNab scion in the near future.

'So let's face it, Meredith, you've lost. Love, loyalty and courage have defeated you. With these examples before you – particularly my dear Wilma's – does it not occur to you that the time has come to spurn the darkness? To move into the light? Good God, woman, do you never wonder, as I do, what it might be like to rest?...'

Sholto sank back into his chair, apparently exhausted. He closed his eyes and laid his head on the back of his chair. 'Any word,

311

Jenny? From herself, I mean?'

'Nothing so far.'

He sat up and waved his hand in the air. 'Oh, switch the damn thing off! Whatever Meredith has to say, I'm not interested. But I doubt she'll respond. She wasn't stupid. She'll know she's beaten. Now, could someone please hand round the sandwiches? I'm *famished*.'

I did as instructed and put the laptop away in my bag, then, unobserved in the general *mêlée*, I took out a pen and my chequebook. Wilma stood and reached for the sandwiches, but Sholto laid a restraining hand on her arm. 'No, Wilma, the boys can do that... Ah, *thank* you,' he said helping himself from the plate Alec offered. 'Tuck in, everyone.' He glanced at his watch. 'This is our long-past-midnight feast. In fact, it will soon be dawn. At daybreak Rev. Sheridan is going to perambulate around the castle, blessing it and saying prayers. You are all cordially invited to join us.' Sholto helped himself to another sandwich, remarking, 'Meredith can't complain about not being given a good send-off, can she?... These sandwiches are delicious! Do you know, the last time I was this happy, I was on top of Mount Everest!... What's this?' Sholto asked as I presented him with a folded piece of paper. 'A note from Meredith?'

'No. It's my dowry.'

'Dowry?' He peered at it and frowned, then, rubbing his eyes, he handed the cheque to Alec. 'How many noughts is that?'

Alec stared, then whispered, 'Six.'

'I thought so.' Sholto turned to me and said slowly and clearly, as if speaking to someone of limited intelligence, 'Jenny, this is a cheque made out to me for one million pounds.'

'Yes. I'm sorry to behave in such an ostentatious way, but since your son has taken a vow to marry me, like something out of a fairy tale, I feel at liberty to behave like a fairy godmother. I wish to use my personal wealth for the good of my future family. I also think my future home could do with a bit of refurbishment, frankly. So I'd like you to put that in train while I do things like sell up my London house and organise my Highland wedding.' I took Alec's hand. 'Perhaps ours could be the flagship wedding. The first of many at Cauldstane.'

Fergus' eyes lit up. 'A *double* wedding. You have to admit, that would be a grand publicity stunt. It could get the business off to a flying start.'

'But, Jenny,' Sholto protested, waving the cheque in the air. 'We can't possibly accept this!'

'Why ever not? I'm to become family. What Alec needed to do was marry money. But he had no idea how well off I am. Did you?' I asked, turning to my stunned fiancé.

'D'you think if I'd known, I would have proposed?'

'Exactly. That's why you had to make that vow. Because you're unfamiliar with the ways in which writers can make money, you never suspected a humble ghost writer could be wealthy. You're presumably also unfamiliar with London property prices, so you had no idea of my potential worth. Nor did you care. But I didn't want you going back on your proposal when you found out.'

Sholto looked down at the cheque again and murmured, 'Well, I'm flabbergasted. Would somebody please pinch me because I think I must be dreaming... This delightful woman is about to become my daughter-in-law and the future mistress of Cauldstane *and* she's going to bail us all out? I don't believe it. *Can't* believe it.'

'You have to, Sholto. I admit that cheque pretty much cleans out my personal savings account, but once I've sold my house in London – it was my parents' house, four bedrooms in Crouch End – I'll have a large sum from the proceeds. I suggest some of it should be invested in setting up Cauldstane as a business enterprise, one that will enable us all to continue to live in the castle, or on the estate, for as long as anyone wants to.' I turned to Alec. 'I'm terribly sorry to spring this on you. But you did rather put pressure on me by proposing. And so did Meredith.'

'Och, I dare say I'll learn to live with your wealth. Given time,' he added with mock solemnity.

'Blame Imogen Ryan. She wrote a pile of bestsellers. They sold all over the world and some were made into films. Then there were the DVDs, another lucrative sideline. My parents had already left me well provided for and I inherited a large house in a desirable part of London. Unlike you and Fergus, I was born with a silver spoon in my mouth. And that,' I said, turning to my future father-in-law, 'was one of the things my mother collected. Silver. She had a passion for it and left her collection to me. I think it will look very well at Cauldstane. So *please*, Sholto, do allow me to help. It would make me so very happy.'

'Who am I,' said Sholto, 'to deprive this young woman of her happiness? Welcome to our family, Jenny – and a special welcome to your money!'

Rupert called out from the open window, 'The new day's dawning... Come and look.'

I went to Rupert's side and stood shivering as the dark sky, heavy with cloud, turned pink, lavender and duck egg blue. From the top of the castle we could see for miles, but everything was blanketed with snow. I breathed in the sharp, cold air and felt profoundly grateful for the new day, for the snow, for the improbable sky.

Rupert closed the window, rubbed his hands together and said, 'To work!' He walked back to the fireplace and stood facing into the room. 'I'm going to begin the blessing of Cauldstane outside, then we'll move indoors, passing through all the rooms, one by one, sprinkling holy water and saying prayers. In each room I'd like to open all the windows and we'll leave all the doors open. This serves two purposes: it lets the light in and any unwanted spirits out. But on a day like today, it will be a chilly job, so I suggest you all wrap up very warm. I've brought my own equipment,' Rupert continued. 'But if you have a container you'd like to use – something that has a special meaning for the MacNabs – I'll use that for the holy water. I'd like to use a twig or small branch from the castle grounds to sprinkle the water. I noticed some shrubs in the courtyard. Perhaps we could take something from one of those? Alec, can I leave you to supply these things?'

'Gladly. I'd like to use a twig from our old rowan tree.'

'Just the job! Shall we assemble in, say, fifteen minutes? Let's meet in the kitchen and fill our water container there. Any questions?... Very well, I'll see you all in the kitchen in quarter of an hour.'

Sholto hobbled over to the door, then paused. He turned back and said, 'God bless you, Rupert. You can have no idea what all this means to me. To the MacNabs.'

'And I doubt you have any idea, Mr MacNab, how happy it makes me to be able to serve you all in this way. Thank you for giving me the opportunity.' Then Rupert went to Sholto, offered him his arm and escorted him from the room.

314

Alec and I were the last to leave. When we got to the door, he laid a hand on my arm and said in a low voice, 'Do you believe in all this, Jenny?'

'No, not really.'

'But you still think it will work?'

'Yes, I do. What was it the man said to Christ, before he performed the miracle?... *Lord I believe. Help thou mine unbelief.* My unbelief isn't going to stop this working, Alec. Nor is yours. Come on, we have a castle to bless...'

Chapter Thirty-two

In the next fifteen minutes Fergus found and washed a pewter porringer, a two-handled bowl from which broth or porridge could be eaten. It had been given to Sholto and Liz as a wedding present and was engraved with their initials. Rupert said it would be an ideal vessel for the holy water.

Alec cleared snow in the courtyard so there was an area for us to stand in and a path to the armoury. He also gathered a few small rowan twigs and bound them together with a thin strip of leather. This improvised tool looked something like a pastry brush, but Rupert seemed perfectly satisfied with it.

Wilma cleared the kitchen table and covered it with a fresh linen cloth and a table runner of MacNab tartan. Zelda brought a bowl of white chrysanthemums from the dining room and placed them in the centre.

And so we gathered in the kitchen at the appointed time, wearing coats and scarves and carrying our hats and gloves. We stood round the table and watched as Rupert filled the porringer with tap water. (I must confess I was surprised. I'd expected him to bring something special. A bottle of Evian at least.) He set the porringer down on the table, then bowed his head. After a moment's silence, he began to pray.

'I come to bless this home and pray that the presence of God may be known and felt in it, that all that is evil and unclean may be driven far from it. Creator God, as you breathed your Spirit over the waters in the darkness, now sanctify this water that it may signify to us the cleansing power of your Holy Spirit, which we ask you to pour forth for this home. Grant this we pray, in the name of your only son, Jesus Christ our Lord. Amen.'

Then Rupert put on his coat and his green bird-watching hat. He led the way out of the kitchen, holding the porringer in both hands, with the home-made water sprinkler sitting in the vessel. The sun wasn't high enough yet to have penetrated the courtyard and it still seemed cold and gloomy. We gathered round without speaking and when we were all still, Rupert said, 'Peace be to this house and all who dwell in it. Lord, you gave to your Church authority to act in your Name. We ask you therefore to visit today what we visit, and to bless whatever we bless; and grant that as we enter this house in lowliness of heart, all powers of evil may be put to flight and your spirit of peace may enter in.' He then approached the back door and, sprinkling water on the threshold, said, 'Defend from harm all who enter and leave by this door, and give your protection to the members of this household in their going out and their coming in; through Jesus Christ our Lord. Amen.'

Before entering the castle, we went over to the armoury where Rupert said another prayer and sprinkled water in the doorway, then inside, he sprinkled more in the four corners of the workshop. He asked Alec to open the grimy window, then we moved on, leaving the door and window open behind us.

The kitchen was next. There was a collective but discreet sigh of relief as we basked once again in the warmth of the Aga. Rupert removed his hat, then, to Wilma's obvious delight, said a special prayer for the kitchen: 'Grant, Lord, to all who shall work in this room that in serving others they may serve you and that in the busyness of the kitchen, they may know your tranquillity; through Jesus Christ our Lord. Amen.'

Thus we processed through the castle in silence, apart from prayers and instructions to open windows, some of which proved intractable. Many hadn't been opened in years and Alec had to use the blade of his *sgian dubh* to force some of them open.

There were special prayers for the library, the dining room and the drawing room and the same prayer was said in each of the bedrooms. Rupert didn't turn a hair when he saw all the swords in Alec's room, but he sprinkled water generously in those corners and at the window, saying, 'Bless the bedrooms of this house and guard with your continual watchfulness all who take rest within these walls, that refreshed by the gift of sleep they may wake to serve you joyfully in their daily work; through Jesus Christ our Lord. Amen.'

Alec took down the sword propped against the window, sheathed it in its scabbard, then threw open the window. We heard the sound of the river, now in full spate, augmented by melting snow. I suffered a sudden shivering fit, unrelated to the temperature in the room.

It was hard to tell if Meredith responded. With doors and windows open all over the building, there were odd bangs and rattles. Cold spots were of course quite undetectable. I thought we might encounter trouble in the music room, but when we got there, I saw that someone – Wilma, I imagine – had covered the harpsichord with a thick blanket, perhaps to protect it from the elements. Rupert said a short prayer, we opened the windows and moved on.

Whether by accident or Rupert's design, we came to Meredith's old bedroom last. By the time we got to the top floor, Sholto looked very tired. No one had had much more than a nap before the gathering in the Great Hall and only Alec and Rupert looked alert. I don't suppose I was the only one distracted by thoughts of a big pot of tea and a restorative bowl of porridge eaten beside the Aga.

Before entering Meredith's room, Rupert turned to us and said, 'I understand this was Meredith MacNab's bedroom. I will repeat the bedroom prayer in here, but I will also say a prayer for the repose of her unquiet spirit, asking her to depart. Could I ask you all to look into your hearts and try, if you will, to let go of anger and any other negative emotions. I realise that will be very hard, but try to bear in mind that we are dealing here with a human soul which needs salvation. Our object is to direct this soul away from her obsession with earthly matters and into the mercy and peace of Christ. We want to replace her present existence of unrest and disquiet with rest in eternity and light perpetual. Now, in a moment we shall enter the room. We've met with no trouble so far, but it's possible we might be challenged in here. Do remain outside, if you prefer, but if you wish to enter, can I recommend the Lord's Prayer? That will stand you in good stead.'

Rupert turned to face the bedroom door, took a moment to gather himself, then nodded to Alec who opened the door. The room was dark and Alec reached inside to switch on the light. The crystal chandelier lit up a room that was exactly as I'd left it. The cardboard boxes containing Meredith's journals sat in front of the bookcase. The heavy velvet curtains were still drawn and this time I noticed the sickly smell Alec had mentioned. ("Like something's rotting.") Was this really just Meredith's stale perfume?

As we filed in, the many mirrors reflected the presence of a congregation, not a family. A wardrobe door swung open and would have hit Sholto had Wilma not pulled him out of the way. There followed a faint tinny rattle which I identified as the coat-hangers jiggling inside the wardrobe. Wilma must have heard it too because her mouth started to move. You didn't need to be a lip-reader to know she was reciting the Lord's Prayer.

Rupert said the bedroom prayer, then a specific prayer for Meredith. 'Go forth from this world, Meredith, to that place appointed you by God; in the name of the Father who created you, in the name of Jesus Christ who died for you and in the name of the Holy Spirit who gives life to the people of God. May the light of God go with you as you journey from this world and may you rest in peace.' That was followed by a heartfelt *Amen* from us, then Rupert turned to face the photographic portrait of Meredith which hung above the bed. As he sprinkled water onto the bed, the picture began to swing, then the hook appeared to come loose so that the picture fell forward. Wilma cried out as it fell, but it landed quite safely, face down on the gold satin bedspread.

Unperturbed, Rupert walked to a corner of the room, sprinkled water and said, 'May the light of God go with you as you journey from this world and may you rest in peace.'

As he left the first corner, there was a tearing sound. He didn't look back but prayed continuously for the repose of Meredith's spirit. The cause of the sound soon became apparent. Where the portrait had hung, the stained red damask covering the wall was peeling away, starting at the ceiling and rolling downwards until the fabric hung from the wall like a parched tongue.

Alec put a protective arm round me, Sholto held Wilma and Fergus held his aunt, who'd buried her face in his coat, overcome by the spectacle, as one after another, strips of fabric crept down the walls. Rupert proceeded from one corner to another, then, after he'd sprinkled water in the final corner, he said, 'Alec. Fergus. The curtains, if you please. Open them, then open all the windows.'

Alec strode to the nearest window and yanked at a curtain. It fell down, bringing the brass rail with it, enveloping him in a thick cloud of plaster dust and burying his feet in a heap of burgundy velvet, but he laughed in triumph as daylight entered the room at last. He stepped over the fallen curtain and pulled hard at the next,

came down just as easily. Then he climbed onto the window
kicked Meredith's photographs and ornaments aside and
d open the window. We were at the top of the castle where
urrents were strong and a gust of freezing air swept round the
m, ruffling the strips of fabric so they danced wildly, like flames.

Alec was already at the next window and Fergus at the last.
ey pulled down the remaining curtains and tossed them onto the
ed. The room was thick with dust now and loud with coughs and
sneezes. All three windows were open and the wind swept round
the room, knocking over photo frames and launching old theatre
programmes into the air. There was a loud bang as the folding
screen went over, then another as the dummy clothed in
Meredith's silk kimono toppled. The wind caught her paper parasol,
lifted it into the air and hurled it against the wall, shattering its ribs.

Above the wind and the now audible recitation of the Lord's
Prayer from Wilma, I heard Rupert's firm, even voice praying
steadily: 'Be gone from this place, every evil haunting and
phantasm. In the name of God, Father, Son and Holy Spirit: we
order you to leave this place, harming no one. Go to the place
appointed you and may you rest in peace. Amen.'

The wind subsided gradually and sunlight filled the room,
gilding the tawdry wreckage. We stood holding on to one another,
braced for more, but nothing happened. The pages of one of
Meredith's journals flapped and her kimono slithered across the
floor, but it was just the wind.

'For our final prayers,' Rupert announced, 'I'd like to return to
the Great Hall. Would you all please follow me?'

We trooped downstairs to the Hall, where the fire still burned
but all the candles had blown out. We huddled round the fire, but
Rupert took up a position in front of an open window and said,
'Lord God, bless, hallow and sanctify this house that in it there may
be joy and gladness, peace and love, health and goodness, and
thanksgiving always to you, Father, Son and Holy Spirit; let your
blessing rest upon this house and those who dwell in it, now and for
ever. Amen.'

We all joined in heartily with "Amen". Rupert remained at the
window but turned round and looked out. After a moment he said,
'What an absolutely *glorious* day. St Andrew's Day too! Do come
and look.'

We gathered in front of the open windows and looked out across the snowy Cauldstane estate, dazzling now in the sunshine.

'It all looks so *clean*, doesn't it?' said Wilma. 'Clean and new.'

'It's a new day, Wilma,' said Sholto, his voice unsteady. 'A new era...'

Rupert continued to scan the sky, then pointed and said, 'Good gracious, I do believe that's a red kite up there!'

'It is,' said Alec. 'There's a pair of them. They're often to be seen over Cauldstane. We think of them as a good omen.'

I looked up at him. 'I saw one when I came for my interview.'

'See what I mean?' He put an arm round me, pulled me to him and I rested my head on his chest, exhausted and relieved.

Looking up at the sky, I watched the red kite glide lazily. 'You see, Rupert? I told you you'd get some bird watching in on this trip.'

The bird hovered, impossibly still above Cauldstane, then it flicked its forked tail, swooped and was gone.

~~~~~

ACKNOWLEDGEMENTS

The author would like to thank the following people who offered information, advice and support during the writing of CAULDSTANE:

Lyn Baines, Clare Cooper, Gregor Duthie, Amanda Fairclough, Margaret Gillard, Amy Glover, Philip Glover, Roz Morris, Jonathan Salmond and Rachel Thomson.

~~~

Follow Linda Gillard on Facebook:
https://www.facebook.com/LindaGillardAuthor

Find more information about Linda on her website:
www.lindagillard.co.uk

Also by Linda Gillard...

HOUSE OF SILENCE

Selected by Amazon for *Editor's Pick Top Ten BEST OF 2011*. (Indie Author category.)

Orphaned by drink, drugs and rock'n'roll, Gwen Rowland is invited to spend Christmas at her boyfriend Alfie's family home, Creake Hall – a ramshackle Tudor manor in Norfolk. Soon after she arrives, Gwen senses something isn't quite right. Alfie acts strangely towards his family and is reluctant to talk about the past. His mother, a celebrated children's author, keeps to her room, living in a twilight world, unable to distinguish between past and present, fact and fiction.

When Gwen discovers fragments of forgotten family letters sewn into an old patchwork quilt, she starts to piece together the jigsaw of the past and realises there's more to the family history than she's been told. It seems there are things people don't want her to know. And one of those people is Alfie...

REVIEWS

"HOUSE OF SILENCE is one of those books you'll put everything else on hold for."
CORNFLOWER BOOKS blog

"The family turns out to have more secrets than the Pentagon. I enjoyed every minute of this book. It's written with considerable panache and humour, despite the fact that there's a very serious underlying thread to the book - how do we, as individuals and families, deal with tragedy?"
Kathleen Jones, author of MARGARET FORSTER: A LIFE IN BOOKS

EMOTIONAL GEOLOGY

Short-listed for the WAVERTON GOOD READ AWARD 2006

A passionate, off-beat love story set on the bleak and beautiful island of North Uist in the Outer Hebrides.

Rose Leonard is on the run from her life. Haunted by her turbulent past, she takes refuge in a remote Hebridean island community where she cocoons herself in work, silence and solitude in a house by the sea. A new life and new love are offered by friends, her estranged daughter and most of all by Calum, a fragile younger man who has his own demons to exorcise. But does Rose, with her tenuous hold on sanity, have the courage to say "Yes" to life and put her past behind her?...

REVIEWS

"The emotional power makes this reviewer reflect on how Charlotte and Emily Bronte might have written if they were living and writing now."
Northwords Now

"Complex and important issues are played out in the windswept beauty of a Hebridean island setting, with a hero who is definitely in the Mr Darcy league!"
www.ScottishReaders.net

STAR GAZING

Short-listed for *Romantic Novel of the Year 2009* and *The Robin Jenkins Literary Award*, the UK's first environmental book award.

Blind since birth, widowed in her twenties, now lonely in her forties, Marianne Fraser lives in Edinburgh in elegant, angry anonymity with her sister, Louisa, a successful novelist. Marianne's passionate nature finds expression in music, a love she finds she shares with Keir, a man she encounters on her doorstep one winter's night.

Keir makes no concession to her condition. He's abrupt to the point of rudeness, yet oddly kind. But can Marianne trust her feelings for this reclusive stranger who wants to take a blind woman to his island home on Skye, to "show her the stars"?...

REVIEWS

"A joy to read from the first page to the last... Romantic and quirky and beautifully written"
www.LoveReading.co.uk

"A thinking woman's romance that lingers in the memory long after the last page has been turned."
New York Journal of Books

"A read for diehard romantics with a bent towards environmental issues."
Aberdeen Press & Journal

UNTYING THE KNOT

Marrying a war hero was a big mistake. So was divorcing him.

A wife is meant to stand by her man. Especially an army wife. But Fay didn't. She walked away - from Magnus, her traumatised war hero husband and from the home he was restoring: Tullibardine Tower, a ruined 16th-century tower house on a Perthshire hillside.

Now their daughter Emily is getting married. But she's marrying someone she shouldn't.

And so is Magnus...

REVIEWS

"This author is funny, smart, sensitive and has a great feel for romance... Highly recommended!"
RHAPSODYINBOOKS blog

"Another deeply moving and skilfully executed novel by Linda Gillard... Once again, she had me committed to her characters and caught up in their lives from the first few pages, then weeping for joy at the end."
AWESOME INDIES book blog

"Daring to write characters like this is brave. And it works. Beautifully."
Indie Ebook Review

A LIFETIME BURNING

A BOUQUET OF BARBED WIRE meets THE FORSYTE SAGA in this powerful and haunting novel spanning the 20th century.

Flora Dunbar is dead. But it isn't over.

The spectre at the funeral is Flora herself, unobserved by her grieving family and the four men who loved her. Looking back over a turbulent lifetime, Flora recalls an eccentric childhood lived in the shadow of her musical twin, Rory; early marriage to Hugh, a handsome clergyman twice her age; motherhood, which brought her Theo, the son she couldn't love; middle age, when she finally found brief happiness in a scandalous affair with her nephew, Colin.

"There has been much love in this family – some would say too much – and not a little hate. If you asked my sister-in-law, Grace why she hated me, she'd say it was because I seduced her precious firstborn, then tossed him on to the sizeable scrap heap marked 'Flora's ex-lovers'. But she'd be lying. That isn't why Grace hated me. Ask my brother Rory."

REVIEWS

"An absolute page-turner! I could not put this book down and read it over a weekend. It is a haunting and disturbing exploration of the meaning of love within a close-knit family... Find a place for it in your holiday luggage!"
www.LoveReading.co.uk

"Probably the most convincing portrayal of being a twin that I have ever read."
STUCK-IN-A-BOOK blog

THE GLASS GUARDIAN

Ruth Travers has lost a lover, both parents and her job. Now she thinks she might be losing her mind.

When death strikes again, Ruth finds herself the owner of a dilapidated Victorian house on the Isle of Skye: *Tigh na Linne*, the summer home she shared as a child with her beloved Aunt Janet, the woman she'd regarded as a mother. As Ruth prepares to put the old house up for sale, she discovers she's not the only occupant. Worse, she suspects she might be falling in love. With a man who died almost a hundred years ago.

REVIEWS

"As usual with Gillard's novels, I read THE GLASS GUARDIAN in almost one sitting. The story is about love, loss, grief, music, World War I, Skye, family secrets, loneliness and a ghost who will break your heart."
I PREFER READING book blog

"A captivating story, dealing with passionate love and tragic death... An old, crumbling house, snow falling all around, and a handsome ghost...Curling up with this book on a dark night would be perfect!"
THE LITTLE READER LIBRARY book blog

"The ending? Beautiful and completely satisfying. I cried tears of joy."
AWESOME INDIES book blog

Printed in Great Britain
by Amazon.co.uk, Ltd.,
Marston Gate.